The Stories We Hold Secret

Tales of Women's Spiritual Development

Edited by
Carol Bruchac, Linda Hogan, Judith McDaniel
The Greenfield Review Press
Greenfield Center, N.Y. 12833

P9-CRT-379

Publication of this anthology has been made possible, in part, through a Literary Publishing Grant from the Literature Program of the New York State Council on the Arts.

ISBN 0-912678-66-6

Library of Congress # 85-70356

FIRST EDITION

Typesetting by Sans Serif, 2378 East Stadium Blvd.,
Ann Arbor, MI 48104
Printed in the United States of America
Cover: Sand painting by Clara Cohan

ACKNOWLEDGEMENTS

In all cases, unless otherwise noted, permission to reprint previously published work has been granted by the individual authors. We are grateful to the magazines and presses listed below for their commitment to the writing of American women.

Andrea Freud Loewenstein: "Crab Queen" from *Conditions*.
Beth Brant: "A Simple Act" from *Sinister Wisdom*.
Judy Grahn: "Boys at the Rodeo," reprinted with the permission of The Crossing Press from *True to Life Adventure Stories*.
Harriet Malinowitz: "Coffee and Cake" from *Conditions*.
Kathleen Shaye Hill: for "Taking Care of Business."
Meridel Le Sueur: for "I was Marching" and "Annunciation" from *Salute to Spring*, International Publishers.
Barbara Smith: "Monday" from *Between Ourselves*.
Grace Paley: "Anxiety" from *Later the Same Day*, Farrar, Straus and Giroux.
Audre Lorde: "Tar Beach," reprinted with the permission of The Crossing Press from *Zami: A New Spelling of My Name*.
Roberta Fernández: "Amanda" from *Quentos*. Kitchen Table Press.
Sylvia A. Watanabe: "The Prayer Lady" from *The Greenfield Review*.
Joan Sauro: "Inner Marathon" from *Inner Marathon*, Paulist Press.

CONTENTS

EDITOR'S NOTE

When I first approached Linda Hogan and Judith McDaniel with the idea of doing an anthology of women's short fiction little did I know the journey upon which I was about to embark. The importance of a theme for the book was proposed, ideas discussed and finally Linda's idea of a book dealing with the theme of spirituality was enthusiastically agreed upon. Long phone conversations, letters and talking about exactly how to define spirituality and how women would respond to such a theme followed.

It was one year ago, the summer of 85. An important summer for me. Joe away at Yaddo Writer's Retreat for the month of July and my sons finally old enough for summer work and leisure time away from home with friends. I had the luxury of time, quiet time, my time to read, to fill my head with the hundreds of stories submitted to this book. Extraordinary stories, wonderful, powerful stories, some sad and some with profound humor. I floated through that month, my head filled with these women's stories. In the middle of it all I returned to my home town, Ithaca, N.Y., to attend my 25th High School reunion. More stories face to face from women who looked like family, so familiar after 25 years. Ithaca, a place of geographic and spiritual power for me. The renewed contact with these special people felt tribal and related to the work I was so immersed in with this book.

Through a sometimes complicated relay system, we all managed to read and discuss every story. Excellent stories were rejected because they just did not work with our theme. Others fell into those sections we devised. We did not agree on all of these stories. There were long discussions and some compromise. The strongest agreement came with those stories in our last section. We knew this was what our book was about. Little discussion was needed— the messages of these stories were right. The lives of strong women and healers inspire us all.

I want to thank Linda Hogan and Judith McDaniel for making this journey possible for me. Our patience with each other and shared commitment to a project we all believed to be an important contribution to the literary community has resulted in what I feel to be a unique book of great significance.

I also want to thank my mother-in-law, Marion Bowman Bruchac, for her time spent proof-reading, my friend Kate O'Connell for listening during my more frustrating times with this book, and a special thanks to my husband Joe for his excellent editorial advice and his emotional support at those times when I felt inadequate for such an undertaking.

And to *all* of you who submitted work, your creative power has afforded me an unforgettable year of learning through your vision.

Carol Bruchac

WOMEN: DOING AND BEING

The stories we hold secret are stories of our growth as women, our transformations, the waking moments of realization that change the direction of our lives. They are sacred stories. They are hidden stories, sometimes even from ourselves. They have been concealed while we search for a language that will speak the unnamed mystery, for words that will release grief or anger, words that, like a rosetta stone, help us decipher the inside story that must be told.

When that language arrives, it has many voices. It may be recalling of people or events, or what writer Meridel LeSueur has called "re-membering the dismembered." Or it is the telling of inner and symbolic events that preceded changes we made. It might be the voice of our ancestors in the leaves of evening. Sometimes it is the voice of our own pain saying, No more.

These stories rarely fit the form and language we have been told that literature is supposed to fill. At first, this seems like a count against them. And they tell the forbidden. They are the stories that have been silenced and now their voices are waking up and insisting on speaking what they know. They are as familiar as our own lives because we have lived them or we have heard them from friends in moments of quiet secrecy. We have almost forgotten them because they have not been valued or believed. Like Cassandra, when we are soothsayers, we are accused of lying, it goes so much against the veneer we are told is real.

Now we are the "betrayers of the lie." In our speaking and writing, we betray what has harmed us and held us down. We tell on those who hurt us. We give away the truths of oppression, and we betray our own denial by allowing our art and literature, our often unconscious internal creative processes to express what we ourselves have held in. We are in the middle of overthrowing an internal dictatorship that has been forced on us, and in that revolution we are becoming whole.

This is just a beginning, this truth-telling, this courageous facing of inner reality and outer facts. It is sometimes like Gandhi's "clinging to the truth." It insists on change. It is a form of quest and of illumination in that sense of the word that means light-bearing. The women in these stories bear light. They are in various stages of knowing their inner truths and seeing the outer world. Many are, for the first time, believing their own voices. Some are facing their own victimization. Others are caught in a decisive moment, a telling moment, a truth-telling moment. Some are creating a new self, a new community with others, a new way of loving. Still others are in that reverie so important to women's spiritual strength, reflecting on the lives they live, the directions they have gone and are going, the losses and loves they have sustained. In these stories, change is being made, decisions are being made, life is being lived. Women are doing and being.

ON DOING AND BEING: It is this Doing and Being that we must pay close attention to. In our growing many of us have taken side roads and detours and been lost. It is the North American way of Doing that has gotten us in trouble on the path of our living. By this, I do not mean to criticize action, but the way in which we often substitute real action with the kind of Doing I am talking about, that busyness and work, that having to get things done. It is Doing dominating Being. It is when we define ourselves by what we do or measure ourselves by outside standards that we must beware. We think these will empower us. In reality they have caused us to lose the center, the core of self. This shunning of our own internal feminine* energies and principles has been costly. It has been a selling out of intuition, instinct, and life energy, a sacrifice of our gifts to those who judged these qualities inferior. Now there is something lacking which many are seeking to reclaim.

Helen Luke, in her book *Woman, Earth and Spirit*, writes about this reclamation as a searching that takes place in "a time such as ours when every kind of experimentation is encouraged and pro-

---

*By "feminine" I mean those qualities discussed by Jungian Marie Louise Von Franz and others who have returned to us the value of the so-called female qualities that were judged as inferior by the patriarchal consciousness."

moted." False spirituality, she says, "threatens a far greater number of people who . . . have been largely deprived of the rituals and collective symbols by which their souls were unconsciously nourished. [They] seek everywhere to rediscover a numinous sense of meaning in life. Charismatic movements, and mystical or occult teachings of all kinds, spring up to meet the need of thousands who have lost contact with the spiritual in the deserts of materialistic rationalism." p9

This materialistic rationalism has led us into a barren land, a dried and eroded place in the self. It is a place deprived of imagery of the feminine self, and of connectedness with all life. For some time, women writers have been searching out ways of creating new images and connections. Part of that searching has been a movement away from the western religious traditions and from male literary traditions. It has been a redefinition of the meaning of God, sometimes as Goddess, the creation of new ways of seeing the self, the creation of new art and literature, a transformation of mythic materials. Margaret Atwood's book *Surfacing*, was one of the novels that carried this movement forward:

> No gods to help me now, they're questionable once more, theoretical as Jesus.

For her, the gods are a cluster of people, deities and beings, inner and outer. Her main character knows that for her own wholeness she must discard and sacrifice old things, even old beliefs, "Even the guides, the miraculous double woman and the god with horns, they must be translated."

It is this translation we require. Even in women's search for the goddess we need a new translation. We need to interpret our inner lives differently, to translate our perceptions in a new way. For many women who have searched for the meaning lost to them, it has been ironic, or perhaps it is a paradox, that the methods and techniques being used to achieve spiritual growth have not been enough.

It is a step-by-step life process to waking consciousness and it can't be speeded up. When we go searching for new ways, we leave behind the deepest secrets of all, the secrets of being. We forget that we are all sacred beings and do not have to search out new ways of "getting there." In fact, that is one of the dangers of a searching spirituality. Where is there to get? There are no goals to be set and attained, no bargaining, no new ritual that will, once and for all, wake a person to her spirit.

Nor has it been appropriate for women to turn to traditions other than their own, often calling themselves shamans and attempting to impose themselves into the world of old and complex spiritual traditions, simplifying and diminishing the religions they seek to gain strength from.

Now there are workshops promising instant spirituality as if we could find lasting wholeness rather than temporary emotional release in a weekend. These are symptoms of a kind of "Doing" that I mean, the one that is taking the place of Being for so many women who are searching for that which they already possess. We have devalued ourselves. We have not paid homage to the earth. We have not paid homage to our lives or works. We have not developed compassion, even for ourselves. We have felt we can never be enough of anything. So we are back in the circle, standing at the beginning, starting to once again define and revise our spiritual selves, beginning the long process of inner nurturing, and learning again and again that none of the steps can be bypassed or hurried. Nor can we measure our growth with that of others, for we each have our own design and blueprint that is unique to us.

There are no short cuts. In all traditions, growth takes time. And for women, it happens when we give ourselves up to the process of it, the uprooting, the limbo world of the unknown we cannot control. Our journeys are ripenings and each has its own natural way. The constant fixing, doing, pretending, denying, lying, and working for change or against it only serves to show us how much and which parts of the old values remain; we still cling to the idea that our acts will save us, a form of salvation. But for the soul, these actions do not feed it.

When we sent out a call for stories, I expected that we would receive stories with strong women characters, with healers and wise women and women who remembered their connection to the earth, women who were wakened by extraordinary internal events as well as those external to themselves. I thought these stories would be filled with the women we are in the process of becoming. I thought they'd be full grown.

I was brought back to reality by these stories. They reminded me that everyday life is the spiritual, is the waking and transformation, that it is filled with growth and perception that is wise and healing, and that, for us, the spirit works in quiet but transforming ways. Reading these stories I have felt reminded that our growth does not come from putting on any spiritual clothing. Growth comes from removing and removing, ceasing, undoing, from letting ourselves drop down, or even fall, into the core of our living Being.

I was reminded that our renewal often really does flow from loss, pain, ashes. We are like giant redwood trees, with new life springing from our fallen selves. I was reminded that writing is, in itself, part of our growing, part of our spiritual strength. And I was given the images of strong women in all their various ways and stages of becoming rather than being given the finished women I had imagined. I was reminded that we are never finished, and that we carry the brilliant soul within us, buried in matter, as in Gertrud Kolmar's poem of emergence, "The Toad," where she says "I am the toad, and wear a precious jewel . . . "

It is this jewel we need to uncover and our life is a journey whose task is to find this gem, mine it, and let it shine. There are no previous maps or landmarks for this journey. We can look to the myths, Psyche's journey, and the ancient stories of women. But we see that in each story, women are helped by the inner voices, the spirit world, the voices of earth. Magical help is passed down by a feminine wisdom, and the task is to listen, to unravel information, to separate one thing from another, and to Be.

This is the significance of Being. It allows us to fulfill our task. It allows us to listen to the ancient voices of guidance, and our listening is all that will save us.

These stories about women remind us that when we doubt or ignore these demands from our center, we get into trouble because it is the inner voice that makes real the demands of the growing and it insists that we follow. That following is the challenge to us, living as we do in a place that values individualism, but not individuals, where pursuit of happiness is a constitutional priviledge, but a woman's growth to wholeness is against cultural conventions and has hardly even begun to be described.

For each of us the direction is different, but for many women the inner voice demands periods of silence and contemplation. It requires prayer and faith in creation. It requires a respect for land and life. Earth consciousness is the foundation of women's growing, and it is an honor for us to give back to the earth, to care for the animals, plants, people, minerals, to fight with all our will, politics, and the many forms of education we have earned in order to preserve life inside and outside ourselves.

This innerness, this Being, requires an awareness of the human condition in the entire world, and for many, this awareness will lead to action, political work, anti-war efforts, or the undertaking of some one of many tasks or labor. Our Being may demand of us that we participate in the evolution and revolution taking place in and around us, that we question our own ways of being, our own learned perceptions. Or it may demand of us that we provide service for others, or that we live a life of contemplation. Whatever it requires, we only know we must follow, and that our way is different from that of any other. As I said, we cannot measure ourselves against each other. Gandhi once said that it is better for a person to have their own Dharma, well-lived, than to imitate that of another.

Still, we can see from the stories we tell and re-tell that other women have had similar tasks, have been through the same stages of growth as we have, and we can compare notes on how we live, how we survive, how we passed through the fire of transformation. Our sharing is important on this threshold of life and change.

We have survived and in that survival is our life, strength, our spirituality. And we are telling about it, from the first stages of self-recognition, of the boundaries between self and others, to those strong and wise women, "The Prayer Lady" who achieves enlightenment while emptying the trash in Sylvia Watanabe's story, that healing woman in Shay Youngblood's "Born Wid Religion."

Without pretensions, the stories in this anthology speak the inner truths of women. They contain themes of familial love, loss, death, trauma, sexuality, power. They are stories of daily living. The stories tell how it has been and are telling how it can be. They are not stories about the creator, but about creation. They are stories about breaking, breaking down, breaking open, breaking out, and breaking free. They remind us of where we stand in our own living between birth and death. They ignore what was commonly thought to be landmark transitions in women's growing and instead, address the inner response to these events. They remind us to pay attention to our holy dailiness. The stories are our healing, our searching out love, union, self-knowledge. They return us to the inner core. These stories let the soul find us and find us out as if we were the last item in Pandora's box, and we are. They are our medicine.

Linda Hogan

I'd like to offer a special thanks to Michael Dennis Browne for the use of his cabin retreat where we read the manuscript, and to Joseph Bruchac for his assistance. And special love for the inner life of the three of us women who brought this project together, and for all the women whose work appears here, and for those strong writers whose work did not fit our needs, and for those women who will come after us with their own words and stories.

Linda Hogan

INTRODUCTION

. . . we are all born into communities, whether we like it or not and whether or not we get along with the community. And when I speak of 'doing one's first works over,' I am referring to the movement of the human soul, in crisis, which then is forced to reexamine the depths from which it comes in order to strike water from the rock of the inheritance.

James Baldwin, from *The Evidence of Things Not Seen*

Start with shame. That as an adult I have always been ashamed of the spiritual community into which I was born, in which I was raised. To be Christian, to be Protestant has seemed to me an assertion of the privileges that go along with being white, middle-class, North American, an assertion I have spent much of my life attempting to redesign.

Did my religion ever mean anything to me? I was taken to Sunday school every week with my sisters. I learned the stories in the bible, I suppose, but I know that my present knowledge of those stories is not from those days, but from a course in comparative religion I took in college and from my later interest in archetypes and mythology. When I was twelve I was intensely involved in a fundamentalist church for a summer, but I know now my interest was in a thirteen-year-old cousin with whom I was infatuated. I would have followed her anywhere and consider myself lucky she only took me to bible study class.

Shame. I graduated from college in 1966 and went to spend the summer with my family. They were stationed in Teheran, my father a military officer somehow on loan to the Iranians even though we weren't supposed to have a military presence there. I flew on Pan Am flight #1 half way around the world with my younger sister. On the first Sunday we went to church as a family, as we always had when I was growing up. The minister was a military chaplain, as he had always been. We sat in the pew in front of the American ambassador and his wife. There were the desultory songs, the offering, the sermon, and then the closing prayer. The chaplain called for "death and damnation to our enemies in Vietnam." I know he said it.

In 1961 I had gone to Antioch College wearing my U.S. Air Force sweatshirt, proud of what I thought it meant. But this was five years later. I had travelled in East Germany in 1965, and at every train station I had seen the signs sending "Greetings to our friends in North Vietnam in their struggle against the American aggressor." I didn't know where Vietnam was and had no idea how to respond when student friends asked me why the U.S. was invading Vietnam. That was the summer of the Watts riots. Reading about the riots in the East German press, I distrusted the reporting. I knew they were exaggerating. Police in my country simply wouldn't fire on crowds. I told my East German friends confidently that they were being lied to by their press. Then a friend's mother sent him the clippings from his home town Iowa newspaper. It was all true. And more. I began to wonder where Vietnam was.

That summer in Teheran, I thought a lot about Vietnam and about the chaplain's prayer. I had to think about it, since refusing to go to church with my family required an explanation. What it meant to me, I realized, was that the religion I had been brought up in served the interests of my government before it served any spiritual need I might have experienced. And I thought then that if that was what prayer was—a petition to god to bring death and damnation to the enemies of my government—then prayer was an obscenity.

I have learned many things about prayer since that time. When my mother was dying and no longer able to talk with us, I sat with her in the hospital and remembered how when I was a child she had told me that she prayed every day. "I talk with god," she said. When I asked what that meant, she explained that when she walked down the street she told the grass how beautiful it was and thanked the flowers for being there and talked with the birds and squirrels. It took a long time for me to understand what she was telling me: how she kept a "right relationship" with the world around her was through her daily prayer.

I called my friend Linda Hogan once and told her I didn't like the word prayer, that it embarrassed me. Didn't she find it embarrassing? There was a pause, then an exasperated, "Oh, you Christians!" I rushed to be offended, but she cut me off. "Judith, what do you think your poems are?" Of course. My poems are about creating a right relationship with my world, all parts of it. I imagine if I could have heard them, my mother's chats with the grass and the birds and squirrels might have sounded like poems.

In August of 1985 I went to Nicargua with Witness for Peace, an organization which describes itself as an interfaith group committed to nonviolence whose objective is to change U.S. policy toward Central America. The decision to make this trip with Witness for Peace was a difficult one for me. I prefer to think of myself as someone who believes in political solutions to problems; and while praying on the border between Honduras and Nicaragua has a certain dramatic symbolism, it was not clear to me how it was going to seriously challenge the reality of contra invasions and terrorist attacks on unarmed Nicaraguans. I was more convinced by the Nicaraguans' belief that when North Americans were present in their villages, the contra attack less frequently, a reality they attributed to contra reluctance to kill citizens of the country providing their primary funding and support. When our delegation was asked to be an unarmed presence on the southern border, the Rio San Juan, the border between Nicaragua and Costa Rica, I was relieved. This was an action I could support unambivalently. We would travel a river that had been closed to civilian traffic for 30 months due to contra harassment, a river that was vital to the survival of peasant families farming along its banks. When we were fired on by U.S. backed contras and captured and forced to march into the jungle on the Costa Rican side of the river, the political reality of our action became even more pointed. Costa Rica could not now claim that contra did not operate in and out of its territory.

When we were released and returned to the United States, I was surprised at how angry some people, many people, were at what we had done. Our local congressman said we had "holes in our heads" to have gone into a war zone and we deserved what we got. A caller on a radio talk show said no one would have been upset if we hadn't come back at all. Months later my sister said, "Well, you wouldn't call what you did religious, would you?" "Yes," I said, "I would." "No." She was quite firm. "That was a political action." And a woman in our delegation reported that a man at one of her talks wanted to know how much we had actually prayed on the trip. If we had prayed enough, the implication was, we could be called religious, but the minutes devoted to prayer had to equal more than the minutes devoted to political discussion. "I couldn't think how to answer him," she said, "and then of course in bed that night I knew what I wanted to say. I wanted to tell him that the action was the prayer."

The action was the prayer. I know that is true for me when the action is another way of creating a "right relationship" with my world. I had known it to be true when I was in college during the Civil Rights Movement and dozens of my classmates were "going south" on another kind of witness at lunch counters and on picket lines and marches and in prison, a witness that carried serious consequences, even death, for some. And I knew it to be true in my first years as a college professor when news of Vietnam mobilized the college campuses and we went out on strike and faced the riot police's bludgeons and marched with candles the night the president said he would not run for office again.

My shame at Christian hypocrisy and apparent self-servingness began to be transformed into a greater complex of feelings when I discovered liberation theology several years ago. Although I do not consider myself a Christian today, the realization that some North American Christians do indeed live in communities of resistance and solidarity with oppressed peoples made it possible for me to affiliate with Witness for Peace. And I am relieved that feminist theologians are helping all women who are members of patriarchal religions to struggle for their own liberation and to recognize their connections to other liberation movements. But for me, my most significant spiritual connection remains an action which helps me be in right relationship to my world.

I began this dialogue with my heritage by recognizing that I was raised in a religion, a faith, that was meant to be devoid of political content—unless that political content supported the status quo, the established power of the state, and remained implicit, not stated. That was the inheritance of my childhood. But the inheritance of my early adulthood was feminism and in these recent years I have had to struggle also with the richness and limitations of that movement.

I believe it was that energy for transforming our world, that energy that comes from transforming our world, which so informed the early feminist movement and drew me – and so many others – passionately into feminism. Most of the feminists I knew and worked with then certainly did not call the energy of our work "spiritual," although the language of liberation theology could have described our experiences: we worked with love for change, change that enhanced the entire community. We sat in consciousness raising groups and valued each woman's individual participation. Issues of class and race were briefly a focus of that early feminist movement. For feminism to become a radical and radicalizing force in the world, white women discovered that race and class issues had to be central to our thinking, our discussions. But there were many failures, and those failures continue today. Our theory is too seldom connected to our planning for action. Women's health care systems, rape crisis centers, women's buildings and other projects are frequently established by and for white middle class women. Because we had seldom made conscious or verbal the intersections of privilege and oppression, we are, I believe, also unprepared as a community to discuss or act on the realities of anti-Semitism as they affect Jewish women in a predominantly Christian society. And because we were trained in the duality of the patriarchy, we allow the separation of theory and action. Our words speak of our connections to one another; again and again our actions deny those connections. Sin, in liberation theology, is the denial of solidarity. I think that denial has been the continual failing of the broad based feminist movement in the U.S.

To say the action is the prayer is one way for me to begin to make the essential re-connections. It requires me to act as well as speak against racism, for example. It requires that I make the changes in my life which will create my personal community as one of "right relationship" – with me and within the larger world. It is this work, finally, which I see as "doing one's first works over." None of us is responsible for being born into a particular community, but we are responsible for and to the communities in which we choose to live and love and work.

When we began working on this anthology, I understood that redefining the "political" to include what was for me an essential "spiritual" element would be an important part of the work I wanted this book to be doing. We sent out the announcement calling for submissions and asked for stories of women's spiritual consciousness, for work that speaks about our connections, our waking and growth, moments of healing and transformation. We wanted stories that show women walking new paths, doing new work. If anything surprised me about the submissions we received it was that so few of them were about women working in political communities, feminist or otherwise. Georgiana Sanchez's "The Heart of Flowers Singing" portrays a woman whose personal epiphany leads her toward a political action and a political community. Yuri Kageyama's "Asian American Art Story" is set in the middle of a political collective. It was the only unsolicited story we received that used such a setting. When I asked friends who I knew wrote stories that I would describe as "political" or "feminist" if they would submit something for the anthology, each told me she had nothing that would be appropriate.

And so I began to reevaluate, to wonder at my own preconceptions, and to look at the stories we had received in new ways. This reflection brought me full circle back to my mother's talks with god. So many of the stories in this anthology are the teller's attempt to come into "right relationship" with her world, that I could not ignore the spiritual and political importance of that telling. It was, after all, just such an urge that sent women to consciousness raising groups in the late sixties and early seventies, an urge to tell the story, to know the story had been heard, and in the telling and hearing to transform the participants and the event.

We did also receive and find some wonderful stories about women who are healers, both of themselves and their communities, women who are strong and powerful, women who believe in themselves and their own power. Someday, I believe, in the not-too-distant future, women will be writing more stories like these and we will be able to read volumes of short stories about women who claim their power and shape their worlds.

Judith McDaniel

I. UNKNOWN TO MYSELF

Susan Marina Wolfe's words "unknown to myself" sum up how our lives sometimes move, often without our knowledge or consent. The stories in this section are pivotal episodes. They tell of growth stimulated by inner recognitions. They are stories where the inability to act is in its last life. This transition takes many forms. Some of these stories are filled with pain so intense that psychic numbing seems the only way to survive. Other stories remind us that we are in trouble every day and that we share a common pain: lives thwarted by the long history and vise-like grip of the patriarchy which still struggles, in many forms, to hold us back and down. Nonetheless, qualities of openness and vulnerability typify all the stories in this section. That openness seems to go hand in hand with reaching this turning point in women's lives. Here we are given an open mind, heart, and eyes so that the world can enter with all the facts we may have tried to deny or ignore at other stages in our lives.

Susan Marina Wolfe

Susan Marina Wolfe studies social and agricultural history at the University of Minnesota and the University of Wyoming. She has just turned forty, travels with her fourteen year old dog, Ben, and is trying to replace her '77 Civic.

"PIES"

There's a small old woman in my head.

This woman knits hats for her grandchildren's Christmases. She knits pink and blue hats with pompoms for men in their 30's. The hats are too small. The knitting is tight and harsh and rough enough to scour the burnt sugar from a pan.

It is September. This is the day for dipping cattle and giving injections. Ten of us are gathered at a mid-day table.

There is no plumbing here. There is no electricity. All morning an old gas stove has boiled up fresh-dug potatoes and carrots and beans from the garden. Homemade noodles are mixed with chicken. Pies are in the oven.

The workers wash their faces clean in a basin by the door as they enter the kitchen.

"Smells good," they say. "Looks like good eats."

The old woman, married to this family for 57 years, looks down and mutters firmly "Not fit t'eat."

Women pull the table from the wall and squeeze ten chairs around it.

"Do we smell apple pie?"

"Gran makes the best pies."

"Gran you make the best pie crust."

"Did you know she uses vinegar?"

We pass the dishes up one side and down the other. Arms bump against arms. Spoons clink against heavy bowls. Outside is a wind that will not stop until the work this day is done. There is dust in the wind.

"I'll take some of them potatoes down here."

"Mrs. Bates used vinegar and egg in her pie crust."

"Egg too? I never heard of that."

"I remember Mrs. Bates. She had all them kids didn't she?"

"She made the best pie crust. Been a lot of years since she gave me that recipe."

"I went to school with some of her kids."

"Lived in a shack down in town. Didn't have water—electricity—nuthin. Them six kids was always clean."

"Her husband wasn't much. Did he ever work?"

"She worked two jobs. Both down in town. I remember them kids. They was always clean."

"And she's the one who told you about vinegar and egg in the pie crust?"

"She was sickly for years, but she never missed a day of work. Them kids was always clean. Been a lot of years since she gave me that recipe."

"Didn't anyone try to help her?" I asked. Who had tried to help a sick woman with six clean kids, a useless man and two jobs?

Conversation stopped. Eating stopped. The wind outside continued.

"Fine eats, gran. Fine eats."

"Weren't much there fit t'eat."

Fifty-seven years she has spent with the tall man at the end of the table. He was drunk for fifty-five of them. There's a rusted car on top of a hill where he dragged it years ago when his dog died. He is sober now but the car is still on the hill. The woman makes pie crusts.

Five children came from this 57 years. Two drink, one paints the hills, and two are never mentioned. A grandson went through treatment, but he drinks. A grandson went through treatment, and he's dry. The daughter of one who isn't mentioned went to college, and we hear she picked up with a black man. A daughter learns to be a waitress in the town. "She carries them trays real good I hear." Praise from the old grand sire at the end of the table. Praise for the woman who carries trays and for the pie crust.

A son stretches his hands across his chest. "I'm about ready to try some of that pie."

"Smells awful good."

"Probably not fit t'eat."

The pies are cut. Hot slices of sugared apple slide from the crust and touch the plates she passes round the table.

4

"This dark one's got more cinnamon. Too much maybe. You don't want all that cinnamon. I knew it wouldn't be right. Too much cinnamon. It's too dark."

"Gran you make the best pies."

"Not fit t'eat."

"Vinegar and egg?"

"Got the recipe from Mrs. Bates. You remember Mrs. Bates? Them six kids of hers was always clean."

"She sure did a nice pie crust. Mom, you outdid yourself. Good eats."

"Weren't much there fit t'eat."

The wind outside pulls tighter round the house. The air is thick with dust. In the afternoon the men and women who know their jobs move back into the wind, pushing cattle through the chute with prods and shouts. Cows are being separated from calves. A woman gives injections for Black Leg and Red Nose. An implant is shot behind the ear for growth. Strong solution, dipped from a bucket, is ladled like broth onto the backbones of the cattle. It seeps through hide to kill the grubs beneath it. It seeps through human skin and burns. Dust blows into eyes and ears. There is bawling of cattle and wind.

This is Cow Camp. This is where they work the cattle. For 100 years this camphouse has stood on the homesteaded plain. It is two rooms filled with beds and a kitchen. Behind the hill is an outhouse. It's old and it leans. "You don't want to sit down too hard." So goes the family joke. No one is willing to start a new joke or dig a new pit.

The man I have chosen in my life is a grandson to this family. He is outside working in the wind. I sit with Gran.

She perches lightly on the edge of a bed. Beneath it is a chamberpot. Her feet don't touch the floor. Her left hand plucks at the fabric of her trousers.

We talk about strange dreams. We all have dreams. City or country, we all sleep and dream.

I tell her my recurring dream of being on a great ship that stops awhile but never docks. She clucks her tongue and looks confused. She does not dream of ocean liners.

Her foot begins to kick. "I dream," she tells me, "over and over that the kids are all small again. Ain't that something? We're going to go someplace and I get them all dressed. But we never get ready and we never go."

The windows are shut tight against the wind and dust. I hear the sounds of cattle and the shouts of those who work them, including the quiet man I love.

In the morning I will rise at four and pace his house until the light. I will cry when he finds me and shout to him in rage and fear that I will never make a pie crust. He will not understand. I will look at him and wonder at my life and at that moment, unknown even to myself, I will begin to leave.

Pam Brown

In May of 1983 I found myself arrested for sales and possession of a controlled substance. Something I thought would never happen to me. Jan. 26, 1984 I was sentenced to C.I.W. (California Institute for Women). Due to overcrowding I was sent to CRC (California Rehabilitation Center).

I became interested in the writing program known as Bright Fires. Writing has always been something I have been interested in. As a result of the Bright Fires program directed by Sharon Stricker and Co-directed by Stephanie Roth I learned how to express my writing voice. Without the fear of rejection.

I was released from CRC on Aug. 12, 1985 and I have taken with me the lessons I learned through writing in Bright Fires. I am still writing. I am writing to save my life.

JUST ANOTHER DAY

Maybe when I get out of here it would be nice to go to Berkeley and walk down Telegraph Avenue and remember the things I tried so many years to forget. Why not leave them where they are for now? Anger, fear, falling. I have this terrible fear of falling when I lay down at night and close my eyes. I see myself falling off of cliffs and high buildings. I have to shake away my vision so that I won't keep falling because it scares me. It hurts me. I don't want to fall and be crushed so I make myself stop and not see that any more. Then I change the scene in my head to something more pleasant and then all of a sudden here comes the falling again. I can be anywhere and all of a sudden I am falling and afraid of that falling. I back off from it.

That is how I handle most things in my life that are unpleasant. I just push them off to the side somewhere and keep going on like everything is ok even when it is not. Then I get to the point where I am numb. I don't feel any more. It is as though I am an outside observer in my own mind. I am like a message trapped in a bottle thrown out to sea, tossed among the waves and finally washed up on the shore waiting for someone to open the bottle and take out the message and read what it says: *RAGE fear cliff path falling sorrow anger hate deep root cancer death dying a little every day*

There is one of the roots! Dying a little everyday. Prison is like a cancer that grows into your heart and stops the breath from flowing. I am standing at the edge of a cliff right now. What I want and need to say is right on the edge of my mind but I just can't find it. What will bring it up and out of the dark regions of the mind . . . RAGE RAGE RAGE RAGE tearing the hair out by the roots.

I see this ragged cave woman tearing her hair out by the roots and foaming at the mouth.

I stuffed rage down into the bottom of my soul. When I had the last abortion, I did it so easily. Murder the baby I wanted to keep but couldn't. Don't keep it. You will never be able to handle it. It will only make life worse for you. Didn't I feel some amount of rage when the father of the baby looked at me and said, "You can do one of three things: 1) give it up for adoption when it is born; 2) marry me and sign over all rights to the child when it is born and then divorce me; 3) have an abortion.

I walked up the steps of the abortion clinic alone, full of cocaine so I wouldn't feel the rage that was building up inside? As I took each lonely step up the stairs and through the narrow corridor didn't I feel some sort of rage at being alone? I remember not feeling any thing. I remember doing such a good job of not feeling anything—with 3 or 4 grams of coke in my purse and probably at least a gram up my nose I could handle anything even rage. Alone I sat in the waiting room waiting for my turn. I paid my $200 and made several trips to the bathroom to keep stuffing more coke up my nose, to make sure that the rage stayed in the proper place.

Sitting in the waiting room at the abortion clinic. Wearing a pair of designer jeans and a silk top, sunglasses on top of my head, waiting. Finally I am led down the hall by an over-thin tall dark-skinned lady—into the room where a child in my womb will be torn away again for the fourth time. I don't think about it being the fourth time. I hate myself.

I smile at the doctor when he comes into the room. In my mind, I am trying to make it like a day at the beach. Like this is an everyday thing that I am doing and telling myself that I won't feel a thing. I probably have at least 2 grams of coke in me at this point. I am ready for anything. I am alone. No one knows where I am today. I lied to my friends and told them that I wasn't PG (pregnant) and that I had to go to the doctor. Later today I am going to make a large drug deal. All in a day's work. I laugh to myself. Back to the table. I am laying on the table now and the vacuum starts. I barely feel the pain. My legs are spread and in stirrups. The doctor looks at me and says, "Does that hurt?" "No, it's ok."

It's over. We start the small talk now. Something about me being a buyer for a boutique. I like that blouse that you have on. See I told you, Pam, this is not ever going to have to be felt. You breezed right through it, see? You can talk to the doctor about what she has on. Aren't you strong aren't you normal aren't you alone. Sit up now. Dizzy. I need to get out of here. I have so many things to do today. Don't feel a thing. I am then led down the same narrow corridor to the recovery room. I am alone. I have just had an abortion and I have to drive myself home. I am not mad. I am not sad. Why am I alone today of all days? I have too many things to do. I don't need anyone here. What good does it do? I wait about 15 minutes and then I ask if I may leave. If you're feeling ok you can leave.

Feeling ok?

I walk back down the same stairs I came up and somehow they seem a little lonelier to me than they did when I walked up them. I walk outside into the sunlight shake my head. I get into my sky blue duster, start the engine, put the car in reverse and squeal the tires taking off out of my parking space. I feel reckless self-destructive but mostly wreckless. Driving too fast hoping I die in a car that I know is not safe I head for home.

Esther K. Willison

I am one of the founders of an alternative public school in Schenectady, New York. I have two grown daughters (ages twenty-six and twenty-two), am politically active, enjoy sports and play the recorder with friends. I have worked some summers as the program director at a camp for handicapped children and young adults. Currently I am on sabbatical, in graduate school (English Literature), and working on my first novel. I was married for eighteen years and have been living for the past three years with another woman.

THE DROP

Nola and Seymour waited in the living room of the small house. They could hear their two daughters thumping around upstairs.

"I wonder where they are," Nola said, looking out the window.

"Oh, they're usually later than they say, aren't they?" responded her husband.

"I guess so. The later the better. I'm glad they have to leave early tomorrow." Nola stood up and tugged her blouse down from under her skirt.

"Oh, they're not so bad," Seymour answered. He liked his in-laws. He liked everyone.

"No, not for you," Nola said sharply, "you go in your study and close the door." A loud crash was heard above them. Whatever dropped had been broken. At the same time a black and brown Lincoln pulled up in front of the house.

"You go greet them. I'll go upstairs. At least they weren't hurt. No one's crying." Nola ran upstairs. Sy waited for her parents to come to the door. He wished Nola was able to confront her mother although he realized why it was easier for him. He wished she would disagree with him sometimes, too, instead of retreating. Her silence scared him. Occasionally she receded so far into her tunnel, his arm was not long enough to reach her to pull her back. And he didn't like stretching.

Nola's mother and her stepfather, Don, came jumbling through the door, bringing December's cold, windy air with them. Pam and Leslie came bounding downstairs, two at a time, in the matching dresses grandma had given them the last visit.

"Hello, hello," Don said, putting down the packages and small suitcase. He wore a bright blue cap over his fuzzy white hair. His eyes were also blue, but duller than the cap. Emily hugged her grandchildren, not too hard, lest they tip askew her blond wig. She was a small woman with a tall ego, her pretty face in a perpetual pose, as if the photographer might be just around the corner. Nola, hanging up her mother's long fur coat, asked, "How was the trip?"

"Well, not bad," Don replied. "Em took a good snooze like she always does . . . "

"Don! You exaggerate! I was resting. I can't sleep with you driving. You nod off. We'd never get here alive!" She looked around the house. This was their first visit since Nola and Sy moved in.

"Mmm. Cute. Small. No bedrooms downstairs?" Nola looked at Seymour but he was preoccupied, hanging up the garment bag.

"No, no bedrooms. Want to see the upstairs or are you hungry? You both look good."

"Thank you. You've put on a little weight, haven't you," her mother responded, adding, "let's go up—Oh, I see you'll have to put carpeting on these stairs." The children followed her up, scampering into their own rooms at the top, each calling to "come and see my room!" Sy stayed downstairs to start a fire in the small fireplace.

"Nice," Emily said, looking around, "interesting arrangement." Leslie, who was ten, kept her room like piano keys, everything in order—all the time, the orange crates stacked in straight rows, the strings of beads hanging from her loft bed, protecting her secret hideaway, exactly the same length. Pam, four years younger, had cleaned her room for Grandma's visit and never noticed the lumps and wrinkles in her bed until Grandma said, "Oh, I see you are trying to make your bed. That's nice." There were bits of paper and crayons sticking out here and there and three boots lay huddled together in a corner of the room.

After glancing into Seymour and Nola's bedroom and Seymour's study, Em stood in the bathroom.

"But there's no shower curtain in here."

"That's true. We have to get one."

"We'll go tomorrow. You need a rug for the hall downstairs too, a gold one would be just right."

"That's fine," Nola replied smiling, although she began to conjure up her anger. Her large, dark eyes blinked too often. She bit down on the left side of her thin lips. She quickly finished giving her mother a tour of the house.

"You have to buy some plastic covers for your dining room chairs. If you don't they will look ragged in no time."

"I don't like plastic," Nola said, trying to sound like she was saying, "What a grand idea that is!"

"You can get clear plastic made to size. I'll send you some."

"The chairs look fine. They won't wear out." Nola felt her long, sharp nose tingle, her nostrils enlarge.

"If you don't take good care of them, they'll look terrible. Plastic covers are wonderful. I have them."

"No, but thanks anyway."

"I'll send you some."

Next Em asked her daughter why she didn't have a glass top on the tea cart she had brought for them when they moved in.

"Your brother has one on his. You must protect the wood, Nola, it will stain." Nola tried to keep from using her power but it was getting harder and harder. Maybe lunch will help, she thought. She had started to confide in Sy about her power but he wouldn't let her finish. He was a pragmatist.

"You don't expect me to believe that, do you? Besides, why would you do that even if you could? Try to understand people a little more. You have to put yourself in their world." His full features and curly brown hair rounded his words even more. "And if you get mad, just say so. Scratch the most obnoxious person and find a pleasant surprise underneath, right?" (Once she had called his optimism the baby fat of his mind—too plump for her lean analysis.) "Now don't bother me with fantasy," he continued, flicking his hand out towards her, "I have work to do."

They ate tuna fish sandwiches and drank coffee. The children were laughing and kicking each other under the table. Sy and Don talked about the recent presidential election. Emily asked, "Don't you have any whole wheat bread? This rye bread is too hard for me to digest."

"No, sorry, Mother. I'll get some when we go out."

"So, how's your school doing, Nola?"

"Very well. We have a big enrollment now because . . . "

"Do you have skim milk? Leslie, that dress is getting too small for you. Here, pull the sleeves down." Em tugged at Leslie's sleeves. When lunch was over, Nola's mother stood up.

"Oh, I have to go *upstairs* to the bathroom, don't I. I would never buy a house with just one bathroom. Your brother has two." Nola waited until her mother was halfway up the stairs before she dropped her. Ffut! Swish! Gone. She had dropped a few people before, but never so quickly, never without reconsidering. The stairs sank in less than a second through the floor of the house, sank through the ground and disappeared, her mother with them. It always surprised Nola that she was the only one who saw it happen, and the only one who could make it happen, for that matter.

She looked over at her two children, her husband and her stepfather. They had not even noticed. She was also astonished to see the instant replacement of anything she sank; an identical set of stairs had reappeared already. Her mother was gone, vanished, underground — yet all appeared the same. The disappearances were silent except for a barely audible swoooosh sound, like a car at high speed going through a puddle.

Nola had realized she could drop people about six months before her mother's visit. Louise Saniniap, the parent of one of her students, had called her and threatened to have her fired if she failed to teach her young son to read. Nola hadn't taken the threat seriously at first and told Louise she couldn't give her any guarantees. The child was nine years old and a new student in the small, private school where Nola taught. The Saniniaps were financial backers of the school. Louise began to call Nola every day. She organized a group of parents who claimed they could prove that Nola was not a qualified teacher. They complained about her "inability to maintain discipline." Nola, threatened by Louise's verbal attacks, was physically afraid of her as well. She looked like the sharpest totem pole bird come to life, especially when she flapped her broad winged arms menacingly.

One Saturday morning, when Louise came to the house to ask Nola to resign, Nola imagined dropping her through the living room floor where they sat. Ffut! Swish! Chair and all, down she went. The chair reappeared, empty. Nola had thought about this drop for several weeks. She had been concerned for Louise's family and her co-workers at her job. She was not worried about them discovering her — how could anyone ever find out? She was a little bothered by the morality of it. Did she have the right to drop people? The community was still looking for Louise.

But after the first drop, it became easier. She dropped her sister-in-law, Monique, without any moral qualms. For years Monique pushed her husband to earn more and more. She refused to make any adjustments after his first heart attack. More and more was her motto, no matter who suffered. He wanted children, but she wouldn't take the risk of sacrificing her career. Finally, he wanted to end their marriage but didn't know how. So Nola had dropped Monique. Nola's mother mourned for a month or so, but she had important work to do and expensive clothes to wear. She recovered quickly and incorporated her daughter-in-law's disappearance into her already long list of "terrible things that have happened to me."

Nola had almost dropped Sy in a restaurant a week before her mother's visit, but she had remembered, at the last moment, that she hated living alone and that they were, after all, friends, in spite of their disagreements. It was unusual for them to eat out as Sy did not believe in it. He got up suddenly when she had said, "this casserole is cold. But don't call the waitress. I don't want you to tell her."

"That's just fine," Sy snapped. "How do you expect me to enjoy my meal when you're unhappy but refuse to do anything about it!" He threw his napkin on the table and marched out. Later, when Nola got home, she had given Sy a pre-drop stare but then she remembered that the children were quite fond of their father.

After lunch everyone began to look for Em. The search continued all afternoon. Don's theory was that someone had hurt her feelings and she had gone back to New York.

"But how did she get there?" Seymour asked him.

"Oh, she could have walked to the train station. When she decides the world is against her, there's no stopping her from suffering. It's what she does best." Sy wasn't satisfied. Her disappearance was too reminiscent of Monique's. He wondered if there was a relationship. Nola was busy comforting the children. They were worried about themselves disappearing.

"That will never happen. I promise you," she told them.

"You don't seem to be too concerned about your mother," Seymour spoke up, looking at her, searching her eyes. He noticed that she had become even more quiet recently, rarely offering a comment, or opinion. But the disappearance of her mother was a serious matter.

"Oh, I am concerned," she said. I just know that she can take care of herself, wherever she is. You would think she might have left us a note, though."

Seymour reported his missing mother-in-law to the local police and to the New York police, but she never turned up. Don inherited her savings and lived for a long time, comfortably, eating and drinking all the food and drink his wife had forbidden him to touch. He wore his socks for more than one day and he continued driving absentmindedly without mishap.

A dozen years went by; the children were grown and away at school. Nola, as she got older, dropped more and more people, some of them indiscriminately. Each time she felt a sense of relief and satisfaction. But each time the feeling was temporary. Sy watched her becoming more and more withdrawn. He had always been somewhat impatient with her personal probings anyway, so part of him was relieved. She was no longer interested in his work and she never talked about her own job. She was losing weight. Her nose, even thinner now, was beaked.

Sometimes Nola had a rationale for her drop. One late afternoon, her neighbor, Bunny Togib, came over to visit. "Did you see that new family," she asked Nola, "the one up the street on the left, the Handlers? Once we start letting the coloreds in here, it's all over for us." Ffut! Swish! Right through the floor went Bunny. Nola smiled. She folded her arms contentedly.

Nola saw a group of high school kids chasing someone. She was driving home from work. She didn't like the way the kids were shouting at the young boy fleeing from them. She stopped her car and dropped all five at once. One by one their families noticed they were missing. Some of the parents were also friends—they wondered if the teenagers had run away together. Fearfully they asked each other if they could have been kidnapped. The police found no trace of them. The other families in the neighborhood became so frightened they stayed in their houses for two weeks.

Other times she would drop someone because of their tone of voice or because she didn't like the way they looked. The local newspaper began printing articles about so many disappearance. They published photographs of the missing people.

Nola isolated herself more and more. She ate little. Seymour tried to get her to talk about it. But nothing he did helped. He never knew how close he came to disappearing himself.

"What's bothering you?" he asked gently.

"Nothing," Nola answered. "Or everything. Everything *is* nothing. Everybody is nobody."

"That's true," Sy agreed. "But could we make something out of nothing if it weren't? How could anyone become somebody if they didn't start out as nobody?" But Nola didn't hear Sy. It was too late. The anorexic mind cannot accept baby fat. It's too rich. A few weeks later Sy tried again. "If you're not happy you can change."

"No, I can't."

"Why not?"

"I don't have *that* kind of power. Mine is magic."

"What do you mean, magic? There is no such thing."

"I know."

At last, Nola, having dropped everyone with whom she disagreed, sat alone in her house. It was summer; school was out. The air was warm and still. Seymour was working in the garden. Every flower, every weed, was coddled by his chubby hands. The daughters, finished with school, led busy lives in other towns. There was no one now at whom to be angry. And she had become so thin that there was no excess left on her body to replace the anger. A sense of loss frightened and depressed her.

Seymour came in from the garden and called Nola. He called a second time. After a few moments of silence he heard a faint swoosh sound. His wife did not answer the third call either. He searched the house and contacted all their friends. They printed her picture in the local paper. Seymour never recovered from her disappearance. He often wondered about the sound he heard that day, but he never told anyone about it. He had, at last, found a way to protect her.

Bismillan IR Rahman IR Rahim

Translated: In the name of God most gracious most merciful.

Yasmeen Jamal

My name is Yasmeen Jamal; I am an artist; Irish American, a believing woman to the teachings of Quran and an ex-con.

I started writing in prison to keep tabs on my sanity. I continue to write for the same reasons although I am now part of society called the "free world."

I, as a woman did not at times realize the full potential of being that mother/daughter/bearer of life/backbone of society. The worth of women is a true blessing. I pray to always be reminded of our worth.

THE CONVERSION

"Yes, Baby Cakes, you have the smell of a fish. You can always tell the new dames on the yard. They all have the air of fresh flowers just waitin' to be picked. How long have I been here? Let me see. Fifteen years this comin' Spring. I came just after the prison was built in nineteen sixty-nine. Hell of a year to get busted for more reasons than one, let me tell ya'. The tax payers raised all kinds of hell and the legislature patted themselves on the back for getting the bill approved to build this tin-can. At first they kept the women housed at the men's joint, but that didn't work out too well. Too much nature takin' it's course; know what I mean?

"Just the other day, Big Mamma, she's the Superintendent, gets busted dippin' her hands where they don't belong. She had a habit for years taking our money and spending it her way. She finally got caught. Heard tell, they're thinking about filing charges. It would serve her right to get convicted and walk this yard with us. She never would walk the yard before without her henchmen to back her. She has the sliest smile in the world and eyes that never flinched about nothin'. And when she spoke, the earth trembled. Yes indeed, she was a cold piece. Personally, I liked the fat bitch, but I was one of a very few, you can believe that. I understand she was a crook and I always did understand. Game recognizes game Baby Cakes, all over the world. Don't ever forget that."

"Listen Honey, you stick with me and you'll do just fine. Listen to what I tell you and keep your mouth shut. Those are the first rules you learn about doing time. You are pretty, young, and tender; these women will be on you like white on rice. I know what I am talkin' about. Your schooling starts right here with me. I don't want you gettin' out of line; I'll teach you the ropes. What are the ropes? Damn Baby, you don't know too much do you? I see I gotta take you real slow."

"You know I used to be a pretty, young thing like you. Still don't look too bad, for an old dame. Don't laugh. It's true. I was fine as wine and just your kind. That was before I came to prison. I have spent all these years on the yard and looks like I am going to die here. Do I feel bad? Honey, I stopped feeling anything years ago. And you better do the same if you want to survive. Listen, I came in doing two life sentences. Both of them running wild. It means, Dimwit, that after I do one life sentence, I have to start the other one. Ha, I often wonder how they intend on collecting that last life sentence. Dig me up after I am dead to start it? I might just decide to live long enough to find out."

"How did I get busted? All right, let me run it to you. I was a ho'. What is it? It's a whore, Stupid. A woman who sleeps with men for money and or favors. I preferred the money. Some real kinky fellas out there Baby, and I got paid for taking care of their kinks. Now you understand? Good, I knew you could hang in there. Anyway I stayed on the road. I went to different cities; stayed in the best hotels; and worked my trade. I was well paid and respected by my circle of friends. Most of them gangsters, like me, appreciating a woman knowing how to take care of herself. See it is not what you do, but how you do. A woman can maintain respect no matter who she sleeps with. All you got to do is follow rules and regulations of your profession. Codes, you might say. Cons have codes too. You'll learn them soon enough."

"Getting back to me. I had missed a flight to New York and decided to spend the night at a hotel near the airport. About 9:00 P.M. I get a little antsy sitting in my room. So I go downstairs to have a soda at the bar. I never drink liquor. Takes a woman's age faster than anything I know. This man was alone and he starts a conversation with me; I feed into it, figuring I can make me a couple of hundred extra bucks. What the hell, I was bored anyway. I bring him up to my room for some fun and games. He is more than a little drunk, which should have clued me then not to mess with him. I had set a rule for myself never to pick up a drunk for a client. Should have followed my mind; never would have been here if I had. Anyway, he starts to rough me up a bit. I tell him to back off and I start to get dressed. He gets angry and tells me; check this out; "That he didn't get his monies worth." The creep wasn't marrying me, so he got more than he paid for. Some of those bastards never get enough. He was one of them. The more belligerent he gets; the more I act a fool. Finally, I pull my derringer out. Not to hurt him, but to get the idiot away from me. I always carried a neat derringer for my own protection, me being a woman by myself. We start to struggle and the gun goes off. Guess who caught the fuckin' bullet? The jerk bled to death, I find out later. Soon as I saw the red of blood, I booked out of there ninety goin' north. I mean, quick, fast, and in a hurry. I was so scared I left the money he had paid me."

"I catch a ride with some truck driving chump who has more on his mind than just giving me a lift. I am; in no way, shape, or form ready to be gogled. I am not in the mood; plain and simple. This guy starts to get real physical, so I grab a whiskey bottle that was laying in the front seat and belt the shit out of him. He croaks too. When they catch up with me, I am holed up in some two-bit hotel room in Albuquerque. During my trial, I find out the first man was some Senator's son from Wisconsin and the trucker owned half the state of Georgia. Still can't figure out why he was driving a truck that day. But to make a story short; I get two life sentences runnin' back to back."

"There is another woman here doing three hundred and ninety-nine years total. She blew up a factory, full of folks, during working hours. So I am not the only one with a lifetime contract with the penal system. There are plenty of lifers to keep me company. But do me a favor, do not look so out done when you hear stories of woman doing long time. It is an every day occurence around this camp. We treat it like a cut. It hurts, but only for a little while. A lot of things happen behind bars that the free world find shocking. It is no big thing to us doing time. Remember what I said; keep your eyes open and your mouth shut. Life will be a lot healthier."

"Girl, will you quit staring? No, that is not a man. That is Sonia and she is a stud broad. A woman who dresses up in men's attire is what she is. But Honey, let me tell you, she sits her butt on the toilet seat just like you and I do. Haven't you ever seen two women kiss before? I see I have got to take you so slow, that we damn near stop in the middle of the stream. You know you can drown like that don't you? The women that you are so obviously gawking at are married. How do I know? I married them last week. That's why they call me the Preacher. Let me hip you to who I am.

I am the official, un-official, Justice of Peace around here. I handle divorces too. It can get to be quite profitable. I charge a fee. Game don't stop just cause you are locked up Baby Cakes. I got to survive. So do you. In the summertime someone is always getting married and/or divorced. I call it my three F season: fixin', fightin', and fuckin'. The Preacher helps these women do all three."

"Everybody on the yard has a hustle. Got to. Keeps the mind sharp and you on your toes. What's a hustle? A trade, so to speak. Like me and the marriages I perform. I supply a demand. These dames wanna play dress up and get married? Cool, I marry them. I know it don't mean a damn thing but you tell one of these life doin' bitches they can't get married. Sometimes, the women hustle each other. They raw-dog to the max. Some call it "canteen pimpin". It goes like this. A new woman comes to the yard; like yourself for example. Fresh and green, like summers grass. One of the more aggressive women will peep her to see just what she is about; which means how much money she has on her books. The next thing you know, the new fresh dame is not so new and fresh any more. She has had her drawers pimped from her. It happens all the time. It is not hard to find out how much money a woman has either. How much do you have? That much huh? Do me a favor and don't tell anyone else, you hear?

"See that dame over by the fence. The woman in the blue pull over sweater. Yeah, that's the one. You stay away from her, you understand? I want you to stay away from any woman who can't remember how to put their lipstick on. If you want a man, I'll see about getting you one. But you stay away from the fakes. How will I get you a man? Don't worry your sweet head about it. There is nothing the free world has, within reason, that the Preacher can't get a hold of, including a man. You just gotta know how to go about it. I see you still don't know who I am. You'll learn. I have a reputation Baby Cakes; and it ain't too shabby. You'll have everything you need and then some if you play it smart."

"Another thing, while its on my mind. Don't ask a con nothin'. Let them offer the information to you. You'll stay pretty longer, if you follow my advice. You will get all the grapes just by bein' around me. Nothin' happens on this yard that I don't know about. It comes with the territory. I call it privileged access."

"And listen Doll Face, if anyone brings you anything to make you feel good, by all means take it. Don't turn nothin' down but your collar. But don't consume a thing. Not until the Preacher has a chance to check it out for you. I don't care what it is. Pills, powder, perfume; it matters not. Just hold on to it until I have a chance to get at you. Stay away from the hooch though. Hooch, Lame Brain, hooch. You are dumber than I thought. Hooch is alcohol made from fruit and yeast. Hooch, primo, what ever the name; you stay clean away. I already told you it can make you old before your time. It can kill you too. A friend of mine keeled over in seventy-two from a bad batch. This penitentiary can make you or break you. Depends on you; how you choose to do your time. We are going to get you enrolled in school; I can see that now. That way I can keep an eye on you. It will keep you off the yard and out of folks business.

"Yesterday they took Betty to the hole for beating up her woman. She swept the floor with Yaya's butt. Used it like it was a broom. That's what will happen if you stick your nose in business that don't concern you. But you'll be all right; as long as you listen to the Preacher. I take care of mine."

"Lot of dames you see are career criminals. In other words, they are not in prison behind crimes of passion. If they caught their husbands with Sally Mae, the next door neighbor, most of them would just get them a new husband. Damn going to prison behind a man cheatin'. They are here because prison is an occupational hazard. They feed their kids, pay their bills, send Lil' Mary to dance classes, and take yearly vacations, just like normal people; except on money made illegally. They are professionals in what they do. Listen Baby Cakes, their life style beats slingin' beef jerky any day of the week. They look at life as a gamble; you win some and you loose some. Always remember, a professional lives by the codes of their profession, no matter what it is. If I had lived by mine, I wouldn't be here. What was mine? One was never to mess with drunks, remember? I did and I got charged. Prison is my charging; not my occupational hazard. Dope dealers, forgers, thiefs; they all have codes they live and die by. That's what makes you a pro. Law of the land Baby Cakes; that's what time it is."

"You know you are not so bright as you are pretty. By the time I finish with you, you'll be one bad bitch. But you gotta listen to the Preacher. See a hard head will make a soft ass. Don't be no fool."

"First thing we gotta do is put some money from your books on to canteen. Canteen is where you shop once a month. Don't worry, I'll show you how. You have to fill out a money draw slip and put it in the box next to the canteen building. Here, get me a slip and I will fill it out for you. We want this done right. We'll put the full amount allowed which is one hundred ten dollars. That way we don't run out of money when we shop. Never can tell when you might run out of cigarettes and coffee and need to re-up. Especially the way these women borrow. If anybody asks you for anything, tell them to see me; I'm running this show. I don't care what it is; don't loan nothing out. OK, you got the slip signed? Good we can take it to the box on our way to dinner. Next Tuesday you can shop and I'll go with you. I'll even help you write a list for what we need. What brand do you smoke? That's a coincidence. Me too."

"It is going to be such a pleasure doing time with you. We have so much in common. The Preacher is going to take special care of you. You're going to be my Sugar Pie. Don't worry about a thing. By the way, what is your name?

Andrea Freud Loewenstein

Andrea Freud Loewenstein is a lesbian-feminist writer who just returned to the Boston area after living in London for two years. Her work life consists of balancing teaching and writing. As a teacher she has worked primarily with women who have been deprived of a voice, trying to help them get it back. As a writer, she has published one novel, THIS PLACE, and is at work on a second novel and a collection of short stories.

28

CRAB QUEEN

(Tuesday morning) Last week in our rap Rev. Tom suggested that I keep a diary of my spiritual progress so here goes nothing. I told him I was never very good at compositions at school, my sister was the creative one, not me, I was just the pretty one and hope I have still got my looks as I am thirty-two now and can still fit into the dress I was married in. But he said to just pretend I was having a rap with Jesus, the way I do with him. To talk to Him freely from the bottom of my heart and He would excuse errors of spelling punctuation and etc. And besides he said not to worry because this diary will be for my own eyes and His alone, Rev. Tom said it was alright not to even show it to Billy (that's my husband) but I could share selected passages with him (Rev. Tom) if I felt the need in our next rap but not to feel I must.

I think Rev. Tom must be the best Spiritual Advisor around and you would think that even more if you knew Bill before he got saved with his Red-Neck ways and every other word out his mouth a cuss and the way he would stay out drinking a lot with the boys. Which was one main reason Mom and Dad threw such a fit when we had to get married plus his family is sort of low-class from the South Bay which is where mostly the Red-Neck and Hill-Billy families that are on welfare live. Rev. Tom says no one will find The Way until their ready and you can only lead a horse so far into the water but he has to drink his own self, but I bet no other Rev. could of led Bill this far to where he has turned 100% around and has not touched a drop of liquor in over two and one half years, and coaches the North Bay Little League that Billy Jr is in for recreation plus takes us all out on his outboard fishing in the bay, in other words has become a real "Family Man". To tell you the truth now I sometimes feel he has left *me* behind the way I lose my temper at times (which I have always had a problem with) at him and the kids but especially at Shirlye which is Dad's wife that he married only less than two months after Mom died of her liver and who is enough to try the patience of a Saint which as I just said I am not.

Which brings me back to: Why I Am Writing This. It is because even *inside* me I have feelings that are not Christian for instance sometimes I feel like just taking and shaking my kids until they snap in two specially Kate my second girl who always trys to pick a fight with the whole world and does her best to aggravate me and I almost always stop myself and don't lay a hand on her but I still *feel* that way. And when Shirlye is at her worse for instance after Dad had offered to help Bill out on the mortgage on the house just during the Winter months which are the worst time for the Station because there are no Summer People here, galivanting around and not caring how much they spend on gas then. Well that time she forced him to call back after we had already been counting on the help and planned accordingly and take it all back, and even had the nerve to imply that it was *me* behind the whole thing that had *pressured* Dad to give us *her* money as she put it although everyone knows when you marry your money passes right into your husbands hands and is his as much as yours to do what he pleases with. Say what you want about Mom she was never tight with money, she'd as soon give it away as keep it, specially when she'd been drinking. Sometimes *she'd* talk mean to you too, but it was when she was drunk, and didn't know what she was saying, it would just sort of slip out by accident. But Shirlye is the same drunk or sober—just as mean and nasty as she can be.

So when she did that I just kept trying to remember Rev. Tom's sermons, and repeated to myself over and over, "Forgive her she know not what she does", and "Love they neighbor as thyself", only I put in Stepmother for neighbor. But still I woke up like I sometimes do at night with this feeling like a rock in my stomach and just couldn't fall back asleep. It is no point waking Bill at these times, because he just doesn't understand, even though he is as sweet as can be, and will get the Pepto Bismal and even make me a cup of tea if I ask him to. But if I told him it was being angry that was upsetting my stomach he just would not comprehend what it was I was talking about. But Rev. Tom does understand and he says that is why I should keep this diary: as a sincere effort to rid myself of these feelings and develop a truly loving and Christian attitude plus to get an Outlet. He says an Outlet is very important. That it is a constant struggle and battle with your self to be a good Christian. That everyone has feelings like mine even him and it is not wrong to have them as long as you constantly struggle against them and be sure to get an Outlet. Because or else it can get to you and drive you nuts or make you sick, like for instance in my case I could get stomach ulcers. Or Migraine Headaches like Shirlye gets, or Sugar like my neighbor down the road Misty Brown. Or Heart like Dad or else turn to drink like Mom did. Because sometimes you can get to feeling like a pressure cooker with four kids under twelve and a husband to take care of plus a new home with a mortgage that takes more than half his salary and nothing but relatives that don't even realize that a gas station does not bring in that much and you could use a little help but instead try to make things harder than they already are (not that it's Dad's fault that Shirlye won't give him a penny.)

Also my only sister Kate who Katy's named after that went away to college then moved to New York city to live when Mom was at her worse. Of course everyone has a perfect right to just look out for theirself, but the burden has to fall somewhere, and Dad never could cope with Mom when she was drunk, it just plain upset him too much and brought on his Heart and there I was living three blocks away at the time in our old place so it was up to me. *I* would of liked to go to college too but I guess the Lord didn't intend it that way, and now of course I have Billy Jr and Timothy and Katy and Barby who I wouldn't trade a hair on their heads for all the college education and BA in this one and MA in that one and PHD that Kate is working on right now and all the fancy ways she went and developed as soon as she left home such as being a liberal and a vegetarian and an atheist and a woman's libber, plus a Homosexual which thank goodness Mom died before she found out although come to think of it, she probly might not of objected if it was Kate doing it. Now when *I* got pregnant they were ashamed to show their heads outside the door and couldn't ever consider me their real daughter again. Plus, they'd knew I would end up that way all the time because of the horish way I acted. (That's the very words Dad used to me, and I haven't ever forgot them, either.) But as for Kate, you would of thought she never did anything to disappoint anyone, the way they treat her. Mom used to wear her honors society key around her neck and had those degrees of her framed and up on her bedroom wall where she wouldn't even hang pictures of her own grandchildren. So probly if she'd found out that Kate was a homosexual that liked girls, that would of been peachy-keen, too.

Well there comes Barby with her blanket in her mouth and dragging down the stairs picking up dog-hairs as she goes and that means the others are sure to follow. What reminded me about Kate is she is coming in two days for a short visit, which will mean extra work and effort on everyone's part with her being a Vegetarian and all, so we never know what to give her to eat and have to cook special. It's just as well she never stays more than a day or two though of course I will be just tickled to see her. It's been more than a year now, and the kids don't even know their Aunty Kate. Last time she came the first thing out of Timmy's mouth was "Mommy, is that a boy or a girl?" before I could get to him. But who could blame the kid seeing that Kate does dress like a man and wears her hair short enough for one, though she is a petite blond like me who could be cute enough if she ever did anything with herself, so she never looks like a full-grown man, but more like a boy that I bet takes about the same size as Billy Jr big as he is this year.

One person that will not be tickled to see Kate is Shirlye, who has been complaining about it for a week now. She says Kate acts like she's too good for us and even talks Northern now, and she shouldn't even bother to come home if she can't act like folks. Then too, she threw a fit over a letter Kate wrote to Dad last year all about how she never gets to talk to him alone without her (Shirlye) being there which is all too true, by the way, that woman will but in everywhere, you can never snatch a moment alone with your own Father. Plus Kate wrote its impossible to talk about Mom when Shirlye is around because it upsets her and she wants to be able to talk about Mom with him. Well I know just what Kate means, and I think it's darn spooky the way no one will mention her name like she was a ghost that never existed or something but in a way you can see Shirlye's point too in this case, after all she is Dad's wife, and I might feel the same way if Bill had been married before, and not want to be reminded of Her all the time.

(Wed. 3:30 PM)   I read what I wrote so far and prayed hard to get rid of my anger and unforgivingness. I have decided not to show it to Rev. Tom until I improve in my feelings. Rev. Tom says all the feeling sorry in the world doesn't help a mite unless you change your actions too, so I called Shirlye right up and talked with her for at least one half hour after the kids left for school. Mostly she complained about Kate. It was hard to put up with but I know it is worth it for how else will the kids have a "real" relationship with their grandparents like all kids deserve to. Billy Jr. still remembers Mom who used to just love him to pieces whenever she was sober, but as for the others, Shirlye is all the "Grandma" they've got, since Billy's folks passed. And too, I can understand how Shirlye feels. You'd think Kate would at least try to adjust to the life we live here which used to be her own, and just eat what is served, which used to be plenty good enough for her.

I had to interrupt to separate Katy and Timmy. Seems like I am always telling *her* to sit still and be a lady and him to fight back which he should seeing that he is a boy and almost a whole year older. And Katy! One time last year she got sent home from school for fighting a little boy in her class, that she said took her lunch which is the way of little boys and the teacher could of got it back for her if she would of just gone through the right channels. But that girl won't ask you for the time of day, she never has, she rather fight. Well that time thank the Lord I remembered what Rev. Tom says and instead of hitting her just talked to her very quiet about how hurt Jesus felt at what she did, and how ashamed He was of her for not acting like a little lady which I think did have its effect more than a beating would of done, just like he said it would. I sometimes worry that she will take after Kate (I mean in her mannish ways) but come to think of it now, Kate was more like Timmy in that way, shy and small for her age and with that way of sitting so still in one spot all buttoned up and so quiet you almost forget their there. But in how she hates to wear a dress Katy takes after Kate all right.

I remember how Kate used to go and hide under the porch when it was time to get dressed for church because she said the ruffles hurt her legs and I would be the only one who could get her out. By the time she was born, Mom was drinking pretty steady which was why the Dr. had her tubes tied, he said her system wouldn't support another birth. They used to call me Little Mother and think it was cute because I was only four years older than her, but if you ask me it was not cute but sad because who was going to look after that child if I didn't? Mom never noticed if we ate or not, or how we looked. I used to just love getting dressed up myself, and always had the hope that Mom might notice, and say I was cute, but I don't remember her ever doing it. Barby is just like me that way, now. She wants to wear her church dress and shoes to nursery school every day and her favorite game is bride which she plays with little Malcolm Boyd next door, cause she gets to dress up for it, and I tell her she is just the cutest thing alive.

Rev. Tom asked me if Kate had these tendencies when we were young, and it *is* true she didn't date much, nothing like I did, but I think that just because of the contrast between us, so to speak. At the time, my looks meant a lot to me, a lot more than they should of, seeing that it's not what you look like on the outside but how pure your soul is inside that counts for much. I was all involved in entering these beauty contests they used to hold. And then, too, I had a good personality, and was outgoing and friendly to one and all no matter who it was, while Kate used to be so quiet and stand-offish that some people thought she was a snob, or kind of hard, with that blank look on her face that you could never tell what she was thinking. She was that way even at home, like when Mom would be off her head raving about snakes in the bed and Dad would be clutching at his heart and sobbing and I'd be half-hysterical myself, just pleading with her to go to the hospital, you could look over to the sofa and there would be Kate, just sitting there reading on one of her books or staring off into space with that buttoned-up look. It wasn't that she didn't have any feelings, though, she just never used to like to show them. And boys do like a girl that at least knows how to smile, so maybe that was what started her off on the wrong foot, not being popular, especially with a big sister that was.

Sophomore year I got picked Miss Virginia Beach and Junior year I was Crab Queen, picked out of all the girls in five counties besides ours and riding in the lead float of the parade we have each Summer for the Crab Festival, that people come from as far as Richmond and Charlestown, North Carolina, to see, with a white, floor-length decolte gown with two skirts and little red velvet crab insignia all around the neckline, and a crown and sceptor made out of crab claws and five ladies in waiting that wore purple, pink, and orange, to represent the three colors crabs are before and after you cook them, that rode lower than me in the Royal Coach. I'm a natural blond anyway, and I used to just give myself one of those 'Toni' rinses which enhance the natural lights of your own hair, and more than one person told me I looked like a princess out of a book. Although I was the Queen, of course, the Crab Queen.

(Wed. night)   Well, there is more news. Kate just called to say she was bringing a "friend" home with her, and you know what that means. I would just like to see the look on Shirlye's face now! I wonder if this is the same "friend" she brought to Mom's funeral which a lot of people were surprised she would do instead of a boyfriend and at the way she didn't shed a tear. But as Rev. Tom says, "be not the first to cast stones" which is one thing the people in this town could use a sermon on, the way they run their mouths. Bill and I had the both of them sleeping over here and Bill took some time after the funeral to talk to Kate about the comfort there is in Christ, although I don't believe she heard a word the state she was in. She was upset all right, although you wouldn't of ever known it unless you knew her like I do. Probably regretted running off instead of staying home when Mom needed her. That's what I said to Rev. Tom at the time, that I was able to grieve with a clear heart because I knew I'd done my best and stood by her when she needed me. I would say that grieving like that has a different flavor to it than the kind you do when you're all full of regrets.

Well I stood by my sister Kate then and wouldn't let a word be said against her just like I always have and always will, now that I'm the closest thing to a Mom she's got. I have never mentioned her liking girls to anyone out loud except to Bill of course and Rev. Tom which doesn't count. Not even to Dad or to Kate herself, just excepted everything with no questions asked.

When Dad called I asked him how Shirlye was taking the news that she's bringing this girl and he said, "not so good," and that his heart was already acting up. Well, that poor man has had a hard life what with Moms drinking and me getting pregnant when I wasn't married and now this too and I'll pray to be a better daughter to him and try and ease things for him by getting along with Shirlye and even try and forgive him for the way he used to beat me for coming in late and running with the wrong type of boy. Seemed like the first time anybody really noticed me was when I got my shape, and then seemed like he used to take and beat me every weekend. And that is the only time I remember either of them touching me, come to think of it. Which is probably why I can't stand for anyone to touch on me now. I hate that part of the sermon where you have to get up and embrace your neighbor and I always try to get an aisle seat with Bill on the one side, so I don't end up having to hug up to some sweaty old wart hog of a woman or someone. I know you're sposed to like it, but I just can't stomach it myself. They gave one of those talks at the PTA how it's good for children to get a lot of physical affection even when they get big so I try to make myself but it comes more naturally to Bill. Though I do like to hold Barby on my lap, she's still so little and will stay still without squirming unlike the others. I don't believe it's good for boys past babies, though. It could turn them funny. I am having a real good time writing this diary, and beginning to think I could of been a writer if anyone had ever encouraged me. It feels good to have someone to talk to that will listen and not tell me I'm stupid or get away or else pull on me telling me their hungry or Katy just hit me Mom, or help me with this paper for school or are the kids uniforms dry yet. Which is what Bill just wanted to know, and I haven't even put them in so time to go.

(Thursday, 2:37 PM)   Well I re-read this whole diary and am still not satisfied with my attitude. I just sat down and prayed and prayed on it and I believe it helped because when Katy came in with her new school things all dirty I didn't even scold her, just sat her down for a real nice mother-daughter talk. She asked me did I love her as much as Barby and I told her the story how Christ loved all his lambs in the flock just as much even the little bad one that wandered off. And I told her if she would only strive to be a good Christian little girl I would love her even more. I just bet we will be seeing some improvement from a certain person!

Then when Kate called from over Dad and Shirlye's where she just got in, we had a real nice talk too, at least until she asked me did I have those picture albums from when we were growing up. I told her I did and she was welcome to look at them when she came over, which she will do tomorrow, but in my mind I said, "Those were Mom's albums and they will stay right here where there meant to be with me who cared for her and not go back to no New York City!" Kate said the visit was OK so far except there wasn't anything in the house she could eat except maybe some lettuce and Shirlye and Dad were drinking already. I told her Dad was probly nervous from expecting her and just don't pay no mind to Shirlye. And then she put her friend on, a different one from last time. She is a Writer, and talks even weirder than Kate does herself now, like she was holding her nose all the time, and said she was looking forward to meeting me because Kate had told her so much about how I used to take care of her when she was a kid and practically brought her up. So I'm glad at least someone is giving me some credit around here! I have to go now because I need to get dinner before my meeting for the Bible-Summer-School which is at 7:30.

(Thurs. 1:30 AM)   Bill is asleep which I don't know how he can do but I am so wrot up I know it will do me good to write because I need an Outlet now if I ever did! Well what happened started when I was still out. Bill had put the kids down and was sitting watching TV when he heard a terrible comotion at the door. And there was my sister Kate sobbing hysterically with her girlfriend who had her arms around her and all etc. right out on the lit front porch for all to see. Well he brought them in and sat them down on the sofa and at first he couldn't get a word out of Kate she was crying so hard except for "can we stay here tonight?" And of course he assured them they could with no questions asked.

Well apparently what happened was Sara (that's her friend) went up to bed right after dinner and Kate stayed up hoping to talk to Dad a little because there were some things she wanted to ask him, like why didn't he answer that letter! Well, Shirlye was listening outside the door which didn't surprise me at all knowing her, and bust in and started shouting all about how it was her home and Kate had no right to insult her the way she did in that letter and take her own husband aside and poison him against her. And how Kate had always thought she was to good for *them* when to tell the truth they ought to be glad they even let her stay there the way she looks and now bringing her girlfriend there that they were supposed to just overlook and pretend it was a man or something! How Dad cried every night at what his daughter had turned into and everyone in town believed it was Kate drove her mother to drink and brought her to an early grave but she wasn't going to do the same to Shirlye and etc etc. Well I wouldn't even know it all seeing how Bill never remembers what you want to hear when he's telling something, but when I came home she had to tell it all again and was still crying which is not the Kate I know! Even when she used to fall off her bike and scrape all the skin off her knees where any normal kid would just ball and run to Mommy, she used to just go right on riding as if nothing happened and maybe at dinner I'd notice and ask her and she'd just mumble I fell off, and that would be that.

So I knew all of this wasn't necessary and told her to control herself it wasn't that bad, and Shirlye was just like that and would say anything when she lost her temper. And then this girlfriend who is a strange looking girl with lots of wild hair like wire and sort of dark-skinned though she talks white enough and dresses funny but not as mannish as Kate, had the nerve to turn to me and say, "Please let her cry, it's good for her", just as if it was her that had known Kate all these years and just about brought her up, and not me. I was just about to say I had enough, and maybe *they* had nothing better to do than to stay up all night and wake up the kids, but I for one had to get up early, when Kate asked me how did Shirlye treat *me*, and didn't *I* think she was an evil woman. Which you can imagine got me going and we both agreed that ever since Mom had died Shirlye had been doing her very best to spoil things between Dad and his own daughters wanting to have him all to herself. Once we got that settled we started to talk about Mom, and how sweet and sort of sparkling she could be at times. How when she was in a room when she was sober it just seemed like the whole place was lit up. How she just loved Billy Jr. when he was born and forgot all about how she felt when I got pregnant with him. Well, maybe it was dredging up the past, but it felt good, though of course sad, too, and pretty soon the both of us were sniffling and crying together. Well, after a while of this I looked up, and that Sara and Bill were both gone. They had just quietly left the room when we were goin on. I peeked in the kitchen and there they were, just sitting and talking, like two men that had married two sisters, and were giving them a chance for some hen talk together. Like Bill couldn't even tell the difference or something.

When we got to bed I asked him didn't he feel funny sitting there talking to her like that, but he had to play dumb, and wouldn't say anything but "huh?" and "like what?" So I asked him what he thought of Sara, and he just said, "Oh, she seems like a nice girl, seems to really care for Kate." Which all it turned out to be was a way to work it round to "but not as much as I care for you, sweetheart", which is the way he talks when he wants It. But four is enough for me even though the church does teach us to produce and multiply and the more kids you have for Jesus the better and not to interfere with God's natural process. Well it isn't Jesus that's gonna bring them up, so I did get one of those things, but I can't seem to put it in so it doesn't hurt me so I just pushed him away and said, "not with them right next door."

When he'd fell asleep I had to get up to go to the bathroom which used to be part of the guest room before we renovated it, so now you can hear everything that goes on in there when you're sitting on the john. And what I heard was this little rustling noise and a kind of steady mumbling which when I listened close was words mumbled over and over sort of like singing, like the way you might do a child that had a bad dream to put it back asleep. I couldn't hear all the words, but some were, "It's OK now, go to sleep. It'll be OK, I love you, it's over now, go to sleep. I'm right here, go to sleep." Like that, and I figured the noise was probably Sara's hand, going round and round as she rubbed Kate's back.

I don't know why, but it made me sad. I went in to see if all the commotion had woke up the kids but they were all asleep. I just stood there looking at the girls and trying to remember when I had done that with them, sort of soothed them to sleep like that, or when they were awake even. Barby yes, cause she's the youngest and we knew a little more by then. Which is probly why she's such a sweet-natured, affectionate little thing. But I didn't cuddle with Billy JR too much. I was only seventeen, and the summer before I'd been Crab Queen and then here I was all of a sudden, married and tied down. He used to cry, and I'd just look at him and think, "I'm not going to pick you up, you little pest. If it wasn't for you I'd be in a beauty contest right now." But Mom used to pet him a lot, and maybe that's why he's pretty easy-going too. And Timmy was born right when Billy was at the age that they're into everything and we weren't Saved yet, and Bill and I would be fighting like cats and dogs every night and I just didn't have the time to hold him that much which is maybe why he's so quiet now and still wets the bed and is the one of my kids that people always forget about. And then Katy who was born the year Mom died and who seems like she was just born stubborn, fighting and the first word out of her mouth no, like she got the bad part of me and nothing else. I just stood there looking at them, and I started to feel all sorry for myself cause I swore I'd be a good mother to them like Mom couldn't be to us, and I started to feel like maybe I failed.

Then I went in the bathroom but that noise had stopped and I got into bed and tried to remember a time when I wasn't like I am now, when I really wished someone would touch me, but I couldn't remember ever feeling that way once I was grown. But Kate must of, and maybe she went and turned into what she is because it's different with a man. They don't give you that kind of attention, the way you want your Mom to do when you're a kid, just to cuddle and pet you and really listen to what you have to say and how you feel and how you look, and just plain notice you the way a woman will.

(Fri. afternoon)   This morning after the kids were in school and Bill had gone to work, Kate and Sara wanted to look at that old album. And of course Sara went crazy over the pictures of Kate as a little kid, although she doesn't look like much, just small and sullen with her hair down over her face half the time. Then we came to the ones of me as Crab Queen cut out from the paper, and they wanted to know all about that. Kate said she remembered when I was crowned, and then *I* remembered how she was the only one of the family that came out to see me and didn't even watch the whole parade, just ran alongside of my float with that hair falling in her eyes and the cute smile she has when she ever gets around to smiling.

Then the girls got home from school early today and Sara took them out on the lawn to play which I guess won't do them any harm except that it looked funny the way she was rolling around on the grass with them considering that she is thirty years old. Well I guess if you have no other responsibilities you can afford to act like that. Then Dad came over to talk to Kate and try to patch things up, and I just came right out and told them I wanted to be in on it too, cause she isn't the only one around here that doesn't like how she's being treated. So they said the two of them would talk a while, and then all three of us would. When I was writing the above Sara came in with the girls hanging to her like little crabs asking could she take them on a walk. I said OK since it will be easier having a serious talk with all of them out of the house. She asked me what I was writing and I told her a diary and she said she keeps one too being a Writer. She said she takes hers everywhere and writes down her impressions and then she can refer to it later when she's writing a story or something. Boy would I like to find out what she has written down about me and my family!!! Lucky for her I am saved or I might be tempted to look.

(Fri. 5:00 PM) Well I was good and sorry for my decision when that girl brought my kids back covered with mud and wet clear up to the knees! She'd gone and took them down the Bay where they are strictly forbidden to go what with those tides and not knowing how to swim. I almost had a heart attack when I saw it and I only thank goodness Bill wasn't home because the one time he will really lose his temper is when someone exposes his kids to danger. I really let Katy have it and scolded her but good for exposing her little sister to get drownded and told her what if Barby had fell in it would be her fault. I guess that Sara knew who I was really talking to because she kept saying it wasn't their fault and she was watching them all the time while she was telling them stories and they only played at the edge and didn't go in the water. Which just goes to show. A girl like that who is a Writer and not used to kids could get so involved in her stories that she might not notice if there was one less on the way back!

Then Katy wouldn't stop crying until Sara finally said she'd tell her another story, and then shut right up and scooted over on her lap, which is real unusual for her. So in the end it all ended up with me looking mean and in the wrong just for not wanting my own little girls to get drownded! It would be easier to be loving and forgiving if other people would at least admit their trespasses. But how can you forgive someone when she probably thinks she's the one that should be forgiving you? A girl like that could twist anything around to make herself look in the right and I just wonder how she did this in her diary?

In the talk, Kate was yelling and Dad was crying and then Dad was yelling and Kate was crying. He told her he Loved Her about three times which he never has said to me ever but of course that was not good enough for Miss New York City who wanted him to prove it and how are you supposed to prove a thing like that. I did not get in a word edgewise. Kate has sure changed, and nor for the better, either!

(Fri. 12:00 midnight) Well I did something I shouldn't have. They all went ahead because Billy JR had to practise before the game and the uniforms were not dry yet. I had to check something in the guest room bureau and her diary was right out there on top which was careless if you ask me. It's almost asking somebody to read it to leave it out like that. Maybe she kind of hoped I would. I always hide mine but good in a different place each time. She just started it last month so there wasn't very much, just a whole lot about this big fight her and Kate had I'm not sure about what. The part about us was sort of like a story. This is it.

—Two sisters and one stayed and one went away. Both daughters of a charming powerful drunk whose mark they'd carry all their lives. Kate who goes away into herself and Jean who lashes out but both of them women who inspire devotion and both with the magnetism of that mother, who made everyone wait—
—The story of Jean, a powerful woman whose high point in life was when she was crab queen at 17, and nothing's been the same since—The way she makes the kids and the big clumsy man wait on her moods, watch to see if she's gonna smile or snap . . .
—And behind it all the whine of children and the repetition of prayers like a sedative—and always the lapping of the bay—

Well I must say it wasn't as bad as I thought it would be! Who knows, maybe I'll open a book someday and the main character will be me! All through the game I kept saying it to myself: "The story of Jean, a powerful woman."

(Sat. noon) Well, it's over. They left. And it's just like I knew it would be. All on me. Shirlye called to say that if I hadn't let them stay here Kate would of had to face reality and apologize to her, and she knows I was behind it all and had never liked her. I had to go and patch it all up and bring her roses from the garden. For the sake of the kids.

Katy whined all afternoon and asked me why didn't I tell her stories like that lady. And Timmy took the book that Kate gave him (something wierd about a boy that likes dolls or something, wouldn't you know) out back and missed his ball practise. I just let them be and went in the kitchen and tidied up a little. There was the picture album, and wouldn't you know it, there were three pictures missing. Well, at least they were just of Kate and not of me or Mom.

Then I tried to imagine what they were doing. Still driving back, I guess, maybe fighting about something, yelling and saying things just like the rest of us do. I can't say that I envy Kate, all in all. I have a few things to look forward to. I have my rap with Rev. Tom on Monday and I guess I'll have to tell him about reading that girl's diary. I know he'll feel bad about it but I guess he'll forgive me, just like the Lord. And I guess he'll be surprised at how much I wrote! I know it's not the way it should be, but at least it is an Outlet and Jesus loves those who try, and you can tell I did that! A whole books worth, almost. And every so often I'll stop and say part of what that Writer wrote about me to myself. "A woman who inspires devotion." "A powerful woman." And then I feel good, like an important person. One that gets noticed. One that when a Writer met her one time she wanted to write a book about her.

B. G. Mares

Hi! I'm B.G. Mares.

I've never sent anything in to be published. I mostly write things for my own satisfaction.

My parents live in a small town in New Mexico. I grew up with an aunt one hundred miles from there. I have five brothers and one half sister. My aunt didn't have any children.

I met my husband when I was sixteen and we married when I was eighteen. We have two children. I'm in the process of getting my degree in Home Economics with a minor in Physical Education.

THROUGH MY EYES

It all began with the Christmas rush. School for the semester ended just a few days before Christmas, which didn't give my husband and I much time to get ready for the holidays. I was beginning to feel worn out and thought I was coming down with strep. I really didn't want to be sick for the holidays so a friend of mine offered me an antibiotic. I ended up having an allergic reaction and spent the Christmas holiday in the hospital recovering. From then on I felt really weak and tired. I'm usually pretty healthy, but this felt like I was never going to feel healthy again.

In the hospital I took the recommended blood tests to make sure that my organs had not been damaged by the allergic reaction. The tests showed that everything looked fine.

In mid January, I went in for a pregnancy test because I hadn't had a period for a month and a half. I had an IUD, so I really didn't think I was pregnant. The result of the test was negative. The doctor said it was possible that I was pregnant, but he doubted it.

The following week-end we went to get groceries, which is a forty-five minute drive one-way. When we returned I was suppose to babysit, but I really wasn't feeling up to it. While making dinner, I began to feel weak. I was making a batch of tortillas and I literally had to sit down before I passed out. I was feeling nauseated and feverish. I thought I had the flu. My husband ended up taking care of all the kids, our two and the three I was baby-sitting for.

The next day was our son's fourth birthday party and I had the same symptoms. Everyone at the party was talking about the "bug" going around, so I naturally thought that was what I had.

The following Monday I went to see the doctor and he said I had a virus, just something that was going around. He prescribed an antispasmodic, which didn't help. That evening I really got sick, but I was still convinced that it was the flu. He recommended that I go in for another pregnancy test in a week. As the symptoms continued, I convinced myself that the antibiotic had damaged something and that it just wasn't showing up in the tests.

When I went in for another pregnancy test, I thought I had a pelvic infection because I was feeling tender. I asked the doctor if the antibiotic could have caused some damage to my insides. He said, "No, that's what we were looking for in the blood tests we took." Then he did a pelvic exam along with a pregnancy test. He looked at me and said, "You're pregnant."

The first thing I said was, "I'm not going to have it."

The doctor said, "I have information on that for you." Then I asked him, if he was going to take the IUD out. He said, "If you're not going to have it, there's no point in taking it out."

With a quick response I said, "I might go ahead and have it."

"Let's go take it out then," he said and began to pull it out. But it wouldn't come out. So he stopped and said, "You should probably look towards having an abortion, because it seems embedded in the fetus."

I sat up and said, "That's relieving. Now I don't have to feel guilty about having an abortion."

The doctor shook his head in agreement, but also in shock, at my response. He excused himself saying, "I'm going to check this under the microscope to make sure you don't have an infection."

When he returned he said, "You don't have an infection." While writing information in my file he asked if Dr. Smith would be okay for the abortion? I said, "It doesn't matter, whoever you recommend is fine." He said, "Dr. Smith is good, Oh no! you can't go to her. She doesn't do abortions, but Dr. Bringham does."

I left the doctor's office and drove home, saying to myself, "I can't believe this is happening. Paul is going to have a heart attack." It was a cold winter day in February and this made it feel even colder. I drove into the drive way feeling butterflies in my stomach. I walked in and saw Paul sitting in front of the television. I started feeling mad at him and I didn't really want to talk to him. Just at that moment the receptionist telephoned. "You need to come back and get your referral papers," she said. On my way out the door Paul said, "Hey, where you going, what did the doctor say?" I yelled back, "He said I'm pregnant." I could hear him reply, "Mmmmm" in a discouraged voice.

When I returned from getting the referral papers the first thing Paul said was, "Is it safe to have the baby since you had such a bad reaction to the antibiotic at Christmas?" I replied in a snobby voice, "It doesn't matter, the doctor said the IUD was probably embedded in the fetus, so we're off the hook." Paul looked numb.

I made all the necessary arrangements so I could go in and see the doctor by myself. We didn't want anyone asking questions. Paul took the morning off so he could stay home and watch the kids.

That night Paul was feeling my stomach and saying, "I hope the baby's okay." I would reply coldly, "Why? We're not having it."

The next morning I drove to town. It was a nice quiet ride, the sun was out and the roads were dry. The snow was really pretty on the sides of the road. A couple of tears came to my eyes as I said, "Why me?" When I arrived at the doctor's office I was very nervous.

When Dr. Bringham walked in to check me, he said, "How are you?"

"I'm nervous," I replied.

"Well, I'll try to make it as comfortable as possible." When he checked to see if he could take the IUD out he said, "It's already half way out." He checked for a tubal. "The fetus is in the right place," he assured me. After removing the IUD, he said, "There's a twenty-five percent chance of miscarrying. If you make it through the first trimester, you should have a normal pregnancy." He also told me that most women who get pregnant with a Copper-7 IUD usually go ahead and abort.

I looked at him, teary eyed.

"I know its a tough decision to make." He looked down at the referral paper. "This Dr. Gordon said, Patient wants abortion."

"That was yesterday," I replied. There was a moment of silence, which I broke by saying, "I babysit all day and I hate to take off. I would have to have it done at the end of the day on Friday." He said to talk to the receptionist.

I went into the reception area ready to burst into tears. The receptionist was talking to another patient about making an appointment for her second abortion. This person was young and didn't seem to have a conscience about the situation. She told the receptionist she also needed another doctor's excuse for missing work again.

The receptionist looked at me and said, "That'll be twenty-two dollars." I began to write a check hoping the room would clear so I wouldn't have to make the appointment with everyone listening. It was apparent no one was going to leave so I told her in a very shaky voice, "I need to make an appointment for 3:00 on Friday for an abortion." I left the building feeling empty.

On the way home I felt as if someone had hurt my feelings. I cried almost all the way home. I kept saying to myself, "It's not my fault, I'm innocent here, I had the IUD put in so I wouldn't get pregnant, the medical profession got me into this, they can get me out." I got a "hold" of myself by the time I got home.

When I got home I was very calm in front of Paul. I walked in and flopped on the chair. I explained everything to him and told him, "It doesn't matter, I'm not having it anyway." He said, "Okay."

During the next three days, I kept looking for a good excuse to have the abortion. I called for a second opinion hoping someone would say that I should abort because of the bad reaction to the antibiotic. But their opinion was the same. That it was up to me whether I wanted to have it or not. It's my body and I'm the only one that can make that decision. That I still had the legal right to abort. Also that they never heard of anyone having any psychological problems from an abortion.

I kept thinking about what other people would say. Would I be strong enough to live with others passing judgement. Can you imagine what everyone would tell Paul at work. Being that we're the only Chicanos in town, with two kids and another one on the way and a wife that just babysits. "Gosh! Don't they believe in birth control." And my in-laws on the other hand, "Doesn't she know any better, she's not even working, poor Paul." My mother would be delighted since she had seven of us. My sister would be a total snob about it. She would say such things as, "I told you so, you should of gotten your tubes tied after your second. You can't afford anymore and two kids is enough." I didn't think I was strong enough to go through any humiliating moments.

It was a hard decision, I didn't want to have the abortion

because I felt like the baby growing inside of me, chose me to be its parent. I should feel honored that it picked me and nobody else. I must be doing something right for this little one to have picked me to nurture and care for it as it grew to be an adult.

But I also knew financially we couldn't afford anymore children. If I had it, I would have to stay home another three years before I would feel right about leaving the baby and returning to work. This would hold us back financially, but I still want to have at least one more.

The two nights before the abortion were restless. When I was with Paul I didn't get too emotional. I felt strong and knew the abortion was the logical thing to do and so did he. He just kept saying, "If we do it, let's do it and forget it."

The day before the abortion, Paul asked me if I had a sitter for the kids. I kept saying no. Obviously, I was stalling, hoping I would get talked out of it. I finally got around to calling someone the night before. I asked the sitter, "Are you sure you can babysit tomorrow?" Of all times to not have any trouble finding a sitter.

On the day of the abortion Paul brought home some magazines that were being thrown out at the library. One magazine had the development of the embryo. I kept saying, "I can't believe it looks like this already."

We were both pretty quiet on the way to the clinic. I was starting to feel nervous as we arrived. Finally we were in the examining room. I did okay through the numbing procedure. As my adrenaline came back to normal I started having hurt feelings again. I couldn't stop the tears this time. Paul said, "We can still stop if you want." I turned to him and said, "No, this is the right thing to do, what if this one has bad eyes like you, how would you feel then?"

He looked at me, hurt, and replied, "I know, I'm going to have the vasectomy so we don't have to go through this again.

We went through the entire procedure with tears. There was no backing out once the scraping started. I asked Paul if he wanted to see what was taken out and he said no, but I just had to see what I had let someone do to me. I felt a little relief after I saw how small it was. It really didn't look like anything.

Everyone kept asking if I felt any cramping. I said, "It's very mild." The assistant said, "Boy, you're tough." I just felt numb inside. I told Paul, "I'm glad that's over with."

The following day Paul had to take care of business, so I was left alone at home taking care of our kids. Out of loneliness I called almost everyone on my side of the family. Fortunately we had good conversations. I didn't mention the abortion but I felt better after talking to them. I felt fine physically. I just kept saying, "Oh Gosh" to myself everytime I thought about the abortion.

When I took showers was when I cried. As the water from the shower poured down my body the hurt feelings rose in my chest. I would put my hands over my face and rub my eyes to stop the hurt and tears. It was my only consolation in this time of mourning and I would say, "Oh God," as if asking for forgiveness. I couldn't tell anyone what I was feeling because I didn't want anyone passing judgement. I felt bad enough as it was.

As time passed I stopped thinking about it. I will always wonder if my reasons for the abortion were sound. Was I really being strong or was I at my weakest?

Jim Roaix

Karen Cooper

I was born in Oklahoma. Came East when I married. After a dozen years as an adult I returned to college and chose to study anthropology. I am of Cherokee descent. I work in a museum and present programs on Woodland Indian life and history. I also fingerweave and write poetry. Connecticut is home to my nearly-grown children, but I look forward to living in other places in other times. Life is always an exciting adventure.

A TWIG BREAKS

Something in me strives to connect with the past. Not my past, but another's past. An ancestral past. And so, after all, it is my past.

A twig breaks a hundred years ago. And I hear it today.

I hear rippling water. Yet I am in my living room.

The coyote calls. They don't live here anymore. I live here.

But the twig breaks. I hear it. And after the twig breaks, I hear a soft footfall. My eyes cease to see; my ears see for me.

I am alone in my house. I seem to be always alone. I have no family here. No connections. I do not go to bars. I was not raised that way. But neither do I go to church. I have left that way.

I am alone. And so, I think, it shall always be. I lay on my sofa in the living room, having just vacuumed. Now I am resting.

My eyes are closed, but my ears are seeing. Before I might drop the book I am reading, I lay it on the table next to me.

And the twig breaks, as it has so many times before.

Someone comes through the woods from the East. Quietly he comes. And only my ears see him.

He is in the rising sun. Coming toward me. I face the South. He is from the East.

In front of me I hear horses. They are far away. The thunder of their hooves grows louder. Even so, I hear the snapping twig in the East. It snapped only once, but I hear it again — as an echo in my head.

The horses come closer. Toward me.

I look at the rising sun. I cannot move and I look toward the stranger. He stands in the rising sun. And the thunder grows before me. Slowly they come, and yet swiftly. Dustily they come, and yet clearly. Animated. Dreamlike. Yet very real. And I am afraid.

The horses' nostrils are flared. I can see their nostrils. The horses have black bodies with white heads and two white spots on their black sides. They thunder toward me. I am afraid, but I do not move. I cannot move. They are before me. I think I can touch them if I stretch out my hand. But I cannot move. And they are before me. Coming, rocking, flowing.

I look to the East. He is there. He raises his arm. And the horses stop.

Their white heads bend down to snip grass. They graze. Their black sides with the two white spots do not heave. They are not winded.

But they are thirsty. I look to the East. He is there and I melt into a pool of water. The horses step toward me, but I ripple away. The sound of water. And the coyote calls. And I am here. I am here.

I open my eyes. I see my living room. I am lying on the sofa. I do not hear the snapping twig now nor see the horses. The past is gone. It is gone. I want it gone. I will it gone.

I don't want to hear the snapping twig, so I turn on the radio. The music is loud. I sing with it. I fill my mind with a grocery list. I will go shopping. I will fill myself with Today.

I go to the store and begin filling my cart with cans and boxes. I turn into an aisle and there He is. The man in the East. I know it is He.

He wears a shirt with horses imprinted upon it. Black-bodied horses with white heads and two white spots upon their sides. And high on one shoulder is imprinted the yellow sun. And the horses are running on the front of the shirt and grazing on the back of the shirt. And on the back is a blue stream.

He sees me looking at his shirt and smiles at me. It is a pretty shirt, but I don't care for it. It fills me with nausea and fear.

I leave the cart there. I leave the store. I drive away. But down the road I must pull over. My eyes are filled with tears. I cannot see the road. I hear the snap. The distant cracking of a twig. The coyote calls my name. I must go home.

Judith McDaniel

Judith McDaniel is a political activist and writer who lives in Albany, New York. She has published two books of poems, November Woman *(The Loft Press) and* Metamorphosis and Other Poems of Recovery *(Long Haul Press), and a novel,* Winter Passage *(Spinsters Ink).* Sanctuary, *her book of poems and essays which includes her account of being captured by contra terrorists in Nicaragua, will be published in the Spring of 1987 by Firebrand Books.*

FIRST TRIES DON'T ALWAYS WORK

[*First Tries* is a novel about teen alcoholism written for young adults. In the following excerpt, the two protagonists are fifteen year old Chris Jablonsky and Officer Katie Lynde, the county sheriff.]

The pounding in her head was the first thing Chris noticed. It was so loud she couldn't tell at first if it was in her head or if she was in a room submerged by the sound of it, thrumming away behind her eyes. When she tried to open her eyes, tried to see where she was and if she could stop the noise somehow, she couldn't get her eyes open. Or if they did open she couldn't see. Just breathing hurt too. Her throat was so dry.

After what seemed like a long time she ran her tongue over her dry lips, trying to moisten them, but her tongue was dry. Then she felt a hand behind her head, raising her up a little, and there was water on her lips, trickling down her throat. Chris swallowed gratefully and felt tears start.

What was wrong with her? Where was she anyway? The next time she opened her eyes, there was some light in the room and she could sort of see someone sitting beside her bed. Someone she didn't know, Chris thought first, then gradually she began to think the person looked a little familiar.

"Chris?"

She opened her eyes again, peering toward the figure by the bed. Who in the world? Who could want her at this hour? It must be the middle of the night. She was much too tired for this. She closed her eyes again.

When she woke the second time, the noise had become less intense, the pain less sharp. Again the hand was there and the water to drink. This time she took several swallows and said, "Thanks." The voice that said thanks didn't sound at all like hers.

The cop. The figure by the bed was that cop, Chris realized, and she felt her heart start to beat faster with this new information.

"Good morning," Katie said.

She didn't look angry. Chris wondered why she was there, then began to look around her, realizing this was not her bed at home. She saw the hospital tag around her wrist first, then the metal frame of the bed. She closed her eyes, trying to remember. But there was no memory. She could tell from the way her head felt that she had been drunk, really drunk. The hangover, at least, was familiar. Whatever news this cop was waiting around to tell her wasn't going to be good, Chris could tell that.

"I really blew it?" Chris asked the question in a small voice.

"Yeah." Katie's answer was soft, not gruff, and Chris thought she could see some sympathy in the cop's face. "Do you need some more water?"

Chris nodded, glad she wouldn't have to talk for a moment. How could she make up a good story to get out of this one when she didn't have the slightest idea where to start. God. She sighed and rested her head back on the pillow, eyes shut. Maybe if she went to sleep again . . .

"So, are you going to get up some day and try again?" Katie's question interrupted Chris's doze. Her voice wasn't so gentle this time and Chris opened her eyes, trying to concentrate.

"I don't know. How can I? I don't even know what happened?" Chris tried for a look of boredom and indifference, her usual way of discouraging adults who got too nosey.

"Hmmm." Katie had been looking at her like that for a long time, Chris thought, with her head tilted to one side. "We can probably figure out what happened," Katie said finally. "Would that help you?"

Chris fought to keep the tears out of her eyes. She didn't trust her voice, so she nodded. Her throat felt swollen and all closed up. It was hard to imagine she would be able to talk again in her old voice any time soon. She didn't want Katie to go away, Chris realized suddenly. She didn't want to be left with her own thoughts and her vacant memory. It scared her, this empty place in her mind where there should have been at least some notion of where she'd been and what she'd done.

"Let's start at the beginning." Katie's voice was warm again and Chris began to feel better.

"O.K." she agreed.

"You left the game when it was over. Liz went with somebody else and so did your brother. Did you go with Gregory or McDuff then?"

Oh, yeah. Now Chris was getting the outline back. It was just a sketch, though, with blurred edges and none of the detail filled in.

"Where did you go? Do you remember?"

"I asked them to take me home." Chris remember this at the same moment she said it. "I had chores to do." There. She'd remembered. She went on with more confidence. "Duffy said he had to make one stop first. We had some beer." The image of the six pack, the lids being snapped off, flashed into her mind like a neon sign. She remembered how much she had wanted a beer, remembered how warm and comfortable she felt after the first swallow. What was wrong with that, anyway? "We just had some beer after the game," she said defiantly to Katie. "You know, to warm up. And celebrate."

Katie just nodded this time. Chris could see she meant for her to go on.

"We went to a trailer." It was funny how she couldn't seem to remember these things until she said them out loud. When she said the word trailer, she could see the littered front yard, the cabinets with beer cans and dirty glasses on them. "It's the trailer north of the village, I think," she told Katie. "There are two of them, actually, with all that wood in the front yard."

"I know the place."

"Well, we must have gone in. It's such a creepy place," Chris shivered at the memory. "I didn't know what they were doing there. Why did we stop?"

Chris was distracted, puzzled. So much had happened. And she couldn't remember if it had been a long time they were there or just a few minutes. "This guy, Mike, was showing them some stuff. He had a whole suitcase full of pills. Like a portable drug store." Chris thought that was kind of funny and looked over to see if Katie was laughing. She wasn't. She was looking at Chris real seriously, waiting for her to go on. Uh, oh.

"What kind of pills, Chris? Can you remember that?"

"He was telling them the names when I came out of the bathroom," Chris remembered, and rushed to add, "I didn't know what was going on. Names like Black Beauty. Like that."

Katie nodded. "What else can you remember?"

"Then he went to a cabinet and there was a ton of pot in it. Every shelf." Her voice was awed in memory. "All stuff with foreign names. They all smoked a joint." She wrinkled her nose. "That stuff is so stupid."

"You didn't smoke?" Katie sounded surprised and Chris let herself feel a little superior.

"I never do that stuff. I was drinking a beer." Then Chris remembered the glass of coke and something. "Oh, yeah. I had some other kind of drink. One of the guys was making them." Her mind flashed on the purple and gold letter jacket, just at nose level. Then it flashed to those arms locked around her, rubbing up and down, the hands trying to get under her jacket, pulling her bra away. Who was that? She couldn't remember and the frustration brought tears back to her eyes.

"I can't remember."

"Can't remember what?"

"Who he was. The one who gave me the drink. Who kept *grabbing* me." Her voice was low and disgusted. All she could remember was Gregory, stoned, laughing, sitting down at the table with her and Mike, saying . . . oh, god, that was it. "They put some in my drink. One of those uppers. That's when it all started getting confused." There. It *hadn't* been her fault at all. Surely this cop would see that now, anybody would know it hadn't been her fault. It could have happened to anybody.

And Katie was sitting forward on her chair, not casual at all now. "They put it in your drink? You mean you didn't take any of the amphetamines yourself?"

"God, no. I never took any of that. It was like . . ." She couldn't think what it was like, to describe it. She looked to Katie for help, but Katie was just sitting there, nodding encouragingly. "Everything started going faster. That's why they call it speed, isn't it?"

"Yeah."

"It was exciting. It felt good at first, I mean." Chris was confused. The words seemed to be coming out before she had a chance to think them and she didn't know how much she wanted this cop to know. But if she didn't remember in time to hold it back, how could she control it? She was quiet for a moment, then confessed. "But it scared me."

She was remembering sitting at the table talking to Mike and how grown-up she'd felt. Then she remembered walking on the road alone, like a kid who was lost. But what came in between? That was what she couldn't remember and she felt the fear rising in her again. Shit. What was wrong with her? Her hands were shaking and . . . what had happened that made her so afraid?

"Chris, what's wrong?

"I can't remember." Chris heard her own voice high-pitched like she was yelling at Katie across a long distance. "Why can't I remember?"

"What are you trying to remember?"

"What happened after the trailer. How did I get out on the road?" She was running her hand through her hair, pulling nervously on the end of it as though she could pull the memory out of her head.

"I don't know exactly why you were on the road, Chris. But I do know the doctor said you weren't raped. Is that it? Is that what you're trying to remember?"

Chris stared at Katie, speechless. The hands. She remembered the hands, and the wet mouth. Shame crept up her face, reddening it.

"That doesn't mean you weren't sexually . . . uh . . . abused. It sounds like that guy was pretty awful."

Chris appreciated the soft, concerned way Katie was talking to her. Not like she'd done something wrong, not like that at all.

"Yeah," she said finally. "He was creepy." She ran her tongue over her dry lips. She still didn't understand. "Why can't I remember this stuff?"

Katie was quiet for a minute and Chris could tell she knew the answer, but was deciding whether to say it or not. When she took a deep breath and looked Chris in the eye, Chris knew she was going to tell her, and probably Chris wasn't going to like what she would hear.

"It's called a black-out, Chris. An alcoholic black-out. Alcohol affects the brain. It stops certain parts of it from working in the way you're used to. That's why when you drink, sometimes you do things you wouldn't do otherwise. You know how at parties when people get high they do silly or goofy things. If you keep drinking, other parts of your brain stop working. You had a lot to drink, so your brain quit remembering. That part of it quit working. We call it a black-out."

There was silence for a moment. Chris was playing the words back through her head, trying to make sense of them.

"Does that mean I'm an alcoholic?" Chris asked finally. It was a question she'd thought to herself a couple of times, but never meant to ask outloud. She wanted to keep her voice casual, like the answer didn't matter, but it cracked and wavered instead. She stared at Katie. There had to be some answers somewhere. She was more than scared. She felt as if she'd awakened in a whole new world. None of the things that were familiar to her seemed quite the same and that was why she could ask the question.

"I don't know, Chris. Only you can answer that question."

Chris started to protest, but Katie motioned her to wait a minute. "But I think we can look at some of the evidence together. And we can talk about what it means to be an alcoholic, o.k.?"

"O.K. But first I want . . . do you know?" Chris paused. What *did* she want? "What happened to me?" she pleaded, finally. "Do you know what happened to me?"

"Partly." Katie settled back in her chair and Chris could see she was going to get the rest of the story. She took a couple of deep breaths and hoped she could hear it all.

"After you left the trailer, you drove north. Up in Tylerville you got in another truck. You stole a truck. That is," she corrected, "whoever was driving it stole it. It belonged to someone who knows McDuff. You drove it around for a while. It must have been quite a drive. I found the truck and then followed pieces of it back to where you started from."

Katie was trying to joke a little, but Chris said nothing. She could find nothing familiar in Katie's words.

"Then somebody set the truck on fire. I don't know if you were there then or not. I found you about a mile and a half from the wreck, so I assume you were with them for part of that time."

Chris ran the words Katie had just said through her mind, but they didn't feel familiar. She knew Katie wasn't speaking a foreign language, but it just didn't seem like the words made any sense. Stole a truck? Duffy had said he would take her home. Why didn't he take her home? Maybe they had just borrowed the truck? Maybe Duffy's truck had broken down? But a fire? Somebody set the truck on fire. Chris sighed, the effort too much, her whole body exhausted by the attempt to remember the night, to rearrange the events Katie was describing so that they would fit into her old familiar world. But they wouldn't go into place, somehow she just couldn't make them fit into place. She leaned back on the pillow again and closed her eyes. Maybe if she could rest for a moment . . .

The next time Chris opened her eyes she thought Katie was still standing by her bed. But she got the body in focus and saw it was her mother, standing, hands clasped behind her back. She was looking down at Chris, her face worried. For a moment neither of them spoke and Chris felt her throat getting clogged again. She wondered how much her mother knew about what had happened. What had Katie Lynde told her? Almost at once her mind started going in the old tracks, trying to figure out how she could get out of this one, whether she could tell a lie big enough for her mother to believe it wasn't her fault.

Finally her mom stopped staring at her and brought her chair over and sat down. "How are you feeling, Chris?" she asked, and Chris was surprised to hear her mother's voice shaking a little, like she was scared too.

Chris shrugged, hoping her mom would go on talking. But she didn't. "I'm o.k., I guess." O.K. if you ignored the pounding in her head, the bruises on her thigh and right forearm, the twisted right ankle. She had to be o.k. since she couldn't explain those things to her mother.

"I want to talk with you, Chris."

"Sure." Chris tried to sound nonchalant, like her mother asked such a thing of her everyday, but her heart started pounding a little harder.

Lois Jablonsky opened her mouth as though she was going to

start talking, then closed it again. The second time she did that, Chris knew it was going to be bad. She wasn't sure what it was, but the tears moved from her throat up to behind her eyes.

"Chris, have you . . . how long . . ." Lois stopped and swallowed. "Have you been drinking long, Chris?"

"Mom, I only had one drink," Chris lied. She tried to sound urgent and honest. "I told that cop this morning. Those guys put something in my drink. It wasn't my fault. I didn't know I was drinking it?"

"What do you mean?" Lois was thrown off-track. "What did they put in your drink?"

"I'm not sure. Something like speed. It freaked me out. I didn't know what was happening." Chris was sitting forward in the bed now, leaning toward her mother, getting some of her energy back as she tried to explain, to get rid of what she thought her mother was suggesting.

"Chris, I'm talking about something else. Last night the doctor told us how much alcohol was in your blood test. Enough, he said, that you would have passed out if you hadn't had the drugs." She paused and in the silence they could hear the soft hum of the hospital all around them. An intercom was calling Dr. Sullivan, calling Dr. Sullivan over and over. "They didn't make you take all those drinks, Chris. Honey, why did you drink so much? Do you know?"

Chris couldn't answer. She didn't know. She just shook her head back and forth, wishing it were over, that her mother would go away now. Prying. Always prying. Didn't she know she'd better stop asking those questions? She might not like the answers.

But instead of asking any more questions, her mom started to cry. She tried to cover her eyes with her hand, like she didn't want Chris to see. "I tried so hard. I thought if you kids didn't see your father . . . I told him he couldn't drink like that in the house. It wasn't good for you kids, I told him it wasn't." She was crying hard now.

"Mom, mom," Chris said urgently. She was scared. "What's wrong? I'm o.k. Honest, I'm fine."

Lois shook her head, no. "You aren't o.k., Chris. Last night I went up to your room when I went home. I was so scared for you,

I didn't know what to do. I didn't know how to help you. I looked and looked. Finally I found it. Your jar. I found it behind some books." She stopped talking again after she jerked the last words out.

Chris stared at her mother. Oh, god, she thought, this was the worst. This was what she had wanted never to happen, what she thought would kill her. But here she was, not dead. Just ashamed. Ashamed in her whole body. She wished the police car had never found her, wished she could have just curled up out in the woods and fallen asleep and never awakened. Die. Let me die, please. She turned her back on her mother and curled up in a ball on her side, head tucked down toward her knees. "Go away," she muttered, just loud enough for her mother to hear. "Go away. I never want to see you again." But she felt her mother's hand stay on her shoulder. Then finally the tears broke out and she sobbed and sobbed. It wasn't fair. Why should this happen to her? She cried until all the tears ought to be gone, but whenever she paused to breathe, it seemed like the sobs started pulling at her chest again and she couldn't stop them.

Chris wasn't surprised to see Katie when she put her head around the door of the hospital room just as the supper dishes were being taken away. When the aide moved on to the next patient, Katie came in, lifted the lid off one of the discarded dishes, peered in at the contents, then made a face.

"Do you think you'll survive the hospital food?" she asked Chris.

"I don't know," Chris answered, trying to be casual, like it didn't matter why Katie was there. "The lady down the hall went into cardiac arrest when she saw she'd gotten chicken livers instead of chop suey."

"Oh, yeah," Katie was laughing now. "I think either one would give me heart failure."

Chris watched her pull the chair up beside the bed, sit and fidget with her hat for a minute. Then she looked up at Chris. "Did your mother tell you why I was coming tonight?"

Chris nodded. "She said you had a warrant to serve me. For my arrest." So much had happened in the last few hours, Chris spoke those words as if nothing could ever surprise her again. First her mother saying she wasn't mad about the booze in Chris's room, she was just scared for her and wanted to help her. Then Tad coming all the way over to the hospital on his motorcycle— checking to see no one else was around before he snuck in to see her. He'd scared her when he started saying what he was going to do to Duffy and Gregory the next time he saw them. He sat in the chair—where Katie was now—and slammed his fist into his hand a few times, trying for tough. But when he left, he cleared his throat over and over, and said, "I'm sorry. I'm sorry I didn't bring you home." Then he flung his head back to throw his hair out of his eyes and stomped out of the room.

"Yeah, well. I want to tell you what I told your parents. They'll be up in a while. Andy and Gregory started talking about stealing the truck. Gregory didn't remember much, but Andy did. And then McDuff got worried and he started talking. So I don't have a lot of choice about what comes now. I want you to understand that."

Chris nodded, her eyes fixed on Katie's face. Her whole world was changing, she knew it was, and there was nothing she could do to stop it now. She wasn't even sure she wanted to. It was a relief, in some way, not having to lie about everything and remember what she said to who about which story she'd made up that week.

"You were asking me before what happened during that time you can't remember. I guess I can tell you now. At least we know what the guys say happened. You all drove up to Tylerville in McDuff's truck. He got in the truck of a guy who hadn't paid him for cutting some wood and drove it off. Gregory was driving McDuff's truck. You parked McDuff's truck in the woods and all got into the stolen truck for a joy ride. McDuff was still driving, but that makes the other three of you accessories to grand larceny."

Katie paused and Chris thought she ought to ask a question, but she couldn't think of anything that sounded nonchalant enough.

"Gregory sort of remembers that Andy was getting rough with you. He won't say what exactly. But at some point he remembers you yelling and McDuff stopping the truck and making you get out."

Chris was listening to everything Katie said, trying to find a place in her memory to plug in the words. But it was like she was hearing a story about somebody she didn't know. Who was this person sitting across from her in the dark blue uniform with the gun bulging out of the holster at her side, the shiny badge tacked to her jacket? For a moment Chris felt like she was back inside the nightmare of last night, where nothing connected to anything else. Then, gradually, the fog began to clear and she was Chris Jablonsky again, sitting in her hospital room and the aide was clearing away the dinner dishes from the bed across the aisle.

"What's going to happen?" she asked Katie.

"I've talked to your parents. They say it's pretty much up to you. If you are willing to help us in the case—and help us get some evidence against the guys in the trailer who are selling drugs—I think we can get you probation. And some counselling. You know, somebody who can talk with you about that question you asked me this morning."

"What question?" Chris was impatient. How could she be expected to remember when there was so much happening?

"You asked me if I thought you were an alcoholic."

"Oh." Oh, yeah. That. Chris was thinking about that when she saw her mom and dad standing in the door of the room. Her dad had cried last night, that's what her mother had told Chris when they finally started talking. He thought he had done something wrong. Her mother thought *she* had done something wrong. Chris said, no, it was *me* that did it. It all seemed so confusing, the love and the hurt and the shame.

"Are you ready for us?" Lois Jablonsky asked. They were both dressed up, Chris saw, and they looked nervous too. Funny, Chris thought all of a sudden, maybe it wasn't so easy being an adult either. She'd always thought adults knew what to do and could do anything they wanted. Her parents didn't look like that now.

"Yes, I'm ready." Katie put her official voice on. "Come over here." Then she turned back to Chris. "Chris, I have a warrant for your arrest and before I ask you any questions I want to read you this warning of your rights."

It was like being at a play, Chris thought, as she nodded her permission for Katie to continue. The roles were all written out and all she could do now was follow the script. Only half-sure of what she could expect, or of what would be expected of her now, she listened to Katie's words.

"You have a right to remain silent and refuse to answer any questions. Anything you do say may be used against you in a court of law. As we discuss this matter you have a right to stop answering questions at any time . . ."

II. A SIMPLE ACT

"A Simple Act" is what each of these stories becomes, even in the writing of them. In Beth Brant's title story, writing is itself the act of keeping life alive, of recording history, of change-making, and of breaking down all the walls requiring personal and historical amnesia. Thus, this section contains stories of action, of creation, of making. Some of the women here are angry and their act of creation is to find a direction for their anger. In all of these stories, the women know what is happening around them and they are not in conflict about what the facts of the outside world happen to be. This knowing and seeing becomes the action which we celebrate in these strong stories.

Beth Brant

I'm 44 years old, a lesbian mother, a Bay of Quinte Mohawk. I am the editor of A Gathering of Spirit *(Sinister Wisdom Books, 1983) the first anthology devoted to the writing and art of North American Indian women. I am also the author of* Mohawk Trail *(Firebrand Books, 1985) a collection of prose and poetry. I live in Detroit with my lover Denise, and one of my three daughters. I write because it is a gift from the spirits.*

A SIMPLE ACT

for Denise Dorsz

Gourds climbing the fence. Against the rusted criss-cross wires,
the leaves are fresh. The green, ruffled plants twine around
the wood posts that need painting. The fruit of the vine
hangs in irregular shapes. Some are smooth. Others bumpy
and scarred. All are colors of the earth. Brown. Green.
Gold.

A gourd is a hollowed-out shell, used as a utensil. I imagine
women together, sitting outside the tipis and lodges, carving
and scooping. Creating bowls for food. Spoons for drinking
water. A simple act—requiring lifetimes to learn. At times
the pods were dried and rattles made to amuse babies. Or
noisemakers, to call the spirits in sorrow and celebration.

I am taking a break from my hot room, from the writing,
where I dredge for ghosts. The writing that unearths pain,
old memories.

I cover myself with paper, the ink making tracks, like animals
who follow the scent of water past unfamiliar ground.

I invent new from the old.

STORY ONE

Sandra

In the third, fourth, and fifth grades, we were best friends. Spending nights at each other's houses, our girl bodies hugging tight. We had much in common. Our families were large and sloppy. We occupied places of honor due to our fair skin and hair. Assimilation separated us from our ancient and inherited places of home. Your Russian gave way to English. Your blonde hair and freckles a counterpoint to the darkness of eye and black hair massed and trembling around your mother's head. My blonde hair, fine and thin, my skin pink and flushed in contrast to the sleek, black hair of my aunts, my uncle, my father. Their eyes dark, hidden by folds of skin. We were anachronisms . . . except to each other. Our friendship fit us well.

We invented stories about ourselves. We were children from another planet. We were girls from an undiscovered country. We were alien beings in families that were "different." Different among the different.

Your big sister Olga wore falsies. We stole a pair from her and took turns tucking them inside our undershirts. We pretended to be big girls, kissing on the lips and touching our foam rubber breasts. Imagining what being grown meant. In the sixth and seventh grades our blood started to flow, our breasts turned into a reality of sweet flesh and waiting nipples. The place between our thighs filled with a wanting so tender, an intensity of heat from which our fingers emerged, shimmering with liquid energy, our bodies spent with the expression of our growing strength. When we began to know what this was—that it was called love—someone told on us. Told on us. Through my bedroom window where we lay on the bed, listening to the radio, stroking blonde hair, Roger, the boy next door, saw us and told on us. Our mothers were properly upset. We heard the words from them: "You can't play with each other anymore." "You should be ashamed." "WHAT WILL PEOPLE THINK?"

We fought in our separate ways. You screamed in Russian as your father hit you with his belt. You cursed him, vowing revenge. Your mother watched, painfully, but did not interfere, upholding the morality of the family. My mother shamed me by promising not to tell the rest of the family. I refused to speak to her for weeks, taking refuge in silence, the acceptable solution. I hated her for the complicity we shared.

Sandra, we couldn't help but see each other. You lived across the street. We'd catch glimpses of the other running to school. Our eyes averted, never focusing. The belt marks, the silences, the shame, restoring us once again to our rightful places. We were good girls, nice girls, after all. So, like an old blouse that had become too thin and frayed, an embarrassment to wear, our friendship was put away, locked up inside our past. Entering the eighth grade in 1954, we were thirteen years old. Something hard, yet invisible, had formed over our memory. We went the way of boys, back seats of cars, self-destruction. I heard you were put in the hospital with sugar diabetes. I sent a card—unsigned. Your family moved away. I never saw you again.

Sandra, we are forty-one now.
I have three daughters.
A woman lover.
I am a writer.
Sandra, I am remembering our loss.
Sandra . . . I am remembering.
I loved you.

We have a basket filled with gourds. Our basket is woven from sweetgrass, and the scent stirs up the air and lights on our skin. This still life sits on a table in front of our bedroom window. In late afternoon, the sun glances around the hanging plants, printing designs on the wall and on our arms as we lay on our bed. We trust our love to each other's care. The room grows heavy with words. Our lungs expand to breathe the life gestating in the space connecting your eyes to mine. You put your hand on my face and imprint forever, in memory, this passage of love and faith. I watch you come from your bath. I pull you toward me, my hands soothed by the wetness on your back and between your thighs. You smell of cinnamon and clean water. Desire shapes us. Desire to touch with our hands, our eyes, our mouths, our minds. I bend over you, kissing the hollow of your throat, your pulse leaping under my lips.

We touch.

Dancers wearing shells of turtles, feathers of eagles, bones of our people.

We touch.

STORY TWO

My House

The house I grew up in was a small frame box. It had two stories. My sister, cousins, and I shared a room on the second floor. A chestnut tree rubbed its branches against our window. In the summer, we opened the glass panes and coaxed the arms of the tree into the room. Grandpa spoke to the tree every night. We listened to the words, holding our breath and our questions in fear of breaking a magic we knew was happening, but couldn't name.

In our house, we spoke the language of censure. Sentences stopped in the middle. The joke without a punch line. The mixture of a supposed-to-be-forgotten Mohawk, strangled with uneasy English.

I was a dreamer. I created places of freedom in my mind. Words that my family whispered in their sleep could be shouted. Words that we were not supposed to say could be sung, like the hymns Grandma sang on Sundays.

The secrets we held to ourselves. We swallowed them. They lay at the bottoms of our stomachs, making us fat with nerves and itching from inside.

The secrets we held to ourselves.

The secret that my mom's father refused to see her after she married a dark man, an Indian man.

The secret that my uncle drank himself to oblivion—then death.

The secret that Grandma didn't go out because storekeepers called her names—*dumb Indian, squaw.*

The secret that Grandpa carried a heart inside him clogged with the starches, the fats, the poverty of food that as a young boy, as an Indian, he had no choice about eating.

All of us, weighed down by invisible scales. Balancing always, our life among the assimilators and our life of memory.

We were shamed. We didn't fit. We didn't belong.
I had learned the lessons. I kept my mouth shut. I kept the
    quiet.

One night in August, 1954, a fire in the basement.
Things burned.
Secret things.
Indian things.
Things the neighbors never saw.
False Faces. Beaded necklaces. Old letters written in
    Mohawk. A turtle rattle. Corn husks.
Secrets brought from home.
Secrets protecting us in hostile places.

"Did you lose anything?" The neighbors stood, anxious to not know. The night air was hot. The moon hung full and white. The stars in a crazy design over us.

"Did you lose anything?" The question came again.

"Just a few old things" . . . and Grandma and Grandpa stepped into the house, led by my mother's and father's hands. My grandparents tears were acid, tunneling holes in their cheeks.

"Don't forget this night, *kontirio.** Don't forget this night."

Grandfather looked at me, the phrase repeated again and again. "Don't forget this night."

Grandfather's back became a little more stooped. He lapsed into Mohawk at odd moments. His heart stopped in his sleep. Heavy. Constricted. Silenced.

Grandmother's back became a little thicker. Her shoulders were two eagles transfixed on a mountain, checked in flight. Her hands became large and knobby from arthritis. Still, she made the fry bread, the corn soup, the quilts, and changed the diapers of her great-grandchildren. She never spoke of that night. Her eyes faded, watery with age. She died. Her heart quitting in her sleep.

I closed the windows and covered my ears to the knocking of the tree.

In my room overlooking the back yard.
Through the open window, I smell the cut grass, hear
the vines on the fence make a whispery sound. The
gourds rattle as a breeze moves along quickly, bringing
a promise of autumn and change.
I sit at the desk, pen in my hand, paper scattered underneath. Trying to bring forth sound and words.
Unblocking my throat.
Untying my tongue.
Scraping sand from my eyes.
Pulling each finger out of the fist I have carried at
my side.
Unclenching my teeth.
Burning the brush ahead of me, brambles cutting across
my mind.

Each memory a pain in the heart. But *this* heart keeps pumping blood through my body, keeping me alive.

I write because to not write is a breach of faith.

Out of a past where amnesia was the expected.
Out of a past occupied with quiet.
Out of a past, I make truth for a future.

Cultures gone up in flames.
The smell of burning leather, paper, flesh, filling the spaces where memory fails.
The smell of a chestnut tree, its leaves making magic.
The smell of Sandra's hair, like dark coffee and incense.

I close my eyes. Pictures unreeling on my eyelids.
Portraits of beloved people flashing by quickly.
Opening my eyes, I think of the seemingly ordinary things that women do. And how, with the brush of an eyelash against a cheek, the movement of pen on paper, power is born.

A gourd is a hollowed-out shell, used as a utensil.

We make our bowls from the stuff of nature. Of life.

We carve and scoop, discarding the pulp.

Ink on paper, picking up trails I left so many lives ago.

Leaving my mark, my footprints, my sign.

I write what I know.

Norma jean Ross

I am Norma jean Ross, a 43 year old inmate at California Rehabilitation Center, Norco, CA. I became attracted to writing after attending Bright Fires Creative Writing Program directed by Sharon Stricker, within the confines of the institution. With Sharon's guidance and individual teaching methods, I was able through writing and keeping a journal to tap into many buried and secret thoughts. This exposure of repressed feelings through writing has allowed me to be able to free myself from many shames and guilts that I have carried inside myself for my adult lifetime. I am especially pleased that "My New Daddy" was selected to be printed because this is and always will be, the hardest thing I've ever written. My writing has been published in "Poppy" Bright Fires Creative Writing Program's book of Poems, Prose and Art, of which I am Art Editor and Assistant Editor, Cafe Solo, series no. 2. I won awards in both writing and fine art in the William James Statewide P.E.N. competition 1985, and finally with much pride, now the Greenfield Review. My birthplace is Stidham, Oklahoma and I have five children, 2 boys and 3 girls. I am 1/16 Cherokee Indian. I will close for now, once again "Thank You."

MY NEW DADDY

I was molested at eleven years old. Not raped, molested. You may not understand the difference. Molestation is intimidation of a child by threats, coercion, bribery, manipulation of many different forms.

I heard him breathing deeply. My eyes opened just enough to see my stepfather sitting naked in a chair by my bed. I shut my eyes tightly and lay trembling in the darkness, praying to God for help. I was sure that my stepfather could hear my heart banging inside my chest. His breathing quickened, the noises he made scared me. I thought he was having a fit and was going to kill me.

He made sure that I was never alone with my mother when she was home. His eyes would narrow into an unspoken threat when she would come home from the bar she worked at. My mother worked nights so she was asleep most of the day. By the time I got home from school she would be getting ready to go to work and usually be in a hurry as she had to walk three miles into town.

My stepfather slapped me around after she went to work. I remember him making me pull my panties down so he could spank me for being bad. I got spanked for a lot of things like, sweeping the floor wrong. He was left-handed and I was right-handed. But if he caught me sweeping the floor right-handed, I got spanked.

After I cleaned the house he would make me bathe while he watched . . . making sure that I'd get myself clean. Sometimes he would wash me himself . . . just to be positively sure. Then he would make me sit on his lap like a little girl. He would tell me not to let boys touch me in my private places, touching them himself, so I'd know where he was talking about. Before sending me to bed he would kiss me goodnight and push his tongue into my mouth. If I jerked away he slapped me full across the face for being mean to him when all he was doing was trying to be a good father to me.

One morning after my mother came home from work she found me passed out drunk on my bed with blood all over the sheets. My stepfather told her that I had tried to entice him and had put something up inside myself. They got into a fight in the living room. He was beating her up really bad, I grabbed a frying pan and hit him until he let go of her. I must have been half-crazy because he ran out the door with blood pouring from his head. My mother lay thrashing and screaming on the floor hysterical. I ran out the back door. I ran and ran and ran.

All during my involvement and the classes with "Bright Fires," a women's prison writing workshop, I wrote bits and pieces and occasionally shared them with the women.

Some things though, I hadn't shared. A few parts of my journal were painful for me to read, even to myself. I put some well hidden feelings on paper. Pieces titled, "Whose Pretty Little Girl is That?" and "My New Daddy," were feelings and memories that I had hidden deep inside of my soul—words I thought caused a look to enter other people's eyes. Over the years I thought it was bad to pity yourself, people would say, "Oh, she just feels sorry for herself."

I had to identify and name my pain in order to release it. I had to feel it and I had to allow the hurt to come out of my body. I had to learn it's good to cry when you're hurt. That is what Tears are for.

When I read out loud the part of my journal about being molested by my stepfather, my friends and teacher all gathered around me. I could not contain it all any longer. I cried and cried. At forty-two I cried in loving arms.

Ann Meredith

Judy Grahn

Judy Grahn is author of numerous books of poetry including Edward the Dyke and Other Poems *and the recently dramatized* Queen of Wands. *Her nonfiction includes the groundbreaking Gay and Lesbian cultural history* Another Mother Tongue *(Beacon Press). She is hard at work on* The Queen of Swords, *poetry that requires her to make a number of descents to meet the shadowy Lady of the Underworld.*

BOYS AT THE RODEO

A lot of people have spent time on some women's farm this summer of 1972 and one day six of us decide to go to the rodeo. We are all mature and mostly in our early thirties. We wear levis and shirts and short hair. Susan has shaved her head.

The man at the gate, who looks like a cousin of the sheriff, is certain we are trying to get in for free. It must have been something in the way we are walking. He stares into Susan's face. "I know you're at least fourteen," he says. He slaps her shoulder, in that comradely way men have with each other. That's when we know he thinks we are boys.

"You're over thirteen," he says to Wendy.

You're over thirteen," he says to me. He examines each of us closely, and sees only that we have been outdoors, are muscled, and look him directly in the eye. Since we are too short to be men, we must be boys. Everyone else at the rodeo are girls.

We decide to play it straight, so to speak. We make up boys' names for each other. Since Wendy has missed the episode with Susan at the gate, I slap her on the shoulder to demonstrate. "This is what he did." Slam. She never missed a step. It didn't feel bad to me at all. We laugh uneasily. We have achieved the status of fourteen year old boys, what a disguise for travelling through the world. I split into two pieces for the rest of the evening, and have never decided if it is worse to be 31 years old and called a boy or to be 31 years old and called a girl.

Irregardless, we are starved so we decide to eat, and here we have the status of boys for real. It seems to us that all the men and all the women attached to the men and most of the children are eating steak dinner plates; and we are the only women not attached to men. We eat hot dogs, which cost one tenth as much. A man who has taken a woman to the rodeo on this particular day has to have at least $12.00 to spend. So he has charge of all of her money and some of our money too, for we average $3.00 apiece and have taken each other to the rodeo.

Hot dogs in hand we escort ourselves to the wooden stands, and first is the standing up ceremony. We are pledging allegiance for the way of life — the competition, the supposed masculinity and pretty girls. I stand up, cursing, pretending I'm in some other country. One which has not been rediscovered. The loudspeaker plays Anchors Aweigh, that's what I like about rodeos, always something unexpected. At the last one I attended in another state the men on horses threw candy and nuts to the kids, chipping their teeth and breaking their noses. Who is it, I wonder, that has put these guys in charge. Even quiet mothers raged over that episode.

Now it is time for the rodeo queen contest, and a display of four very young women on horses. They are judged for queen 30% on the horsemanship and 70% on the number of queen tickets which people bought on their behalf to 'elect' them. Talk about stuffed ballot boxes. I notice the winner as usual is the one on the registered thoroughbred whose daddy owns tracts and tracts of something — lumber, minerals, animals. His family name is all over the county.

The last loser sits well on a scrubby little pony and lives with her aunt and uncle. I pick her for the dyke even though it is speculation without clues. I can't help it, it's a pleasant habit. I wish I could give her a ribbon. Not for being a dyke, but for sitting on her horse well. For believing there ever was a contest, for not being the daughter of anyone who owns thousands of acres of anything.

Now the loudspeaker announces the girls' barrel races, which is the only grown women's event. It goes first because it is not really a part of the rodeo, but more like a mildly athletic variation of a parade by women to introduce the real thing. Like us boys in the stand, the girls are simply bearing witness to someone else's act.

The voice is booming that barrel racing is a new, modern event, that these young women are the wives and daughters of cowboys, and barrel racing is a way for them to participate in their own right. How generous of these northern cowboys to have resurrected barrel racing for women and to have forgotten the hard roping and riding which women always used to do in rodeos when I was younger. Even though I was a town child, I heard thrilling rumors of the all-women's rodeo in Texas, including that the finest brahma bull rider in all of Texas was a forty year old woman who weighed a hundred pounds.

Indeed, my first lover's first lover was a big heavy woman who was normally slow as a cold python, but she was just hell when she got up on a horse. She could rope and tie a calf faster than any cowboy within 500 miles of Sweetwater, Texas. That's what the West Texas dykes said, and they never lied about anything as important to them as calf roping, or the differences between women and men. And what about that news story I had heard recently on the radio, about a bull rider who was eight months pregnant? The newsman just had apoplectic fits over her, but not me, I was proud of her. She makes me think of all of us who have had our insides so overly protected from jarring we cannot possibly get through childbirth without an anesthetic.

While I have been grumbling these thoughts to myself, three barrels have been set up in a big triangle on the field, and the women one by one have raced their horses around each one and back to start. The trick is to turn your horse as sharply as possible without overthrowing the barrel.

After this moderate display, the main bulk of the rodeo begins, with calf roping, bronco riding, bull riding. It's a very male show during which the men demonstrate their various abilities at immobilizing, cornering, maneuvering and conquering cattle of every age.

A rodeo is an interminable number of roped and tied calves, ridden and unridden broncoes. The repetition is broken by a few antics from the agile, necessary clown. His long legs nearly envelope the little jackass he is riding for the satire of it.

After a number of hours they produce an event I have never seen before—goat tying. This is for the girls eleven and twelve. They use one goat for fourteen participants. The goat is supposed to be held in place on a rope by a large man on horseback. Each girl rushes out in a long run half way across the field, grabs the animal, knocks it down, ties its legs together. Sometimes the man lets his horse drift so the goat pulls six or eight feet away from her, something no one would allow to happen in a male event. Many of the girls take over a full minute just to do their tying, and the fact that only one goat has been used makes everybody say, 'poor goat, poor goat,' and start laughing. This has become the real comedy event of the evening, and the purpose clearly is to show how badly girls do in the rodeo.

Only one has broken through this purpose to the other side. One small girl is not disheartened by the years of bad training, the ridiculous cross-field run, the laughing superior man on his horse, or the shape-shifting goat. She downs it in a beautiful flying tackle. This makes me whisper, as usual, 'that's the dyke', but for the rest of it we watch the girls look ludicrous, awkward, out-classed and totally dominated by the large handsome man on horse. In the stands we six boys drink beer in disgust, groan and hug our breasts, hold our heads and twist our faces at each other in embarrassment.

As the calf roping starts up again, we decide to use our disguises to walk around the grounds. Making our way around to the cowboy side of the arena, we pass the intricate mazes of rail where the stock is stored, to the chutes where they are loading the bull riders onto the bulls.

I wish to report that although we pass by dozens of men, and although we have pressed against wild horses and have climbed on rails overlooking thousands of pounds of angry animalflesh, though we touch ropes and halters, we are never once warned away, never told that this is not the proper place for us, that we had better get back for our own good, are not safe, etc., none of the dozens of warnings and threats we would have gotten if we had been recognized as thirty one year old girls instead of fourteen year old boys. It is a most interesting way to wander around the world for the day.

We examine everything closely. The brahma bulls are in the chutes, ready to be released into the ring. They are bulky, kindly looking creatures with rolling eyes; they resemble overgrown pigs. One of us whispers, "Aren't those the same kind of cattle that walk around all over the streets in India and never hurt anybody?"

Here in the chutes made exactly their size, they are converted into wild antagonistic beasts by means of a nasty belt around their loins, squeezed tight to mash their most tender testicles just before they are released into the ring. This torture is supplemented by a jolt of electricity from an electric cattle prod to make sure they come out bucking. So much for the rodeo as a great drama between man and nature.

A pale, nervous cowboy sits on the bull's back with one hand in a glove hooked under a strap around the bull's midsection. He gains points by using his spurs during the ride. He has to remain on top until the timing buzzer buzzes a few seconds after he and the bull plunge out of the gate. I had always considered it the most exciting event.

Around the fence sit many eager young men watching, helping, and getting in the way. We are easily accepted among them. How depressing this can be.

Out in the arena a dismounted cowboy reaches over and slaps his horse fiercely on the mouth because it has turned its head the wrong way.

I squat down peering through the rails where I see the neat, tight-fitting pants of two young men standing provocatively chest to chest.

"Don't you think Henry's a queer," one says with contempt.

"Hell, I *know* he's a queer," the other says. They hold an informal spitting contest for the punctuation. Meantime their eyes have brightened and their fronts are moving toward each other in their clean, smooth shirts. I realize they are flirting with each other, using Henry to bring up the dangerous subject of themselves. I am remembering all the gay cowboys I ever knew. This is one of the things I like about cowboys. They don't wear those beautiful pearl button shirts and tight levis for nothing.

As the events inside the arena subside, we walk down to a roped off pavillion where there is a dance. The band consists of one portly, bouncing enthusiastic man of middle age who is singing with great spirit into the microphone. The rest of the band are three grim, lean young men over fourteen. The drummer drums angrily, while jerking his head behind himself as though searching the air for someone who is already two hours late and had seriously promised to take him away from here. The two guitar players are sleepwalking from the feet up with their eyes so glassy you could read by them.

A redhaired man appears, surrounded by redhaired children who ask, "Are you drunk, Daddy?"

"No, I am not drunk," Daddy says.

"Can we have some money?"

"No," Daddy says, "I am not drunk enough to give you any money."

During a break in the music the redhaired man asks the band-leader where he got his band.

"Where did I get this band?" the bandleader puffs up, "I raised this band myself. These are all my sons — I raised this band myself." The redhaired man is so very impressed he is nearly bowing and kissing the hand of the bandleader, as they repeat this conversation two or three times. "This is *my* band," the bandleader says, and the two guitar players exchange grim and glassy looks.

Next the bandleader has announced "Okie From Muskogee", a song intended to portray the white country morality of cowboys. The crowd does not respond but he sings enthusiastically anyway. Two of his more alert sons drag themselves to the microphone to wail that they don't smoke marijuana in Muskogee — as those hippies down in San Francisco do, and they certainly don't. From the look of it they shoot hard drugs and pop pills.

In the middle of the song a very drunk thirteen year old boy has staggered up to Wendy, pounding her on the shoulder and exclaiming, "Can you dig it, brother?" Later she tells me she has never been called brother before, and she likes it. Her first real identification as one of the brothers, in the brotherhood of man.

We boys begin to walk back to our truck, past a cowboy vomiting on his own pretty boots, past another lying completely under a car. Near our truck, a young man has calf-roped a young woman. She shrieks for him to stop, hopping weakly along behind him. This is the first bid for public attention I have seen from any woman here since the barrel race. I understand that this little scene is a re-enactment of the true meaning of the rodeo, and of the conquest of the west. And oh how much I do not want to be her; I do not want to be the conquest of the west.

I am remembering how the clown always seems to be tall and riding on an ass, that must be a way of poking fun at the small and usually dark people who tried to raise sheep or goats or were sod farmers and rode burros instead of tall handsome blond horses, and who were driven under by the beef raisers. And so today we went to a display of cattle handling instead of a sheep shearing or a goat milking contest — or to go into even older ghost territory, a corn dance, or acorn gathering . . .

As we reach the truck, the tall man passes with the rodeo queen, who must surely be his niece, or something. All this non-contest, if it is for anyone, must certainly be for him. As a boy, I look at him. He is his own spitting image, of what is manly and white and masterly, so tall in his high heels, so *well horsed*. His manner portrays his theory of life as the survival of the fittest against wild beasts, and all the mythical rest of us who are too female or dark, not straight, or much too native to the earth to now be trusted as more than witnesses, flags, cheerleaders and unwilling stock.

As he passes, we step out of the way and I am glad we are in our disguise. I hate to step out of his way as a full grown woman, one who hasn't enough class status to warrant his thinly polite chivalry. He has knocked me off the sidewalk of too many towns, too often.

Yet somewhere in me I know I have always wanted to be manly, what I mean is having that expression of courage, control, coordination, ability I associate with men. To *provide*.

But here I am in this truck, not a man at all, a fourteen year old boy only. Tomorrow is my thirty second birthday. We six snuggle together in the bed of this rickety truck which is our world for the time being. We are headed back to the bold and shakey adventures of our all-women's farm, our all-women's households and companies, our expanding minds, ambitions and bodies, we who are neither male nor female at this moment in the pageant world, who are not the rancher's wife, mother earth, Virgin Mary or the rodeo queen — we who are really the one who took her self seriously, who once took an all-out dive at the goat believing that the odds were square and that she was truly in the contest.

And now that we know it is not a contest, just a play — we have run off with the goat ourselves to try another way of life.

Because I certainly do not want to be a 32 year old girl, or calf either, and I certainly also do always remember Gertrude Stein's beautiful dykely voice saying, what is the use of being a boy if you grow up to be a man.

Harriet Malinowitz

In 1980, preparing to get my Masters of Fine Arts (M.F.A.) degree, I submitted "Coffee and Cake" to my (male) advisor for inclusion in my thesis. He returned it with a note saying that it was "thin, typical, predictable and didactic," and told me that if I didn't "get off that track" and write something "acceptable" I wouldn't get my degree. Since he'd made a career of writing about little boys from Brooklyn who made adorable and ingenuous observations, I pragmatically but miserably wrote a couple of stories about adolescent girls from Queens who likewise spouted precious remarks. My thesis was then accepted—"With distinction!" he told me, pumping my hand—and I emerged with an M.F.A. and a dead weight of 50% rag bond paper bound in red leather.

The same year, "Coffee and Cake" was published in Conditions *magazine, and two years later it was anthologized in* Nice Jewish Girls: A Lesbian Anthology *(Persephone Press). In writing, as in conversation, it's good to have a healthy sense of audience.*

Neither I nor the four male mentors who presided over the entire M.F.A. in Fiction program were going through paces that were in any way unusual. The redeeming part of the experience was that it crystallized for me in a deeper way than ever before the fact that my spiritual survival desperately depended on the existence of women's publishing, a feminist literary canon, and in short, women's culture. For this tradition is reserved my ultimate "Without Whom . . ." acknowledgement.

I now teach English and writing at Hunter College and New York University. I'm politically active in the women's movement and in Central America solidarity work. For recreation I watch The Bill Cosby Show, *where on Thursday nights I tune in along with millions of other neurotics across America to see how healthy, normal, well-adjusted people live.*

92

COFFEE AND CAKE

I have not seen my brother Steven since last Thanksgiving, when he forgot to buy the turkey. My mother, my uncle, and I flew out to Tucson for four days. It was one of the very few times all year that it rained, and it rained continuously, the four of us thrown into a more intensive proximity than we'd counted on. I brought a pumpkin bread I'd baked in Massachusetts, carefully wrapped in foil, and winter squash and gourds I'd picked up at farm stands. But when we got there Steven had forgotten to buy a turkey. It was almost midnight on Wednesday.

"It doesn't matter, I'll take us all out to eat," said my uncle—his characteristic gesture, his cure-all for all of life's ills. I had to try to flush out the raw anger and disappointment in my eyes; I couldn't answer the magnanimity of that offer, the pleasure beaming from my uncle's face at the pleasure he was giving us. There was no way I could tamper with his kindness. Steven, sensing my disturbance, said, "You're only here for a few days, anyway. You wouldn't want to spend a whole day inside cooking, would you?"

The next day we took a dismal ride through the rain to Bisbee, where everything was closed for the holiday. Sitting in the only restaurant open in town, we ate slices of turkey in pasty gravy, canned sweet potatoes, frozen peas. My mother was getting enthusiastic about the salad bar, while I sat beside her, furious, humiliated for her, wishing she could be more collected about salad bars. I felt the weight of many salad bars behind me. I wanted to tell them not to be too easily satisfied—but didn't know how to press without stabbing. I was afraid of doing some real damage. Instead, I sat there, miserably watching them in their enjoyment as they absorbed the soullessness of all they touched, knowing that I, by proximity to them, absorbed it too. In the end, I made weak jokes, caustic barbs punctuated by ameliorating laughs. They sent me puzzled looks but they held me to my laughter. Nobody actually choked on the indignity of the food. The event, after all, was not serious.

Now I am seeing Steven again, after seven months, at my mother's house in Queens. He arrived last night at 3 AM, having driven almost continuously from Arizona. I have driven in for the weekend from Massachusetts, and I arrive in time for dinner. We embrace, the ceremony so old that we can use it to camouflage the embarrassment of our real warmth. A dog is barking; it runs in and jumps on me. This is Willie, the puppy Steven has recently bought. It's strange to see a dog in my mother's house; stranger still to see it and Steven playing with each other so intimately. I go into the kitchen, where I find my mother cutting grapefruits. We also kiss each other, and then immediately the dog is there, hurling himself at us in his excitement. Steven appears behind the dog and admonishes him to get down. There are four of us in the kitchen; this morning there was only my mother, but now her daughter has come from Massachusetts, her son has driven all the way in from Arizona, and there is this new personage who runs in and out of the room. He runs in and we pet him, talk to him. He comes over to where my mother is standing and puts his paws up around her leg.

"Sit for Grandma!" commands Steven, and we all begin to laugh.

"Sit for Grandma!" Steven says again, when Willie doesn't pay attention to him, and then he pulls Willie on the floor where they wrestle for a minute. The disciplining parent. My mother is still laughing at hearing the word "Grandma" spoken. I see in her face that this is very funny and very absurd to her, and yet the name itself is like a code word nobody's dared to speak before. Grandma. Someone she wishes to be. She laughs, a little confusedly now, at Willie. Her grandchild? All three of us are redistributing our weight, shifting to make room for a new member of whose inclusion in our circle there can be no question.

I watch Willie and Steven for a little while; then I look again at my mother, who is also watching them, removed from the action now, her lips slightly curving, her eyes soft with absorption. Abruptly, I feel a twinge of fear—the fear that here is a new contingency upon which our survival depends, a new element which must be preserved in our fragile chain of love. I am afraid of the looks upon all our faces, the expressions which confess our helpless awareness of each other.

Steven is teasingly twisting a bone out of Willie's teeth and tossing it so it skims the rug and lands near the piano. We all laugh, and I am afraid. We are too close. I am afraid of their pain. I am afraid too of their joy, because once I see it I know it will be tragic if it goes away. I think of Petra, my lover. With her my fear is of loss, of the unpredictable movements of our personalities. With family, not many changes are expected. The continuance of the relationships is assured; no one else can threaten them. They are utterly pre-determined, pre-guaranteed.

Yet, with all this certainty, all this knowledge, there is still something in the particularity of their pain I can't understand. I see the looks of anguish on their faces, which I perceive even when they are unaware of them. I know too well the delicately honed variations in their expressions. Too well, too, do I know their happy looks. If only I could know for sure that the happy looks would remain, then I could go away, finally, at peace, and not come back.

We don't *want* to be moved by each other. We strive endlessly to be superficially touched, less than profoundly affected. Our joy is always shadowed by death, by geographic mobility, by a dangerous world in which we cannot offer each other real protection, where we play by disparate rules. And I am afraid that later tonight, when my mother goes up to bed and Steven and I go out for coffee, and I finally tell him that I am a lesbian, he won't understand.

One month before, long distance, Massachusetts to Arizona: *This has been a big year for me. A lot has changed. I want very much to talk to you when you come in.*

What is it? Tell me now.

No, it's nothing I can spit out over the phone. I shouldn't have brought it up. I'm sorry. It will have to wait.

But he continues to tease me, playing 20 questions. *Does it have something to do with your career?* Yes. *Is it political?* Yes. *Is it revolutionary?* Yes. *Is it physical?* Yes.

"Now you've got me really confused," he says. "Are you going around planting bombs?"

Yes.

We slide into a booth at The Greasy Spoon Diner. The waitress takes our order: coffee and two slices of hazelnut cheesecake. She puts her pad in her apron pocket, takes our menus, and walks away.

All around us are plump, middle-aged Jewish people of Queens, drinking coffee, eating cheesecake, babka, apple strudel. Tomorrow they will go back on their diets; tomorrow night they will return and break them. Steven and I both pretend to feel alienated among them but between us lies the secret of their familiarity. We've constructed our lives around being different from them, and yet in a minute the pastry smells waft over and seduce us back. I wonder if the smells make him think of what I'm thinking: the week we sat *shiva* for my father, the friends and neighbors and relatives coming to pay condolence calls, bringing cakes and pies from Jewish bakeries all over the length and breadth of Long Island. About 50 visitors a day; which meant five times throughout the afternoon and evening sitting down to coffee from the huge borrowed percolator and cakes on fluted trivets carefully lifted from pastel-colored cardboard boxes tied with flecked string. Did we ever eat dinner? Lunch? Breakfast? Was it a collective plot of our guests to ensure our proper mourning behavior by depriving us of protein and inducing a protracted sugar fit? I don't remember minding or objecting. I only remember loving those cakes for being so inordinately civilized; for being so attractive; for being so expensive. Within those boxes with their script saying "Ida's" or "Mitzi's" or "Ratner's," I sensed my culture.

Yet rarely would my mother have bought such cakes. I had known them all my life from visitors who brought them, from houses I had visited as a child in which they were served. That only my mother, among all mothers I knew, did not identify herself with those pastries branded our family as an anomaly within German and Eastern European Jewish society. Sometimes even now I forget that before my struggle to separate and become an assimilated American, there had been the converse struggle to integrate, to transcend the limitations of a family which was ethnically incorrect.

My family: a year ago, Steven's birthday, the three of us in my mother's house. Steven has been living in the Village for a year but he has come home to re-live the birthday ritual. My family, so fond of form, so oblivious of content. My mother has an Entenmann's Marshmallow Fudge Cake for him. I groan, remembering to smile humorously as I do so, and she turns to me with a laugh and says, "Well, it's his favorite." Boys will be boys. There it sits, sugary, fudgy, tacky in its tin plate. The candles stuck in this skimpy little mass of junk make me want to cry—because this is the cake of his dreams; it is the aspiration of his birthday, and she is so acquiescent in fulfilling it. Our mother, who was supposed to teach us about life. And Steven, whose window on Cornelia Street draws in air perfumed with Italian breads, baguettes, challahs, cannolis, ruggaluch, croissants, tortes, napoleons, brioches. Steven, Steven, Steven! How is it, why is it that the three of us are gathered around this birthday cake in this kitchen, still going through the paces of this ritual? What is it that sabotages our imaginations, preventing us from inventing new celebrations?

Now, hazelnut cheesecake between us on the very un-greasy tabletop in The Greasy Spoon Diner. Steven leans back against the shiny leather seat. "So what's new?" he says.

He is so relaxed that I think he must know. Yet unless I *know* he knows, which I don't know, I have to proceed on the assumption that he doesn't.

I had said to Petra: "The problem is that there are certain words which mean very different things to me than they do to him, and I'm not sure how to use them."

"Like what?" she'd asked.

"Like 'lesbian,' " I'd admitted.

I look at him and decide that that is not a good place to start.

"You remember Petra," I say, and he says yes, he does. The way he acknowledges it, as if clearing an irrelevant detail out of the way so we can get to the point, tells me that he doesn't know at all. So I say, quickly, "Well, last year we became friends and then we became lovers."

Somewhere along the sentence there has been a jolt in his look of blank expectancy; perhaps a fraction of a second before I got to "lovers."

"Really?" he says, in an unnatural voice, and chugs his glass of water like beer.

"Yes," I say, "really."

Then I launch into a synopsis of this year of my life, and I hear, as if from a distance, the words and phrases spilling from my mouth: "structuring my life," "defining myself," "made a decision," "political statement." I have become, quite clearly, a paragon of control. I talk and talk, words of power and strength tripping over themselves in their eagerness to make themselves clear. I don't say, "I fell in love with Petra and I was terrified to realize that whether I wished it and willed it or not, I was a lesbian. That I *had* to learn these things because without them I couldn't live." No, not me; I was a right-on radical lesbian feminist from the day I was born. On and on I go, skipping the fright, the confusion, skipping even the love because it is too bare, too vulnerable, and too true. I tell him only the things I have learned, the perceptions I have been injecting into my veins like new, life-giving blood. Maybe if I can reassemble my molecules so that I look like a Holly Near record, it will all miraculously click with him.

But that look on his face. A look of shock, and a confusion he is struggling valiantly to conceal. There is something about that look—how do I know it? Oh yes, now I remember, it's the look on the face of the man Marjorie Morningstar marries, after she confesses to him that she's not a virgin. Never again, we are told, will that look of pure happiness he had when he believed Marjorie to be pure reappear upon his face. I read that book five times between the ages of 13 and 18 and it always made me feel furiously futile. It was as if I could see that man standing not very far away from me, and I wanted to go and shake him, only I knew I'd have to walk all the way around the world to get to him, instead of simply crossing the street.

Now I get that same feeling, only it is more diffuse and not really directed at Steven. I suddenly realize it's not going to be all roses after all. I haven't seen that look on anyone's face yet—and on his face it cripples me, makes my bones feel weak.

"You haven't told Mom, have you?"

"No, but I'm going to eventually."

"I wouldn't do that. Don't forget you're living in a different world than she is. She'd be really crushed."

I feel the terrible sense of power I felt in the restaurant in Bisbee, as he reminds me of the damage I can do. I am sickened to hear the fear in his voice, to hear his conviction that the possibility of telling my mother is a lethal weapon I possess. I'm trying to tell him I've been born, while reflected in his eyes I watch my own death. And this, we both somehow know, is at the root of the protective instinct we both feel for my mother. I think of Chava, the daughter in *Fiddler on the Roof* who marries a gentile. Her parents sit *shiva* for her, heartbroken as if she had died. I used to despise Tevya for that—for being so fanatic and bullheaded, letting ritual and ceremony prescribe his feelings for his own daughter. Now I understand how words like "daughters," "marriage," "family," and "Jewish" came glued together in their heads, so that when one beam slipped the whole roof fell in. I wonder if "heterosexual" is glued into my mother's definition of me in the same way. I am sure that it is. Steven's face tells me that it is. Which means that when I cease to be heterosexual, I cease to exist.

"Tell me honestly how you feel," I say. My voice proclaims: Spare me nothing. I can take it. Nothing can mar my confidence, so let's be candid. "Are you really that surprised?"

"Yes," he says, "yes, I am. I'm sorry if I seem negative—this will take some getting used to. If you want me to be honest, I guess I can't help admitting I'm somewhat disappointed."

Disappointed. About what? That I've exploded his illusions about my heterosexuality? That I'm flawed?

"I just don't understand how you can *decide* to *define* yourself as a lesbian," he says, hesitating over the word but coming through in the end. "How can you say that's what you *are*? I've had only heterosexual relationships, but I don't *define* myself as heterosexual. I wouldn't say I *am* heterosexual."

"But you don't have to say it. Everybody assumes it anyway.

You're very defined—so defined you never even have to mention it."

He thinks about this. I think what confuses me most in this conversation is the careful consideration he is giving to everything I say. I have had friends tell me about coming out to brothers who were football players and corporate executives, men who simply dismissed them across the board as loony dykes. There is something reassuring about having an antagonist live up to your expectations of him. If my brother were to get belligerent, derisive, or abusive, I could dismiss him with equal conviction. Then I could say he didn't matter. But he matters.

"I guess you're right about that," he says. "I never really thought of it. It's just this idea of a political concept settling who you're going to have relationships with that gets me."

I launch into a lecture about the personal being political, but he's right, because there's one thing wrong with my argument: I have expounded on the political and neglected the personal. It's the one part I can't seem to get out. It's perfectly reasonable that he doesn't understand. I'm touched that he's still trusting in me enough to sit rubbing his cheek thoughtfully as he tries to digest what I have not really prepared for consumption.

So I explain why I feel it's important to fully acknowledge all the components of one's identity. "I'm white, I'm middle-class, I'm Jewish, I'm a woman, I'm a writer, I'm a feminist, I'm a native New Yorker, I'm a lesbian," I say. "Each of these is absolutely fundamental to my concept of myself as a person in the world." I add that coming out as a lesbian was what finally made me throw out the last vestiges of my anti-Semitism. Finding out what lesbian separatism meant made me think of what Jewish separatism meant to me all my life. The two reflected so much on each other that I was finally able to really look at separatism—what it was for the separatists, and for the ones being separated from.

"Sometimes I think of those stories they used to tell us in Hebrew school, about the Jews in Europe during the war who were 'safely' assimilated with changed names and false histories, who finally put *mezuzahs* up on their doors and got carted away. They used to make these people sound like heroes, and I always thought they were just crazy. But now I understand. Not that I'd be putting any *mezuzah* up on *my* door, or coming out if the government were going to execute me for it. I'd still be scared and cowardly. But I understand the point now. I understand what it means to deny who you are." There, it was subtle but he might have caught it.

"I still think it's crazy," says Steven. "You're not denying who you are to yourself. Why would you willingly bring more problems into your own life? I think it's more important to do what you want to do, know who you are in yourself, but protect yourself at the same time."

I tell him then about Rema, a friend from high school who is a lesbian now. I saw her once last year, by accident, in a restaurant in Chinatown. She works for a jewelry company, wears makeup and excruciatingly high heels, and is only out to her closest friends, who are all lesbians and none of whom consider themselves feminists.

"I don't see how anyone can live like that," I say.

"I do," says Steven, "I really do. Not everyone's like you. Not everyone wants to fight. Some people just want to have an easy life."

"At the cost of feeding the world's stereotypes. Rema gets chalked up as straight. When people in her office look around and take stock of the world, they're going to believe it's homogeneously straight, as long as everyone in it claims to be. For all we know, half the earth could be gay and no one will ever know, because everyone's so busy acting straight."

"But that's her decision," says Steven.

"It's not just *her* decision. Rema's not only perpetuating her own oppression—she's perpetuating mine!" Oh my God—I've actually used the word "oppression." It sounds ridiculous uttered here in The Greasy Spoon, with my brother. It's one of those words you generally pitch only when there's someone around who's trained to catch it.

"But can't you understand why someone might not want to deal with being a social outcast?"

"I'm not an outcast!" I yell, hitting the table. A couple in the next booth turns around and looks at me in surprise. If there's one thing I want Steven to understand, it's that I'm no outcast and have no intention of being an outcast. But how can he really come to understand this? How can I convey a sense of my own feminism when there is a hurt look in his eyes every time I say the word "men"? I don't mean him—but I don't know how either of us will react to excluding him from the category. How can I possibly make him understand what a women's community means? What it does? Here is a man I don't *want* to be divided from—but how can I help it, within the terms in which I've chosen to view the world—and now, even in his terms? How can we both remain whole and healthy and still be undivided?

Driving home in the car we talk, unbelievably, of other things. Neither one of us has seized the oars and rowed away, but neither of us has dropped anchor, either. What had to be said has been said; even if it never gets spoken of again, it is there, a little packet of information tied and labeled and irrevocably welded into our relationship. I feel a little ill, physically, although I can't exactly locate the source of my discomfort. I'm not sorry I told him. If I hadn't, I would have gone on month after month, probably year after year, always planning to, perennially on the verge. And that would have been like pushing a rock uphill through all of eternity; or like writing a book that is all preface.

And there he is at the wheel, still driving, still liking me, not going through any red lights. And I still like him too, even if it would be more convenient at this moment not to. I look at him, his face washed in wave after wave of streetlight as we ride down the Queens avenue we have ridden down since we were born. We aren't waiting to grow up any more; we aren't wondering who we'll become, what profession we'll choose, whom we'll marry. These questions haven't been answered; but we've lived long enough to know that life is not a symphony that plays itself out in three movements. The answers, when they come at all, are unearthed in fragments, like archaic fossils or chips of Greek pottery, and at random, often after many days of fruitless digging. And if Steven and I aren't digging in the same place, at least we share some sense of the theory and the process of the dig, and looking back to where we started our eyes come to rest on the same point.

What I didn't know until now, until I came upon this fragment, is that what I hoped for will most likely never happen. Steven and I have already been socialized. Lies are already firmly woven in the fabric of our past together, insisting upon the shape of our present. Yet there are also truths buried in our history which have spun a binding web around us. We are the world's only two bona fide products of the union of Selma and Larry Edelman, the only two ever to have grown up in our house under our circumstances. We are the central intelligence bank of the idiosyncracies of these two individuals, and we carry these idiosyncracies around somewhere in our own personalities. At best it is like a legacy; at worst, a genetic disease. In either case, certain secrets will always hover between us. Some we'll learn to speak, others will remain silenced, but we will always be pressed into remembrance of their existence by each other's mere presence. There is no one else that either of us can ever be connected to in this way, just as nothing can ever separate us from the common ground of our knowledge—even when the intensity makes us wish to be divided.

My mother used to tell me the story of how I had interrupted my brother's circumcision by crying out at the crucial moment, "The doctor is going to cut the baby!" This was Steven's *bris*, the first major event in a Jewish boy's life and generally the occasion for a party. If he, the boy, had been the firstborn, the *bris* would have been followed by a *pinion aben* a month later. No one in my family has ever been clear on the significance of a *pinion aben*; they only know that it is a tradition, another excuse to celebrate. At the age of 13 Steven was worth $1500, mostly in bonds given to him at his Bar Mitzvah—the ceremony invented so that the Jewish boy can proclaim: "Today I am a man."

I have been told that my turn too will come. My grandmother, who is senile and often doesn't remember who I am, has one message to impart when she recognizes me at her nursing home: "Remember, I want to dance at your wedding." She has said this to me over and over, like a broken record, sometimes a dozen times in one visit. Ninety-one years old and in a wheelchair, but if I marry she will dance. Sometimes I have the impulse to gather my family and say: "Today I am a lesbian," and see who starts to dance. I would like to see someone rent a catering hall, give me a salad bowl, say, "*Mazel tov, mazel tov,* health and happiness always!" with tears of joy in their eyes. My birth, my marriage, my death — these are the events which did, would, will chart my existence; they are my demarcation lines on the genealogical map.

"Why is it so important to you to tell the world?" had been Steven's question. "What do you get from it?" And I know the crazy thing I hoped to get from telling him. I hoped to see him dance.

Kathleen Shaye Hill

Kathleen Shaye Hill is Klamath/Paiute/White and an enrolled member of the Klamath Indian Tribe. She has done work for her tribe at the Federal Archives in Seattle, Washington and has just completed working for one full year to have the Klamath recognized by the Federal Government. (In 1986, Congress passed a bill reinstating recognition of the Klamath.) She is raising her two children, writing short stories, and working on a novel.

TAKING CARE OF BUSINESS

The morning of the funeral Reeva went upstairs, stepped into her closet, closed the door as she always did and under the dim light of a 25 watt bulb, got herself dressed. Even though it was warm outside, she put on a gray flannel suit and a shocking pink blouse. With a quick wrist she wrapped her hair up and stuck a few hairpins in it.

She had paid a high price for what he'd done. To begin with, she had lived a life of jealousy—resentment, really—directed toward the women she met who had been protected, who'd held onto their innocence throughout childhood. She had lost a good man, a good husband, because she'd never learned what it meant to make love, never known physical intimacy that didn't leave her feeling violated. And now she even seemed to have lost her children. They thought she was crazy. They hadn't said so but she knew it was true. Each time she stepped out of the room she heard them hurriedly whispering, and as soon as she stepped back in they clammed up and acted as if no words had passed between them. They came to visit less and less often and when they did they no longer asked what the graphs and charts on her walls were for. She had been very clever on that issue; she'd kept them color-coded and the only keys were on the lists which she slid under the rug in her bedroom each night. The memos were important, too. They contained the explanations that rounded out her project. These she kept rolled up like scrolls in the ankles of her steel-toed woodchooping boots.

This morning, for the first time, all the facets of what had become her life-project, her reason for being, were united. Still stockingfooted, she laid them out on the bed—the final chart propped on the left pillow, the list underneath, the graph on her pillow and the memos (but only the most recent ones) lined up below it.

It had taken her a good many years to realize the extent of what he had done to her. Although she'd been paying for it all along, it hadn't been clear just how much she'd paid until five years ago. That's when Jim had left; because, as he'd very gently put it, she just didn't seem to love him the way he needed to be loved. They shared no intimacy, no passion, he said, and now that the kids were grown, they should both be free to seek the kind of love that would fulfill their later years. There were no fights, there was no cruelty, and all along she had known he was right. Even before he brought it up, she'd known there was something wrong with her. Another kind of man would have used the word "frigid" but Jim didn't have that in him. It didn't matter, though, because the hurt in his eyes and the agony she felt couldn't have been worse if he'd chopped up her heart and served it on that night's salad plate.

She knew it was too late with Jim, but the desperate sorrow got her to that woman psychologist and in a matter of months they'd dredged up her past, waded through it and finally set it aside. At least that's what her goodhearted counselor thought. Only Reeva knew better. As hard as she tried, she just couldn't accept the past and move beyond it in the way that White woman wanted. And even though the counselor was good and kind and sensitive, she seemed unable to understand the double-damage a White man could do an Indian girl. It wasn't that she didn't care; she just didn't understand that his Whiteness made a difference. After a few months Reeva got tired of trying to teach her. Instead, she went along with her, said the things the counselor was able to accept, and, afterward, turned to her graphs, charts, memos and lists.

Every night after work she'd come home, fix dinner, call her mother, then go upstairs and work on the project. It hadn't been easy at first. There had been no words, no way of pinning down those feelings, those memories of night after night spent waiting and never knowing. So it started with the lists of words: fear/isolation/violation/denial/recrimination. Those were the first words, there were many to follow.

Then there were the memos. A description of a memory or emotion was written on a memo for each word. Like the "F" memo for "fear": "Every night, not knowing if he'd be there or not. No more baby dolls; it was flannel from here to there. And tucking the blankets in tightly, so tightly I could hardly breathe. Then

108

pushing the bed against the wall and sliding in under those tight, tight covers and laying up hard against the wall and listening to every sound. When I was almost asleep they'd turn the radio off downstairs and I'd wait, as I knew he'd wait, for her to go to sleep. Sometimes I'd hear him, hear the stairs creak, and I'd know he was creeping up those stairs. It was scary to know how much like a rodent, a nightcreature, he was. So I'd close my eyes and wait and breathe heavy like I thought sleep sounded. If I cried or whimpered or said 'please, don't,' he'd say 'shut up or I'm going to tell your mother on you.' Some nights I'd hear him when he wasn't there. I'd peek out of the corner of my eye expecting to see his pasty-white body, dressed in nothing but freshly bleached undershorts, scampering across the linoleum to my bed. But there was nothing. No one. And I knew I was getting crazy." That was fear.

On the chart, fear was olive-green because every time he touched her, each time his corpse-colored fingers pried inside the elastic of her pajamas or between the buttons on her nightgown, she wanted to throw up. Now, each time she woke up at night, scared, still hearing him even though all of this was thirty years past and her house was four miles from his, she took that wide-tipped felt marker and added a horizontal stripe of olive-green to the bottom of the long, broad, "F" column on her chart.

Each word had its own column and she did her best, really put a lot of thought into deciding just what color was appropriate. The hardest was "H", the "hate" column. That color turned out to be sludge-brown. She could think of nothing more appropriate for the hate she felt than the color of the sludge in the bottom of Klamath Lake, because he'd done to her what the White farmers and ranchers had done to her tribe's beloved lake. The color had been hard to find in a wide-tipped felt marker, but it was worth the search that took her all the way to Portland because it was exactly right.

Reeva looked across the chart one last time and admired the murky, muddled colors for the chance they'd given her to visualize the anguish.

She turned to the graph. The line of it was her gauge of happiness. She couldn't remember before age four so that's where it started. The line was above the minimal-happy point until she was eleven, two years after her mother had married him. He was a little strange but he was good to her mother as her own father had not been and, even though he was White, her younger brothers found it easy to call him Daddy.

Reeva and Lani, her best friend, had a lot of silliness together that eleventh year. It was great fun changing into women and when they showered or changed clothes they laughed at how funny their breasts were; how different they looked than the round, lightly-marked momma-breasts of their mothers. They had giggled themselves senseless over their bodies and they could hardly wait to grow up and nurse their own babies. But all of that changed. He changed it. That's when he started coming around, poking and prying, and she hated him and she hated her breasts and she never wanted babies anymore.

At sixteen, she tried to tell her mother—only once—what he'd been doing, how he'd been messing around with her. But Momma couldn't believe it. Maybe she just loved him too much. At different times she tried to tell her brothers too, but they seemed not to have heard. Each time they just started talking about something else. The funny thing about it was all of them, in their odd little ways, seemed to have thrown her, not him, out of their lives.

Then Jim came along and got her away from him so she let him have her. But she never could get herself to nurse those babies.

Reeva let out a long, deep sigh and it filled the room with heavy air. She chastised herself for being self-indulgent. After all, her mother had just died. Her mother had loved that man and, in his own way, she supposed, he must have loved her mother. He'd taken care of Momma all those years and had been a good father to her brothers. That counted for something; at least at the time.

Well, today would be the end of that. She had waited all these years and today he was going to be the one to pay. She was tired of wearing his shame. Let him see how comfortable he was dressed up in it. She reached under the mattress and pulled out the speech. It had taken hours to write. She no longer needed the lists, the graphs, the charts and memos. Once Momma was safely in the Earth, once they had all gathered in Momma's home after the final meal in her honor, once everyone had eaten their dessert and finished their coffee, Reeva was going to make a toast. "This," she would start out, raising a glass of wine high into the air, "is to pay tribute to the god-damn son-of-a-bitch who robbed me of my childhood, who stole my sensuality before I even knew I had it." Then she would go into detail. She would tell each thing he had done to her. Like how he'd threatened her with Momma, knowing Reeva couldn't bear to face the answer if Momma had to make a choice between him and her. But death had removed that fear. Now, without having to worry about Momma, she'd tell everything. Even how she'd cried and begged and prayed and neither he nor the Creator had listened or cared.

Already, she could picture the faces of the folks at the funeral. Some would stand there with their mouths hanging open. Some would get indignant and leave. Her kids might try to shut her up in order to protect "their Grandpa". But she wouldn't listen.

One way or another, she'd get it said and they'd all just have to listen up. All of them would pay for the fact that when she had needed it—when she, too, had been young and sweet and vulnerable—no one had cared enough to protect her.

Reeva was unable to cry. Momma was gone, forever, but no matter how hard she tried she couldn't cry.

They'd finished the final meal at the church and only the closest friends and family members were at Momma's house. His family was there, as were her aunts and uncles, the people who'd known her since childhood, her kids, her ex-husband Jim, her brothers, sisters-in-law, nieces and nephews. A fine audience.

The first glass of wine was to take the edge off, the second to steel her nerves. She looked around at the solemn faces, at the half-finished plates of dessert, half-full cups of lukewarm coffee. No one else was drinking wine today, but she didn't care, didn't give one damn. She'd brought her own. She kept scouring the room with her eyes and now, they landed on him. He was sitting all alone in that recliner Momma'd bought one Father's Day. There he was, sniveling away, whining how life wasn't worth living anymore. Reeva downed the little bit of wine left in her glass and let the dry-edged flavor bite into her tongue for a moment. If he thought life wasn't worth living now, just give her a half-hour.

She refilled the glass in the kitchen, this time sipping it very slowly. People were mulling around now but none of them spoke to her. For a long while she watched him. He was a homely little man, ugly and frail. He'd die soon. It showed all over him. He knew it, too—that showed as well. Her kids were hovering over him now, patting him on the back, holding his hand. Giving him the kind of tender care they had never been able to give her. On second thought, maybe she'd never been able to give them that kind of tenderness either.

She looked at him again and he was watching her. He held his hands out toward her. "Daughter," he said. "My daughter . . . " There were great salty tears rolling out of his sad, bloodshot eyes. She turned away and went back to the kitchen to pour what was left of the bottle into her glass.

On re-entering the living room she glanced around at the plates once more. They were all empty. Her moment had come. Reeva cleared her throat and stood up. She was no longer invisible to the group, all heads turned to her. Her eyes had become weapons. She looked at him and he winced. It was clear that he didn't recognize the woman she'd become. In his sorrow and old age, they both knew that he had become the vulnerable one.

Very slowly, she raised the half-empty glass into the air. Her eyes swept the room, skimming over each brown or white face, each pair of worn, painfilled eyes that raised to meet hers. *Their pain*—she had forgotten all about THEIR PAIN. She paused for a moment, but knew nothing except to forge ahead. After all, there the glass was, dangling from her hand, high up over her head. She let her eyes settle on him once. "This," she said—just as she had planned, raising her glass even higher—"this is to pay tribute," she coughed, cleared her throat, looked about, and accidentally saw Momma's portrait above his chair. "This is to pay tribute to the memory of my mother, a woman who suffered but endured, whose only strengths were love and patience. May the Ancestors be watching over her as she travels to the AfterWorld."

Nobody said anything. Nobody even had a glass to toast with. Someone murmured "amen" but mostly they just stared, dumbfounded. Finally, her brothers came to her and each put his arms around her, holding her close. Then Jim came and hugged her.

She sank into his arms in a way she'd never been able to sink before. Her children came next and each of them held and kissed her. Finally the gathering cleared and he was standing there. It was just the two of them. He reached out to her, put his arms around her and said, "Thank you, daughter. Thank you." Reeva let him pull her close although she felt her back tighten up in the old way. He held her as tightly as his weak old arms could hold her.

She pulled back and took a long look at his little rodent face. Life had, indeed, given him the face he'd deserved all along. She smiled then leaned into him, putting her lips right next to his ear. "I'm not your daughter," she whispered. "Don't call me that again. And don't think I've forgotten the childhood you robbed me of. Your funeral is next. If you ever so much as cross me, you'll pay for it then."

She didn't need to look at him again. His silence and the limp way his arms fell to his sides made it clear that he knew she meant business.

Reeva pulled her shoulders up, took a deep breath and turned to the roomful of people. She smiled, thanked each one of them for coming and said she needed to go home and have some time alone now.

They smiled back and nodded their heads as if they understood.

Akira Yamada

Yuri Kageyama

Yuri Kageyama was born in 1953, in Aichi-ken, Japan and grew up in Tokyo, Maryland and Alabama. She is a magna cum laude graduate of Cornell University and holds a Master's degree in Sociology from the University of California, Berkeley. Her works have appeared in The Greenfield Review, Breaking Silence: An Anthology of Contemporary Asian American Poets *(The Greenfield Review Press),* Y'Bird, Yellow Silk, River Styx, Bridge, *etc. Her first book of poems is forthcoming from I. Reed Books. In the past, she has collaborated with a dancer, a visual artist, an actor and musicians in presentations of her work. Currently, she is working with an independent film-maker on a film of one of her stories, an off-beat romance. She has also translated works from Japanese into English, such as poetry by the contemporary woman poet, Hiromi Ito. She lives in San Francisco with a musician/carpenter and their son Isaku.*

ASIAN AMERICAN ART STORY

A summer night, cool, though from the ocean breeze and the fog that, like a moving smoking mountain, merges avenue by descendingly numbered avenue, all the way to San Francisco's Japanesetown.

I'm already feeling pretty good from the cheap Chablis. I know even my skin stinks with alcohol. I'm in good shape then, that being some years ago. My one bare shoulder is brown and shiny.

I'm in my gypsy-look stage, so I'm wearing a big soft white top—a little satiny—that hangs lopsided off the shoulder and a bigger skirt, that's mostly black with a neon yet kimono-like chrysanthemum print—an attempt to maintain the Japanese ethnicity in my apparel; another being the jangling earrings, silver, that're molded into the shape of fans. A thick purple sash with pink and gold tassels encircles a thin waist that's never experienced pregnancy beyond six weeks.

I'm standing with most of my weight on my left leg and a wrist cocked on a hip, because it's nearing eight o'clock, the time the reading's supposed to start, and no other poet from our workshop has shown up, except for myself and Pacifico, who's settled himself down next to the wine jug and already looks so dazed I'm afraid he won't make it to the microphone. The technician from the city's arts program has, thank god, shown up, and is busy setting up, tripping over the black snake-like cords and going, "Testing, testing," into the phallic mikes.

On second thought, maybe it'd be better if no one shows up at all. There's always a few—I see familiar faces, now, peering into the dark seating area; one waves to me; I nod—so readings end up resembling a wake for some distant relative—sad but not overwhelming, just enough to leave an unpleasant aftertaste.

The one that waved walks up to me. "Nervous?" she asks, flipping her black hair over her shoulder. The silky strands fall together, like a curtain.

I shake my head. "How come nobody's responsible enough to be on time for these gigs? I always get stuck holding the bag."

"No one's here, anyway," she points out, meaning to be comforting.

"Thanks."

"They'll come. There's an understanding, you know. We all operate on Colored People's Time. You're being crazy expecting everyone to be here on time, Misty." She nudges my elbow. "See? Here's Dan Yamaguchi. Armed with his pile of right-on poems!"

I turn and see Dan, sure enough carrying a worn out folder under an arm that's in a worn out work-shirt. The layered ends of his hair rustle at his shoulders. I smile, but naturally he ignores me and moves towards Pacifico near the wine. I watch Dan pouring himself a paper cupful and Dan and Pacifico exchanging the power handshake and slapping each other on the backs, saying stuff, probably like, "What's up bro?" "The same, man," or whatever, and I feel a slight nausea in my diaphragm.

"What about the lights?" the tech is asking me. They're always asking me, as though I should know.

"I don't know."

The Chinese American tech's face visibly expresses disgust. Poor guy. He has the thankless job of teching for all these untogether community groups. I don't blame him.

"Well—can you just leave that center area lighted, sorta in general, for the whole thing?" I suggest, trying to be helpful.

He still looks disgusted but runs up to the tech booth, plays with some switches and calls down if that's what I want.

"Fantastic. Fine, fine," I say. "Thanks." I feel that I'm going against my feminist principles, but, when he comes down, I hug the tech, demonstrating my gratitude by letting his arm push against the softness of my breast, and he looks a lot less disgusted. Maybe he'll do his job right, while he's here. The extent I have to put myself out for this workshop, when no one else seems to give a fuck.

I was the one who'd typed out the press releases, xeroxed them, folded them, stapled them, stamped our bulk-rate non-profit organization stamp, and delivered the pack to the post office. I was the one who'd attempted to design the poster, but it looked so awful, I had to go to Barnaby Kim, and I had to bring him the grass, out of

116

my own pocket, to help urge him to contribute his talents for this worthy literary cause. *I* was the one who traversed what felt like every corner of San Francisco, risking my life on the infamous twenty-two MUNI bus rides, to tape Barnaby's silkscreened posters advertising this memorable event, to occur, I glance at my watch, excuse me, to have occurred, beginning two minutes ago.

To confess, it wasn't that bad. Sharyl helped me a lot. And I look at my friend with the long hair, standing before me, in her skin tight jade dress and black stockings and heels. "What are you going to read?" she asks lazily. "Not that it matters. The audience is only going to be your friends, who'll forgive you for anything." With another one of her supposedly soothing remarks, she slides away into the darkness, to find a seat.

"Tell me when you folks're ready to start," the tech instructs me, his tone taking on a slight friendliness.

By the stage is a cluster of people, wearing Army jackets, paint-speckled coveralls and Hawaiian shirts that have long lost their impact in color. They are studying type-written sheets with rather uptight concentration. I sigh with relief that everyone's here.

"When do we go on?" a voice interrupts my thoughts. His thinly elongated Japanese eyes are barely visible behind thick wire-rimmed glasses and masses of hair that connect into a moustache and beard below. The only discernible flesh are the nose and the pinkish lips, and, boy, can he blow that saxophone with those lips — the reason I hired his trio for our performance, fighting some objections from the group that our grant money could be put to better use than feeding some bum musicians.

Let's give credit where due, though. These musicians showed up over an hour early, laid out their equipment, did a quick sound check with the tech and had lots of time left over, to grab something to eat, if they'd wanted, before the poets trickled in.

"Six poets're scheduled to read tonight, so three'll read, then music, then three more; how's that?"

"Sounds good," he says.

I wish I'd kept my mouth shut, because now everyone's going to blame me for dictatorially and dogmatically deciding the program, without taking a democratic vote or anything. But, damn it, we're going on any second; how can they expect me to hold a meeting?

Too late, now. It's not my fault. Everyone asks me because either no one else is there or else whoever's there's too drunk or spaced out to take control.

The saxophone-player walks off to tell the rest of the group. And I follow his gait, not because I'm interested in him, but because I want to see the guy on the guitar. He's very quiet and always stooped over his guitar, even while they're waiting around, so you can't see his cute face, and I wish he'd look up when the saxophone player talks to them, and he does, and I think I'm going to melt on the spot, I mean, all my juices seeping from my vagina and my bones turning to hot wax, starting from pelvis on out.

He has a skimpy undershirt on, very sexy; his muscles are tight without being overly bulging and masculine—just the way I like them— and what's sexier are his straight-legged jeans (Lee's, I remember), an old pair, nothing to it, except his ass is—his ass is—is—superb. You know what I mean. The way some men are into legs or tits, women are the same. Personally, I'm open. It might be a neck I notice or a sinew on an arm. With him, it was his ass; okay?

He's turning around to place his guitar in his case, and there it is—his cutest ass—and I dream it's me, not the Fender Stratocaster, he's laying, so gently, into the red velour of his bed, I mean, case.

"Let's start." It's Dan Yamaguchi, and he's got the nerve to sound impatient and irritated, as though he's the one who's done all the work, and I've kept *them* waiting. Jesus!

I usually have a good time when I read. Or rather I make it a point to have a good time. No one's really listening, so might as well. Besides, it's my Baby, going out there. My poems, my Baby. Why make it all any more like a funeral than it has to be? I respect my work for the simple reason that no one else does. No one's going to come pat me on the back, except for the horny guys who mistake a woman's reading an erotic poem for an open invitation to the world for a slumber party in her bed. "I'm interested in lending a hand to get your work published," is the come on, aimed to be lethal. Sad; huh? Even, "What's your sign?" beats that.

I have this friend who's basically extremely bitter, something to do with growing up in a Japanese American farming community in California and having a suppressed father who acted like his family were invisible, instead of acting like those middle class American fathers, like the one Beaver Cleaver had. And the Japanese American Nisei mother—that's another long story, but, in short, she's not like Beaver's mom either.

Anyway, this friend used to say—more than once, during our midnight sessions over camomile tea—that she could've been a dancer, if only her parents'd given her the chance while young, because she had the inborn talent, except now, in her mid-twenties, it's too late, even if she's taking two classes a night, after work. Her parents used to laugh at her when she'd tap dance on their porch steps, pretending to be a Mouseketeer. Worse, they taught her to be ashamed. She wasn't even supposed to be angry, let alone artistic. She was supposed to remain a constantly stoic Noh mask of proper Japanese serenity and submissiveness.

I keep on going off on tangents about this friend, but, as I said, she's very bitter. She'd spit that artists are in it for power, to be in the limelight, to bask in the glory. What power? What glory? This filthy stage that hasn't been swept in weeks? Really, I'd hate to be a dancer and have to do a move like slither on this floor and get up with year-old gum globs and cobwebs on my leotard!

She doesn't understand. No one does.

We do it for the love of it.

It's the faith of believing in the unbelievable.

There are much easier ways to make money than getting fifteen dollars for a poem published in some obscure small press offset job, courtesy of some state arts council, or five dollars for being a runner-up in a local fiction contest.

I write because I live to write and write to live. And poetry pulsates in my blood—which reminds me, in an offhand kind of way—I better catch that guitarist before he takes off. I'm searching in the crowd for the Lee jeans ass.

I see him. He's laughing. He must be a little drunk. His wine cup dangerously tips in his hand. He's standing with three or four guys—being very mellow and community.

I dig out the already signed checks from my huge cloth bag ("The bag's bigger than you," guys'd tease me, assuming that they were being clever and inspired) and distribute each check to each mellow, community musician, saving the one for the ass til the last.

I'm not a bit nervous when I approach him. I don't reach out and grab his ass, a distinct possibility. I hand him the check with one hand and place the other casually on his shoulder—merely a cordial gesture. My advice: be cautious with Asian men. They have a tendency to be easily intimidated by aggressive women, even gorgeous ones.

"Are you gay? My friend says you're too cute to be straight," I whisper into his ear, practically licking his lobe, knowing damned well he's heterosexual. Otherwise, you might get wacked in the face. After all, this is San Francisco. Actually, I'm thinking my come-on is inspired and clever. I'm asking him if he's available in a way that's flattering and slightly offbeat. No? Maybe it *was* a dumb thing to say. Who cares? It worked.

This story could end here. A crazy girl who's convinced herself she's a poet—synonymous with viewing herself as a prophet, goddess, witch and nymph ("nymphomaniac," my enemies would sneer, but skip that) (some would also say, "revolutionary," but skip that, too)—this madwoman meets sensitive, good looking, creative gentleman, musically inclined, endowed with quality equipments of inorganic and organic specimen, open to working on a relationship, possibly a commitment, meanwhile offering fun and crazy times together. Wonderful story, n'est-ce pas? Except we Japanese say, "Ne?"

But it doesn't end here. My story, of course, goes on and on, I suppose, until death, and I'm not dead yet, but I don't mean it that way. This story has a really nasty ending.

What I mean is, all of a sudden, I get this queer letter in the mail, signed by Dan Yamaguchi, for an emergency meeting for the workshop. I don't pay much attention to it, when I open the envelope, except to mark it in my calendar, next Tuesday night at seven-thirty at the workshop, because just then my lover pulls me close to his smell. The smell of his sweat and skin and mouth and hair—like tasting seaweed on your tongue, feeling wet sand in between your fingers, hearing the fog horn go off, echoing inside your brain, til you're gone, gone, gone.

As soon as I get to the meeting, I sense something's wrong. First of all, there're too many people. The dingey room is half-filled with cigarette smoke. I'm only ten minutes late, but every workshop member is present, probably the only meeting with perfect attendance in the history of the workshop. I sit on the broken down sofa and smile at no one in particular. Maybe it's paranoia, but everyone's critically eying my leather pants, perhaps as an indication of my decadent, bourgeois ways? My intuition, unfortunately, is pretty much on target, as it turns out, because, sooner or later, the discussion moves in that direction.

When I just sat down, however, I couldn't pretend to fantasize what was coming. I tap Pacifico's arm, ask him for a cigarette. He happens to be sitting next to me. He shakes his box, waits til I choose a cigarette, then lights a match for me, cups the flame with his brown hands that are unexpectedly delicate for his solid build. I should've read the pity in his eyes, the guilt in his manner, as he watched the innocent and stupid lamb prancing up to the sacrificial altar, in her leather pants and cleavage-revealing purple blouse.

I blow the smoke towards the cracks in the ceiling and try not to notice the silence, as though everyone were holding their breaths to hear the metallic clanging of my earrings, all those Asian eyes on me, like alley cat tigers out for the kill. I also try to block out the fact that community cadre-types are sitting in the room, the vaguely recognizable faces of those perpetually hanging out in J-town, with their red, always red,-splattered leaflets and newspapers. They've certainly never been members of our poetry workshop.

"We've been in existence for nearly two years now, and I called this meeting to have an opportunity to reflect upon our past activities and especially to talk about the direction we'd like to be heading in the future. It's my feeling that, some time during the course of the workshop's development, we may have lost sight of our original goals and values—which centered on our work for the community."

That is Dan Yamaguchi talking, and I have to pinch myself almost, not to tune out. By now, I'm catching on that I, Misty Mandai, this nymph, prophet, goddess, poet, witch might've walked right into a Salem hunt. "There are certain members in the workshop that have taken over the leadership," here, he stares right at me, then continues, facing the crowd, "and I question that leadership. Where it's taking us. In light of our goals that we set up as a group earlier."

There're some comments from the floor. A couple of guys aren't hip yet to what's happening and are making random remarks about the workshop goals, the community and what have you, and Dan lets them voice their off-the-wall viewpoints, for he knows there's no hurry. No one's going to come to my aid. Not even the ones that like me.

The cadres speak up now with their practiced rhetoric. They emphasize Dan's points, in an attempt to bring the flow of the meeting back to the main purpose—purging me. Dan speaks again, "In the beginning, we were formed to serve the community. Now, certain people are saying, we can write whatever we want because, hey, we're community, too. There has to be a line drawn somewhere, as to what's politically correct and what's politically incorrect."

People are nodding, looking serious and impressed.

"Bullshit!" I say, and my voice is trembling. For once, I hate being in a room full of Asian men. (The women are there, but are few and silent, and they, too, stare at my leather pants, not bothering to disguise their disdain.) I feel weak, being a woman, and I am afraid. "How do you draw the line? Who's to say? That a poem with barbed wires is a correct poem because it refers to the camps, but a poem about loving a man isn't because loving a man isn't a Japanese American experience? Do we have to have 'ojii-chan' and 'obaachan' in our poems to make them valid? I'm sick of all this." My words come out fast, shaking and tumbling, one after the other.

I touch Pacifico's arm again to ask for another cigarette, and he jumps. He hands me the cigarette but won't light it for me. I have to fumble in my big bag for my lighter and, while at it, wish I could climb in there and hide, burying my head among my cosmetics, and cry. But I guess I appear strong and calm from the outside. That's what I've been told.

"You guys don't even know your Marx and Lenin backwards or

forwards and you're throwing all this dogmatic shit down. It's just going to hold us back. We're still in the formulative stage. We have to try everything. Take risks and experiment." I cross my leather legs. Subconsciously I admire my pants. They are beautiful, and they were cheap. Fifty per cent off sale.

I'm thinking about the joy of having purchased my pants because what I'm forced to confront right now is too horrible. I am hurt.

"Speaking of dogmatic," Dan focuses his gaze right into my eyes, freezes it there, "I didn't think that was right, the way you handled that last reading."

Here it comes.

I'm too numb to be hurt.

They're saying totally weird shit, now—that I'm writing for the white mainstream, the worst insult attributable to a non-white poet; that my poems aren't fit to wrap Chinatown fish in; that I'm ego-tripping, probably praying I'd make it on to the Tonight Show, one particularly malicious cadre-type jeers.

I'm happy he's home when I get back. He has Jimi Hendrix on full blast, and he's playing the solo, note for note, along with the record. I wait by the threshold. He notices me and puckers up his mouth, stoops over suddenly, magically running his fingers over the guitar neck, up and down, up and down, and then leans back, arching his spine, his face pinched in pain, as his guitar wails then groans. He smiles what he thinks is a devastating smile any groupie would swoon over, wiggles his hips a bit. That last move makes me smile—a bit.

He reaches over, unplugs the amplifier. "Hi, baby. How'd the meeting go?"

I shrug.

He comes over and kisses me. My hand on his naked back contacts beads of perspiration. With my fingertips, I trace the groove on his skin, left by the strap of his instrument. His lips taste salty. I want to tell him everything, pour it all out, but there's too much to say.

"Hendrix was a genius," he mumbles with his eyes closed. "Did I tell you I went to the same high school as did Jimi Hendrix?" He grew up in Seattle.

"What is Asian American art?" I speak into his mouth, and our teeth bump.

"Hell if I know."

Just then, some birds take off the tree that's right outside our window, and their wings flap the air, energized with a desperate vibration. "Doves," we'd started to call them, even though they're just dirty pigeons from Gold Gate Park.

I start to open my mouth, but he places a calloused finger. "Shhh . . . " He waits til the last sound of the birds fades, and he lights a candle that's stuck in a plastic orange juice bottle, then turns off the light switch. The shadows of his plants loom larger than life, growing jungles on the walls and ceiling.

Jessica Jopp

I was born in Connecticut and have lived most of my life in various places in New York. I've been writing poems for many years and have had a few published: one in Maine Life *and two in a recent issue of* The Greenfield Review. *For a little more than a year I worked for a publishing company in Binghamton.*

126

TIME·CLOCK

When we sat on the railyard wall at lunch today Katy had a cigarette and said things are back to normal. I don't like that word but I'm younger, and maybe when I am 19 I will like normal too. I don't want to be here then. If they could see these words I might be treated bad, the way Doris was or worse. And that was because she started saying stuff. We all talk, just not loud or when we're working. But she yelled once over the sound the shrink-wrapper made that she felt like throwing up every time the boss's son pressed up against her back when there was plenty of room for him to get by. It was like the beat of the books rolling down the belt was a cover for her. Like an instrument could cover a voice and she felt safe, I guess, in the beat and it frenzied her. She started standing at the folder whenever someone had it on to make 3-fold flyers for the mailing. She stood—not really looking at the woman folding, but just there in the rhythm—and would tell about the time the son grabbed her in the lunchroom. She said the smell of his cologne was enough to knock the instinct out of a salmon, and she slapped him. That was the first time he grabbed at her between the legs.

And once I saw her down below with the presses. The printers went about their gears and knobs and counting, and Doris stood there in the rhythm with the stacks of paper and greasy rags hanging on the basement posts. She had on a red t-shirt and a few pieces of her hair came out from where it was pinned up and caught the afternoon light coming in the windows. And she said there wasn't a place on her body anymore that he hadn't pawed over with his pudgy hands. She said it over and over to the sound the sheets made coming through the rollers—"not a place, not a place." I was at the collator and stood there watching a page printed *Civil Procedure Law* go by and by and by, and lost count from listening to her. After a half hour or so one of the printers touched her shoulder and led her back upstairs. The more she talked like that the worse the boss's son was to her.

I was there when it happened. It was on a Friday and some of the women were joking around and talking about going to Ritzie's for a beer and taking their jackets off the metal rack when they punched out. And Jeannine and some of them were talking about getting out ten thousand penal codes by the end of next week and Katy was saying shit for the rain and the walk to the bus, when Doris came up from the basement with a big hammer in her hand. She walked over and got in line to punch out. When she came up to the time-clock she put her card in and pulled it out slowly and carefully put it back on the rack. Then she looked over her shoulder and said, real casual, "Stand back ladies." And nobody had time to think to ask her what she was doing. She just raised the heavy thing above her head and started smashing the grey square time-clock. And all the clicks and hums of the wrapper and the folder and the presses and the trains going by all day were in her, and she let them out with the hammer. The curve of glass covering the numbers flew into a million tiny birds and the hands fell from the face onto the wooden floor. Springs and gears split and cracked and crumbled and Doris raised the hammer over her head again and again, and the frenzy was with her. The metal holder with the time cards in it fell off the wall and all our names were on the floor with the numbers and the broken glass. Somebody was screaming and somebody else was laughing and the boss came down from the office and waddled over to her and grunted, "you crazy bitch," and grabbed the hammer from her. Then it was quiet and all you could hear was Doris's quick breathing like a kid and she looked tired of crying, her hair all over and the wild beating in her eyes. I could hear the 4:30 Lackawanna and Lake Erie go by outside and I knew it was a dark green car in front and loads of coal behind. Then the boss started screaming "get out" and "you'll pay for this" over and over. And we went out, not talking except for Claire who took Doris by the arm and said she'd drive her home.

Walking downtown in the rain to get the 5:20 Robinson Street, I told Katy I had to stop and walked over to the lot by the Red Star taxi place and threw up my peanut butter sandwich and coke. Katy said better there than on a crowded bus. So we missed the 5:20 and she had a cigarette while we waited for the 5:50. But the ache stayed in my stomach the whole weekend.

We have another time-clock now to mark when we come and when we go. Now I look at all the women as if they are Doris and are pulled by a beating and I can save them before it turns wild. They don't know this of course. Maybe I shouldn't write about them behind their backs like this, or say I understand their hands, because do I? At fifteen one doesn't really know, but I feel it. I close my eyes now at home and see the brick warehouse walls near the railyard near work and see how it looks from the third floor storage room when the afternoon light shines all the way down the rails. And I close my eyes and still hear—like constant water but not as smooth—the binder wrapper and the flyer folder and the collator and presses. Sometimes lately it seems when I think of Doris and the others I am like maple buds, red and hanging heavy ready to burst into whatever maples have.

Sometimes lately when I think of Doris and the others, I think of them all in one place, and not at work. I mean they are all standing in the grass out by the pond at Chenango Park, and it was me who led them there. Me who walked them over the downtown bridge and out towards Chenango. Past all the second-hand stores on Clinton and past the empty shoe factories where you can see bare bulbs hanging still lighted in the stairway landings. Out and past town. And I'd get to the edge of the pond first and them following me and no one else around. I'd sort of test the water, but of course the water would be cool at night. And so we'd have the moon too, way up there, going about a moon's business, but coming down here too in the park a few places light and yes on the water. And yes on the women. And I'd take each one like she was a child grubby with summer dirt, and slowly I'd peel off all her sticky layers and her shoes which I know make her feet hurt. And then I'd pick her up, the nearest one, and I'd stand near to the pond with its lilies a ways off and its water skimmers over the top. And some cattails too and even I'd put in a frog at the edge of the pond. And I'd throw her in. Then her hair would come loose from being pinned all day and it would drift out on the ripples her body made. And she could swim if she could or she could just float if she wanted. And she would laugh or just say nothing or talk about work even. But she'd be cooler than she'd ever been. Then I'd up with the next one and in she goes too, even though some of them are big and some sort of fat. All of them and my arms would never feel tired like they do sometimes after packing boxes. All of them in the cool evening water would be there easy. Doris too. Everything just then would be easy for them the way it is for the queen anne's lace growing along the tracks in late summer.

That's how it would be. But I could never say anything to them. Maybe they wouldn't want to know. I couldn't even tell Katy with her long brown hair that makes her neck so hot in the summer. Sometimes sitting out on the wall eating with her I think it. She goes on about a guy she met a few weeks ago, and all I hear is Tom this and Tom that and I nod. Sometimes at work I smile at one of the women and say in my head like I say here—I'll throw you in Chenango Pond sometime, I say, when it is hot and then your feet will be easy and your hands cool. I say it just like that, but never so they hear. It's in my head. They go about with the clicks and beats of rollers and pages and we all talk numbers and updates, but it's in my head even then. Sometimes I feel funny for thinking of them this way, feel like they look at my head and it is clear and they can look right in and see the bright shiny working of my wish. But I know they can't. They don't know. Just right here I say.

Linda Greenwald

Although I have had some poetry published in Combinations, Rolling Stone Magazine *and in regional magazines, I have not had a short story published. At present, now that my four children are grown and I am widowed, I have gone back to school and am working on a novel based on the life of Emily Dickinson. That unfinished work is my current nearly full-time activity and is my project as a candidate for an MFA in fiction at Bennington College.*

THE COBALT BLUE DISHES

A shower falls over me. Water cools as it falls. One more minute before all of the hot runs out. It is of course the students. There are four rooms of them in my house and again they have used all the water. One day soon the electric water heater will need replacing. Nothing in this house works as it should. I must learn how to use a wrench.

This old house near the stockade. Just outside the stockade of old Schenectady. Near the elegance. My elegance needs fixing. The divorce money made a down payment. And my parents, I've borrowed from them. I think about the money due. The end of the month tomorrow. Easier when the students stay long. Union College. But from the Community College, they are in and out and gone sometimes before the last month's rent is in my hands.

The water is getting cold. I curse my tenants. There is shampoo in my dark hair. I can hear the bubbles crackle in my hair. Shit, I rarely use this word aloud. Unless aroused. I gasp for breath, the water is so cold and I dry myself. The room smells of lavender soap, lavender powder. Poofs of lavender fall on the wooden floor. I wonder where the money for the mortgage will come after the students leave in June.

I stand naked in the bedroom. I have made tracks of powder on the cold floor. White tracks on gray painted wide boards. There is my bed. My marriage bed. Sometimes I see Jed sleeping there back in our house on the farm. Fonda. Montgomery County. I see his red hair and his beard bright as feathers on the white pillow. Sometimes I dream he's kissing me and when I awake I'm crying. And then I lie around and think of him and his young wife and that new red-haired baby. Or maybe the baby's hair is blonde and straight like Ellen's. Ellen. Ellen and I. We were close once. I thought like mother and daughter. I showed her how to make meat loaf. And now they eat it off my blue platter. I see my cups and saucers on the round oak table in the farmhouse kitchen. They are eating on lovely old blue plates. She likes to be called

Cookie. I cannot think of someone called Cookie sleeping next to him.

I have turned my heart against Ellen—his Cookie. I am now working on Jed. I'll feel better when I don't long for him with my body.

All this is on my mind because of the anniversary. Today. Twenty-fifth. We made it to twenty-four. I should be happy over that. But I'm not; I wanted more years. To share grandchildren with him. Oh God do I love him still?

I dress for class. I'm studying computer programing. Practical. I think of buttons to push and all those cards and sheets—acres of them. All that software. I yearn for my loom at home—no, not home, *there*. Or if I could be a weaver instead.

I remember the first signs our marriage might go. Restless. He was getting restless. Forty and restless. Once my mother said, I think he has a wild streak. Red hair wild, she said. Hair like a fox. You watch out. You'll have children and then he'll go.

We had changed from dairy farming to sheep. All of Jed's studying at Ag and Tech and the dairy business was failing. Not failing exactly. Jed never failed at anything. But he knew it was time for sheep. I liked those days. I bought a loom. I was weaving that night when he said, let's go dancing. I love dancing too. I was weaving a dreamy soft scarfy cloth, loose knit and transparent. We went dancing. My weaving was nearly finished. I left it on the loom. Sheep's colors. Strands of soft gray, creamy straw, dusky brown, charcoal. Fat strands and lean. I was weaving air and sunlight—a wall hanging. I could hear the sheep bleat as I wove.

As we danced at the tavern I thought of my weaving. While we whirled I saw the wool and the design in the soft world I was weaving.

Jed held me and I told him, Melanie is going to have a baby. She called me this afternoon. His beard stiffened. His blue eyes snapped.

"Well have a good time Grandma," he said. "That'll suit you fine. But I'm too young to be a grandpa."

He swung me around and around. And he did look young.

"Yes, forty's too young for that," he said.

I couldn't believe his words. Was he going crazy? I grew dizzy as we danced faster and faster. I remember thinking: his fatherhood whirls by me. Who is this man who holds me now? He has been so caring with his children. This does not sound like Jed. I could see him leading our three children on expeditions to the tops of mountains like Slide and Peekamoose. Going into the Adirondacks as they are older. All four of them with their back packs.

"This is not real," I said aloud and I left the dance floor and the tavern altogether for the coolness of the air outside.

But that was years ago. Dressed in my jeans and sweat shirt, I am ready for breakfast. I pour the coffee. I hate my cup. So utilitarian. Happy Anniversary, Alma, I say. The coffee tastes of anger. I think of the dishes I abandoned. Jed, Jr. and Tim, our sons, helped me move. Why did I leave my dishes behind? I bought them with my own money. In Bennington. We were there in Vermont. Buying sheep. Cobalt blue—hard and shiny pottery. This coffee is bitter in this ugly white cup. I throw it in the garbage though it isn't even chipped. Then I eat toast. I always burn my toast a little. I spread peanut butter thin. Before I can think, I have left the house and am walking fast on sneakered feet toward State Street.

Cookie and Jed are married a year already. A week after the divorce they went off someplace and said the words. But they consummated the marriage quite some time before that.

Thinking about it, I jog faster and faster toward the college.

I hadn't been spying on Jed. I really didn't expect to see them on the couch in the playroom over the garage. Cookie, then our son Tim's fiancée, and Jed. No voices. So quiet and tender with each other. So passionate. I backed down the ladder and sat at my loom in the kitchen. I couldn't see the wool for my blurring eyes. My hands so cold, my heart so dull, my mind so numb.

I did nothing said nothing.

Events took over. I kept Tim from killing his father but I couldn't make him love Jed again. Tim was not the same after that. Not for a long time. He never sees Jed any more.

I see the old Hotel that is now my college. One more block to class. I slow to a walk then wait for the light on State while I catch my breath.

I have made a decision to celebrate this anniversary day my way. I don't expect to make the papers and I don't—not exactly. Later Mother sends me this clipping. I wonder who has written those mean things about Cookie. I mean Ellen. She's not that stupid.

Weekly Journal, May 3:

State Police responding to a call late Thursday afternoon reported an unusual break-in at the home of Jed and Ellen Thompson of Parson's Road.

Mr. and Mrs. Thompson found their kitchen door open and unlocked when they returned to their house after lambing. Ellen Thompson said an entire set of antique blue dishes was missing. Included were plates, cups and saucers which had been set on mats on the kitchen table for the evening meal. On these mats and in the cupboard the intruder had set an equivalent number of new white dishes which the couple had never seen before. A large loom was also taken at this time.

No damage to buildings or signs of forced entry were recorded. Mrs. Thompson said no charges would be filed against an unnamed suspect because none of the items taken were considered of value to her as they previously belonged to the first Mrs. Thompson. A neighbor could not identify the driver of a large blue truck seen by several witnesses in the area.

Corporal Mark Anders and Sergeant James Harrison of West-field barracks investigated.

These days I like the taste of herbal tea in my blue cups. Wild mint or strawberry leaves from my small garden. Sometimes rose hips. When I get home in the afternoon I work on my designs. I am teaching weaving and I'm in a poetry workshop. So far I've finished one poem.

Spectrum Blue

In the tea leaves
of her mind
his first wife wonders
if they breakfast
on her pottery,
Old Bennington
curved saucers
antique bowls.
Don't think of me
as toast crumbs
grease my plates.
Once I washed each
cup by hand
airy sun falling
from the open faucet.
Wavery flowing blue
watery grotto, cobalt
spattery ink on cream
splashed in soft cerulean.

Kally Kendall

Meridel LeSueur

I was born in Iowa February 22, 1900 so have lived through this bloody century. Also a time when the concepts of matter and reality have changed entirely. And also the colonial struggles have roused the people of the earth to defend themselves and the very destruction of the earth, with a level of global consciousness never visible before on this planet.

I have been part of the struggles of my people in the middle west. I am deeply rooted in that history and struggle and out of it has come my work. I am a witness. I look upon writing as a witness for the people and the time.

Writing witness now has become global. The communal pain has forced a cry out that is deep and communicative. We as writers have come to re member not dis member and have risen out of the corpse of the old as singers of the new image the living image of humanity.

I WAS MARCHING

Minneapolis, 1934

I have never been in a strike before. It is like looking at something that is happening for the first time and there are no thoughts and no words yet accrued to it. If you come from the middle class, words are likely to mean more than an event. You are likely to think about a thing, and the happening will be the size of a pin-point and the words around the happening very large, distorting it queerly. It's a case of "Remembrance of Things Past." When you are in the event, you are likely to have a distinctly individualistic attitude, to be only partly there, and to care more for the happening afterwards than when it is happening. That is why it is hard for a person like myself and others to be in a strike.

Besides, in American life, you hear things happening in a far and muffled way. One thing is said and another happens. Our merchant society has been built upon a huge hypocrisy, a cutthroat competition which sets one man against another and at the same time an ideology mouthing such words as "Humanity," "Truth," the "Golden Rule," and such. Now in a crisis the word falls away and the skeleton of that action shows in terrific movement.

For two days I heard of the strike. I went by their headquarters, I walked by on the opposite side of the street and saw the dark old building that had been a garage and lean, dark young faces leaning from the upstairs windows. I had to go down there often. I looked in. I saw the huge black interior and live coals of living men moving restlessly and orderly, their eyes gleaming from their sweaty faces.

I saw cars leaving filled with grimy men, pickets going to the line, engines roaring out. I stayed close to the door, watching. I didn't go in. I was afraid they would put me out. After all, I could remain a spectator. A man wearing a polo hat kept going around with a large camera taking pictures.

I am putting down exactly how I felt, because I believe others of my class feel the same as I did. I believe it stands for an important psychic change that must take place in all. I saw many artists, writers, professionals, even businessmen and women standing across the street, too, and I saw in their faces the same longings, the same fears.

The truth is I was afraid. Not of the physical danger at all, but an awful fright of mixing, of losing myself, of being unknown and lost. I felt inferior. *I felt no one would know me there, that all I had been trained to excel in would go unnoticed.* I can't describe what I felt, but perhaps it will come near it to say that I felt I excelled in competing with others and I knew instantly that these people were not competing at all, that they were acting in a strange, powerful trance of movement together. And I was filled with longing to act with them and with fear that I could not. I felt I was born out of every kind of life, thrown up alone, looking at other lonely people, a condition I had been in the habit of defending with various attitudes of cynicism, preciosity, defiance, and hatred.

Looking at that dark and lively building, massed with men, I knew my feelings to be those belonging to disruption, chaos, and disintegration and I felt their direct and awful movement, mute and powerful, drawing them into a close and glowing cohesion like a powerful conflagration in the midst of the city. And it filled me with fear and awe and at the same time hope. I knew this action to be prophetic and indicative of future actions and I wanted to be part of it.

Our life seems to be marked with a curious and muffled violence over America, but this action has always been in the dark, men and women dying obscurely, poor and poverty marked lives, but now from city to city runs this violence, into the open, and colossal happenings stand bare before our eyes, the street churning suddenly upon the pivot of mad violence, whole men suddenly spouting blood and running like living sieves, another holding a dangling arm shot squarely off, a tall youngster, running, tripping over his intestines, and one block away, in the burning sun, gay women shopping and a window dresser trying to decide whether to put green or red voile on a manikin.

In these terrible happenings you cannot be neutral now. No one can be neutral in the face of bullets.

The next day, with sweat breaking out on my body, I walked past the three guards at the door. They said, "Let the women in. We need women." And I knew it was no joke.

At first I could not see into the dark building. I felt many men coming and going, cars driving through. I had an awful impulse to go into the office which I passed, and offer to do some special work. I saw a sign which said, "Get your button." I saw they all had buttons with the date and the number of the union local. I didn't get a button. I wanted to be anonymous.

There seemed to be a current, running down the wooden stairs, towards the front of the building, into the street, that was massed with people, and back again. I followed the current up the old stairs packed closely with hot men and women. As I was going up I could look down and see the lower floor, the cars drawing up to await picket call, the hospital roped off on one side.

Upstairs men sat bolt upright in chairs asleep, their bodies flung in attitudes of peculiar violence of fatigue. A woman nursed her baby. Two young girls slept together on a cot, dressed in overalls. The voice of the loudspeaker filled the room. The immense heat pressed down from the flat ceiling. I stood up against the wall for an hour. No one paid any attention to me. The commissary was in back and the women came out sometimes and sat down, fanning themselves with their aprons and listening to the news over the loudspeaker. A huge man seemed hung on a tiny folding chair. Occasionally someone tiptoed over and brushed the flies off his face. His great head fell over and the sweat poured regularly from his forehead like a spring. I wondered why they took such care of him. They all looked at him tenderly as he slept. I learned later he was a leader on the picket line and had the scalps of more cops to his name than any other.

Three windows flanked the front. I walked over to the windows. A red-headed woman with a button saying, "Unemployed Council," was looking out. I looked out with her. A thick crowd stood in the heat below listening to the strike bulletin. We could look right into the windows of the smart club across the street. We could see people peering out of the windows half hidden.

I kept feeling they would put me out. No one paid any attention. The woman said without looking at me, nodding to the

palatial house, "It sure is good to see the enemy plain like that."
"Yes," I said. I saw that the club was surrounded by a steel picket
fence higher than a man. "They know what they put that there
fence there for," she said. "Yes," I said. "Well," she said, "I've got to
get back to the kitchen. Is it ever hot?" The thermometer said
ninety-nine. The sweat ran off us, burning our skins. "The boys'll
be coming in," she said, "for their noon feed." She had a scarred
face, "Boy, will it be a mad house?" "Do you need any help?" I said
eagerly. "Boy," she said, "some of us have been pouring coffee since
two o'clock this morning, steady, without no letup." She started to
go. She didn't pay any special attention to me as an individual.
She didn't seem to be thinking of me, she didn't seem to see me. I
watched her go. I felt rebuffed, hurt. Then I saw instantly she
didn't see me because she saw only what she was doing. I ran after
her.

I found the kitchen organized like a factory. Nobody asks my
name. I am given a large butcher's apron. I realize I have never
before worked anonymously. At first I feel strange and then I feel
good. The forewoman sets me to washing tin cups. There are not
enough cups. We have to wash fast and rinse them and set them
up quickly for buttermilk and coffee as the line thickens and the
men wait. A little shortish man who is a professional dishwasher
is supervising. I feel I won't be able to wash tin cups, but when no
one pays any attention except to see that there are enough cups I
feel better.

The line grows heavy. The men are coming in from the picket
line. Each woman has one thing to do. There is no confusion. I
soon learn I am not supposed to help pour the buttermilk. I am
not supposed to serve sandwiches. I am supposed to wash tin cups.
I suddenly look around and realize all these women are from
factories. I know they have learned this organization and speciali-
zation in the factory. I look at the round shoulders of the woman
cutting bread next to me and I feel I know her. The cups are
brought back, washed and put on the counter again. The sweat
pours down our faces, but you forget about it.

Then I am changed and put to pouring coffee. At first I look at
the men's faces and then I don't look any more. It seems I am
pouring coffee for the same tense dirty sweating face, the same

body, the same blue shirt and overalls. Hours go by, the heat is terrific. I am not tired. I am not hot. I am pouring coffee. I am swung into the most intense and natural organization I have ever felt. I know everything that is going on. These things become of great matter to me.

Eyes looking, hands raising a thousand cups, throats burning, eyes bloodshot from lack of sleep, the body dilated to catch every sound over the whole city. Buttermilk? Coffee?

"Is your man here?" the woman cutting sandwiches asks me.

"No," I say, then I lie for some reason, peering around as if looking eagerly for someone, "I don't see him now."

But I was pouring coffee for living men.

For a long time, about one o'clock, it seemed like something was about to happen. Women seemed to be pouring into headquarters to be near their men. You could hear only lies over the radio. And lies in the papers. Nobody knew precisely what was happening, but everyone thought something would happen in a few hours. You could feel the men being poured out of the hall onto the picket line. Every few minutes cars left and more drew up and were filled. The voice of the loudspeaker was accelerated, calling for men, calling for picket cars.

I could hear the men talking about the arbitration board, the truce that was supposed to be maintained while the board sat with the Governor. They listened to every word over the loudspeaker. A terrible communal excitement ran through the hall like a fire through a forest. I could hardly breathe. I seemed to have no body at all except the body of this excitement. I felt that what had happened before had not been a real movement, these false words and actions had taken place on the periphery. The real action was about to show the real intention.

We kept on pouring thousands of cups of coffee, feeding thousands of men.

The chef with a woman tattooed on his arm was just dishing the last of the stew. It was about two o'clock. The commissary was about empty. We went into the front hall. It was drained of men. The chairs were empty. The voice of the announcer was excited. "The men are massed at the market," he said. "Something is going to happen." I sat down beside a woman who was holding her hands tightly together, leaning forward listening, her eyes bright and dilated. I had never seen her before. She took my hands. She pulled me towards her. She was crying. "It's awful," she said, "something awful is going to happen. They've taken both my children away from me and now something is going to happen to all those men." I held her hands. She had a green ribbon around her hair.

The action seemed reversed. The cars were coming back. The announcer cried, "This is murder." Cars were coming in. I don't know how we got to the stairs. Everyone seemed to be converging at a menaced point. I saw below the crowd stirring, uncoiling. I saw them taking men out of cars and putting them on the hospital cots, on the floor. At first I felt frightened, the close black area of the barn, the blood, the heavy moment, the sense of myself lost, gone. But I couldn't have turned away now. A woman clung to my hand. I was pressed against the body of another. If you are to understand anything you must understand it in the muscular event, in actions we have not been trained for. Something broke all my surfaces in something that was beyond horror and I was dabbing alcohol on the gaping wounds that buckshot makes, hanging open like crying mouths. Buckshot wounds splay in the body and then swell like a blow. Ness, who died, had thirty-eight slugs in his body, in the chest and in the back.

The picket cars kept coming in. Some men have walked back from the market, holding their own blood in. They move in a great explosion, and the newness of the movement makes it seem like something under ether, moving terrifically towards a culmination.

From all over the city workers are coming. They gather outside in two great half-circles, cut in two to let the ambulances in. A traffic cop is still directing traffic at the corner and the crowd cannot stand to see him. "We'll give you just two seconds to beat it," they tell him. He goes away quickly. A striker takes over the street.

Men, women, and children are massing outside, a living circle close packed for protection. From the tall office building business-men are looking down on the black swarm thickening, coagulating into what action they cannot tell.

We have living blood on our skirts.

That night at eight o'clock a mass meeting was called of all labor. It was to be in a parking lot two blocks from headquarters. All the women gather at the front of the building with collection cans, ready to march to the meeting. I have not been home. It never occurs to me to leave. The twilight is eerie and the men are saying that the chief of policy is going to attack the meeting and raid headquarters. The smell of blood hangs in the hot, still air. Rumors strike at the taut nerves. The dusk looks ghastly with what might be in the next half-hour.

"If you have any children," a woman said to me, "you better not go." I looked at the desperate women's faces, the broken feet, the torn and hanging pelvis, the worn and lovely bodies of women who persist under such desperate labors. I shivered, though it was ninety-six and the sun had been down a good hour.

The parking lot was already full of people when we got there and men swarmed the adjoining roofs. An elegant café stood across the street with water sprinkling from its roof and splendidly dressed men and women stood on the steps as if looking at a show.

The platform was the bullet-riddled truck of the afternoon's fray. We had been told to stand close to this platform, so we did, making the center of a wide massed circle that stretched as far as we could see. We seemed buried like minerals in a mass, packed body to body. I felt again that peculiar heavy silence in which there is the real form of the happening. My eyes burn. I can hardly see. I seem to be standing like an animal in ambush. I have the brightest, most physical feeling with every sense sharpened peculiarly. The movements, the masses that I see and feel I have never known before. I only partly know what I am seeing, feeling, but I feel it is the real body and gesture of a future vitality. I see that there is a bright clot of women drawn close to a bullet-riddled truck. I am one of them, yet I don't feel myself at all. It is curious, I feel most alive and yet for the first time in my life I do not feel myself as separate. I realize then that all my previous feelings have been based on feeling myself separate and distinct from others and now I sense sharply faces, bodies, closeness, and my own fear is not my own alone, nor my hope.

The strikers keep moving up cars. We keep moving back together to let cars pass and form between us and a brick building that flanks the parking lot. They are connecting the loudspeaker, testing it. Yes, they are moving up lots of cars, through the crowd and lining them closely side by side. There must be ten thousand people now, heat rising from them. They are standing silent, watching the platform, watching the cars being brought up. The silence seems terrific like a great form moving of itself. This is real movement issuing from the close reality of mass feeling. This is the first real rhythmic movement I have ever seen. My heart hammers terrifically. My hands are swollen and hot. No one is producing this movement. It is a movement upon which all are moving softly, rhythmically, terribly.

No matter how many times I looked at what was happening I hardly knew what I saw. I looked and I saw time and time again that there were men standing close to us, around us, and then suddenly I knew that there was a living chain of men standing shoulder to shoulder, forming a circle around the group of women. They stood shoulder to shoulder slightly moving like a thick vine from the pressure behind, but standing tightly woven like a living wall, moving gently.

I saw that the cars were now lined one close-fitted to the other with strikers sitting on the roofs and closely packed on the running boards. They could see far over the crowd. "What are they doing that for?" I said. No one answered. The wide dilated eyes of the women were like my own. No one seemed to be answering questions now. They simply spoke, cried out, moved together now.

The last car drove in slowly, the crowd letting them through without command or instruction. "A little closer," someone said. "Be sure they are close." Men sprang up to direct whatever action was needed and then subsided again and no one had noticed who it was. They stepped forward to direct a needed action and then fell anonymously back again.

We all watched carefully the placing of the cars. Sometimes we looked at each other. I didn't understand that look. I felt uneasy. It was as if something escaped me. And then suddenly, on my very body, I knew what they were doing, as if it had been communi-

146

cated to me from a thousand eyes, a thousand silent throats, as if it had been shouted in the loudest voice.

They were building a barricade.

Two men died from that day's shooting. Men lined up to give one of them a blood transfusion, but he died. Black Friday men called the murderous day. Night and day workers held their children up to see the body of Ness who died. Tuesday, the day of the funeral, one thousand more militia were massed downtown.

It was still over ninety in the shade. I went to the funeral parlors and thousands of men and women were massed there waiting in the terrific sun. One block of women and children were standing two hours waiting. I went over and stood near them. I didn't know whether I could march. I didn't like marching in parades. Besides, I felt they might not want me.

I stood aside not knowing if I would march. I couldn't see how they would ever organize it anyway. No one seemed to be doing much.

At three-forty some command went down the ranks. I said foolishly at the last minute, "I don't belong to the auxiliary—could I march?" Three women drew me in. "We want all to march," they said gently. "Come with us."

The giant mass uncoiled like a serpent and straightened out ahead and to my amazement on a lift of road I could see six blocks of massed men, four abreast, with bare heads, moving straight on and as they moved, uncoiled the mass behind and pulled it after them. I felt myself walking, accelerating my speed with the others as the line stretched, pulled taut, then held its rhythm.

Not a cop was in sight. The cortege moved through the stop-and-go signs, it seemed to lift of its own dramatic rhythm, coming from the intention of every person there. We were moving spontaneously in a movement, natural, hardy, and miraculous.

We passed through six blocks of tenements, through a sea of grim faces, and there was not a sound. There was the curious shuffle of thousands of feet, without drum or bugle, in ominous silence, a march not heavy as the military, but very light, exactly with the heart-beat.

I was marching with a million hands, movements, faces, and my own movement was repeating again and again, making a new movement from these many gestures, the walking, falling back, the open mouth crying, the nostrils stretched apart, the raised hand, the blow falling, and the outstretched hand drawing me in.

I felt my legs straighten. I felt my feet join in that strange shuffle of thousands of bodies moving with direction, of thousands of feet, and my own breath with the gigantic breath. As if an electric charge had passed through me, my hair stood on end, I was marching.

Georgiana Valoyce Sanchez

I am Pima/Papago and Chumash, born in California and raised in a home where stories were told. My Pima/Papago mother taught me to love the desert of the O'otham with its awesome, terrible beauty. My Chumash father, born in 1898, taught me to love a California long gone, to love the mountains and sea-coast that have been the home of the Chumash since earliest memory. The stories nurtured me and, in many ways, compelled me to follow my dream.

Several years ago, when my five children were still quite young, I went into my backyard to pray. It was a windy night, but I remember that the air was clear and stars could be seen. A storm must have been stirring over the Pacific Ocean because I could smell salt water. I prayed that night to be shown what I was meant to do on this earth. Though I loved my husband and children very much, I felt strongly that I was being called to do something more.

The answer to my prayer was very clear. I was to follow my dream, the dream that I was afraid to voice for fear of ridicule. My secret dream was to write, to write particularly about my experience as an American Indian person.

As a high school drop-out I did not have the skills to be the writer I dreamed to be, so, despite much fear, I began a long journey to educate myself by attending an English class at my local high school. Years later, in 1984, I graduated with honors from California State University, Long Beach with a Bachelor of Arts degree in English/ Creative Writing. I expect to receive my Master of Art degree in English Literature in the winter of 1986. Throughout the years of study I have been keenly aware that I am only acquiring a very limited knowledge and that the real wisdom comes from my faith in God and in the old stories of my people.

My life as wife, mother, daughter, sister, writer, student and community activist has been difficult at times, but always blessed. It is in that dynamic tension of my life where my stories are born and where my dreams come true. I am grateful.

THE HEART OF THE FLOWER

It was Thursday, March 8, 1973. Word had come to us slowly and in confused fragments from across the nation. The siege at Wounded Knee on the Pine Ridge Reservation in South Dakota had been underway for nearly a week before the full drama of what was happening there began to unfold on the West Coast. The siege at Wounded Knee was now into its ninth day.

I went through all the familiar rituals. Putting on the morning coffee. Two slices of bread in the toaster. Frying the eggs. Standing by the door as my husband Ed drove off to work. But, now, changing the sheets on our unmade bed, I daydreamed about joining the American Indian Movement activists at Wounded Knee. I sidestepped my way between bed and dresser to tuck one corner of the bottom sheet secure; sidestep, echoing the rhythm of some distant dance around the drum. A dance that took place in spite of, because of, the United States Army troops and artillery that surrounded the village of Wounded Knee. I snapped the top sheet out over the bed and it swept upward—a bird's wide wing against the sky—before the slow settling to earth.

Outside, beyond the shadowed frame of my front porch, mountains had bloomed. Distant fire trails were as clear as the lifeline on the palm of my hand. Brush stubbled sides caught the light, the shade. A strong wind had come up during the night, clearing the Los Angeles basin of the gray smog that made us forget the mountains had ever existed.

The air breathed. Everywhere was movement and the crisp feel of March wind. Across the street, neat rows of stucco houses sat complacent as cows beneath the restless trees. And I saw feathered prayer sticks, eagle-winged petitions of victory vibrating through the air, planted in my front yard; only not. For fear of cries of blasphemy from Mrs. Johnson across the street, or eyesore or blight, or calling attention to myself as no proper Indian woman should. But mostly because Ed would be embarrassed and angry. I leaned against the door frame and rested my hand against the screen. Beyond the housetops and telephone poles and electric wires, beyond the distant mountains, far to the northeast, lay Wounded Knee.

The child within my womb fluttered. A small movement like a butterfly's wing against the wind. I placed my hand on the small mound of my belly and stood very still, listening with every nerve of my body for the next movement. Again, the small lonely movement. I was filled with wonder at the thought of a child growing, moving inside me. Separate, and yet, so mine. I turned from the open front door and closed it.

I made my way into the kitchen and sat down at the table, waiting for the next movement. None came. The child was still. I cleared the plates of dried egg and toast, collecting the leftover food for the dog. The window next to the kitchen table was sunlit and alive with the patterns of leaf shadows moving in the wind. The wind was a living presence on the Morongo Indian Reservation where I had been raised—where my parents were buried. Sometimes, the wind would come up the Pass between the San Gorgonio and San Jacinto mountain ranges sounding like an old woman singing a wailing song for the dead. Times like that my parents would gather the family together in the warm old house and Mama would make hot fry bread over the wood stove and serve it with honey and mugs of good strong coffee. And we would sit close and tell jokes and stories.

Shadows flitted back and forth across the kitchen table like large gray moths. I leaned forward in my chair and rubbed the pain in my lower back. Leaf branches played against the window, making soft scratching sounds like field mice in an acorn shed. I sat there a few minutes more, watching the shadows dance in the wind. Finally, I took the dishes to the sink and washed them.

On Friday, March 9, I called Doctor Bergman and told him of the low back pain I was feeling. He told me to stay off my feet and to come in the next day if I was not feeling better. I hung up the phone. Bowls of limp cereal adrift waited patiently on the kitchen table for rescue. I wiped up the soggy wake of our breakfast and carried the bowls to the sink. There was so much to be done. The books on my nightstand were piled so high they nearly obscured the small gooseneck reading lamp Ed had bought me for Christmas. The books would have to be sorted and put back into the large walnut bookcase that quietly ruled the living room.

Above the sink an eagle flew over wheat fields of gold and rust. Two orange butterfly plaques hung beside it. I ran warm water into the sink, the water warm as the pain in my lower back, each sting of the water-rush on bowls and spoons an echo of the persistent radiating wave within.

That night, Ed made dinner while I lay blanketed on the couch watching the Five O'Clock News. One commentator reported that the United States Government had issued an order that everyone was to leave the village of Wounded Knee or it would "come in shooting." The National Council of Churches had sent representatives who pledged to stand between the besieged Indians and the Federal Marshals when the shooting began.

I raised myself on my elbow and called to Ed. "Quick, come and listen to this. They're going to start shooting if the people don't leave."

Ed stepped into the livingroom, wiping his hands on his faded work jeans. His dark face was lined and haggard. He planted his legs apart next to the television set and folded his arms—Geremino, *Goyaathle*, embattled—looking much like a photograph he had once sent me from one of the rural settlements along the Mekong Delta, except, now, his hair was longer and there were no fair-haired buddies grinning over his shoulders, no deserted village in the background.

A reporter was interviewing a group of Onondagas that had traveled to Wounded Knee from upstate New York. "Those crazy AIM bastards are dragging everyone into this," Ed said. "What right have they got to call themselves the 'American Indian Movement?' They have no right to speak for us." The Onondagas moved on. Ed turned his head in my general direction, a side glance, his eyes still on the television screen. "You should hear the guys at work. It sounds like they're just itching for another Indian war."

"It's about time someone spoke up and took a stand," I said, knowing I would anger him. Not caring.

Ed turned fully toward me. His eyes a dark fire. "You're a dreamer, Joanna. You'd think with all that reading you do you'd understand. The old days are gone. There's no bringing them back. This is the *real* world we're living in. We've got enough trouble just trying to make it through the day."

On the television screen there were lines of Indian people walking and cars, bumper to bumper, trying to get to Wounded Knee. There was snow on the ground and many of the Indian people walking had only thin blankets as covering against the cold. Federal Marshals in fur-fringed parkas were blockading the roads to the Pine Ridge Reservation. I pulled the blanket up around my shoulders and straightened my pillow. Ed turned from me and went back into the kitchen. Pregnant or not, if I could, I would be there, now, walking the roads to Wounded Knee.

My bedroom was a dark cave. I lay in the large bed, isolated in the darkness. From beyond the open doorway came the low murmur of the television set. The flickering light from the screen was a campfire that danced shadows against the cave wall. Wounded Knee was far away. I was suspended in time and space, not fully realizing what was happening to me.

It was a strange sensation; the knowing and not knowing. My mind was like a small alert bird perched atop the headboard, watching. As my mind watched and marked the darkness, the flickering light of the television, the shadows on the wall, my body knew the subdued bands of pain, the moontide and the blood flow. And when the water bag broke, warm and gushing between my legs, the small bird perched atop the headboard flew quickly to my side, and I knew. I knew with the clear mind of the bird that the fetus within my womb was being carried on the tide.

I made my way out of the warm cave into the cold light of the white bathroom. I locked the door. No Grandmothers in the birthing hut. Alone. I sat on the toilet seat and reached between my legs to catch the child, denying it even as it happened. My silent screams deafened me, blurred the stillbirth of the fetus. I didn't question that the child was not attached to the placenta, didn't question the break of so vital a link, only felt the small wet body cradled in the palm of my hand. Saw the child's eyes closed, swollen, its hands reaching as if to be held. Its strange sad dignity.

I began to tremble, violently.

154

I carefully placed the fetus on a flower of pale pink bathroom tissue and rested the tissue on the clothes hamper. I tried to clean myself, flushing away all evidence. Finally, I stood and pulled the rose-colored towel from the towel ring and wiped the floor with it, calming myself in the doing. I threw the dirty towel into the bathtub and called Ed.

What could I say? I should have rested more? I should have dreamed less? I should not have harbored thoughts of death and killing? — of eagle feathers trailing in the wind?

I unlocked the door and let Ed in. I pointed to the fetus and, again, the sense of separation came over me. Small bird eyes noted the concerned look on his face, the shock that rippled through his body and settled in his eyes — and that instant of curiosity at the small dead thing.

Ed cried, hurting man sobs, and I held him, my body weeping but straight and still. From where his sorrow welled I could not say, for I was separate, holding him. There and not there. A wavering ghost, my long white nightgown stained with blood.

The next morning, the bedroom was flooded with light. It was not a clean light. It poured through the smudged windows and reflected off the mirror, dust flecked and hazy. The house was still for a Saturday. Quiet. From the direction of the kitchen came the soft clatter of dishes. Like the tick tock of a clock in an empty room it had the effect of intensifying the silence. Ed.

He had been so kind the night before, anxious to do whatever was needed. I had wrapped the dead fetus in the bathroom tissue and had carried it to the hospital in my purse. I could feel the small body, the heat of its near-life faintly warm and fading, through the tissue, the thin cloth purse. I did not cry the long drive to the hospital. Ed was silent.

They took the child from me. A young nurse's assistant picked the fetus from the tissue with a pair of steel tongs. She placed the fetus in a steel bowl and carried it from the room. It was like the tearing of a limb. Flesh and bone and muscle ripped from my body. And all I could do was cry, deep wrenching sobs.

Now, lying in bed, grief seeped through my pores and clung to the bed, the blankets, the walls. A gray film of a shroud that touched everything. It was inside of me and outside of me. It would not leave. And there was anger, too. A cold deadly fire.

Minute specks of dust drifted in the sunlight. A memory from my childhood assaulted me: me, walking up the stairs of a museum with my parents. Walking through a maze of rooms, looking for a special display of Indian artwork; beads and baskets and old deer hoof rattles. For some reason we did not ask for directions. We came across a dark windowless corner of the museum where a long shelf was stocked with jars of preserved fetuses in different stages of growth. The fluid in the jars had reflected the light of an overhead bulb and the fetuses had seemed to float in the hazy light. The larger babies were perfect—every finger and fingernail, every toe, the two small ears like flower petals, the closed dreaming eyes. I could not grasp the meaning of why dead babies would be bottled for all to see. The act seemed to contain within it a violence so profound, so calculated, that there could be no possible defense against it. At the same time that I was horribly fascinated, I was repulsed and very afraid. My parents had rushed me out of the museum, my mother visibly shaken and my father grim and silent.

I turned away from the hazy drifting light, curling my body around the remembering, the hurt, the anger. But no matter how tightly I shut my eyes, the light seeped through.

I could not sleep. I could not rest. I was an open throbbing wound. I sat up in bed and put on my robe and slippers. As I passed the large dresser, I caught a glimpse of an old woman in turquoise looking at me from the mirror. I smoothed back my hair and continued into the kitchen.

Ed was standing at the stove, frying eggs. I turned away. "You okay?" Ed asked. Stupid, stupid question. "I'm fine," I said.

I sat down at the table and looked out the window. The wind had stopped blowing. "You know," I said, "we're like those fetuses scientists put into bottles." I felt Ed's wondering look. He brought me my breakfast. Two eggs, sunnyside up. Sausages. I pushed the plate away. "Did you hear what I said?"

"Yes," Ed said. He sat down beside me. "Why do you want to talk about things like that?"

"Because that baby is nothing to them." I started to cry. "Don't you see? Don't you see, that's what they're doing to us."

Ed moved his chair closer to mine. He pulled me towards him and held me close. His strong arms were a shaded mountain place; tobacco and sage. Our legs touched. "It's okay," he said. "It's okay."

I pulled away from him. "It's not okay. Can't you see that? What's wrong with you?" I wiped the tears from my face, dim tapes of anger at my father playing; times when he could not ease the pain, make things better.

Ed leaned his elbow on the table and rubbed at his forehead. "Honey, you're tired. You've been through hell. I know that."

"Aren't you listening to what I'm saying? They bottle dead babies for God's sake. I'm dying inside and you just sit there." Ed made a move to hug me again, but I pushed him away. "What are we doing here? What kind of life is this? Right now, there are men, strong Indian men, at Wounded Knee, trying to do something for all of us. And what do you do—fry eggs like an old woman." I pushed hard at the plate of eggs and sausages and sent it flying across the table. Yes: the flying sausages, the sharp thud of plate on wall, the hollow cracking of dish and splatter of egg, Ed's startled face in the foreground. Yes.

I nearly stumbled over my robe as I ran out of the kitchen. I locked the bedroom door and leaned against it, a strange triumph drumming.

On Sunday, March 11, Dennis Banks of the American Indian Movement at Wounded Knee announced on national television that the Oglala Sioux Nation was to determine its own borders, as defined by the Treaty of 1868 with the United States, and that it would stop anyone who violated its borders.

Ed found me in my nightgown, packing canned goods and beans and macaroni into two large shopping bags. He leaned against the doorway. "You planning on going someplace?"

I stood up and braced myself against the cupboard door, lightheaded and dizzy from bending over. "You know perfectly well what I'm doing," I said.

Ed came and stood by me. His face was troubled.

I started rearranging the canned goods still left in the cupboard. Peas with peas. Corn with corn. "I know you think I'm crazy. I've tried to make you understand how important this is, but you're blind and deaf to me." I faced him. "Indian people from all over the nation are sending food and blankets and . . . "

"Guns," Ed said. His eyes were hard, his mouth set against me.

I wanted to slap him. "I don't want killing. I don't think anyone really wants killing. There's something bigger going on there. For the first time since I was a little girl I feel good about being Indian. Most of the time I don't really know what that means. I'd like to think it means something." My hands and legs were shaking. I walked over to the table and sat down.

Ed stood by the cupboard, looking down at the shopping bags. He pushed at his hair and smoothed it behind his ear; there were strands of gray in the raven blackness. "How in the hell do you intend to get this stuff to them?"

I folded my hands in my lap, steadying them. "There's an AIM regional office in L.A. I thought we could take it there."

"You're really determined to get us into this thing, aren't you?" Ed shook his head. "I don't know. Yesterday, when you were so upset, I thought it was because of the baby." He looked fully at me. There was a pleading in his eyes, a weary sorrow. "There are no clean lines, Joanna. Sometimes it's hard to know who the enemy is."

I looked away toward the empty stove to the right of him. "We can't pretend anymore that everything is fine. It's not." Surely, I had explained the years of hurting inside, the slow dying that had begun as far back as my first day of public school. All of the years when I walked close to the edge of a dark abyss where surely I would fall and die because teachers and white students and everyone with power in the outside world told me, in word and action, that I was dirty, stupid, of no worth.

Ed nudged at a bag of groceries with his foot. "And you think that this will make everything right?" The pleading had gone from his eyes. His hands were clenched.

"It's something. It's better than sitting back and letting everything run over us. Every day we lose a little bit more. I see you. The conflict. Wanting to be accepted by the guys at work. Putting

158

up with their stupid jokes. Hating yourself for pretending. If we don't do something, if we don't enter into a stream that takes us away from this lie we're living, we'll die inside." I blinked back the tears. "And then what have we got to give to each other"—I hesitated—"to our children?"

Ed turned his back to me. He gripped the edge of the sink with both hands, his arms straight out, head down. Above his head the eagle flew. Butterflies trailed. "Don't do this to me," he said, his voice husky, muffled. "It's not as simple as you make it seem."

He pushed himself away from the sink and walked slowly over to the table. He stood over me; an outcropping of desert rock against the yellow sky walls of our kitchen. "You talk as if I've given you nothing," he said. "As if all I've worked for has been some kind of a lie." He looked away, over my head, toward the window. "All I could think about in Viet Nam was our life together. The kids we'd have. The home I'd buy you." He turned back to me. "Is that so wrong?"

"Not wrong, Ed. Good. Everything I wanted, too." My voice faltered. "But just not enough."

"Not enough." He shook his head, the edge of a bitter laugh in his throat. "Not enough." He pointed his finger at me. "Okay, you win. I won't stop you from doing what you have to do. But don't expect me to take any part in this."

For a moment we were equals, looking into each other's eyes, acknowledging our separateness. If not understanding, at least accepting the other's stand. It was a brief moment of union. Before the eyes looked away. Before we fell back into the hurting bones of ourselves, of our roles as husband, as wife.

Ed carried the groceries to the car. He was tight-lipped and silent. An echo of the night he had driven me to the hospital. His sorrow contained to the point where it seemed he had no sorrow. It was as if his helping me pack the trunk with groceries for Wounded Knee was a form of collusion he deeply regretted but from which he could not free himself. He arranged the groceries in the trunk, propping up the bags with the tool box so they would not spill. He closed the trunk and looked up to where I stood on the porch. "Ready?" he said.

"Ready," I said. I gathered my jacket around me and walked down the porch steps toward the car. Ed stepped aside as I reached for the front door handle. It was an awkward moment. A shifting, somehow, of reins. Before the turn. The leap. "I'll call you when I get there," I said, waiting for his move; the kiss goodbye. Ed nodded.

"The roads are being blockaded," he said, retelling what we both knew. All vehicles were being searched out of California. Chances were the Los Angeles AIM members would never make it through the check points.

"I have to try," I said. Again, the awkwardness, the unspoken words that even refused to form. Only the stand, the position, sure on either side. I opened the car door and got in.

Ed bent over the open door. I reached for his hand. It was calloused and deeply ingrained with years of dirt and grease and getting up early to take some other man's orders, to fight some other man's wars. No amount of soap could wash away the stain. And I started to cry because it was what he thought he knew and his way of loving me and there I was going off on some maybe hopeless vision quest only I couldn't pull out because the child had died. Would never be born. And, oh God, I had to do something. I kissed the palm of his hand and he reached around with the same hand and wiped the tears from my cheek with his finger.

"Better get going," he said, pulling his hand away. He stepped back and closed the door. He hit the car with the palm of his hand, as if to spark a horse to run, and walked up the porch steps and into the house.

By now I could hardly see from crying. I started the car and backed it out of the driveway. Mrs. Johnson was on her front porch, sweeping it clean. She looked up, solid in her gray house-dress, all neat white hair and cool niceness.

I drove away from the house, wiping the tears from my face. At the corner, I turned the car into the slow rush of traffic that flowed by. The car parted the air stream and the wind currents that flowed over and around the car entered the window and touched my hair, my face.

A meadowlark called from a burst of weed-flowers growing in a vacant lot, but clear as the notes were, like the dabs of yellow and lavender blooms that blurred in my passing, the notes echoed within and sang of times when I was a child. Times when the harsh stubble growing on the reservation foothills looked as green and soft as moss. Times when school was out and I would run up the dirt road toward our old house, my shoes in hand, and the earth warm beneath my bare feet.

III. IN THE EVENING

These are the stories of being and becoming, stories that do not let analytical thinking get in the way of living. They are stories of our relation to earth, to natural rhythms that are around us and within us. They are about life and death, birth, about how we rearrange the inner puzzle of ourselves after tragedy or shock. They are the open spaces in our lives where the voices of things are allowed to speak. They are, like the title story by Flying Clouds, stories of everyday life grown strong and beautiful by vibrant telling. Hers is a story of life lived, of living disappearing, a story that is in harmony with the moment. It is a story of the evening, the even-ing, the dusky magical time when the world takes on new light.

Flying Clouds

I'm Chickasaw/ Cherokee and white. I am 39 years old. I live in Tuska-
homa, Oklahoma, a small place. I love stories. They are part of my life here.
Yesterday, I heard one about cyprus knees!

IN THE EVENING

It's almost evening. I've eaten pea soup and fresh bread. There is enough for tomorrow. My bedroom is cleaned, the blue sheets and pillowcases and Mother's embroidered flower quilt on the bed. There are shadows of leaves on the floor. *This* (the shadows of leaves on the floor) is my life, and Ramona is a beautiful part of it, just like the leaves, the sun, the patterns. We are simply part of each other's life.

I dreamed we are almost there. I hear a man's voice explaining the rules and then lots of happy, excited voices of children that sound so sweet. I'm eager to be one of them! Then here they come, all flooding the hills and I'm one of them! I feel joy to be there with the others!

It is the beginning of evening. The south end of the garden is covered with trumpet vines which have begun to bloom. I was looking up close into one of the trumpet blossoms, loving them, praying, "May I be granted to see a hummingbird come to you," when I heard a loud buzz and there a few inches from me landed a little hummingbird looking me in the eye! She's female and I imagine has her nest in the little bois arc tree to which she flew. I remember Ramona's description of how very pretty a little nest she makes!

I've been cooking beans and in a few minutes I'll start the cornbread. I love the birds' voices and the sunlight shining on the sides of the trees.

I worked at Evelyn's today. It was long hours of sitting quietly. I felt thankful to the trumpet vine, the hummingbird, to my dreams.

It's evening. Still hot, but the coolness will begin soon. There's one baby bird in the nest on the porch. She sits up out of the nest most of the time. Just now I was watching the little bird and a rabbit was watching me! This morning walking to the post office,

I came across a turtle crossing the road. When I came back, she'd already made it across.

It's Sunday morning. Soon I must get ready to go to Gum Creek. Ramona is going with me. There is a wonderful breeze blowing from the South. It makes me want to sit here forever.

Last night I went to visit Ramona. She had bisquits in the oven, so I ate with her. Lucinda had given her plums from her trees and Elaine had been over to show her how to make jelly. The jelly was good and pretty. When we sat outside, Dale came over. Ramona's black hen sat over her four chicks and went to sleep for the night beside the porch. Dale and Ramona had killed a skunk the night before, so I heard all about that. Ramona showed me the dolls she's made out of beads to sell Evelyn's friend from the city. I showed Ramona how to make French knots. Ramona likes to learn everything. I love the sound she makes to get the dogs to be quiet.

Now it's evening, the first beginning of evening. I have more faith and security now than I have had since I was a child. I have "a good measure, pressed down, shaken together, pouring over."

This week I want to buy fresh vegetables. I haven't been spending any money on food. I eat at Evelyn's when I work there. We were given commodities—cheese, butter, milk, and honey.

I cleaned all day at Evelyn's and I've cleaned my own house and cooked this evening. My feet hurt! Patty came and gave Evelyn an enema and cleaned her up once. After she left, I had to clean her up four more times and wash everything. Evelyn was so appreciative, I didn't mind.

Something special happened yesterday as I was leaving. John had given me three ripe tomatoes from someone's garden and I asked Susan if she had any onions in her garden, as I would like one to go with my tomatoes. Before long both John and Susan were exclaiming and looking here and there in their tiny garden to see what they could give me. It was the first time I had ever seen them doing something together, doing something out of love, out of a desire to please. The way I saw them, the love I felt for those two people who want so much to be loved, was like seeing them against a backdrop of the entire universe. In addition, I got a cucumber, a sweet pepper, two hot peppers, and three little round onions out of it! When I got home, I made a salad using the little butter-lettuce Mother had picked out for me and the other things. It was more than food.

I'm just home from work. Susan gave me an extra $5.00 today. I'll get a frame for the photograph of the dogwood blossoms. I'm going to start staying with Evelyn at night some.

Now it is the beautiful evening time, the beautiful woman time. The insect voices are the music of the dance. My greatest pleasure today was canning four pints of jalapeno peppers whole and six and a half pints of sliced ones. I should have worn gloves when I cut up that many hot peppers. My hands hurt for two or three hours and they still feel tender and raw and sting some. The peppers look great all in their jars there on the counter. Some of them I saved out to use fresh.

Almost time to return to Evelyn's to spend the night. My period made me very sluggish and almost unhappy today. Almost everything I tried to do I'd just get frustrated with and stop. But finally I settled down on the front porch with a rag and a bucket of water and washed the stems and leaves of my little orange tree. I enjoyed that. I made a little platform for its pot to sit on. It has a little bud!

I've been working at Evelyn's a lot, day and night. I'm making a ceramic corn dish and I have a new pin cushion, red tomato and strawberry with emory, and a little package of embroidery needles. I work on my embroidery a lot while I sit with Evelyn. Tomorrow I'm off—thank goodness! Ramona and I are going early to pick berries.

I have a little time left before I return to Evelyn's closed-up house. I am thankful to this gentle evening with a light rain falling and a breeze. I became very peaceful this afternoon with Evelyn. I worked on my embroidery while we played our geography game. I am eager to sleep. I was up late last night driving home in the lightning, thunder, and pouring rain. I'd gone to Mother's church with her—96 little children came to Bible School. They filled the little church house, their bodies all squeezed together on the pews.

A little visitor just came in under the gate—an armadillo. I felt my brother with me all day. It's been seven years now since his death.

When I was giving Evelyn her medicine last night, I felt love leave my body and go to hers. She must have felt it too, for after she'd swallowed, she said, "I'm so glad you're back." (I'd only been gone a day.)

It's 6:30 p.m. I've just finished the marathon at Evelyn's. I want to clean my house and have everything beautiful. Today I've had the feeling about the future, the baby daughter.

I have a bad backache. Physically I am such a mess. I know no one would believe me, but I am going to be a dancer. I want to dance, to express thanksgiving and love in my heart. Oh! to express all sorts of things! "Comes the rain, comes the wind, comes the telling of destinies." There's wind, thunder, lightning, and rain now. The horses are running all over.

It's late afternoon. I spent most of the day with Ramona. We were happy together. We did our errands and ate Indian tacos in town. Ramona had a long driving lesson on the dirt roads to the spring, at her house we canned tomatoes, and she made lunch for us: black-eyed peas, biscuits and butter and jelly, cucumbers, and ice water.

Oh! Now the rain is coming down! I feel close to Mother of Dawn, so very close. She is my friend, the One who takes care of me. Last night it felt so good to lie in the bed (at Evelyn's) and be able to pray. And to know that I am always going to have that comfort. God will always be with me. I will never be alone. I won't lose my way because God will guide me.

Sharon sent me a box of wonderful things from Mexico. My favorite thing, right at the moment, is a black necklace of clay birds.

168

I'm cooking black-eyed peas. When they're done, I'm going swimming! Besides the peas, I've fixed squash dressing, and tuna fish salad. It will be wonderful to sleep in my own bed tonight.

In a dream I see a Japanese woman who is sleeping after her work. She is a potter, the best in all Japan. A young woman, quiet, who simply does her work. She even weaves the bamboo back and forth to make the little house where she works.

It isn't just me anymore. Now it's me and six baby chicks. They are in a cardboard box with an old screen over the top for now.

Yesterday I visited my family. I gave Grandmother the blackberry cobbler I'd made for her. Mother and I ate out at the Chinese restaurant. Dad helped me build a chick-pen. Tonight is the chicks' first night outside since I got them.

My sister spent the week-end with me. When the possum rattled the chicks' pen, she was the first one out there. One little chick lost a wing. They're inside again.

I saw a small deer drinking water, the wonderful curving way of its body. Today I loved Evelyn's little naked body, like some kind of— well, I don't know—I just loved her being alive, loved that there are little 90-year-old bodies around. I finished a blue ceramic flower pot for Susan. I saw a hummingbird come to the morning-glories. I worked a lot on embroidery.

Beautiful moments this morning shared with Susan. We loved the orchid together, admired the ceramic pots I've made her. She gave me dill pickles, bread and butter pickles, and muskedime jelly. I had a wonderful feeling that's still with me at bedtime. I saw the hummingbird again.

Ramona and Elaine just came to see me. Ramona really likes me, though I'm not sure she liked my "tank top." I had the house clean and was cooking black-eyed peas. They came just at dusk but were still able to see the chickens. We sat in the bedroom where it's coolest. They'd just come from picking peas, beans, and tomatoes.

They gave me some tomatoes and purple-hull peas. They told me Mr. Andrews died yesterday, suddenly. These younger people dying, and Evelyn going on all day, "Oh! me! Oh! my! I'm going to die!" Sometimes it is very depressing to be with her. But I saw lots of little children and babies today at the washerteria and that gave me a happy feeling.

Just now, right at dark, I saw a little deer. She saw me too and we watched each other awhile, then she romped over to a clump of something and took a few bites, then romped back to face me, her big ears moving all around. The feeling reminded me of seeing the beavers in their pond that first time very early in the morning.

I have the day off from work. I feel drawn into myself.

I loved being with Ramona. She is warm through and through. We went to Box Spring for water. I loved her appreciation of the spring water. She calls it "real water" and has feelings toward the spring as one would toward her own precious child.

Less than two hours here at home, then I'm going back to Evelyn's. I have tomorrow off. I worked all afternoon cleaning Evelyn's bedroom and kitchen. I became full of peace and now the beauty of evening. John gave me a little watermelon (about the size of a large cantelope) from his Aunt Mary's garden. (Aunt Mary is 90 years old, Choctaw, grows a garden, lives by herself.) That watermelon is more precious than a diamond to me! She'd also sent him home with some spice cake and I had some with a glass of milk. Ramona and I made plans to go to Cedar Lake.

Mother left this morning after spending three days with me. Her pick-up left in one direction, mine in another. I felt very sad. How beautiful my house is to me after being in Evelyn's all day. Though I don't imagine anyone would believe me, hers so fancy and mine so plain. Mother had made the bed and folded the blankets. My plants, the little chickens, the green hills, all seem to welcome me. And there were the pears needing to be canned.

In a dream I see a man and a woman and their little children. She hugs them all and says, "Home! home!" as the train comes into the mountains. The strength of feeling for a place on earth.

I worked today at Evelyn's. I hated being part of that world over there. I try to do my best, but my best feels like nothing against an ocean, an ocean of unhappiness and waste. I'm eager to get away.

It's cold tonight. I have on my strawberry flannel gown. There are two quilts and an afghan on the bed to cover with. I love everything, absolutely everything. I saw a wet hummingbird after the rain this morning. Last night I heard the wolves, all around. They seemed to be gathering near the river. Now I am listening to the owls call each other.

I've been worrying about the chickens all day and all night. I'm never home to watch out for them. Something already got two of them. Ramona says she'll take the remaining ones. I feel like a failure.

After dark, I gave Ramona my three remaining chickens. I felt a little envious of them, being taken care of by Ramona. I shall always remember how she was, stooping down, reaching in the box for them, putting them in the coop. And now I've taken a bath, a cold one.

It was cool and raining all day. Evelyn was in a bad mood. She wants me to get involved with all her contrived concerns, but I don't want to. The people there are bored and unhappy.

Ramona and I had supper together. I love her very much. I told her.

I'm working only nights now. I love being home during the day. I took a walk and then picked pears from Ruth and Kim's trees. I feel elated because I believe I am going to walk everyday and be strong and well.

Saturday night Ramona and I went to Rock Creek. I suffer so much from self-consciousness. We sat in the pick-up awhile, then went to Juanita's cousin's camp house for supper. I thought they didn't really want us, though they'd asked us. The banaha and green beans were delicious. I realized that Ramona is as shy when everyone is speaking Choctaw as she is when it's English. I hadn't realized that before. We saw Bro. James ringing the bell. He preached about God not being dead, don't the leaves still turn gold? That's what they are doing now and the days are becoming sad.

I'm at Evelyn's now. She's feeling peaceful for once. Well, she's gone to sleep. I'm very sleepy too. We only slept two hours last night.

Soon I must return to Evelyn's. It's been a very soft, quiet day, overcast and I've been very subdued. I worked on the ceramic hummingbird and took a walk. I've longed for the baby I want. I'm just tired, from working nights and missing my dreams.

It's early, just getting light, raining gently. I love to come home! It's miserable around Evelyn. She's rude and unpleasant, blows her whistle for me when I'm right there and she knows it. But she slept some on and off and I worked on my embroidery. I finished all the leaves. I'm making "Partridge in a Pear Tree."

Time to go back to Evelyn's. I slept a lot here at home today. I'm over there too much. But I'm sticking it out as long as I can. I wish the shift were only eight hours instead of 13.

I quit at Evelyn's. But that means I have no money coming in and only about $25.00 and all the bills to pay. I guess I'll have to go back and try to reinstate myself. Pride is only for those who can afford it. One can't even hear the insect voices in that closed-in house, no wonder Evelyn's so miserable. I need to be stronger. I feel like giving up, just hitting the road like my brother used to do.

I dreamed Grandmother was still alive and able to read the news-paper. She and I were friends. She talked to me. On the back page of the paper was her picture. She was one of many old Indian women, all in rows, all dressed alike. The picture was cut so that

Grandmother was in the center. She and I were going somewhere about our baskets.

I'm back working for Evelyn. We don't sleep one wink. When I left, she was all put out with me. She can't understand why after so many hours of it, I'm less than enthusiastic about putting her cover on and off again every half minute! I left very early. It was the darkest time of night. No moon or stars. There are muddy places. The wind is high. It is wonderful to hold one's basket in one's arm, to stand tall, to pray, and to walk home safely on such a morning after no sleep. It is wonderful to come to one's own little gate, to unlatch it, to pray full of thanksgiving, to come into the house, to get into one's own sweet bed, and to fall asleep.

Evelyn's a p in the a. It's up and down all night to tend to her made-up "needs," things like "move my head." Everything's a command and never a "thank you." She won't eat. I asked her would she please try not to say "Oh! me! Oh! my!" for two minutes. She said she would try and as a result she fell asleep! Thank goodness! I got a little sleep too, and today I saw Ramona, wearing a new dress she'd made of purple-red material with black designs. I wanted to swing her around and laugh and play! I worked on ceramics. My spirit lifted and I drove at evening time through the mountains covered with golden trees. I got some potatoes and a coke for supper. Susan sent someone to tell me to hurry back up there to Evelyn.

Evelyn died Tuesday morning. When I got to work, I noticed that she didn't wake up like she usually does when I have to clean her. I called Susan to come in there. We couldn't get her to wake up. Her breathing was very loud, a terrible sound. Her feet were already blue. Everyone else went to bed and to sleep. I stayed awake with her all night, listened to her terrible breathing. Her face already looked like a skull, dark rings around her eyes which wouldn't stay closed. In the morning, just as daylight came, with all of us gathered around her bed, she quit breathing, she died. It was the first time I'd ever watched a person die. I have a feeling of thankfulness to her, for sharing her life and her death with me. The feeling surprises me: I thought I'd feel only relief. I'm going to Grandma's land at Wapanucka to pick up pecans for a few days. I'll sleep in the pick-up, build a little fire in the evenings.

Rita Macy

I have been married for twenty-five years, and have three children. I am a life long resident of Whitehall, New York, with only a short eight year stint in Poughkeepsie, New York. For approximately fifteen years I worked in various offices (lots of responsibility, little pay), and then took a part time job as a school bus driver for ten years (more responsibility, better pay). This allowed more time with my family. I quit work altogether and went back to school at Adirondack Community College as a Liberal Arts major and will graduate in the spring of 1986. Having studied Creative Writing with Ms. Jean Rikhoff, I received the Parnassus Medal for fiction last semester. I have been published in the Literary Magazine, Expressions. *This summer, I am working on the second draft of my novel,* Uncommon Women.*

BEWARE OF GOOD ADVICE
AND OTHER CATASTROPHES

I sat on the side of the country road smoking a cigarette. Bill, my husband, was trying frantically to put out the house fire with our garden hose. The fire trucks, volunteer firemen, and various sightseers were stuck on the other side of South Bay. The light on the one lane Bailey Bridge was not working as usual and traffic was backed up at least until the corner by the county building, two miles away.

Even as the flames shot up higher and higher and my hugh pine tree in the front yard went up like a Christmas tree, I was wondering if the firemen would know if my house trailer had dirty ashes or clean ashes. I mean, every ever-loving housewife knows that cleaning house is a merry-go-round for drudges, but I think that I was on to something here.

I had bought into the whole, "cleanliness is next to Godliness," routine from my grandmother, and "keep your house neat and clean," from my mother, and the fifty thousand or so T.V. commercials warning me about everything from body odors to garbage pail odors and from dishes that should glisten and shine to floors that have that, "just waxed look." And now as I watched my own miniature *Towering Inferno*, I was mentally kicking myself for having been a first class jerk.

Bill and I had worked different shifts, sometimes Bill worked two jobs, always plugging away just to keep going. We finally got the trailer paid off, put all new carpets down, and there it went, up in a puff of smoke. It took about fifteen minutes, twenty tops.

I wondered what it had cost me, not in dollars and cents, but in hours. Too damn much, that's what. Would anybody know now if my floors needed mopping, or my drapes needed pressing, or even if I had made our beds that day? With the best of intentions, my priorities had become all mixed up with my duties as a wife, mother, and resident house drudge. Right on the spot I decided that if somebody mentions duty to me ever again, they had better duck.

By the time some of the firemen made it across the bridge, all that was left to do was keep the fire from spreading to the woods. Finally, we'd had enough and decided to take the kids and go to my brother's vacant house for the night. My brother and his wife had managed to get away to Maine without their kids for a little vacation. Their daughter, Polly, was staying with us, so that it was appropriate that we descended on their house for refuge.

Imagine now, after being awake over twenty-four hours and a few hundred miles later they finally arrived home and found that four people had moved in. Not bag and baggage actually, we didn't have any clothes except what we had on, but we were there for sure.

That fateful night, we all managed to bunk somewhere in their house and grab a few hours rest. The next morning we woke up to the smell of bacon cooking. My brother had cooked a hugh break-fast of bacon, eggs, home frys and a loaf of toast for all of us. They searched through their dresser drawers for clothes to fit us and tried to make us as presentable as possible. Their generosity served to remind me to be thankful that no one had been hurt and what did anything else really matter.

Later on that morning, we went back to look around through the smoldering mess of what was left of ten years work. There wasn't a hell of a lot to sift through. It wasn't until I was in what had been the living room, that I remembered my fish tank. Oh, all my little fish were gone. I sat down and cried for the first time, as if my heart was broken. All the time my rational mind told me how absurd I was, I thought of my little guppies and their tiny babies, so small that they could fit on the head of a pin, and cried harder.

When Bill heard me and came to console me about our loss, all I could sputter about was my fish. My cute little guppies, black mollies, neons, angel fish and even my sucker fish that kept my tank free of algae. I raved on about the khole hoops that I had flushed down the toilet because I suspected them of eating the tails off my guppies. Then, after the flush, I found out that the real culprit was my angel fish. I should have known. Anyone that I've ever known named Angel was anything but.

Oh, well, there's no use crying over spilled milk, or fried fish for that matter. Life goes on and we must keep a stiff upper lip and all the rest of those dumb cliches. A nice neighbor let us stay in his new house for a few weeks. He hadn't moved in because the inside was still not finished off. But it was a godsend to us. It gave us a home base at least.

What a strange sensation, to wake up with nothing of my own around me. Not a comb to comb my hair with, or a toothbrush to brush my teeth, not a can opener, or a frying pan, or a knife and fork, no nicknacks around to remind me of warm memories, no pictures of my babies or momentous events, not a purse to carry or anything to put in it. It was a feeling that has changed my whole life. To this day, I don't own or carry a purse. But it goes much deeper than that.

People started coming. The first man who came was the Methodist minister. We didn't belong to his church, in fact, he didn't even know us. He was a jovial fellow who came to us with an exuberance and an order to go to a store in town and pick out a set of dishes, glasses, pots and pans and a complete set of silverware. He told us the store was expecting us and to choose whatever we wanted. With his visit, the taste of burnt ashes left my mouth. And my life long belief in people, good people, was reaffirmed.

Others came with all sorts of things; an end table, an odd lamp, a pop corn popper, a chair, a bed and box springs, coffee pot and a couple of mugs, clothes, sneakers, an iron, and clothes hangers. It was like having my own private yard sale delivered right to my door. Fourteen years later, my refrigerator, stove, and washing machine are second hand left overs from the fire. Well, they still work just fine and I've learned my lesson well. Never go into debt for the necessities in life. Appliances that just sort of work are all right with me. In fact, I take a kind of perverse pride in owning a washing machine that is at least twenty years old, and a sense of adventure every time that I use it. (This time, will it wash my clothes or tie everything into knots?)

I've also learned about the after life of living in a trailer. I should have expected trouble when Niagara Mohawk hooked us up when we first bought it. They had our trailer listed as an appliance. I remember, at the time, I thought this was hilarious. Not so funny, after the fire, I learned that this appliance depreciates just like a car. Even though it was paid for, it was worth exactly the pile of ashes it had become. Bill had built a little screened porch onto the front and we were paid more insurance money for that than the trailer.

Also, another little item never discussed by insurance agents; the refrigerator, stove, washing machine and anything else that is built in, is considered a part of the trailer. In short, we would have been better off to save our insurance premiums all those years and gone to the movies once in awhile.

"Who knows?" That's the sign I wanted to hang around my neck. After the hundreth time that somebody asks, "What caused the fire?" it gets a little tedious. Well, the firemen never could tell from the pile of ashes that was left. And a fire chief friend tells me that they're usually only looking to see if the fire has been set. And in the end, nobody knows for sure how it started. That's all right with me. The last thing I need is a guilt trip about something I maybe did or didn't do right.

I spend my time now going back to school, enjoying my family and good friends, being ever watchful and on the alert for outside influences telling me, for my own good, what my duties are. My path is clear and uncluttered with boring and tedious preachings and people. I haven't any more time to waste.

Judith McDaniel

Barbara Smith

Barbara Smith is a Black feminist writer and activist who lives in Albany, New York. She co-edited All the Women Are White, all the Blacks Are Men, But Some of Us Are Brave: Black Women's Studies *(The Feminist Press); edited* Home Girls: A Black Feminist Anthology *(Kitchen Table: Women of Color Press); and co-authored* Yours in Struggle: Three Feminist Perspectives on Anti-Semitism and Racism *(Firebrand Books). She is currently completing a collection of short stories.*

MONDAY

"So what you think about this Black child being crowned Miss America?"

"Say what?"

"I said, what you think about them crowning one of our girls on t.v. Saturday night. Me and Jim were up to nearly midnight watching the ceremony and then they had it on the news. You didn't see the newspaper?"

"I was too tired to look at it when I got back from work. You say she's Black?"

"Ahunh. Real bright-skinned. But Black just the same. Her folks live on Long Island."

Lossie pressed her lips tight together and made a sucking sound. "You must be kidding. I wonder what these white folks are up to now?"

"Maybe they ain't up to nothing, just picked the best one for the job. Seemed like everybody was real tickled, grinning all over themselves, kissing and hugging her and acting just like this kind of thing happens every day. I have to admit I went to bed feeling kind of proud."

"You did, Earlene?"

"Sure. How often do they choose one of us for that kind of honor, for being beautiful? She's going to represent America to the whole world and you know the runner-up is a Black girl too."

"Somebody must have put something in those white folks drinks."

"But Lossie, ain't you a little bit proud?"

Lossie frowned and suddenly thought about her daughter, Angela, who wasn't here anymore, because when she finally left her no good husband he took it upon himself to put three bullets through her head cause as he explained to the white policemen, if he couldn't have her nobody else was either. She was a pretty girl, too, with smooth dark skin like Lossie's and big, deep eyes that used to follow Lossie everywhere. Even when she was just a baby seemed like she understood most everything that was going on.

Being pretty hadn't saved her or nice neither. In fact that might have been what killed her.

"No, Earlene, it don't really make me proud. I mean I'm happy for the girl and all, but it'll take a lot more than that to make me satisfied about living on this white boy's land. Let me break it down for you. When I go to the supermarket tomorrow are they going to give me steak for my hamburger money because she's Miss America? Is Miss Lady that I work for going to cut my hours, raise my pay, and stop following me around all day whining while I'm trying to work because some other white people say a Black girl is Miss America? I tend to doubt it."

"But Lossie, it's the principle of the thing. Now some other girls will have the opportunity."

Principle? Opportunity? Sounds like luck to me or some other tricky business. Black folks ain't working, got no place to live, their babies starving, everything a mess. So they throw us a Black Barbie doll on the t.v. Spare me. I ain't buying."

"But Lossie, I always thought you was a race woman."

"I am."

Grace Paley

Grace Paley is a well published and highly praised writer of short fiction. She lives with her husband, Robert Nichols, in New York City and Vermont. She has been active in anti-war and feminist causes for many years. She has two grown children and a grandchild. She teaches at Sarah Lawrence and City College.

ANXIETY

The young fathers are waiting outside the school. What curly heads! Such graceful brown mustaches. They're sitting on their haunches eating pizza and exchanging information. They're waiting for the 3 p.m. bell. It's springtime, the season of first looking out the window. I have a window box of greenhouse marigolds. The young fathers can be seen through the ferny leaves.

The bell rings. The children fall out of school, tumbling through the open door. One of the fathers sees his child. A small girl. Is she Chinese? A little. Up u-u-p, he says, and hoists her to his shoulders. U-u-p, says the second father, and hoists his little boy. The little boy sits on top of his father's head for a couple of seconds before sliding to his shoulders. Very funny, says the father.

They start off down the street, right under and past my window. The two children are still laughing. They try to whisper a secret. The fathers haven't finished their conversation. The frailer father is uncomfortable; his little girl wiggles too much.

Stop it this minute, he says.

Oink oink, says the little girl.

What'd you say?

Oink oink, she says.

The young father says What! three times. Then he seizes the child, raises her high above his head, and sets her hard on her feet.

What'd I do so bad, she says, rubbing her ankle.

Just hold my hand, screams the frail and angry father.

I lean far out the window. Stop! Stop! I cry.

The young father turns, shading his eyes, but sees. What? he says. His friend says, Hey? Who's that? He probably thinks I'm a family friend, a teacher maybe.

Who're you? he says.

I move the pots of marigold aside. Then I'm able to lean on my elbow way out into unshadowed visibility. Once, not too long ago, the tenements were speckled with women like me in every third window up to the fifth story, calling the children from play to receive orders and instruction. This memory enables me to say strictly, Young man, I am an older person who feels free because of that to ask questions and give advice.

Oh? he says, laughs with a little embarrassment, says to his friend, Shoot if you will that old gray head. But he's joking, I know, because he has established himself, legs apart, hands behind his back, his neck arched to see and hear me out.

How old are you? I call. About thirty or so?

Thirty-three.

First I want to say you're about a generation ahead of your father in your attitude and behavior toward your child.

Really? Well? Anything else, ma'am.

Son, I said, leaning another two, three dangerous inches toward him. Son, I must tell you that madmen intend to destroy this beautifully made planet. That the murder of our children by these men has got to become a terror and a sorrow to you, and starting now, it had better interfere with any daily pleasure.

Speech speech, he called.

I waited a minute, but he continued to look up. So, I said, I can tell by your general appearance and loping walk that you agree with me.

I do, he said, winking at his friend; but turning a serious face to mine, he said again, Yes, yes, I do.

Well then, why did you become so angry at that little girl whose future is like a film which suddenly cuts to white. Why did you nearly slam this little doomed person to the ground in your uncontrollable anger.

Let's not go too far, said the young father. She *was* jumping around on my poor back and hollering oink oink.

When were you angriest—when she wiggled and jumped or when she said oink?

He scratched his wonderful head of dark well-cut hair. I guess when she said oink.

Have you ever said oink oink? Think carefully. Years ago, perhaps?

No. Well maybe. Maybe.

Whom did you refer to in this way?

He laughed. He called to his friend, Hey Ken, this old person's got something. The cops. In a demonstration. Oink oink, he said, remembering, laughing.

The little girl smiled and said, Oink oink.

Shut up, he said.

What do you deduce from this?

That I was angry at Rosie because she was dealing with me as though I was a figure of authority, and it's not my thing, never has been, never will be.

I could see his happiness, his nice grin, as he remembered this.

So, I continued, since those children are such lovely examples of what may well be the last generation of humankind, why don't you start all over again, right from the school door, as though none of this had ever happened.

Thank you, said the young father. Thank you. It would be nice to be a horse, he said, grabbing little Rosie's hand. Come on Rosie, let's go. I don't have all day.

U-up, says the first father. U-up, says the second.

Giddap, shout the children, and the fathers yell neigh neigh, as horses do. The children kick their fathers' horsechests, screaming giddap giddap, and they gallop wildly westward.

I lean way out to cry once more. Be careful! Stop! But they've gone too far. Oh, anyone would love to be a fierce fast horse carrying a beloved beautiful rider, but they are galloping toward one of the most dangerous street corners in the world. And they may live beyond that trisection across other dangerous avenues.

So I must shut the window after patting the April-cooled marigolds with their rusty smell of summer. Then I sit in the nice light and wonder how to make sure that they gallop safely home through the airy scary dreams of scientists and the bulky dreams of automakers. I wish I could see just how they sit down at their kitchen tables for a healthy snack (orange juice or milk and cookies) before going out into the new spring afternoon to play.

Toles Photography, Cobleskill, NY

Ina Jones

I am a retired secretary, writing a novel, short stories, and poems in Cobleskill, where I live with my husband. Though I've always written, I am able to write more steadfastly at this time in my life.

I have had work published in Epoch, Blueline, Glens Falls Review, Greenfield Review, Sing Heavenly Muse!.

NO STONE FOR MAMA

Reminders are everywhere. Here in the violets, blue in the grass again. Up there in the mackerel sky portending rain. A sheep sky, she would have said. "The little cloud sheep want water. I think we get soon rain."

My mind's ear strains to remember her voice—which was unmodulated. It slid and veered, got too loud when she grew excited. Her language was unique. Her vocabulary, a veritable button box of assorted English and German, into which she dipped at random. She fastened a German prefix to English verbs: *ge*went, *ge*fixed, *ge*baked. Or put an English suffix with German verbs: polishing was *polier*ing; describing was *beschreib*ing.

I, a purist even in my teens, rolled my eyes heavenward at such grammatical abominations. With caution (for children should respect their parents) I corrected and instructed. "So long as you know how I mean it," she brushed me off. And clattered lids, puffed in laundry steam, panted with domesticity—implying she had no time for airs and graces.

Ach, Mama. Over, under, and through everything flows memory. Endless as cloud sheep come my thoughts. I am writing here, at my backyard picnic table, *polier*ing sentences, *beschreib*ing how it all was. A year ago, a year ago, my mind keeps saying.

With the violets, a year ago, she went to the hospital. With the lilacs, she was gone. Not even a grave is left—no stone to record that her years were eighty-two. Nothing. My mother, erased from the world.

How could I let it happen? I should have been firm.

Had we never come to America, she and my father and I, those fifty years ago—had we stayed in Germany—she would lie buried in Unterrissdorf now, among the graves of my father's family. (Though let me not get carried away—side by side with Tante Hedwig would not have been her pleasure.) The pictures of all the graves, sent us by relatives, she kept in her album. The letters edged in black, in a small drawer of the sideboard, under the handkerchiefs. She approved of mourning bands and mourning veils—thought it regrettable that they were not used in America. "Here, what do they know?" She shrugged off certain lacks in American life. Grief should be black and broken-hearted (as in the novels she traded with the *Kaffeeklatsch* ladies). Coffins should be borne graveward on men's shoulders, with a black-clad procession of mourners coming behind, bearing wreaths, their rhythmic steps making crunching sounds on cemetery gravel. I myself remembered such things, having been already eight when we left Unterrissdorf, thus already indelibly imprinted with Germanness. Hadn't I gone with my grandmother the day she planted my grandfather's grave with geraniums? Down on her knees in her apron, smoothing and smoothing the earth as though it were a featherbed covering him.

As I wish now to smooth the cool earth over you, Mama. *Die kühle Erde.* Weren't you always quoting me verses of the grave's cool reward? You deserved better. I should have seen to things. I blame him. I blame my father.

"Your mother and I want no funeral when our time comes." He said that practically every time I visited them in her last years. "We want cremation."

"Yes, but," I explained (with infinite patience) "even with cremation there's a funeral. There's still a service."

"Nothing churchy!" He was quick to wave all christendom aside. "Your mother and I have never been church goers." As though he had to tell me. "Cremation," he said, "and that's it!"

I see him, walking out of the kitchen, a small man in a perennial gray buttoned sweater, stiff-backed, owing nobody. No churchly weakling.

I associate those arguments with drifting potato pancake smoke. I made them potato pancakes often; it was one thing I could do better than Mrs. Dobisher. Though thank heaven we found Mrs. Dobisher. Potato pancakes were a great diversion. It did me good, all that spitting and hissing of the fat in the frying pan when I slapped in the grated raw potato mixture. But I didn't have my mother's generous hand with lard. These latter day pancakes were not the pancakes of my youth, her crisply golden-edged ones that made our lips shiny with fat, our tongues lively with hotness, for we couldn't wait for any cooling, we devoured the oniony salty discs tossed directly to our plates. In school lunch rooms I only nibbled, to keep secret the wolfing I did at home.

Meals cooked hot and neatly served. That was how the German embroidered motto translated, on the splash guard behind the sink. German sayings were all over the house, proclaiming *Gemütlichkeit.* On the cake plate: *Wohl bekomms!* On the pillow cases: *Behüt Dich Gott!* And over their conjugal bed, in thousands of cross-stitches forming garlands and ornate letters, a verse that wished my mother and father, after the day's laughter and tears, sweet roses in their dreams.

Ach, Mama. You with your sentimental heart. You should have had things nicer. Why did *you* never speak up in those kitchen arguments—why did you never say what *you* wanted? But I guess I know.

You were always sitting at the table in your cotton housecoat by then, combed and freshened for your next meal, your walker beside you. You had little to say anymore, debilitated by stroke. In six years, three strokes, and with each you surrendered more. You became like a good child, taking your medicines, eating your food, watching your television.

Who would have thought it? She, who had once had all that energy, that raucous good cheer that used to drive me crazy. For I was young and priggish then. I wanted her genteel. Nice and refined. Not tying on one of my father's bandana handkerchiefs, winding up the Victrola, going *tra-lee* and *tra-laa* with her lemon oil cloth among the Salvation Army furniture. And when she used to put on *The Blue Danube,* that would drive me craziest of all.

"Come once, *Muschi,* you must learn to waltz!" And she would grab me (protesting) and waltz me around and around the square dining room table.

"Mama, nobody dances like that here!"

For hadn't I been to the Grange Hall dances, where they *promenaded,* went *allemande left,* or went *ladies make a basket and gents take a bow?* Or shuffled a gritty two-step to *Red Sails in the Sunset?*

"*Ja,* you are right!" Bosom heaving she would let up finally, take the needle off, put the record back, close the lid down, replace the doily and the Japanese vase of strawflowers. "Here, what do they know?" With a shrug. In a voice full of regret. Full of conviction that in our homeland, a better system prevailed. There, when there was a dance, the girls went together and the boys went together, nobody languished home waiting for a date. Go, go, the edict was. Mix and mingle where eye meets eye, where two hearts soon beat in three-quarter time.

That was how she had met my father. Oh, often I heard about it.

"*Und* he was standing so by the door." She dramatized (plumply) my slender father's standing with arms crossed, shoulders leaned against the wall, on one foot, the other foot crossed over to rest elegantly on his boot toe. In his dashing World War I uniform. With his clipped little mustache.

"Pop was really good looking." I said that once, gazing at the tinted miniature of him in her gold locket. (When we dusted, we often paused like this, arrested by treasure.)

"I," she said, having come to stand and look with me, "was always satisfied."

Her passionate dream, I knew, was that her daughter have a romance as golden. My life must have its own Maytime, its singing and dancing, its love and laughter. And didn't something approaching that finally come about? Didn't Leland Lasher ask me to the Junior prom? Leland of the pansy eyes and brown wavy hair. Never mind that he moved as though constantly through ploughed furrows (even while dancing). And that he pronounced cows *ceows*. He looked quite splendid, standing just inside the woodshed door with his gardenia box, in his dark suit and gleaming white shirt. And there was that way he handed me into his father's flivver. Off we went, into the twilight and through the ruts. And she and my father waving from the porch—at that time we lived in a house with a porch you could stand on safely.

Ach, Mama. How can I bear to think of your sitting behind that cretonne curtain of Arbuckle's Department Store dressing cubicle, with me trying on all those formals? First the blue organdy, then the aqua with net overskirt, then another and another, till finally the rose-colored watered rayon taffeta, the most expensive, the one just right. How you sat on that stool so broadly, cushiony knees spread, emptying your pocketbook into your lap with abandon, counting out loud (exasperatingly bi-lingually): ". . . *zehn, elf, zwölf* . . . wait once . . . thirteen, fourteen . . . " Then counting the dimes from your dime bank on the flat of your hand, in mounting excitement, the tip of your nose red.

"We make it! We make it!" It was like the Valkyrie's battle cry, there behind the faded floral cretonne. The hovering white-haired sales lady, who had gone hippety-hop back and forth between us and the formals rack, peeked in. You reached to bestow your handfuls of money. "My daughter goes by the dance!" And should she not be sufficiently impressed, you added, "She sings by the Village Improvement Society a duet!"

Ach, Mama. No wonder I started to bawl there, leaned against the varnished plywood, my face distorted in the mirror. Over-wrought by my beautiful gown, you thought, rubbing at my tears with your scratchy crocheted lace handkerchief. But it wasn't the dress only, Mama. To that Village Improvement Society tea, where Elise Cunningham and I sang *The Prayer* from *Hansel and Gretel* so movingly; where Elise's mother, in her voile elegance, presided behind the tea tray so smilingly; where I learned what *petit fours* are—to that tea, Mama, you were invited, too. But I never said.

All your life, you were short-changed. Not given your due. You, without whom we would have gone under. My father was the head of our household. But you were the durable one who held it together. You were durable as work off your treadle sewing machine: sturdy, reinforced, guaranteed for good service.

What did she do when the temporary hired man failed to show, and my father looked bleakly uphill toward the cauliflower field? Cauliflower is like birth, it can't wait. The blue-banded cauliflowers were due that day, rain or shine—the cauliflowers that must be on the truck going down to the city at dawn. Off she went, in the cold drizzle, storming up the wagon track.

"Where are you going?" shouts my father. I see him, framed in the drafty barn doorway, trailing harness gear. He never had the right stance for a farmer. He looked too delicate, too clean, too shaved. He with his impractical dream of land and independence.

"Watch once!" Wind-torn comes her exuberant cry. She stands silhouetted against grayness, bandana fluttering, brandishing the machete knife with which she will behead the cauliflower. Were she brandishing a spear, carrying a shield, wearing an iron helmet with leathern chin strap, she could show herself no more Valkyrie-like. *Holla Ho!* Down go blue-banded cauliflowers!

And when the milking machine broke down? When we had to milk by hand till our fingers swelled? "*Schtripp, schtrapp, schtrull!*" she laughed, peering brown-eyed from around a cow's flank. Which cow? *Rosemunde, Hildegard, Waltraut, Gunekunde?* She gave them noble names—the more sway-backed, the more jagged-boned the cow, the more noble her name. "*Alte Kracke,*" she addressed that sort tenderly. Old rickety one. And threw down an extra scoop of grain.

Schtripp, schtrapp, schtrull! It was one of my nursery rhymes. She, with her apt sayings. Caught unawares, I forgot to be glum (glum because of my being permanently mad at the world). I collapsed against the calf pen in a fit of giggles. I threw her the rejoinder, in our homey Unterrissdorfer dialect: "*Is' der Emmer full?*" Is the pail full?

Then we went on like that, back and forth—she with her hoots of laughter, I with my snorts of giggles, my father with his tickled grin at the gameness of his women. Particularly *my* gameness—I, the apple of his eye, showing my smart inventiveness: "*Schtrull, schtrapp, schtripp!* Take a little sip!"

Orttrud, Sieglinde, Margarethe, Ulrike. All the company of noble sisters, made restless by our lantern-lit conviviality, tossed their heads in the stanchions, went *moooo* over their shoulders, crooked tassled tails and peed arcs into the gutters.

She saved us from drabness. Rescued us from deprivation. Poor we were, yes—it was The Depression (though we knew it only as bad times—*schlechte Zeiten*—we had known them already in Germany)—but she looked after us. Why should Sheffield's get all our cream? In the dank milk house she stood and skimmed, a little off each milk can standing in the vat. We needed cream—it was to whip for the wild strawberries. Or for the *Kirschkuchen*. It was to alleviate stress.

All these things being so, honor was due her. Honor, in life and in death. Not this instant whisking away, as *he* wanted. Not this quick obliteration, this erasure from the world.

"You're not being nice to your friends!" More than once I yelled that after his retreating back. (HISSSSSsssss, went the lard.) "When you don't have a service, you're shutting out your friends!"

He would come back to me then, stand behind me by the stove, put a hand on my shoulder and turn me around. "I have talked to our friends. How many are left? Those few, they understand me well. Some are even coming to my way of thinking: better to leave your money to your children than to one of them funeral fellows."

But you were no longer aware, Mama. You sat by the table in your housecoat. You paid no attention to his ridiculous chin-gesturing, toward a greedy world out there beyond the flocked curtains. A world of conniving hand-rubbing undertakers.

And anyway, you would have objected to nothing. Thinking it over, I come to that conclusion. For didn't you always say "yes" and "amen" to everything he wanted?

I, though, understood your secret heart's wish—and that was for a grave—for your daughter to weep by. A polished stone, for her to leave a bunch of violets by. A stone with your name: *MARIA MAGDALENA ACKERMANN*. With a verse. Something like: *And you know the way where I am going . . .* John 14:4.

I always thought there was still time to bring him around. Meanwhile, I made some plans. They had such nice neighbors there—the neighbors would want to come to her funeral. (Or his. Let's not forget, Pop, it could be *you* first!)

What to serve, afterward, at the house? *Rhubarberkuchen? Apfelkuchen?* Spring? Fall? The cakes we knew were seasonal. Which would be hers? Where would everyone sit? I mentally rearranged furniture. After all her years of living in those deplorable houses—once not even in a house at all, but over a sawmill—she finally had this cute little place, with yellow flower boxes and Adirondack chairs, made her by my father.

"Our Papa makes nice work." Lost in admiration, she used to stand back from a piece of his skilled carpentry and smile. She was right, his work was tops. Had he never deviated from his learned trade, we would have been better off. She never said that, though. Never criticized me much, either, except playfully. ("Such a face. Like forty days rain.") She, the heroic smoother of paths, of ruffled feathers, of rising hackles.

"Your Papa means it good," she used to placate me, coming to wherever I sulked, because he had dealt with me unjustly.

Sure, sure, he meant my good. And when he finally handed me those orange-covered undertaker's contracts, *they* were for my good. Everything all taken care of. Convenient instant disposal of my parents, no muss no fuss. *I, Friedrich Ackermann, herewith pay the sum of* . . . the legal lines swam together in my tears. What could I say? What good to say anything anymore?

"Only a box," he explained, his Adam's apple working. "I told the funeral fellow, no fancy coffins, a plain box does the trick."

I guess he felt pushed, Mama, by your being in the hospital again—not with stroke that time, but with things in general. Stomach, kidneys. In the name of preparedness, I guess, he screwed up his courage to go see the funeral fellow.

But once more you rallied, Mama. Once more back home, to the care of Mrs. Dobisher, who never missed a day of employment while you were gone. She cleaned out all the cupboards. Straightened the drawers. Organized the closets. "A hard worker," said my father in approval. I was jealous for you, Mama. You with your starched curtains, your embroideries, your knittings and crochetings—your screens of *Gemütlichkeit* over behind-the-scenes disasters. Didn't I know how each drawer held something of everything? A few hairpins, a few corset garters, a few greeting cards too pretty to throw out, a few rolled socks? I, the prissy one, used to be appalled. But I'm loyal, Mama, grant me that.

Praise God, however, for Mrs. Dobisher. For when you and Pop were no longer able to manage by yourselves, were we not at our wits' end? What next? The nursing home? Round and round Pop went that time, in indecision. Round and round our house—he was with us for Thanksgiving. I watched him from all the windows as he walked against the wind, plaid hat with the little feather pressed low on his forehead, overcoat collar up, leather-gloved hands swinging. The German gentleman. In his middle years he had finally come upon prosperity—had given up his dream and joined the union. Said goodbye to his vision of acres and stock.

Now you were both on Social Security. You my parents, in golden age. But who would have thought it would be like this?

Does someone really look after us? Who sent Mrs. Dobisher to my father's door? God? Mrs. Dobisher, the answer to desperation (my father's). Mrs. Dobisher, the answer to prayer (mine). Sent to us by God to do saintly work. For a great deal of money.

"Mother has a sore under her left breast."

She liked greeting me with efficient reports whenever I went there. She stood before my mother with hands raised, as though about to conduct her like a symphony. I couldn't bear it, her fingers lifting my mother's sagged flesh. But my mother only sat, letting everything occur. On the bed's edge, in the sunny room where the cross stitches of the wall hanging had faded, had grown pale, were no more than whispers now, in their promising of roses.

I somehow hoped it would just go on and on, with Mrs. Dobisher the capable, my father the resigned, me the breathless coming with concern and casseroles. With me sitting knee to knee with her, leaning to talk up into her face, to tease a smile from her. Her hands were silken soft. Her hands that used to be so chapped and rough. "*Verdammt!*" she used to curse, by lamplight, the crocheting thread sticking to her fingers.

When he called to say she was hospitalized again, I wasn't too alarmed. This, now, was a year ago. In the time of violets. In and out the hospital, that was her pattern. Her stomach again. Kidneys. Fluid. Pain. The usual. I had just been to their house, for her birthday, the eighty-second. Had taken another housecoat. What else to buy her? I had baked her *Flaumkuchen*—thawed plums from the freezer to bake her favorite cake. With whipped cream.

"Don't give her any," my father said. "She'll get sick again."

"A little won't hurt."

Hadn't she always told me that? Fat, despondent, filled with self loathing? Have a little cake. A little won't hurt.

At the hospital, that Sunday, we stood around her bed, tweaked her toes, asked, "How are you feeling?" When we were leaving, I leaned to kiss her cheek, which was soft as old damask. "You haven't said anything, Mama. You *can* talk, can't you?"

She looked at me brown-eyed—gave me a long, studying look. Her pupils had a milky edge. "Sure," she said.

Her last word to me. When I went again, I thought they had moved her to another room.

"Where is my mother?"

"Right there, honey, that's mother over by the window, still in the same place."

They had taken out her teeth. A round snoring mouth. Another stroke. Tubes and bottles.

Every day I went to see her. In little shot glasses brought her violets, so their enchanting scent would waken her, recall her to springtime. Every day I thought, this is the last time, but the following day she still breathed, deeply, evenly, her good heart steadfast. Every day I told her things. "Remember how in Unterrissdorf you used to sit me on the window sill, so I could look down to watch the sheep flock passing? All those gray woolly sheep backs, moving like a river? Like a cloud path in the sky?"

"Talk to her," I said to my father. He looked so little all of a sudden. Diminished. "You can't tell. She might be hearing us."

"Maria!" he shouted into her ear. "Maria, can you hear me?" As though calling her to get his breakfast.

"She hears nothing," he said.

"You can't tell for sure."

"She hears nothing."

I turned my back. Spoke only to her. "When you get better," I said, "I'll be so glad I'll jump ceiling-high." It was a nonsensical thing she used to say to me when I was sick. When she used to bed me down on couches by warm stoves. Or come in the night, in the frayed bathrobe that didn't meet in front. "Ach, Muschi, only get well. I will jump ceiling-high."

Under her covers I laid my hands on her belly. Now her fat was gone, that had made her so miserable. She believed women were either fat or lean by nature. She kept track of how much cake the Kaffeeklatsch ladies ate. All more than she. From the catalogs she kept ordering corsets, which promised, per smiling models standing with full thighs, slenderizing effects through lacings, panels, inner belts, gussets, boning. Dressed up, she chafed in her corset and got headaches. "Why me?" she sometimes wept. "You're not so bad," I said, moved to pity despite my glum aloofness. A little cake I would bring her. A little wouldn't hurt.

To remember her face now, I had to lay my hand over her mouth and chin—look at only the upper half. But even her nice nose was changing. Only the bone structure of her forehead was the same. Sparse white hairs showed where her hairline had once dipped, like a heart. Old pictures in her album showed flirtatious curls. Did my father remember her dark full hair? He only sat, over in the corner, looking gray. Did he remember waltzing with her? Did he remember yesterday?

"Shall I sing?" I asked her, when he wasn't there. I pulled the white curtain around us. *Softly, Oh softly, steal through the room; lilting Oh lovely, magical tune . . .*

"What I don't like," he said, pacing, "is all these bottles keeping her going."

And there was her doctor. Dr. Hans Roth, the German doctor. I knew his kind. In Germany, his kind came to the house all in leather. On a motorcycle with a side car. Took home potatoes and wurst from grovelling families. "The patient is not responding," he said, coming on the line finally, if I outwaited him. The patient, the patient. The patient has a name, you pompous ass. You Nazi. Only your Jewishness saved you. Had you not been Jewish, you would have been a top-notch Nazi.

"Your mother has slipped away." At least he didn't call her *the patient* that last time. The line crackled with silence. Oh, answer my dozens of questions crowding in my throat, Doctor. Was she all alone? Did she perhaps open her eyes one more time? Say a word? Call a name? Lie to me, Dr. Hans. Say something kind. Quote me a line from Goethe. You educated fish.

Ach, Mama. Now it was set in motion, that orange-covered plan. Now the funeral fellow came for you, in whatever subterranean cold dark room they had wheeled you to. Now you were bundled into a sack with tapes for tying your ankles and wrists—I know that, my friend Thelma's husband sells hospital supplies. I, Mama, I should have come for you. Carried you out in my arms, you were so light. *I* should have taken you to the funeral parlor. *Here she is, I have brought you my mother.*

The funeral parlor was not so bad, Mama. I knew you liked it there—those chandeliers. That big wide room. What a place for a dance. All those rows of chairs, they could be put around the edge against the walls. For the girls to sit on one side and the boys on the other. When the music strikes up, when the waltz begins, the boys will come over like a wave. Eye to meet eye.

"I put the little arrangement on the casket," says the funeral fellow. *Ach*, Mama, he was so unctious. Like Digger O'Dell from the Fibber McGee and Molly Show. Could you hear, there in your gray pressed wood casket, which was strictly *Povertyville*? I would have been glad to bring flowers, Mama. But I didn't want to make extra bother for Digger. Already he was doing extra, letting me have this private viewing. Nothing like this was in the contract.

"I just want to stand here a moment alone, thank you." But he doesn't leave. I hear him breathing behind me. Does he think I will throw myself on the plastic flowers? That I will claw the casket open in grief? But you wouldn't have minded the plastic flowers, Mama. You who put fake pointsettias in your glass swan every Christmas. Who kept plastic flamingos on the lawn.

In my Father's house are many rooms. I told it all to you under my breath, in German. As you learned it for your confirmation when you were fourteen. In your first black dress. When your life first became earnest.

And I did give you a funeral, Mama. When I scattered your ashes. I didn't even tell Pop I was going to do that. He, who wanted no funeral no nothing. I purposely chose the day when I knew somebody had invited him to go somewhere. That day I scattered your ashes from your house to our house. Didn't you always choose a jolly Christmas card with that sentiment? *From our house to your house.* I thought of all the holidays you came to spend with us, you and Pop, tootling along Route 7 in your red Volkswagen. And here went your remains over that same route. Your "cremains," as Digger had unctiously said, when he handed me the reddish-brown cannister.

From the car window I let a little of your ash fall from my fingers where it would come to rest in wayside flowers. I flung some where the shad had bloomed like bridal veils all those weeks I drove back and forth to the hospital. All those many days, but you never opened your eyes again.

Yet nothing like that mattered now. Only that the air was sweet from a spring shower—and that there was suddenly a rainbow! For your funeral, Mama! It was like the gate of heaven had opened up. I, your daughter, was driving you towards heaven's gate in the Oldsmobile, before a gravel truck, behind a yellow Schuler's potato chip truck. Your cannister was wedged by my side against the car door. Your ash was grainy, all little particles, like ground-up bone. It didn't repel me, which made me glad. Bone of your bone. I let a little of your ash fly from a bridge, so it would float down the valley in the creek. I let some be borne off by the air in every fresh-scented village.

Until I arrived here, Mama, by my house. I scattered some by that white lilac bush, because all your life you loved lilacs passionately. White lilacs were your wedding bouquet.

Forgive my husband for not coming to your funeral. A word, and he would have left his bank and come—you know that. But I told him I had to do this alone. And forgive Midgie, your darling granddaughter. A word, and she would have left her studies in Chicago, flown home for the funeral of her Oma, whose namesake she is. Mary Magdalene, my Midgie. And I, your *Muschi*.

I, in my black dress, Mama, giving you a funeral.

Where the violets are bluest, there where the white bench is that my father made, I turned the cannister up-side-down. It's almost a year ago. The last of you fell into the grass with a little puff, like a sigh, like a coming to rest. When I sit on the bench these days, something comes up through my soles—I don't know what, but something. Perhaps you even prefer my bench to a stone? "Our Papa makes nice work." I hear you say that. Perhaps by moonlight your spirit stands here, head to the side, and smiles.

Meridel LeSueur

ANNUNCIATION

For Rachel

Ever since I have known I was going to have a child I have kept writing things down on these little scraps of paper. There is something I want to say, something I want to make clear for myself and others. One lives all one's life in a sort of way, one is alive and that is about all that there is to say about it. Then something happens.

There is the pear tree I can see in the afternoons as I sit on this porch writing these notes. It stands for something. It has had something to do with what has happened to me. I sit here all afternoon in the autumn sun and then I begin to write something on this yellow paper; something seems to be going on like a buzzing, a flying and circling within me, and then I want to write it down in some way. I have never felt this way before, except when I was a girl and was first in love and wanted then to set things down on paper so that they would not be lost. It is something perhaps like a farmer who hears the swarming of a host of bees and goes out to catch them so that he will have honey. If he does not go out right away, they will go, and he will hear the buzzing growing more distant in the afternoon.

My sweater pocket is full of scraps of paper on which I have written. I sit here many afternoons while Karl is out looking for work, writing on pieces of paper, unfolding, reading what I have already written.

We have been here two weeks at Mrs. Mason's boarding house. The leaves are falling and there is a golden haze over everything. This is the fourth month for me and it is fall. A rich powerful haze comes down from the mountains over the city. In the afternoon I go out for a walk. There is a park just two blocks from here. Old men and tramps lie on the grass all day. It is hard to get work. Many people beside Karl are out of work. People are hungry just as I am hungry. People are ready to flower and they cannot. In the evenings we go there with a sack of old fruit we can get at the stand across the way quite cheap, bunches of grapes and old pears. At noon there is a hush in the air and at evening there are stirrings of wind coming from the sky, blowing in the fallen leaves, or perhaps there is a light rain, falling quickly on the walk. Early in the mornings the sun comes up hot in the sky and shines all day through the mist. It is strange, I notice all these things, the sun, the rain falling, the blowing of the wind. It is as if they had a meaning for me as the pear tree has come to have.

In front of Mrs. Mason's house there is a large magnolia tree with its blossoms yellow, hanging over the steps almost within reach. Its giant leaves are motionless and shining in the heat, occasionally as I am going down the steps towards the park one falls heavily on the walk.

This house is an old wooden one, that once was quite a mansion I imagine. There are glass chandeliers in the hall and fancy tile in the bathrooms. It was owned by the rich once and now the dispossessed live in it with the rats. We have a room three flights up. You go into the dark hallway and up the stairs. Broken settees and couches sit in the halls. About one o'clock the girls come downstairs to get their mail and sit on the front porch. The blinds go up in the old wooden house across the street. It is always quite hot at noon.

Next to our room lies a sick woman in what is really a kind of closet with no windows. As you pass you see her face on the pillow and a nauseating odor of sickness comes out the door. I haven't asked her what is the matter with her but everyone knows she is waiting for death. Somehow it is not easy to speak to her. No one comes to see her. She has been a housemaid all her life tending other people's children; now no one comes to see her. She gets up sometimes and drinks a little from the bottle of milk that is always sitting by her bed covered with flies.

Mrs. Mason, the landlady, is letting us stay although we have only paid a week's rent and have been here over a week without paying. But it is a bad season and we may be able to pay later. It is better perhaps for her than having an empty room. But I hate to go out and have to pass her door and I am always fearful of meeting her on the stairs. I go down as quietly as I can but it isn't easy, for the stairs creak frightfully.

The room we have on the top floor is a back room, opening out onto an old porch which seems to be actually tied to the wall of the house with bits of wire and rope. The floor of it slants downward to a rickety railing. There is a box perched on the railing that has geraniums in it. They are large, tough California geraniums. I guess nothing can kill them. I water them since I have been here and a terribly red flower has come. It is on this porch I am sitting. Just over the banisters stand the top branches of a pear tree.

Many afternoons I sit here. It has become a kind of alive place to me. The room is dark behind me, with only the huge walnut tree scraping against the one window over the kitchenette. If I go to the railing and look down I can see far below the back yard which has been made into a garden with two fruit trees and I can see where a path has gone in the summer between a small bed of flowers, now only dead stalks. The ground is bare under the walnut tree where little sun penetrates. There is a dog kennel by the round trunk but there doesn't ever seem to be a dog. An old wicker chair sits outdoors in rain or shine. A woman in an old wrapper comes out and sits there almost every afternoon. I don't know who she is, for I don't know anybody in this house, having to sneak downstairs as I do.

Karl says I am foolish to be afraid of the landlady. He comes home drunk and makes a lot of noise. He says she's lucky in these times to have anybody in her house, but I notice in the mornings he goes down the stairs quietly and often goes out the back way.

I'm alone all day so I sit on this rickety porch. Straight out from the rail so that I can almost touch it is the radiating frail top of the pear tree that has opened a door for me. If the pears were still hanging on it each would be alone and separate with a kind of bloom upon it. Such a bloom is upon me at this moment. Is it possible that everyone, Mrs. Mason who runs this boarding house, the woman next door, the girls downstairs, all in this dead wooden house have hung at one time, each separate in a mist and bloom upon some invisible tree? I wonder if it is so.

I am in luck to have this high porch to sit on and this tree swaying before me through the long afternoons and the long nights. Before we came here, after the show broke up in S. F. we were in an old hotel, a foul-smelling place with a dirty chambermaid and an old cat in the halls, and night and day we could hear the radio going in the office. We had a room with a window looking across a narrow way into another room where a lean man stood in the mornings looking across, shaving his evil face. By leaning out and looking up I could see straight up the sides of the tall building and above the smoky sky.

Most of the time I was sick from the bad food we ate. Karl and I walked the streets looking for work. Sometimes I was too sick to go. Karl would come in and there would be no money at all. He would go out again to perhaps borrow something. I know many times he begged although we never spoke of it, but I could tell by the way he looked when he came back with a begged quarter. He went in with a man selling Mexican beans but he didn't make much. I lay on the bed bad days feeling sick and hungry, sick too with the stale odor of the foul walls. I would lie there a long time listening to the clang of the city outside. I would feel thick with this child. For some reason I remember that I would sing to myself and often become happy as if mesmerized there in the foul room. It must have been because of this child. Karl would come back perhaps with a little money and we would go out to a dairy lunch and there have food I could not relish. The first alleyway I must give it up with the people all looking at me.

Karl would be angry. He would walk on down the street so people wouldn't think he was with me. Once we walked until evening down by the docks. "Why don't you take something?" he kept saying. "Then you wouldn't throw up your food like that. Get rid of it. That's what everybody does nowdays. This isn't the time to have a child. Everything is rotten. We must change it." He kept on saying, "Get rid of it. Take something why don't you?" And he got angry when I didn't say anything but just walked along beside him. He shouted so loud at me that some stevedores loading a boat for L. A. laughed at us and began kidding us, thinking perhaps we were lovers having a quarrel.

Some time later, I don't know how long it was, for I hadn't any time except the nine months I was counting off, but one evening Karl sold enough Mexican jumping beans at a carnival to pay our fare, so we got on a river boat and went up the river to a delta town. There might be a better chance of a job. On this boat you can sit up all night if you have no money to buy a berth. We walked all evening along the deck and then when it got cold we went into the saloon because we had pawned our coats. Already at that time I had got the habit of carrying slips of paper around with me and writing on them, as I am doing now. I had a feeling then that something was happening to me of some kind of loveliness I would want to preserve in some way. Perhaps that was it. At any rate I was writing things down. Perhaps it had something to do with Karl wanting me all the time to take something. "Everybody does it," he kept telling me. "It's nothing, then it's all over." I stopped talking to him much. Everything I said only made him angry. So writing was a kind of conversation I carried on with myself and with the child.

Well, on the river boat that night after we had gone into the saloon to get out of the cold, Karl went to sleep right away in a chair. But I couldn't sleep. I sat watching him. The only sound was the churning of the paddle wheel and the lap of the water. I had on then this sweater and the notes I wrote are still in the breast pocket. I would look up from writing and see Karl sleeping like a young boy.

"Tonight, the world into which you are coming"—then I was speaking to the invisible child—"is very strange and beautiful. That is, the natural world is beautiful. I don't know what you will think of man, but the dark glisten of vegetation and the blowing of the fertile land wind and the delicate strong step of the sea wind, these things are familiar to me and will be familiar to you. I hope you will be like these things. I hope you will glisten with the glisten of ancient life, the same beauty that is in a leaf or a wild rabbit, wild sweet beauty of limb and eye. I am going on a boat between dark shores, and the river and the sky are so quiet that I can hear the scurryings of tiny animals on the shores and their little breathings seem to be all around. I think of them, wild, carrying their young now, crouched in the dark underbrush with the fruit-scented land wind in their delicate nostrils, and they are looking out at the moon and the fast clouds. Silent, alive, they sit in the dark shadow of the greedy world. There is something wild about us too, something tender and wild about my having you as a child, about your crouching so secretly here. There is something very tender and wild about it. We, too, are at the mercy of many hunters. On this boat I act like the other human beings, for I do not show that I have you, but really I know we are as helpless, as wild, as some tender wild animals who might be on the ship.

"I put my hand where you lie so silently. I hope you will come glistening with life power, with it shining upon you as upon the feathers of birds. I hope you will be a warrior and fierce for change, so all can live."

Karl woke at dawn and was angry with me for sitting there looking at him. Just to look at me makes him angry now. He took me out and made me walk along the deck although it was hardly light yet. I gave him the "willies" he said, looking at him like that. We walked round and round the decks and he kept talking to me in a low voice, trying to persuade me. It was hard for me to listen. My teeth were chattering with cold, but anyway I found it hard to listen to anyone talking, especially Karl. I remember I kept thinking to myself that a child should be made by machinery now, then there would be no fuss. I kept thinking of all the places I had been with this new child, traveling with the show from Tia Juana to S. F. In trains, over mountains, through deserts, in hotels and rooming houses, and myself in a trance of wonder. There wasn't a person I could have told it to, that I was going to have a child. I didn't want to be pitied. Night after night we played in the tent and the faces were all dust to me, but traveling, through the window the many vistas of the earth meant something—the bony skeleton of the mountains, like the skeleton of the world jutting through its flowery flesh. My child too would be made of bone. There were the fields of summer, the orchards fruiting, the berry fields and the pickers stooping, the oranges and the grapes. Then the city again in September and the many streets I walk looking for work, stopping secretly in doorways to feel beneath my coat.

It is better in this small town with the windy fall days and the sudden rain falling out of a sunny sky. I can't look for work anymore. Karl gets a little work washing dishes at a wienie place. I sit here on the porch as if in a deep sleep waiting for this unknown child. I keep hearing this far flight of strange birds going on in the mysterious air about me. This time has come without warning. How can it be explained? Everything is dead and closed, the world a stone, and then suddenly everything comes alive as it has for me, like an anemone on a rock, opening itself, disclosing itself, and the very stones themselves break open like bread. It has all got something to do with the pear tree too. It has come about some way as I have sat here with this child so many afternoons, with the pear tree murmuring in the air.

The pears are all gone from the tree but I imagine them hanging there, ripe curves within the many scimitar leaves, and within them many pears of the coming season. I feel like a pear. I hang secret within the curling leaves, just as the pear would be hanging on its tree. It seems possible to me that perhaps all people at some time feel this, round and full. You can tell by looking at most people that the world remains a stone to them and a closed door. I'm afraid it will become like that to me again. Perhaps after this child is born, then everything will harden and become small and mean again as it was before. Perhaps I would even have a hard time remembering this time at all and it wouldn't seem wonderful. That is why I would like to write it down.

How can it be explained? Suddenly many movements are going on within me, many things are happening, there is an almost unbearable sense of sprouting, of bursting encasements, of moving kernels, expanding flesh. Perhaps it is such an activity that makes a field come alive with millions of sprouting shoots of corn or wheat. Perhaps it is something like that that makes a new world.

I have been sitting here and it seems as if the wooden houses around me had become husks that suddenly as I watched began to swarm with livening seed. The house across becomes a fermenting seed alive with its own movements. Everything seems to be moving along a curve of creation. The alley below and all the houses are to me like an orchard abloom, shaking and trembling, moving outward with shouting. The people coming and going seem to hang on the tree of life, each blossoming from himself. I am standing here looking at the blind windows of the house next door and suddenly the walls fall away, the doors open, and within I see a young girl making a bed from which she had just risen having dreamed of a young man who became her lover . . . she stands before her looking glass in love with herself.

I see in another room a young man sleeping, his bare arm thrown over his head. I see a woman lying on a bed after her husband has left her. There is a child looking at me. An old woman sits rocking. A boy leans over a table reading a book. A woman who has been nursing a child comes out and hangs clothes on the line, her dress in front wet with milk. A young woman comes to an open door looking up and down the street waiting for her young husband. I get up early to see this young woman come to the door in a pink wrapper and wave to her husband. They have only been married a short time, she stands waving until he is out of sight and even then she stands smiling to herself, her hand upraised.

Why should I be excited? Why should I feel this excitement, seeing a woman waving to her young husband, or a woman who has been nursing a child, or a young man sleeping? Yet I am excited. The many houses have become like an orchard blooming soundlessly. The many people have become like fruits to me, the young girl in the room alone before her mirror, the young man sleeping, the mother, all are shaking with their inward blossoming, shaken by the windy blooming, moving along a future curve.

I do not want it all to go away from me. Now many doors are opening and shutting, light is falling upon darkness, closed places are opening, still things are now moving. But there will come a time when the doors will close again, the shouting will be gone, the sprouting and the movement and the wondrous opening out of everything will be gone. I will be only myself. I will come to look like the women in this house. I try to write it down on little slips of paper, trying to preserve this time for myself so that afterwards when everything is the same again I can remember what it all must have been like.

This is the spring there should be in the world, so I say to myself, "Lie in the sun with the child in your flesh shining like a jewel. Dream and sing, pagan, wise in your vitals. Stand still like a fat budding tree, like a stalk of corn athrob and aglisten in the heat. Lie like a mare panting with the dancing feet of colts against her sides. Sleep at night as the spring earth. Walk heavily as a wheat stalk at its full time bending towards the earth waiting for the reaper. Let your life swell downward so you become like a vase, a vessel. Let the unknown child knock and knock against you and rise like a dolphin within."

212

I look at myself in the mirror. My legs and head hardly make a difference, just a stem my legs. My hips are full and tight in back as if bracing themselves. I look like a pale and shining pomegranate, hard and tight, and my skin shines like crystal with the veins showing beneath blue and distended. Children are playing outside and girls are walking with young men along the walk. All that seems over for me. I am a pomegranate hanging from an invisible tree with the juice and movement of seed within my hard skin. I dress slowly. I hate the smell of clothes. I want to leave them off and just hang in the sun ripening . . . ripening.

It is hard to write it down so that it will mean anything. I've never heard anything about how a woman feels who is going to have a child, or about how a pear tree feels bearing its fruit. I would like to read these things many years from now, when I am barren and no longer trembling like this, when I get like the women in this house, or like the woman in the closed room, I can hear her breathing through the afternoon.

When Karl has no money he does not come back at night. I go out on the street walking to forget how hungry I am. This is an old town and along the streets are many old strong trees. Night leaves hang from them ready to fall, dark and swollen with their coming death. Trees, dark, separate, heavy with their coming death. Trees, dark, separate, heavy with their down hanging leaves, cool surfaces hanging on the dark. I put my hand among the leaf sheaves. They strike with a cool surface, their glossy surfaces surprising me in the dark. I feel like a tree swirling upwards too, muscular sap alive, with rich surfaces hanging from me, flaring outward rocket-like and falling to my roots, a rich strong power in me to break through into a new life. And dark in me as I walk the streets of this decayed town are the buds of my child. I walk alone under the dark flaring trees. There are many houses with the lights shining out but you and I walk on the skirts of the lawns amidst the down pouring darkness. Houses are not for us. For us many kinds of hunger, for us a deep rebellion.

Trees come from a far seed walking the wind, my child too from a far seed blowing from last year's rich and revolutionary dead. My child budding secretly from far walking seed, budding secretly and dangerously in the night.

The woman has come out and sits in the rocker, reading, her fat legs crossed. She scratches herself, cleans her nails, picks her teeth. Across the alley lying flat on the ground is a garage. People are driving in and out. But up here it is very quiet and the movement of the pear tree is the only movement and I seem to hear its delicate sound of living as it moves upon itself silently, and outward and upward.

The leaves twirl and twirl all over the tree, the delicately curving tinkling leaves. They twirl and twirl on the tree and the tree moves far inward upon its stem, moves in an invisible wind, gently swaying. Far below straight down the vertical stem like a steam, black and strong into the ground, runs the trunk; and invisible, spiraling downward and outwards in powerful radiation, lie the roots. I can see it spiraling upwards from below, its stem straight, and from it, spiraling the branches season by season, and from the spiraling branches moving out in quick motion, the forked stems, and from the stems twirling fragilely the tinier stems holding outward until they fall, the half curled pear leaves.

Far below lies the yard, lying flat and black beneath the body of the upshooting tree, for the pear tree from above looks as if it had been shot instantaneously from the ground, shot upward like a rocket to break in showers of leaves and fruits twirling and falling. Its movement looks quick, sudden and rocketing. My child when grown can be looked at in this way as if it suddenly existed . . . but I know the slow time of making. The pear tree knows.

Far inside the vertical stem there must be a movement, a river of sap rising from below and radiating outward in many directions clear to the tips of the leaves. The leaves are the lips of the tree speaking in the wind or they move like many tongues. The fruit of the tree you can see has been a round speech, speaking in full tongue on the tree, hanging in ripe body, the fat curves hung within the small curves of the leaves. I imagine them there. The tree has shot up like a rocket, then stops in mid air and its leaves flow out gently and its fruit curves roundly and gently in a long slow curve. All is gentle on the pear tree after its strong upward shooting movement.

I sit here all the afternoon as if in its branches, midst the gentle and curving body of the tree. I have looked at it until it has become more familiar to me than Karl. It seems a strange thing that a tree might come to mean more to one than one's husband. It seems a shameful thing even. I am ashamed to think of it but it is so. I have sat here in the pale sun and the tree has spoken to me with its many tongued leaves, speaking through the afternoon of how to round a fruit. And I listen through the slow hours. I listen to the whisperings of the pear tree, speaking to me, speaking to me. How can I describe what is said by a pear tree? Karl did not speak to me so. No one spoke to me in any good speech.

There is a woman coming up the stairs, slowly. I can hear her breathing. I can hear her behind me at the screen door.

She came out and spoke to me. I know why she was looking at me so closely. "I hear you're going to have a child," she said. "It's too bad." She is the same color as the dead leaves in the park. Was she once alive too?

I am writing on a piece of wrapping paper now. It is about ten o'clock. Karl didn't come home and I had no supper. I walked through the streets with their heavy, heavy trees bending over the walks and the lights shining from the houses and over the river the mist rising.

Before I came into this room I went out and saw the pear tree standing motionless, its leaves curled in the dark, its radiating body falling darkly, like a stream far below into the earth.

Sharon Hashimoto

Sharon Hashimoto is a Seattle native who has comfortably settled down in a house with Emmett, her Labrador retriever. A graduate of the University of Washington with B.A. degrees in History and Journalism, she began writing short stories in high school, long before enrolling in Nelson Bentley's workshops and concentrating on poetry. Her works have appeared in Echoes From Gold Mountain, the International Examiner, Poetry Seattle, the Seattle Review, *the anthology* GATHERING GROUND *published by Seal Press, and others.*

THE LAST INARI AND MAKIZUSHI STAND

The steam from the boiling pot of rice rose in wide, spiraling circles and seemed to blend the droning voices of the television in with the smells of vinegar and sugar throughout the tiny apartment and out the open window. Crammed into the one room were potted plants and hand-crocheted afghans with lacy time-aged designs that hid the bare arms of the sofa and chairs. And on the dull, scratched buffet was a simple flower arrangement and a picture of him.

Across from the bed, in her miniature kitchen, the old woman with the face like crinkled rice paper smiled to herself, her hands busy chopping takenoko into tiny thin strips. She was a small spare woman with hands that could do amazing things with rice and egg and mushroom. Simple magical things for the people she cared for to be stirred, chopped, whipped, wrapped, peeled, salted and shook into a thousand spells.

Inari.

Makizushi

The words were celebrations upon the tongue. It was rice rinsed clean in cool clear water and seasoned through with the richness of custom and tradition. It was the vinegary smell that tickled one's nose and the familiar taste of gatherings on special occasions. It was the Japan of her childhood and of him and her and the family gathered together under one roof. It was something she had made, with her own two hands, that she could pass on to her children and her children's children that smelled and felt and tasted of who and what she was.

She thought back to all the times when tiny smooth brown faces had stood eye-level beside another table, in another time, their dark eyes opened wide with curiosity at all the exotic ingredients spread out before them.

"Shall I stir the rice now, Mama?"

"Is it too early to put in the mushrooms?"

And they would watch, seeming to be fascinated as she murmured her incantations and mixed carrots with mushrooms and kamaboko in with vinegar and sugar-sweetened rice. Deftly, she would stuff the slit age, her hands turning deep shades of flushed red from the heat, until the plate was covered over with little mounds of tannish brown.

I-na-ri. They would pronounce it slow and carefully and laugh to themselves, and she would join them, her brown face seamed and wrinkled like the stuffed age on the plate before her. And she would place one inari in each child's hand and they would bite deep into the rice and smile, perhaps thinking it tasted exactly the way that Mama smiled.

Makizushi . . . inari . . . the syllables flowed over the tongue and bloomed like a flower upon one's palate. She whispered the words softly to herself over and over again, like a smile, like the sun shining through on a wet rainy day.

The dull thud of the knife against the wooden board seemed to echo the words. It seemed to her that she lived in the kitchen, where the aromas changed with each season. There was the scent of ozoni that meant winter and New Year's Day and chilled somen on hot summer days to cool the flesh. But inari and makizushi was for always; for Sunday dinners, birthdays and picnics. She shifted her weight from her right foot to her left foot to her right again, then crossed the room to check on the rice cooking on the stove. The weather forecaster on the television was predicting another rainy April day.

The phone rang six times before she was able to clean her hands enough to answer it. Her daughter's voice spoke to her from far away.

"Mama, what time is everyone supposed to be at your place?"

"Five, five-thirty. Who's coming with you?"

"Susan, Patty. Maybe Paulie."

"Why 'maybe Paulie'?"

"Oh Mama, we can't make him come."

"Why?"

"Mama . . . "

"Ask him nicely. Please. Tell him it would make Grandma happy. Grandpa too."

"Alright Mama. I'll ask him again."

"Good. Come by five-thirty?"

"Yes, Mama."

By 11 o'clock she had finished with the inari and started the more complicated preparations for the makizushi. Outside, the cloudburst was beating against the building and staining the carpet by the window. It would be another colorless day with the clouds hanging low and threatening, as always, to pour more rain upon the grey trees and grey mud and the grey sidewalks. When she had first arrived in Seattle, she couldn't imagine all the rain that fell from the sky. It was like the constant drip of a faucet, leaking noisily, miserably day in and day out, washing the air that never seemed to be clean enough. New beginnings, he had told her when he had first breathed deep in that air. Here, we can start again. And again, and again, and again, she had felt like telling him. But she had said nothing.

He had worked hard in the broken down hotel near the waterfront, painting, mending, and dealing with the troublemakers that wandered in and out, but he had never complained, never told her his problems. But she could always tell, from the way he slumped in his chair, or in the slow stumbling pace he used when he was tired or frustrated. Often he returned home in his damp raincoat with a frown that was always one line deeper than before.

"Smile," she had once told him, "or you'll look like a wrinkled raisin before you're fifty."

He had looked at her then with tired, drooping eyes. "I have little to smile for."

The skillet hissed as the three eggs, beaten slightly with chopsticks, covered the bottom of the skillet. Carefully, she fried both sides, flipped it out to cool, and checked the kampyo bubbling on the rear burner. The pink powdered shrimp stood ready in a bowl beside the spinach and canned eel.

The makizushi rolled easier each time she did it until it had become a reflex action. She spread the prepared rice one half inch thick upon the heated nori on the bamboo mat and arranged the various ingredients in the center, being careful that they were placed evenly in a line. She rolled away from herself, lifted the mat when the bamboo touched the rice and continued the motion until a perfect cylinder was completed.

As she washed the dishes, she looked out the window towards the roads that ran in a straight line that merged and blended with other roads and streets until the city was patchwork quilted with little squares of houses and buildings. Water-wrinkled hands scrubbed hard over the worn pan. The handle was loose and wobbled as she rinsed it. Outside, it was dark with tiny pinpoints of light mingled in with harsh, glary street lights, three to one block. A grey, dappled moon hung in the east beside a telephone pole, reminding her of the color of warm rice wine sipped greedily on cold winter nights.

One rainy evening, with the children tucked in bed, they had sat in the kitchen, him with a bottle of sake before him, watching her polish the dainty teapot brought over from Japan.

"You dream too much of the old country," he had told her. "Things have changed."

"I miss my family and friends in Japan."

"They are not the same . . . "

"Okasan will be walking beside the lake, gathering flowers for ikebana . . . "

"We cannot visit them as planned." He took a long draught from his cup. "We have no money. It has all gone to the hotel."

"Perhaps we can ask the bank for another loan."

He had shook his head. He had been very quiet for a long time, studying the birds painted like m's on his teacup. "We cannot go back."

She had missed the rolling hills of Japan and the blue-green of the water and the soft grey-green of pussy willows growing in the marshes. Seattle was green, she reminded herself, but in a different way—like a watercolor painting left out in the rain where the colors smeared and ran together. It seemed to her now that the city had always been crying.

"Mama," her son had once asked during dinner. "Why did we leave Yakima?"

And he had answered too quickly. "Mama was sick. The doctors said she needed to be in the city where the hospitals are." But that had not been the reason.

220

Carefully, she cut the slender black rolls into three-quarter inch thicknesses and arranged them on her good china. She stooped over the plate and bent her knees slightly because her back was stiff. She rinsed her hands then and stretched slowly, reaching out towards the ceiling, and walked, still stretching, towards the open window. The rain splashed noisily against the sill and sprinkled her face and arms with tiny beads of silver. She shuddered once but stood beside the window and watched the cars and trucks splash through puddles.

From the hospital room, she had looked out onto the rain-drenched streets. He had stood beside her, beaming over his youngest daughter. She was a happy, gurgling baby, with a head full of thick, black hair and brown eyes that watched her father's face. Okasan, she had thought, you're a grandma again. But her mother was many miles and many years gone by. She had looked into the baby's face and slowly it had dawned on her that she would never see Japan again.

She had passed through dark moods that separated her from her family. It seemed that she watched them from behind a curtain of greying mist like the fogs that would settle between the mountains and hang suspended until the winds roughly pushed them away. There was snow on those gently rounded mountains which melted, leaving empty crags and deep ridges that turned from green to blue-green to pale brown.

It felt strange to know that none of her children would watch their grandmother arrange the cherry blossoms and listen to her as she explained that the tall flowers meant the heavens or harvest the rice grown in ankle-deep water. They were different from her, born under clouded skies and raised on the wrong side of the sea. And yet they were a part of her, and a part of him. Out here, behind the mountains, behind the sun, there was nothing to remind her. Nothing but rain and time to think. Japan faded into a dream that walked with her and spoke to the children in her voice.

Off somewhere, a car floated by and splashed a river of water onto the sidewalk.

The clock on the dresser with the broken second hand ticked slowly towards 5:55. Suppertime. The food on the table was cooling and the gossip among sisters and brothers and cousins was slowly dying. Perched upon the sofa and hiding in the corners of the small room, their eyes kept drifting to the door.

"What time did you tell him to come?" she whispered to her youngest daughter for the fifth time.

"Five-thirty. Mama, why don't we just start eating?"

And she nodded reluctantly, gesturing to everyone to fill up their plates and eat the food she had prepared. They gathered slowly, single-file around the oval table, picking at familiar pickles and salads and pausing long beside the plates of rice. Some spread themselves out upon the floor, while others found seats among the potted plants. Some ate, some talked, some laughed or joked. Others were silent, watching the talk flow mostly between the elders.

At seven o'clock the doorbell rang and she half-jumped, half-rose to answer it. Her grandson stood tall outside the doorway in his jeans and longish hair sprinkled with rain.

"You're all wet!" she scolded him, angry still because he had made her wait.

"No, Grandma, it's hardly sprinkling out," he answered as she led him by the hand into the heart of her family.

"Sit," she told him.

He sat. Then watched her leave to get his plate, piled high with food. She saw him frown as she brought his plate.

"Grandma, I can't eat all of this."

"Try," she told him and handed him an inari. "Eat it," she told him as he paused. She watched his face scrunch up. "What's wrong? Here, taste. It's good." And demonstrating, popped it into her mouth. "What do you taste?"

"Vinegar, rice. I don't like that brown stuff," he answered honestly.

"And this?" she thrust at him a makizushi and watched him bite it gingerly.

"What's this dark thing in the middle?"

She shook her head and frowned to herself. Too American, she thought to herself, and not enough of Grandpa or me inside of him. She looked at him and saw baseball at Sick's Stadium and hamburgers at Herfy's and McDonald's. She watched him as he left the rest of the rice untouched, and felt as if it were herself laying there on the napkin, mutilated and dying. But she knew why. This wasn't her land, it was his. He had grown up in Seattle, with the rain in his blood, and he had breathed the cool breezes, smelling of sea, that blew in from the waterfront. She looked at his cousins and wondered how much she had taught them. They seemed so distant, so far away. She remembered what someone had told her, not so long ago. Who will make the rice for our families after we are gone? Who will have the gatherings? Not our daughters, or our granddaughters. And looking at them, she knew this was true.

She touched her grandson's hand and smiled at him. "Eat what you can."

He nodded.

What will happen to the family after I am gone, she wondered. Would they scatter to all parts of the world like kites blown free from broken strings? And nothing to hold them together? She picked out a makizushi from her grandson's plate and smiled to herself, thinking sadly that she was the last inari and makizushi stand left in the world.

IV. SHAKING THE MESS
OUT OF MISERY

This section is full of women who are working at full strength and in full being, full motion, full life. These are whole women. They are strong. They are healers. They are prayer ladies. Their presence strengthens and heals others. In these stories we could say that the energy of healing radiates outward and moves lives everywhere, like a wind circling the planet. In Shay Youngblood's "Born Wid Religion" Big Mama is a true representative of life and religion and of how faith works when we keep it. Big Mama is a woman whose specialty is "Shaking the mess out of misery," a line which sums up all the women in this section: the women we are lucky to have known, the women whose beliefs in self and life have kept us going, have kept us strong, and feed us to this very minute of our living. These are the women we become when we drop all the masks and conventions and fears that want us to stay out of our full powers. May these women help us grow to our full womanhood.

Layle Silbert

Audre Lorde

Audre Lorde is the author of Chosen Poems—Old and New *(Norton, 1982) and* The Cancer Journals. *She lives on Staten Island and teaches at Hunter College.*

TAR BEACH

Gerri was young and Black and lived in Queens and had a powder-blue Ford that she nicknamed Bluefish. With her carefully waved hair and button-down shirts and grey-flannel slacks, she looked just this side of square, without being square at all, once you got to know her.

By Gerri's invitation and frequently by her wheels, Muriel and I had gone to parties on weekends in Brooklyn and Queens at different women's houses.

One of the women I had met at one of these parties was Kitty.

When I saw Kitty again one night years later in the Swing Rendezvous or the Pony Stable or the Page Three—that tour of second-string gay-girl bars that I had taken to making alone that sad lonely spring of 1957—it was easy to recall the St. Alban's smell of green Queens summer-night and plastic couch-covers and liquor and hair oil and women's bodies at the party where we had first met.

In that brick-faced frame house in Queens, the downstairs pine-paneled recreation room was alive and pulsing with loud music, good food, and beautiful Black women in all different combinations of dress.

There were whip-cord summer suits with starch-shiny shirt collars open at the neck as a concession to the high summer heat, and white gabardine slacks with pleated fronts or slim ivy-league styling for the very slender. There were wheat-colored Cowden jeans, the fashion favorite that summer, with knife-edge creases, and even then, one or two back-buckled grey pants over well-chalked buckskin shoes. There were garrison belts galore, broad black leather belts with shiny thin buckles that originated in army-navy surplus stores, and oxford-styled shirts of the new, iron-free dacron, with its stiff, see-through crispness. These shirts, short-sleeved and man-tailored, were tucked neatly into belted pants or tight, skinny straight skirts. Only the one or two jersey knit shirts were allowed to fall freely outside.

Bermuda shorts, and their shorter cousins, Jamaicas, were

already making their appearance on the dyke-chic scene, the rules of which were every bit as cutthroat as the tyrannies of Seventh Avenue or Paris. These shorts were worn by butch and femme alike, and for this reason were slow to be incorporated into many fashionable gay-girl wardrobes, to keep the signals clear. Clothes were often the most important way of broadcasting one's chosen sexual role.

Here and there throughout the room the flash of brightly colored below-the-knee full skirts over low-necked tight bodices could be seen, along with tight sheath dresses and the shine of high thin heels next to bucks and sneakers and loafers.

Femmes wore their hair in tightly curled pageboy bobs, or piled high on their heads in sculptured bunches of curls, or in feather cuts framing their faces. That sweetly clean fragrance of beauty-parlor that hung over all Black women's gatherings in the fifties was present here also, adding its identifiable smell of hot comb and hair pomade to the other aromas in the room.

Butches wore their hair cut shorter, in a D.A. shaped to a point in the back, or a short pageboy, or sometimes in a tightly curled poodle that predated the natural afro. But this was a rarity, and I can only remember one other Black woman at that party besides me whose hair was not straightened, and she was an acquaintance of ours from the Lower East Side named Ida.

On a table behind the built-in bar stood opened bottles of gin, bourbon, scotch, soda and other various mixers. The bar itself was covered with little delicacies of all descriptions; chips and dips and little crackers and squares of bread laced with the usual dabs of egg-salad and sardine paste. There was also a platter of delicious fried chicken wings, and a pan of potato-and-egg salad dressed with vinegar. Bowls of olives and pickles surrounded the main dishes, with trays of red crab apples and little sweet onions on toothpicks.

But the centerpiece of the whole table was a huge platter of succulent and thinly sliced roast beef, set into an underpan of cracked ice. Upon the beige platter, each slice of rare meat had been lovingly laid out and individually folded up into a vulval pattern, with a tiny dab of mayonnaise at the crucial apex. The pink-brown folded meat around the pale cream-yellow dot formed suggestive sculptures that made a great hit with all the women present, and Pet, at whose house the party was being given and whose idea the meat sculptures were, smilingly acknowledged the many compliments on her platter with a long-necked graceful nod of her elegant dancer's head.

The room's particular mix of heat-smells and music gives way in my mind to the high-cheeked, dark young woman with the silky voice and appraising eyes (something about her mouth reminded me of Ann, the nurse I'd worked with when I'd first left home).

Perching on the edge of the low bench where I was sitting, Kitty absently wiped specks of lipstick from each corner of her mouth with the downward flick of a delicate forefinger.

"Audre . . . that's a nice name. What's it short for?"

My damp arm hairs bristled in the Ruth Brown music, and the heat. I could not stand anybody messing around with my name, not even with nicknames.

"Nothing. It's just Audre. What's Kitty short for?"

"Afrekete," she said, snapping her fingers in time to the rhythm of it and giving a long laugh. "That's me. The Black pussycat." She laughed again. "I like your hairdo. Are you a singer?"

"No." She continued to stare at me with her large direct eyes.

I was suddenly too embarrassed at not knowing what else to say to meet her calmly erotic gaze, so I stood up abruptly and said, in my best Laurel's-terse tone, "Let's dance."

Her face was broad and smooth under too-light make-up, but as we danced a foxtrot she started to sweat, and her skin took on a deep shiny richness. Kitty closed her eyes part way when she danced, and her one gold-rimmed front tooth flashed as she smiled and occasionally caught her lower lip in time to the music.

Her yellow poplin shirt, cut in the style of an Eisenhower jacket, had a zipper that was half open in the summer heat, showing collarbones that stood out like brown wings from her long neck. Garments with zippers were highly prized among the more liberal set of gay-girls, because these could be worn by butch or femme alike on certain occasions, without causing any adverse or troublesome comments. Kitty's narrow, well-pressed khaki skirt was topped by a black belt that matched my own except in its newness, and her natty trimness made me feel almost shabby in my well-worn riding pants.

I thought she was very pretty, and I wished I could dance with as much ease as she did, and as effortlessly. Her hair had been straightened into short feathery curls, and in that room of well-set marcels and D.A.'s and pageboys, it was the closest cut to my own.

Kitty smelled of soap and Jean Naté, and I kept thinking she was bigger than she actually was, because there was a comfortable smell about her that I always associated with large women. I caught another spicy herb-like odor, that I later identified as a combination of coconut oil and Yardley's lavender hair pomade. Her mouth was full, and her lipstick was dark and shiny, a new Max Factor shade called "WARPAINT."

The next dance was a slow fish that suited me fine. I never knew whether to lead or to follow in most other dances, and even the effort to decide which was as difficult for me as having to decide all the time the difference between left and right. Somehow that simple distinction had never become automatic for me, and all that deciding usually left me very little energy with which to enjoy the movement and the music.

But "fishing" was different. A forerunner of the later one-step, it was, in reality, your basic slow bump and grind. The low red lamp and the crowded St. Alban's parlor floor left us just enough room to hold each other frankly, arms around neck and waist, and the slow intimate music moved our bodies much more than our feet.

That had been in St. Alban's, Queens, nearly two years before, when Muriel had seemed to be the certainty in my life. Now in the spring of this new year I had my own apartment all to myself again, but I was mourning. I avoided visiting pairs of friends, or inviting even numbers of people over to my house, because the happiness of couples, or their mere togetherness, hurt me too much in its absence from my own life, whose blankest hole was named Muriel. I had not been back to Queens, nor to any party, since Muriel and I had broken up, and the only people I saw outside of work and school were those friends who lived in the Village and who sought me out or whom I ran into at the bars. Most of them were white.

"Hey, girl, long time no see." Kitty spotted me first. We shook hands. The bar was not crowded, which means it probably was the Page Three, which didn't fill up until after midnight. "Where's your girlfriend?"

I told her that Muriel and I weren't together any more. "Yeah? That's too bad. You-all were kinda cute together. But that's the way it goes. How long you been in the 'life'?"

I stared at Kitty without answering, trying to think of how to explain to her, that for me there was only one life—my own—however I chose to live it. But she seemed to take the words right out of my mouth.

"Not that it matters," she said speculatively, finishing the beer she had carried over to the end of the bar where I was sitting. "We don't have but one, anyway. At least this time around." She took my arm. "Come on, let's dance."

Kitty was still trim and fast-lined, but with an easier looseness about her smile and a lot less make-up. Without its camouflage, her chocolate skin and deep, sculptured mouth reminded me of a Benin bronze. Her hair was still straightened, but shorter, and her black Bermuda shorts and knee socks matched her astonishingly shiny black loafers. A black turtleneck pullover completed her sleek costume. Somehow, this time, my jeans did not feel shabby beside hers, only a variation upon some similar dress. Maybe it was because our belts still matched—broad, black, and brass-buckled.

We moved to the back room and danced to Frankie Lymon's "Goody, Goody," and then to a Belafonte calypso. Dancing with her this time, I felt who I was and where my body was going, and that feeling was more important to me than any lead or follow.

The room felt very warm even though it was only just spring, and Kitty and I smiled at each other as the number ended. We stood waiting for the next record to drop and the next dance to begin. It was a slow Sinatra. Our belt buckles kept getting in the way as we moved in close to the oiled music, and we slid them around to the side of our waists when no one was looking.

For the last few months since Muriel had moved out, my skin had felt cold and hard and essential, like thin frozen leather that was keeping the shape expected. That night on the dance floor of the Page Three as Kitty and I touched our bodies together in dancing, I could feel my carapace soften slowly and then finally melt, until I felt myself covered in a warm, almost forgotten, slip of anticipation, that ebbed and flowed at each contact of our moving bodies.

I could feel something slowly shift in her also, as if a taut string was becoming undone, and finally we didn't start back to the bar at all between dances, but just stood on the floor waiting for the next record, dancing only with each other. A little after midnight, in a silent and mutual decision, we split the Page together, walking blocks through the West Village to Hudson Street where her car was parked. She had invited me up to her house for a drink.

The sweat beneath my breasts from our dancing was turning cold in the sharpness of the night air as we crossed Sheridan Square. I paused to wave to the steadies through the plate glass windows of Jim Atkins's on the corner of Christopher Street.

In her car, I tried not to think about what I was doing as we rode uptown almost in silence. There was an ache in the well beneath my stomach, spreading out and down between my legs like mercury. The smell of her warm body, mixed with the smell of feathery cologne and lavender pomade, anointed the car. My eyes rested on the sight of her coconut-spicy hands on the steering wheel, and the curve of her lashes as she attended the roadway. They made it easy for me to coast beneath her sporadic bursts of conversation with only an occasional friendly grunt.

"I haven't been downtown to the bars in a while, you know? It's funny. I don't know why I don't go downtown more often. But every once in a while, something tells me go and I go. I guess it must be different when you live around there all the time." She turned her gold-flecked smile upon me.

Crossing 59th Street, I had an acute moment of panic. Who was this woman? Suppose she really intended only to give me the drink which she had offered me as we left the Page? Suppose I had totally misunderstood the impact of her invitation, and would soon find myself stranded uptown at 3:00 A.M. on a Sunday morning, and did I even have enough change left in my jeans for carfare home? Had I put out enough food for the kittens? Was Flee coming over with her camera tomorrow morning, and would she feed the cats if I wasn't there? If I wasn't there.

If I wasn't there. The implication of that thought was so shaking it almost threw me out of the car.

I had had only enough money for one beer that night, so I knew I wasn't high, and reefer was only for special occasions. Part of me felt like a raging lioness, inflamed in desire. Even the words in my head seemed borrowed from a dime-store novel. But that part of me was drunk on the thighed nearness of this exciting unknown dark woman, who calmly moved us through upper Manhattan, with her patent-leather loafers and her camel's-hair swing coat and her easy talk, from time to time her gloved hand touching my denimed leg for emphasis.

Another piece of me felt bumbling, inept, and about four years old. I was the idiot playing at being a lover, who was going to be found out shortly and laughed at for my pretensions, as well as rejected out of hand.

Would it be possible—was it ever possible—for two women to share the fire we felt that night without entrapping or smothering each other? I longed for that as I longed for her body, doubting both, eager for both.

And how was it possible, that I should be dreaming the roll of this woman's sea into and around mine, when only a few short hours ago, and for so many months before, I had been mourning the loss of Muriel, so sure that I would continue being broken-hearted forever? And what then if I had been mistaken?

If the knot in my groin would have gone away, I'd have jumped out of the car door at the very next traffic light. Or so I thought to myself.

We came out of the Park Drive at Seventh Avenue and 110th Street, and as quickly as the light changed on the now deserted avenue, Afrekete turned her broad-lipped beautiful face to me, with no smile at all. Her great lidded luminescent eyes looked directly and startlingly into mine. It was as if she had suddenly become another person, as if the wall of glass formed by my spectacles, and behind which I had become so used to hiding, had suddenly dissolved.

Audre Lorde 233

In an uninflected, almost formal voice that perfectly matched and thereby obliterated all my question marks, she asked,

"Can you spend the night?"

And then it occurred to me that perhaps she might have been having the same questions about me that I had been having about her. I was left almost without breath by the combination of her delicacy and her directness—a combination which is still rare and precious.

For beyond the assurance that her question offered me—a declaration that this singing of my flesh, this attraction, was not all within my own head—beyond that assurance was a batch of delicate assumptions built into that simple phrase that reverberated in my poet's brain. It offered us both an out if necessary. If the answer to the question might, by any chance, have been no, then its very syntax allowed for a reason of impossibility, rather than of choice—"I can't," rather than "I won't." The demands of another commitment, an early job, a sick cat, etc., could be lived with more easily than an out-and-out rejection.

Even the phrase "spending the night" was less a euphemism for making love than it was an allowable space provided, in which one could move back or forth. If, perhaps, I were to change my mind before the traffic light and decide that no, I wasn't gay, after all, then a simpler companionship was still available.

I steadied myself enough to say, in my very best Lower East Side Casual voice, "I'd really like to," cursing myself for the banal words, and wondering if she could smell my nervousness and my desperate desire to be suave and debonair, drowning in sheer desire.

We parked half-in and half-out of a bus stop on Manhattan Avenue and 113th Street, in Gennie's old neighborhood.

Something about Kitty made me feel like a rollercoaster, rocketing from idiot to goddess. By the time we had collected her mail from the broken mailbox and then climbed six flights of stairs up to her front door, I felt that there had never been anything else my body had intended to do more, than to reach inside of her coat and take Afrekete into my arms, fitting her body into the curves of mine tightly, her beige camel's-hair billowing around us both, and her gloved hand still holding the door key.

234

In the faint light of the hallway, her lips moved like surf upon the water's edge.

It was a 1½ room kitchenette apartment with tall narrow windows in the narrow, high-ceilinged front room. Across each window, there were built-in shelves at different levels. From these shelves tossed and frothed, hung and leaned and stood, pot after clay pot of green and tousled large and small-leaved plants of all shapes and conditions.

Later, I came to love the way in which the plants filtered the southern exposure sun through the room. Light hit the opposite wall at a point about six inches above the thirty-gallon fish tank that murmured softly, like a quiet jewel, standing on its wrought-iron legs, glowing and mysterious.

Leisurely and swiftly, translucent rainbowed fish darted back and forth through the lit water, perusing the glass sides of the tank for morsels of food, and swimming in and out of the marvelous world created by colored gravels and stone tunnels and bridges that lined the floor of the tank. Astride one of the bridges, her bent head observing the little fish that swam in and out between her legs, stood a little jointed brown doll, her smooth naked body washed by the bubbles rising up from the air unit located behind her.

Between the green plants and the glowing magical tank of exotic fish, lay a room the contents of which I can no longer separate in my mind. Except for a plaid-covered couch that opened up into the double bed which we set rocking as we loved that night into a bright Sunday morning, dappled with green sunlight from the plants in Afrekete's high windows.

I woke to her house suffused in that light, the sky half-seen through the windows of the top-floor kitchenette apartment, and Afrekete, known, asleep against my side.

Little hairs under her navel lay down before my advancing tongue like the beckoned pages of a well-touched book.

How many times into summer had I turned into that block from Eighth Avenue, the saloon on the corner spilling a smell of sawdust and liquor onto the street, a shifting indeterminate number of young and old Black men taking turns sitting on two upturned milk-crates, playing checkers? I would turn the corner into 113th

Street towards the park, my steps quickening and my fingertips tingling to play in her earth.

And I remember Afrekete, who came out of a dream to me always being hard and real as the fire hairs along the underedge of my navel. She brought me live things from the bush, and from her farm set out in cocoyams and cassava—those magical fruit which Kitty bought in the West Indian markets along Lenox Avenue in the 140s or in the Puerto Rican *bodegas* within the bustling market over on Park Avenue and 116th Street under the Central Railroad structures.

"I got this under the bridge" was a saying from time immemorial, giving an adequate explanation that whatever it was had come from as far back and as close to home—that is to say, was as authentic—as was possible.

We bought red delicious pippins, the size of french cashew apples. There were green plantains, which we half-peeled and then planted, fruit-deep, in each other's bodies until the petals of skin lay like tendrils of broad green fire upon the curly darkness between our upspread thighs. *There were ripe red finger bananas, stubby and sweet, with which I parted your lips gently, to insert the peeled fruit into your grape-purple flower.*

I held you, lay between your brown legs, slowly playing my tongue through your familiar forests, slowly licking and swallowing as the deep undulations and tidal motions of your strong body slowly mashed ripe banana into a beige cream that mixed with the juices of your electric flesh. Our bodies met again, each surface touched with each other's flame, from the tips of our curled toes to our tongues, and locked into our own wild rhythms, we rode each other across the thundering space, dripped like light from the peak of each other's tongue.

We were each of us both together. Then we were apart, and sweat sheened our bodies like sweet oil.

Sometimes Afrekete sang in a small club further uptown on Sugar Hill. Sometimes she clerked in the Gristede's Market on 97th Street and Amsterdam, and sometimes with no warning at all she appeared at the Pony Stable or Page Three on Saturday night. Once, I came home to Seventh Street late one night to find her sitting on my stoop at 3:00 A.M., with a bottle of beer in her hand and a piece of bright African cloth wrapped around her head, and we sped uptown through the dawn-empty city with a summer thunder squall crackling above us, and the wet city streets singing beneath the wheels of her little Nash Rambler.

There are certain verities which are always with us, which we come to depend upon. That the sun moves north in summer, that melted ice contracts, that the curved banana is sweeter. Afrekete taught me roots, new definitions of our women's bodies — definitions for which I had only been in training to learn before.

By the beginning of summer the walls of Afrekete's apartment were always warm to the touch from the heat beating down on the roof, and chance breezes through her windows rustled her plants in the window and brushed over our sweat-smooth bodies, at rest after loving.

We talked sometimes about what it meant to love women, and what a relief it was in the eye of the storm, no matter how often we had to bite our tongues and stay silent. Afrekete had a seven-year-old daughter whom she had left with her mama down in Georgia, and we shared a lot of our dreams.

"She's going to be able to love anybody she wants to love," Afrekete said, fiercely, lighting a Lucky Strike. "Same way she's going to be able to work any place she damn well pleases. Her mama's going to see to that."

Once we talked about how Black women had been committed without choice to waging our campaigns in the enemies' strongholds, too much and too often, and how our psychic landscapes had been plundered and wearied by those repeated battles and campaigns.

"And don't I have the scars to prove it," she sighed. "Makes you tough though, babe, if you don't go under. And that's what I like about you; you're like me. We're both going to make it because we're both too tough and crazy not to!" And we held each other and laughed and cried about what we had paid for that toughness, and how hard it was to explain to anyone who didn't already know it that soft and tough had to be one and the same for either to work at all, like our joy and the tears mingling on the one pillow beneath our heads.

And the sun filtered down upon us through the dusty windows, through the mass of green plants that Afrekete tended religiously.

I took a ripe avocado and rolled it between my hands until the skin became a green case for the soft mashed fruit inside, hard pit at the core. *I rose from a kiss in your mouth to nibble a hole in the fruit skin near the navel stalk, squeezed the pale yellow-green fruit juice in thin ritual lines back and forth over and around your coconut-brown belly.*

The oil and sweat from our bodies kept the fruit liquid, and I massaged it over your thighs and between your breasts until your brownness shone like a light through a veil of the palest green avocado, a mantle of goddess pear that I slowly licked from your skin.

Then we would have to get up to gather the pits and fruit skins and bag them to put out later for the garbagemen, because if we left them near the bed for any length of time, they would call out the hordes of cockroaches that always waited on the sidelines within the walls of Harlem tenements, particularly in the smaller older ones under the hill of Morningside Heights.

Afrekete lived not far from Genevieve's grandmother's house.

Sometimes she reminded me of Ella, Gennie's stepmother, who shuffled about with an apron on and a broom outside the room where Gennie and I lay on the studio couch. She would be singing her non-stop tuneless little song over and over and over:

> Momma kilt me
> Poppa et me
> Po' lil' brudder
> suck ma bones . . .

And one day Gennie turned her head on my lap to say uneasily, "You know, sometimes I don't know whether Ella's crazy, or stupid, or divine."

And now I think the goddess was speaking through Ella also, but Ella was too beaten down and anesthetized by Phillip's brutality for her to believe in her own mouth, and we, Gennie and I, were too arrogant and childish—not without right or reason, for we were scarcely more than children—to see that our survival

238

might very well lay in listening to the sweeping woman's tuneless song.

I lost my sister, Gennie, to my silence and her pain and despair, to both our angers and to a world's cruelty that destroys its own young in passing — not even as a rebel gesture or sacrifice or hope for another living of the spirit, but out of not noticing or caring about the destruction. I have never been able to blind myself to that cruelty, which according to one popular definition of mental health, makes me mentally unhealthy.

Afrekete's house was the tallest one near the corner, before the high rocks of Morningside Park began on the other side of the avenue, and one night on the Midsummer Eve's Moon we took a blanket up to the roof. She lived on the top floor, and in an unspoken agreement, the roof belonged mostly to those who had to live under its heat. The roof was the chief resort territory of tenement-dwellers, and was known as Tar Beach.

We jammed the roof door shut with our sneakers, and spread our blanket in the lee of the chimney, between its warm brick wall and the high parapet of the building's face. This was before the blaze of sulphur lamps had stripped the streets of New York of trees and shadow, and the incandescence from the lights below faded this far up. From behind the parapet wall we could see the dark shapes of the basalt and granite outcroppings looming over us from the park across the street, outlined, curiously close and suggestive.

We slipped off the cotton shifts we had worn and moved against each other's damp breasts in the shadow of the roof's chimney, making moon, honor, love, while the ghostly vague light drifting upward from the street competed with the silver hard sweetness of the full moon, reflected in the shiny mirrors of our sweat-slippery dark bodies, sacred as the ocean at high tide.

I remember the moon rising against the tilted planes of her upthrust thighs, and my tongue caught the streak of silver reflected in the curly bush of her dappled-dark maiden hair. *I remember the full moon like white pupils in the center of your wide irises.*

The moons went out, and your eyes grew dark as you rolled over me, and I felt the moon's silver light mix with the wet of your tongue on my eyelids.

Afrekete Afrekete ride me to the crossroads where we shall sleep, coated in the woman's power. The sound of our bodies meeting is the prayer of all strangers and sisters, that the discarded evils, abandoned at all crossroads, will not follow us upon our journeys.

When we came down from the roof later, it was into the sweltering midnight of a west Harlem summer, with canned music in the streets and the disagreeable whines of overtired and overheated children. Nearby, mothers and fathers sat on stoops or milk crates and striped camp chairs, fanning themselves absently and talking or thinking about work as usual tomorrow and not enough sleep.

It was not onto the pale sands of Whydah, nor the beaches of Winneba or Annamabu, with cocopalms softly applauding and crickets keeping time with the pounding of a tar-laden, treacherous, beautiful sea. It was onto 113th Street that we descended after our meeting under the Midsummer Eve's Moon, but the mothers and fathers smiled at us in greeting as we strolled down to Eighth Avenue, hand in hand.

I had not seen Afrekete for a few weeks in July, so I went uptown to her house one evening since she didn't have a phone. The door was locked, and there was no one on the roof when I called up the stairwell.

Another week later, Midge, the bartender at the Pony Stable, gave me a note from Afrekete, saying that she had gotten a gig in Atlanta for September, and was splitting to visit her mama and daughter for a while.

We had come together like elements erupting into an electric storm, exchanging energy, sharing charge, brief and drenching. Then we parted, passed, reformed, reshaping ourselves the better for the exchange.

I never saw Afrekete again, but her print remains upon my life with the resonance and power of an emotional tattoo.

Roberta Fernández

Born and reared in Laredo, Texas, on the Texas-Mexico border, Roberta Fernández also considered the San Francisco Bay Area her home for many years. For the subject of her writing she has turned to the deep-rooted culture of the women of the Mexican border born at the turn of the century and to the manner in which they transmitted their culture to the younger generations. Equally at home in English and in Spanish, Fernández attends in her work to the challenge of bilinguality and biculturality. Her short stories have been published both in English and in Spanish versions. They have appeared in PRISMA *(Mills College, Spring, 1979),* THE MASSACHUSETTS REVIEW *(UMass, Spring, 1983);* REVISTA CHICANO RIQUEÑA *(Houston, Summer, 1980) and in a forthcoming issue of* FEM *(Mexico City) dedicated to Chicanas. They have also been anthologized in* A DECADE OF HISPANIC LITERATURE *(University of Houston, 1982);* CUENTOS: STORIES BY LATINAS *(NY: Kitchen Table — Women of Color Press, 1983). Presently, she is finishing up a Ph.D. in Romance Languages and Literatures at UC, Berkeley. She has taught at Mills College, the University of Massachusetts, Smith College, Brown University and is currently at the University of California, Santa Barbara. She values as an inspiration, if not necessarily an influence, the work of other Third World women writers in the United States, and like many of them, considers her giving voice to voiceless generations of women to be the main concern in her present writing. Sooner or later, she will turn to "the California experience" for a change in mood, theme and language.*

242

AMANDA

Transformation was definitely her specialty, and out of georgettes, piques, poie de soie, organzas, shantungs and laces she made exquisite gowns adorned with delicate opaline beadwork which she carefully touched up with the thinnest silvers of irridescent cording that one could find. At that time I was so captivated by Amanda's creations that often before I fell asleep I would conjure up visions of her workroom where luminous whirls of lentejuelas de conchanacar would be dancing about, softly brushing against the swaying fabrics in various shapes and stages of completion. Then amidst the colorful threads and telas de tornasol shimmering in a reassuring rhythm, she would get smaller and smaller until she was only the tiniest of grey dots among the colors and lights and slowly, slowly, the uninterrupted gentle droning of the magical singer and her mocking whispering voice would both vanish into a silent solid darkness.

By day whenever I had the opportunity I loved to sit next to her machine observing her hands guiding the movement of the fabrics. I was so moved by what I saw that she soon grew to intimidate me and I almost never originated conversation. Therefore, our only communication for long stretches of time was my obvious fascination with the changes that transpired before my watchful eyes. Finally she would look up at me through her gold-rimmed glasses and ask "¿Te gusta, muchacha?"

In response to my nod she would proceed to tell me familiar details about the women who would be showing off her finished costumes at the Black and White Ball or some other such event. Rambling on with the reassurance of someone who has given considerable thought to everything she says, Amanda would then mesmerize me even further with her provocative chismes about men and women who had come to our area many years ago. Then as she tied a thread here and added a touch there I would feel compelled to ask her a question or two as my flimsy contribution to our lengthy conversation.

With most people I chatted freely but with Amanda I seldom

talked since I had the distinct feeling that in addition to other apprehensions I had about her by the time I was five or six, she felt total indifference towards me. "¡Qué preguntona!" I was positive she would be saying to herself even as I persisted with another question. When she stopped talking to concentrate fully on what she was doing I would gaze directly at her, admiring how beautiful she looked. Waves of defeat would overtake me, for the self-containment which she projected behind her austere appearance made me think that she would never take notice of me, while I loved everything about her.

I would follow the shape of her head from the central part of her dark auburn hair pulled down over her ears to the curves of the chongo which she wore at the nape of her long neck. The grey shirtwaist with the narrow skirt and elbow length sleeves she wore day in and day out, everywhere she went, made her seem even taller than she was. The front had tiny stitched-down vertical pleats and a narrow deep pocket in which she sometimes tucked her eyeglasses. She always seemed to have a yellow measuring tape hanging around her neck and a row of straight pins with big plastic heads down the front edge of her neckline. Like the rest of the relatives she seemed reassuringly permanent in the uniform she had created for herself.

Her day lasted from seven in the morning until nine in the evening. During this time she could dash off in a matter of two or three days an elaborate wedding dress or a classically simple evening gown for someone's coming-out party which Artemisa would then embroider. Her disposition did not require her to concentrate on any one outfit from start to finish and this allowed her to work on many at once. It also meant that she had dresses everywhere, hanging from the edge of the doors, on a wall-to-wall bar suspended near the ceiling and on three or four tables where they would be carefully laid out.

Once or twice Amanda managed to make a bride late in her own wedding, when at the last minute she had to sew-in the zipper by hand while the bride was already in the dress. Somehow people didn't seem to mind these occasional slip-ups, for they kept coming back, again and again, from Saltillo and Monterrey, from San Antonio and Corpus Christi, and a few even from far-off

244

Dallas and Houston. Those mid-Texan socialites enjoyed practicing their very singular Spanish with Amanda, and she used to chuckle over her little joke, never once letting on that she really did speak perfect English.

As far as her other designs went, her basic dress pattern might be a direct copy from *Vogue* magazine or it could stem from someone's dearest fantasy. From then on the creation was Amanda's and everyone of her clients trusted the final look to her own discretion. The svelte Club Campestre set from Monterrey and Nuevo Laredo would take her to Audrey Hepburn and Grace Kelly movies to point out the outfits that they wanted, just as their mothers had done with Joan Crawford and Katherine Hepburn movies. Judging from their expressions as they pirouetted before their image in their commissioned artwork she never failed their expectations, except perhaps for that occasional zipper-less bride. She certainly never disappointed me as I sat in solemn and curious attention, peering into her face as I searched for some trace of how she had acquired her special powers.

For there was another aspect to Amanda which only we seemed to whisper about, in very low tones, and that was that Amanda was dabbling in herbs. Although none of us considered her a real hechicera we always had reservations about drinking or eating anything she gave us, and whereas no one ever saw the proverbial muñequitos we fully suspected that she had them hidden somewhere, undoubtedly decked out in the exact replicas of those who had ever crossed her in any way.

Among her few real friends were two ancianas who came to visit her by night, much to everyone's consternation, for those two only needed one quick stolen look to convince you that they were more than amateurs. Librada and Soledad were toothless old women swarthed in black or brown from head-to-toe and they carried their morral filled with hierbas and potions slung over their shoulders just as brujas did in my books. They had a stare that seemed to go right through you, and you knew that no thought was secret from them if you let them look even once into your eyes.

One day in the year when it rained more than in the previous four years and the puddles swelled up with more bubbles than usual I found myself sitting alone in the screened-in porch admiring the sound of the fat rain-drops on the roof when suddenly I looked up to find Librada standing there in her dark brown rebozo, softly knocking on the door.

"La señora le manda un recado a su mamá," she said while my heart thumped so loudly that its noise scared me even further. I managed to tell her to wait there, by the door, while I went to call my mother. By the time that mother came, Librada was already inside, sitting on the couch, and since the message was that Amanda wanted mother to call one of her customers to relay a message, I was left alone with the old woman while mother went to make the call. I sat on the floor pretending to work on a jig-saw puzzle while I really observed Librada's every move. Suddenly she broke the silence asking me how old I was and when my eighth birthday would be. Before I could phrase any words, mother was back with a note for Amanda, and Librada was on her way. Sensing my tension mother suggested that we go into the kitchen to make some good hot chocolate and to talk about what had just happened.

After I drank my cup, I came back to the porch, picked up one of my *Jack and Jill's* and lay down on the couch. As I rearranged a cushion my left arm slid on a viscous greenish-grey substance and I let out a screech which had mother at my side in two seconds. Angry at her for having taken so long to come to my aid, I was wiping my arm on the dress and screaming, "Mire lo que hizo la bruja." She very, very slowly took off my dress and told me to go into the shower and to soap myself well. In the meantime she cleaned up the mess with newspapers and burned them outside by the old brick pond. As soon as I came out of the shower she puffed me up all over with her lavender-fragranced bath powder and for the rest of the afternoon we tried to figure out what the strange episode had meant. Nothing of great importance happened to anyone in the family during the following wet days and mother insisted we forget the incident.

Only I didn't forget it for a long time. On my next visit to Amanda's I described in detail what had happened. She dismissed the entire episode as though it weren't important, shrugging, "Pobre Librada. ¿Por qué le echas la culpa de tal cosa?" With that I went back to my silent observation, now suspecting that she too was part of a complex plot that I couldn't figure out. Yet, instead of making me run, incidents like these drew me more to her, for I distinctly sensed that she was my only link to other exciting possibilities which were not part of the every-day world of the others. What they could be I wasn't sure of but I was so convinced of the hidden powers in that house that I always wore my scapular and made the sign of the cross before I stepped inside.

After the rains stopped and the moon began to change colors I began to imagine a dramatic and eery outfit which I hoped Amanda would create for me. Without discussing it with my sisters I made it more and more sinister and finally when the toads stopping croaking I built up enough nerve to ask her about it.

"Oye, Amanda, ¿me podrías hacer el traje más hermoso de todo el mundo? ¿Uno como el que una bruja le diera su hija favorita? ¡Que sea tan horrible que a todos les encante!"

"¿Y para qué diablos quieres tal cosa?" she asked me in surprise.

"Nomás lo quiero de secreto. Ne creas que voy a asustar a los vecinos."

"Pues, mire usted, chulita, estoy tan ocupada que no puedo decirle ni sí ni no. Uno de estos días, cuando Dios me dé tiempo quizás lo pueda considerar, pero hasta entonces yo no ando haciendo promesas a nadie."

And then I waited. Dog days came and went, and finally when the lechuza flew elsewhere I gave up on my request, brooding over my having asked for something which I should have known would not be coming. Therefore the afternoon that Artemisa dropped off a note saying that la señora wanted to see me that night because she had a surprise for me, I cooly said that I'd be there only if my mother said that I could go.

All the time that I waited to be let in I was very aware that I had left my scapular at home. I knew this time that something very special was about to happen to me, since I could see even from out there that Amanda had finally made me my very special outfit. Mounted on a little-girl dress-dummy a swaying black satin cape was awaiting my touch. It was ankle length with braided frogs cradling tiny buttons down to the knee. On the inside of the neckline was a black fur trim. "Es de gato," she confessed, and it ticked my neck as she buttoned the cape on me. The puffy sleeves fitted very tightly around the wrist, and on the upper side of each wristband was attached a cat's paw which hung down to the knuckles, on top of each hand. Below the collar on the left side of the cape was a small stuffed heart in burgundy-colored velveteen and, beneath the heart, were tear-shaped red translucent beads.

As she pulled the rounded ballooning hood on my head, rows of stitched-down pleats made it fit close to the head. Black chicken feathers framed my face, almost down to my eyes. Between the appliqués of feathers were strung tiny bones which gently touched my cheeks. The bones came from the sparrows which the cats had killed out in the garden, she reassured me. She then suggested that I walk around the room so that she could get a good look at me.

As I moved, the cat's paws rubbed against my hands and the bones of the sparrows bounced like what I imagined snowflakes would feel like on my face. Then she put a necklace over my head which reached to my waist. It too was made of bones of sparrows strung on the finest glittering black thread, with little cascabeles inserted here and there. I raised my arms and danced around the room, and the little bells sounded sweet and clear in the silence. As I glided about the room I noticed in the mirror that Librada was sitting in the next room, laughing under her breath. Without thinking I walked up to her and asked what she thought of my cape.

"Hijita, pareces algo del otro mundo. Mira que hasta me acabo de persignar. Me da miedo nomás en pensar del montón que te vas a llevar contigo al infierno. ¡Qué Dios nos libre!"

As I looked at Librada for the first time, I felt that the room was not big enough to hold all the emotion inside of me. So I put my arms around Amanda and kissed her two, three, four times, then dramatically announced that I was going to show this most beautiful of all creations to my mother. I rushed outside hoping not to see anyone in the street and since luck was to be my companion for a brief while, I made it home without encountering a soul. Pausing outside the door of the kitchen where I could hear voices I took a deep breath, knocked as loudly as I could and in one simultaneous swoop, opened the door and stood inside, arms

248

outstretched as feathers, bones and cascabeles fluttered in unison with my heart.

After the initial silence my sisters started to cry almost hysterically, and while my father turned to comfort them, my mother came towards me with a face that I had never seen on her before. She took a deep breath and quietly said that I must never wear that outfit again. Since her expression frightened me somewhat, I took off the cape, mumbling under my breath over and over how certain people couldn't see special powers no matter how much they might be staring them in the face.

I held the bruja cape in my hands, looking at the tiny holes pieced through the bones of the sparrows, then felt the points of the nails on the cat's paws. As I fingered the beads under the heart I knew that on that very special night when the green lights of the linternas were flickering much brighter than usual, on that calm transparent night of nights I would sleep in my wonderous witch's daughter's cape.

Sometime after the Júdases were all aflame and spirals of light were flying everywhere I slowly opened my eyes on a full moon shining on my face. Instinctively my hand reached to my neck and I rubbed the back of my fingers gently against the cat's fur. I should go outside I thought. Then I slipped off the bed and tipped-toed to the back door in search of that which was not inside.

For a long time I sat on a lawn chair, rocking myself against its back, all the while gazing at the moon and at the familiar surroundings which glowed so luminously within the vast universe, while out there in the darkness the constant chirping of the crickets and the chicharras reiterated the reassuring permanence of everything around me. None of us is allowed to relish in powers like that for long though, and the vision of transcendence exploded in a scream as two hands grabbed me at the shoulders, then shook me back and forth. "What are you doing out here? Didn't I tell you to take off that awful thing?"

Once again I looked at my mother in defiance but immediately sensed that she was apprehensive rather than angry and I knew that it was hopeless to argue with her. Carefully I undid the tiny rounded black buttons from the soft braided loops and took off the cape for what I felt would be the last time.

Years passed, much faster than before, and I had little time left for dark brown-lavender puddles and white lechuzas in the night. Nor did I see my cape after that lovely-but-so-sad, once-in-a-lifetime experience of perfection in the universe. In fact, I often wondered if I had not invented that episode as I invented many others in those endless days of exciting and unrestrained possibilities.

Actually the memory of the cape was something I tried to flick away on those occasions when the past assumed the unpleasantness of an uninvited but persistent guest; yet, no matter how much I tried, the intrusions continued. They were especially bothersome one rainy Sunday afternoon when all the clocks had stopped working one after another as though they too had wanted to participate in the tedium of the moment. So as not to remain still I mustered all the energy that I could and decided to pass the hours by poking around in the boxes and old trunks in the storeroom.

Nothing of interest seemed to be the order of the afternoon when suddenly I came upon something wrapped in yellowed tissue paper. As I unwrapped the package I uttered a sigh of surprise on discovering that inside was the source of the disturbances I had been trying to avoid. I cried as I fingered all the details on the little cape, for it was as precious as it had been on the one day I had worn it many years ago. Only the fur had stiffened somewhat from the dryness in the trunk.

Once again I marvelled at Amanda's gifts. The little black cape was so obviously an expression of genuine love that it seemed a shame it had been hidden for all those years. I carefully lifted the cape out of the trunk wondering why my mother had not burned it as she had threatened, yet knowing full well why she had not.

From then on I placed the little cape among my collection of few but very special possessions which accompanied me everywhere I went. I even had a stuffed dummy made upon which I would arrange the cape in a central spot in every home I made. Over the years the still-crisp little cape ripened in meaning, for I could not imagine anyone ever again taking the time to create anything as personal for me as Amanda had done when our worlds had coincided for a brief and joyous period in those splendid days of luscious white gardenias.

When the end came I could hardly bear it. It happened many years ago when the suitcase containing the little cape got lost en route on my first trip west. No one could understand why the loss of something as quaint as a black cape with chicken feathers, bones of sparrows and cat's paws could cause anyone to carry on in such a manner. Their lack of sympathy only increased my own awareness of what was gone, and for months after I first came to these foggy coastal shores I would wake up to lentejuelas de conchanacar whirling about in the darkness, just as they had done so long ago in that magical room in Amanda's house.

Back home Amanda will soon be eighty, and although I haven't seen her in years, lately I have been dreaming once again about the enchantment which her hands gave to everything they touched, especially when I was very tiny and to celebrate our birthdays, my father, she and I had a joint birthday party lasting three consecutive days, during which he would make a skeletal frame for a kite out of bamboo sticks to which Amanda would attach very thin layers of marquisette with angel cords which my father would then hold on to, while I floated about on the kite above the shrubs and bushes and it was all such fun. I cannot recall the exact year when those celebrations stopped, nor what we did with all those talismanic presents but I must remember to sort through all the trunks and boxes in my mother's storeroom the next time that I am home.

Sylvia A. Watanabe

I was born in Hawaii on the island of Maui. At SUNY Binghamton, I had the good fortune to meet and study with Larry Woiwode.

THE PRAYER LADY

In late summer, when the spirits of the dead returned to eat with the living and to walk under the sky again, the villagers in the Japanese plantation camp put food out for the hungry ghosts and celebrated their coming with dance. On the last night of the festival, as time drew near for the lantern procession to light the spirits down to the sea, the old head priest woke from a dream of falling water and called his wife to dress him in his white silk laying-out kimono. It was nearly time for, their boy, Kitaro, to come for him, he said. Okusan stood in the doorway of her husband's study, trying to catch the drips from the wooden spoon she'd been using to stir the red bean soup, and stifled the impulse to point out that Kitaro wasn't likely to come back now that he'd finally gone to the only peace that anybody was ever likely to know. Instead, she said, "Papa, are you all right?" The old man sat in the musty darkness among shadowy stacks of dog-eared journals and sheets of rice paper covered with Chinese characters. "I would be a lot better if other people did not stand around asking foolish questions," he snapped. "Hurry, old woman! Kitaro will not wait."

Okusan walked over to her husband and looked closely at his face for signs of the falling-down sickness. She wasn't sure exactly what she was looking for; three different doctors couldn't name the first attack which had come on suddenly during an argument with the new head priest at the annual huli huli chicken sale a few months before. Sensei had violently opposed his successor's latest revenue-making scheme of bringing in a popular singer from Japan to appear at the festival. "I built this temple with my own hands before you were even a smile in your Papa's sleep!" Sensei had shouted, just before the ocean roared up inside him and the blackness came. The fit, as Okusan called it, had passed as quickly as it had come, leaving him paralyzed in both legs. The villagers said that the old priest had finally been defeated by progress. For Okusan, who did not put much store either in progress or in medical science, her husband's fit had been an almost magical event—like all of the events that made up time; it worried her that she did not yet know the proper rite of propitiation. The old man was not making matters any easier.

"Ugh," he said, as Okusan bent over him. "You smell of chives." Each week, his wife smelled of a different miracle cure for arthritis that she'd heard about on the People Speak radio show. There had been lemon balm, mint, aloe, clove. He remembered favorite smells. The aloe had been worse than the chives. "I must make ready for Kitaro," he repeated.

"Hush, old man," his wife chided. "Why are you in such a hurry to go away from me? The doctors didn't do any good . . . but they never do . . . we can still . . . let's . . . let's . . . " She did not know how to go on. She did not know how to stop losing him. "I know you don't really approve . . . But it won't hurt to try. Let's ask the Prayer Lady to come. I know she will." Taking her husband's silence as a sign of encouragement, she pressed on. "Didn't Uncle Carlton Tamayoshi go to the Prayer Lady for that heart condition that the doctors swore would kill him inside a year, and here he is, fifteen years later. And what about Mrs. Koyama's terrible gout? On a rainy day, it just about killed her to walk . . . got so she wouldn't leave the house. And remember, oh remember Mustard Hayashi?"

Sensei remembered. It was said that the Prayer Lady could heal people just by touching them with her hands, that the woman had acquired her special powers in a moment of revelation on a rainy summer afternoon as she was emptying the trash. As the story went, a sudden gust of wind had blown the torn page from a sutra book across a neighbor's yard into her hand, and as she held the page, the full meaning of the text had flooded into her mind in a sudden infusion of light. From that moment on, it was believed that she had a special connection with the kami, the spirits of the ancestors, who gave her the power to heal with her touch. For years, Sensei had regarded her as a less than creditable rival for the loyalty of his congregation. Who knows, he thought. If it hadn't been for that woman carrying on her services down the road, church attendance might have been higher. Maybe he would have been able to stop . . . The image of the barely pubescent rock star with the duck tail hairdo flooded his consciousness.

254

"Hmph," Sensei snorted.

Okusan pushed on, "I've heard such good things, such encouraging things, really. Cousin Aki-chan and I were just talking about the Prayer Lady the other day . . . "

"Oh, foolishness!" the old man cried. "That old crank! That garbage can Buddha! You will kill me with your foolish ideas before Kitaro even gets here!" His wizened face had drawn taut; his eyes were bright. The air between them shimmered like spun glass, then darkened again.

Outside, the last tour bus rattled in from Kaanapali. The doors hissed open, spilling out a metallic stream of tourist voices that flowed into the hum of the crowd across the temple yard. "That should be Tanji's vegetable wagon bringing the musicians from up-country," Sensei said. He stared directly at his wife. His voice was suddenly very quiet. Tanji had been a friend of Kitaro. The sea had taken them both in the same fishing accident.

Okusan sighed. Old man. Old man, you will scare everyone away with this craziness and that will be worse than being dead. She did not say the words.

"Hot noodles! Hot dogs! Genuine good luck charms!" the hawkers cried, raising their voices above the sound of the crowd. Okusan wrapped her husband in funeral silk the color of old photographs. The old man closed his eyes. The silk flowed like falling water over him. The scent of camphor rose from its deep folds, like memory.

The dream seemed painted on his closed lids. Always the same dream. The sea. The boy. Strong brown limbs flashing against the white sand, hands reaching up to free the luminous white shape into the bright sky, like a prayer, "Oh look!" And up the kite soared—a dancing shape in that dream of blue. The boy had been the last. He had always belonged to the sea. The others were buried in the temple yard.

The old priest had built the temple with his own hands—hauling stone, mixing mortar, sawing wood until his hands bled and it seemed he would never stand straight again. As he raised walls and roof, the temple shaped what he became. His body grew brown and taut. He hammered the roofbeams down, singing to the sky. He married in the temple and buried his stillborn sons in the graveyard, one by one, knowing that it was not the end of things. Each year, time was renewed for that brief while in summer when the spirits of the dead wakened and the dusty glow of the festival lanterns burned into the early morning.

In the dream, time held him like an embrace, continuous and whole. It seemed he could not tell the boy who sang from the roofbeams from that other boy who ran upon the sand, reaching with eager hands toward the sky.

The old woman finished dressing him. "There," she said settling him on the living room couch with a book of sutras on his lap and his legs stretched out before him. "How handsome you look." The reflection from the reading lamp behind him glinted off his smooth, bald scalp like little stars.

From across the temple yard, the bamboo flute sang out, calling the dancers to the dance. The drums began to beat and the singers to chant. Okusan went to the window and peeked out through the blinds. "Is he coming?" the old man called. "What do you see?" Within the ring of lights formed by the festival lanterns, the dancers in summer kimonos circled the musicians' tower, their sleeves fluttering like white birds in the wind.

"Only the dancers dancing, Papa," the old woman said. She sensed, rather than heard, the stirring of the sea that seemed to come from everywhere, like the quickening of touch.

The sound of footsteps crossed the porch and someone knocked at the screen door. "Konban wa!" a bright voice called. The door pulled open. The Prayer Lady stood on the stoop, with the light from the festival lanterns burning in the night behind her. She wore a Mamasan dress with tiny star-shaped flowers, and her white hair was pulled back neatly into a bun. She carried a bag of strawberry guavas and a bunch of golden crysanthemums in her hands. "Hello, Okusan," she said, giving the flowers and the fruit to her. The Prayer Lady looked at Sensei installed in his funeral clothes upon the couch; she looked him up and down. Her voice was grave. "I heard you weren't feeling well and decided to pay my respects, but if I'd known it was this serious, I would have come sooner."

"You . . . " Sensei glared at his wife.

"I'll go and get some tea and things," Okusan said, hastily leaving the room. "I won't be long . . . "

The Prayer Lady turned back to the old priest. "To look at you," she said, "one could never tell . . . "

"Um," Sensei grunted.

"I see it depresses you to talk about it, though I must say you are taking the whole thing very bravely." She went from window to window, pulling up the blinds. "Ah, but it's a splendid night, isn't it?" The night filled the room. The music swelled.

Sensei's lips were an angry white slit. "I heard you were in a retirement home," he hissed.

"The things people say! You wouldn't believe what they are saying down in the village—that you've lost your grip since the attack. No one has faith anymore, you know? Miracles aren't impossible, after all, though they're a bit out of style. But of course, I've considered it . . . Going into a retirement home, I mean." She glanced about the room at the kegs of rice and saké, the plates of sweets, and the fruits that well-wishers had brought. "I've thought about how nice it would be to lie about on a splendid night like this . . . "

The old priest looked furious. "Sachi!" he called for his wife.

" . . . with well-wishers streaming in the door . . . and nice things to eat . . . "

"Sachi!" he yelled louder. Where was that old woman?

" . . . everyone making a fuss over you . . . " The woman was relentless. "You wouldn't have to lift a finger . . . "

"Get out!" Sensei shouted. He was shaking with rage. "Get out, get out!"

The Prayer Lady walked to the door. "Oh, Sensei," she said. "Don't you know?" Her smooth pink face suddenly looked old. "Neither of us could have held back what is happening." She quietly turned and left.

"What is all the fuss?" Okusan asked, carrying a wooden tray of tea and cakes into the room.

The old man did not answer. He sat very still. Then, he laboriously got to his feet, hobbled past the old woman—waving aside her offer of help—and walked out the door. The night was alive with stars and the sound and smell of the ocean. Okusan watched from the porch steps as he made his way across the temple yard and followed the procession of lights down to the bay. "Aryasa, koryaa," the singers chanted. "It has been so. It shall always be." The lanterns glowed on the dark water. The singers said the words, like the chant of memory through time.

Joan Sauro, C.S.J.

Joan Sauro, a Roman Catholic nun, writes and teaches creative writing to widows and welfare mothers in Syracuse, New York. She is the recipient of a CAPS Fellowship in fiction from the New York State Council on the Arts. Joan's latest book is The Whole Earth Meditation.

INNER MARATHON
The Diary of a Jogging Nun

So I started jogging. Mostly to keep body and soul together.

Actually, I have been running all my life. In the family album there is a picture of me in diapers with my left arm in a sling. Big tears are rolling down. I had been running in my aunt's house and slipped on the high gloss. At picnics, I always won the foot races, for girls under six, for girls six to twelve, for unmarried women. By that time I was running on a tennis court, swinging unorthodox strokes, winning only because my legs were faster. I ran from a potential rapist. I ran when the snowball I threw entered the open window of a delivery truck and struck the driver. Then I entered the convent.

One day another novice looked at me with affection. I ran. In habit and old ladies' shoes I ran, faster than at any picnic or tennis court. I ran circles around the old seminary where we all lived, round and round that high towered, austere, stone fortress, like Achilles running around Troy, spending his anger. I didn't know what I was spending.

When I wasn't running, I was kneeling safely in the chapel, kneeling in the stone fortress on strong runner's legs. I knelt for hours without visible support. One Holy Thursday in the middle of the kneeling I became conscious of my breathing, and conscious that a word was being said in the inhale-exhale. The word was "Jesus." I took it for a blessing on my running and kneeling.

A long time after, I am learning to stand and face certain things. This diary is one of those things.

In the old days we used to read the lives of the saints, the better to emulate their outsized virtues. Today it seems appropriate to read the lives of one another. It is in this spirit that I give you my story, that you may be encouraged to tell yours.

February 14. It may have all started with Sister Consilia, my sixth grade teacher, although until last week I had scarcely a clue.

Joan Sauro, C.S.J. 261

She spied me, this Sister Consilia now past eighty, in the mother house dining room, fixed me with frozen eye and bony finger and "Do you say the prayers I taught you do you Jesus meek and humble of heart make my heart like unto thine O most sacred heart of Jesus be my love sweet heart of Mary be my salvation?"

Well no, I don't. But something like it. Somehow it all contracted to "Jesus," or maybe that's all I heard you say, and I don't even know for sure it all started with you, but chances seem good it may have.

Later I met the Russian Pilgrim, but by then the prayer had long since made its way to my heart.

He was a marathoner, this Russian Pilgrim, doing his forty-three or four miles a day with his Bible in one breast pocket and his *Philokalia* in the other. In his heart he carried the wish to pray always and the Jesus Prayer the holy staret taught him to say on his rosary beads. The thumb on the Pilgrim's left hand was worn thin from sliding over twelve thousand beads a day.

Twelve thousand times a day he prayed, "Lord Jesus Christ, have mercy on me," until in no time at all the prayer slipped from his lips down into his heart and started saying itself to the tune of his heartbeat.

Soon his eyes followed suit and dropped down to his heart too, into those many and convoluted chambers where the Jesus Prayer was going on like a broken record and the Jesus of the Prayer started showing him little by little the mystery of his sensuous and spiritual heart. Then the marathon really began, forty-three or four miles a day through the labyrinthine ways of that heart. All the while, the Pilgrim was breathing in on "Lord Jesus Christ," and breathing out on "have mercy on me."

And that is just about where I am now, at the gateway to the convoluted heart, taking two steps and a breath in on "Je" and two steps and a breath out on "sus."

February 15. My feet take me through the broken streets of an unpresuming, hybrid parish called St. Brigid and St. Joseph. The first steps are all downhill, from home to Twin Trees Too Restaurant, where I take a left on ice and skid past Jenny Herron's dress

262

shop where the mannequins pose in lightless windows. Jenny sits in furs at the Saturday night liturgy. Jenny has no idea I send Jesus into her shop every morning. The block ends at the Twin Trees pizza barn where fresh bread is baking and I remember Jesus blessing the loaves and breaking them. I hear him say, "No one is to have the whole loaf. Of you."

Then the long, seemingly endless, one-half mile up Willis Avenue hill, dotted with dogs and little children, past the school and church and convent up near the top, and the Congregational church, abandoned save for birds in the bell tower. A left on Genesee and my legs rest on a down hill toward the DeSantis music house on the left and the old homestead of my dead music teacher on the right. Jesus, have mercy on her.

The United Methodist church is followed by Beebe the dentist, Edward J. Ryan and Son Funeral Home and the policewoman with the leathered face, frozen in every season. I bless her, the librarians in the Hazard Branch and whoever is pulling the bells in the Episcopalian church. I wave to Red Ertinger, pumping Mobil on weekdays, passing the collection basket on weekends. Cookie Caloia at the car wash is marshaling a line of cars headed by Ed Ryan in the hearse.

A sharp left on ice at the Key Bank leads to the Tops Market on the right, and a long strip of interesting shops on the left — everything from TV's and fleas, to upholstery, Jocko's Shebeen and the American Legion Tipperary Hill Post 1361. It all ends at the Casual Inn. I take a quick left up heartbreak hill where Dick Allen is loading the truck at the auction house, and a quick right past Kerstetter cabinetmakers. For one long level mile I sprint on Emerson Avenue, past the Lipe-Rollway Factory where a woman calls 691 over the roar and violent scream of machines.

A sudden clump of trees hides a small dump and a red cardinal. With one steep climb, I am home with cleaner heart and well-oiled limbs.

February 18. Run easy. Thoughtless. Gentle. Jesus. The road seems to lower kindly and the sun pull me up on a string, up toward home. They say that when Edward Villella dances the prodigal son, he moves as if pulled on a string toward his father.

February 19. Below zero every day. It is difficult to protect my hands, so I open and close them, in rhythm, until hands, feet, breath and prayer are synchronized in open-close, left-right, in-out, Je-sus.

There's a ragtag, one-woman band playing on the slopes and slides of this parish.

February 24. Dry as a cold bone, so I jog up the middle of the Willis Avenue hill, past Mom and Dad's green car, parked in front of the church. They are in at the 10 o'clock Mass. I feel better, seeing their car and knowing where they are, as if they were the children and I the parent.

February 27. Grey to black day, sunless, dogless, practically carless, unobtrusive Wednesday, in the middle of the week like a sandwich.

February 28. Three to five inches fell in the night, got run over and half-plowed. Now there are two to three inches of moist brown sugar underfoot in the street, twisting my ankles unmercifully.

My brother asks me why I don't stay home in winter and run in place. I tell him I would not persevere. Once I got a side ache or lost my breath, I would quit. I run outdoors to put myself *out* of place, far from home, so that when a pain comes, I cannot stop. At that point I'm halfway out, with no choice but to run home.

I think I put myself in this apartment with Janet for the same reason. I put myself *out* of place, out of convent, so that when I want to ease off I cannot. I am forced to live responsibly and to depend on others. It is a kind of situation ethics.

March 3.

> there are cardinals all over the place —
> or maybe the same one
>
> the grape ivy, upright till now,
> has thrown itself out the window
> with longing for the sun

March 5. Steady rain at 8. By 8:45 it turns half rain half snow. Not so wet except for the feet.

I say the Jesus Prayer slowly, trying to forget everything else, praying his name to wash me like baptism.

The run is like the weather, half and half.

March 12. It is the same driving wind that belts us with snow today that last Monday poured down rain. In between came sun and 60°.

March simulates all seasons, serves them all up in smorgasbord fashion. Only the houseplants know. Sure of themselves, they slowly unfurl, one shiny new leaf, then another. Plants know spring has nothing to do with the elements. Spring is a quality of light. So is heaven.

March 15. Heaven is cleaning house today, throws down buckets of dirty wash and a fistful of snow on runners. The wind is a roaring vacuum cleaner, cleaning heaven, dumping bagfuls of dirt, paper, cans, a yellow lampshade to leap over and an old man.

I watch him, the old man, slug down the dirt green side of his house, turn back, turn forward, turn back toward the wrong house where he is banged in shut by a loose door. A car rolls slowly up to the house, rolls back, rolls up, rolls out the driver, unsure which house is his. None of them are.

Joan Sauro, C.S.J.   265

March 20. Winter went for good today and took the ice and snow handicap with it. We still have the wind.

March 21. Every day, before I run, I sit as prayerfully as I can and read a Gospel story, for an hour or so. For twenty years I have been turning these pages faithfully, reading God's story. Today I wonder. Does God read my story?

The answer comes out on the road, somewhere in the windy stretch up Willis Avenue. I see a picture of an ageless Jesus, with wire glasses fallen down his nose. He is sitting in profile, in a Rembrandt lighting—dark brown background, warm gold light on his face.

A book is opened on his lap and he is reading, thoroughly engrossed. Now and again he smiles, gets excited, lifts his head up to relish some passage, turns the page slowly, sighs, cries, shifts nervously in his chair, laughs uproariously at an illustration.

There are many, many books of stories on the darkened shelves behind him, but today he is reading my story, and loving it, as each person hopes.

April 6. I hem and haw at the weather, would rather run in snow, ice, sleet, rain, scorching sun, anything than in wind. Today it comes at me in sixty mile an hour gusts. Today I learn a lesson from the wind:

> It is not always possible to go forward.
> It is always possible to go up and down.

April 7. My greatest joy in jogging is when my two feet are in the air.

High or low—there's not a place I won't go. But I want you to know my aim is high, and as soon as this wind dies down, I'm up and out for keeps. That's why I practice these trash can leaps.

266

April 10. The wind is still furious. All night long it banged the windows, shook the house and even the chairs we sat in for prayer this morning.

A child is playing the piano in the DeSantis music house. One small finger exercise, played to the beat of the metronome, comes through the bay window and rides on the wind to me, jogging by in 4/4 time, to the rhythm of Je - sus.

My legs are a metronome too. I slow them down or speed them up, to adjust to the wind. But I do not break the rhythm of my song.

Every athlete knows that the way to win the game is to control the rhythm.

April 15. Easter Sunday. Peter and John start out on their way toward the tomb. They run side by side most of the way. Then John outruns Peter and reaches the tomb first. He sees and believes.

John, patron saint of joggers, saves his kick for the end. Poets always get there first and have to wait for the Peters, the rocks of the world, to catch up.

April 17. I hear the ground breaking as I run by.

a bulb breaks ground soundlessly,
all at once greenly

no bells peal,
not a note
for valor in the field

April 23. Run under a canopy of soft green fuzz, green puffballs exploding, colored balloons, and the parish is a circus. Every dog is out doing his act. I need steel guards on my legs. I need a warden. I need the hound of heaven, chasing me down the nights

Joan Sauro, C.S.J.   267

and down the days, catching me in the labyrinthine ways of my own mind.

April 24. Far away in the heart of the forest, the contemplative nun at Still Point House of Prayer sits in the yoga position. She breathes the Jesus Prayer gently, in and out, Jesus, Son of David, have mercy on us. Then all the nuns chant the prayer together, there mid the murmuring pines and bird song.

Here in the heart of the city, the active nun jogs the broken streets of the parish, breathing the same name of Jesus, gently, in stride, two steps to a syllable, Je - sus, up and down the hills, into the dusty gutters, around parked cars, mid honks and beeps of passers-by, some friendly, some frisky, the name of Jesus breathed on them all.

April 26. All the windows on the way are thrown open to spring. At the Lipe-Rollway Factory the machines scream violently through every window. I stretch out my arms and open my hands all the long length of the factory. Jesus, have mercy on all who work in violence. Protect their hands and eyes and souls.

April 27. Just a little more gentle jogging today, just a little more quiet in praying. Jesus, Son of David, have mercy on her. Chrissy Susnock was hit by a school bus this morning, less than an hour ago, in the street below our apartment window.

Just a little irritated with the speed and screech sounds in the street, I had slammed the porch door shut and tried to attend to the Morning Praise we were saying. Then there came a screech and scream more terrible than the rest. From the porch we could see—Chrissy lay face down in the middle of the street, in between the garbage truck and the head-start school bus. Her face was a mass of purple.

We called Father Libera and went down to the street. The neighbors were making her as comfortable as they could, with pillows and blankets off their unmade beds. Two black men from the garbage truck took up detail at either end of the street, flagging away traffic. One's face was on the other side of the city, looking for his own children, wondering if they made it to school safely.

Just in from the night shift, the child's father came stumbling out of bed and onto the street. The ambulance came, followed by the police. They iced her face and put splints on her arms. The priest talked gently to her. The mother, having raced back from work, tore from the car and shook all the way to the spot where her child lay. She knelt down and buried her face in the disfigured one.

"Take me home, Mommy."

"Get up. They've got to put her in the ambulance." The mother did not move.

"*You* have to go with her in the ambulance." This came from a stalwart neighbor who knew the right approach, to motherly duty. She and the father pulled up the mother, still shaking, who then hugged the teenage daughter who should have been minding her sister and said, "It's not your fault, honey."

After they left, there were only two white pieces of paper blowing in the street, two empty bandage bags to say this morning at 7:50 a child was hit by a bus, here on our street, and her life was spared, maybe because two nuns were praying, however badly, in a noisy room above the street.

May 1. First week in May is 40°. I run with black gloves on, past the blooming magnolia which has more trust than I. The tree stands in a cold trance, unable to go back to bud or forth to full bloom. I wave a black hand to a pink tree.

May 2. At the gynecologist's I wait, sitting on a table top, in gown and socks. After a while I notice a strange thing going on with my legs.

My right leg dangles down from the table, is still, like a heavy anchor, knows very well I should be here for the periodic checkup.

Joan Sauro, C.S.J.   269

My left leg swings back and forth furiously, rhythmically, saying the Jesus Prayer, saying let's get out of here.

After the examination, I jump for relief off the table and jog the three miles home.

May 12. Last night it was 90°, so we sat out the heat on the front porch. At midnight the Allied Chemical whistle blew, and a jogger in trunks went by with his dog. The man's feet splat splat on the hot sidewalk.

At 7 A.M. it was only 10° cooler. Two girl friends jogged together in the street.

At 8 I am on the road, skipping over the purple trash bags the gay grocer carried out. I say the Jesus Prayer slowly, up the hot Willis Avenue hill, down the Genesee strip, and slow down in front of Ryan's Funeral Home to pray Jesus, Son of David, have mercy on James, lying skin and bones in the death house. James Tierney, father of Sister Patricia and Sister Marguerite. They're home eating breakfast now, so I keep watch with running feet.

James is risen. He is not here. Hurry, feet, hurry to proclaim it to the two sisters, feet pounding the sidewalk, beating the name of Jesus over and over into the streets and sidewalks. Long after I'm gone the name of Jesus will stay engraved in the cement, beaten in by rubber cleats.

When I get home, I take my shoes off and find maple seeds lodged between the cleats, sprouting there.

Marilyn Krysl

Marilyn Krysl grew up in Kansas and Oregon. She has published three books of poetry (Saying Things, *Abattoir Editions, U. of Nebraska Press, 1978;* More Palomino, Please, More Fuchsia, *Cleveland State Poetry Center, 1980;* Diana Lucifera, *Shameless Hussy Press, 1983) and two books of stories* (Honey, You've Been Dealt A Winning Hand, *Capra, Santa Barbara, 1980;* Mozart, Westmoreland and Me, *Thunder's Mouth Press, 1985). Her work has appeared in the* O. Henry Prize Stories, The Atlantic, The New Republic, The Nation *and many little magazines. She lives in Boulder, Colorado and teaches at the University of Colorado.*

GENIE WOMEN

Sundays were different. It was the women who were in power. All my aunts and uncles and cousins were there, and of course we had to go to Sunday school and church, but it was the women, my grandmother, their leader, who insisted on attending church and in fact looked forward to it. Church was a social, not a religious occasion. Church was an excuse for dressing up, for making up your face. Everyone knew this, and that was why the women loved it and the men prayed for the day to pass quickly.

My grandfather and uncles and my father got scant pleasure on this day. When they could not work, they were out of their element. My grandfather had gotten the idea from Genesis that man was born to wrest a living from the land by the sweat of his brow, and he took this as a mandate. Work was what there was to do, except Sundays, when work was forbidden. Play was also forbidden, but that was because my grandfather didn't know how. The younger men might have preferred whiskey and indolence, but they knew what was expected of them. They shaved dutifully, put on their graceless white shirts and suits, and that was that.

The women conceived the occasion as a celebration. Sunday mornings, my cousin Ruthie and I met with them in grandmother's bedroom. Lingerie was made of satin and had to be ironed, but the shiny smoothness was worth all the trouble. Lolling on the bed in peach colored satin, they looked like movie stars. These goddesses drew us to their shimmering sides, washed us and patted us dry with thick towels, powdered us with sweet talcum. I rose with the cloud of powder floating, nebulous, in a shaft of sunlight. I liked the downiness of my belly afterwards. They rubbed glycerine and rosewater on our cheeks and noses to protect our baby skin from sun and dry wind. I liked this too, the soft slide of the oil and its heavy smell, the luxurious attention to my sweet flesh.

Then they let us help them powder and perfume themselves. *Bring me the lavender*, Ruthie's mother, Hope, might say. And one of us would hurry to Grandma's dressing table to fetch it. We observed carefully as she perfumed the inside of her wrists, the lobes of her ears. She was a small woman, and delicate. The scent of lavender seemed right for her. We wondered if someday we too would grow up to be small and delicate, if lavender would some-day be right for us too. But why behind the ears, we wondered. *Because*, she said, the man who stands behind you will smell the perfume and want to see your face.

"Give the powder puff to Grandma." It was my grandmother's habit to poke the powderpuff into the cleavage at the top of her slip and let the powder drift down inside unseen. My mother was brisk and extravagant, filling the bedroom with a pale, dry mist until my grandmother called her name: "Evelyn!" Hope powdered her belly and breasts, then asked one of us to powder her back. Soft shoulder blades fanned from her spine, silk smooth, cream white. I dusted her slowly, lightly, wanting to make the experience last. The powder puff drifted like white cumulus across her skin. I imagined sky, light wind, a long afternoon.

Bathsheba and her women. Demeter and her daughters. Face powder and rouge. The bright red oil sticks of lipstick. Black dye for eyelashes. The tinkle of garters, the putting on of white gloves to prevent runs when pulling on stockings. The adjusting of seams in the stockings. Are my seams straight? No, the left one turns out at the ankle.

Strings of pearls, pearl earrings, flower printed dresses, linen suits. And hats with veils. Round boxes lifted carefully from closet shelves. Boxes of hats of all sizes and descriptions. Cloche hats, straws with wide brims, pill boxes, black straw with cherries, pink linen with net veil, white straw with blue ribbons. And the last touch was a handkerchief, in purse or pocket or carried in the hand.

I felt in the presence of ease, luxury, affection, time without duties. I felt our importance. Here women admired themselves. They praised and approved each other. Hope massages my moth-er's shoulders and the headache goes away. They comforted each other with the small amenities of the body.

They comforted each other and they put on power. If at other times they were depressed or terrified into silence, here they were not afraid. No one judged, no one condemned. We were at ease, did as we pleased, and we took time, great, lazy amounts of time. There was no one to tell us we were wasting it. Each at leisure studied her own nature. A color or cut that was right for one might be wrong for another. Each worked out her particular series of allurements. Each helped the others perfect their particularities.

I came to understand the power of presence. That one's presence had overtones, undertones, reverberations. That to walk into a room meant the room changed. That even if acknowledgment was unspoken, still presence imposed in space and time, demanded and exacted acknowledgment. I understood presence was enhanced by color, by jewelry and scent, that these things encouraged the manifestation of an essence that was invisible but real.

As the toilet progressed, their power increased. By the time these women left the bedroom, they knew who they were. They were not afraid of themselves or each other and certainly not of the men. The men were, in turn, bewildered, uncomfortable in their starched white shirts and ties, not up to their ladies. And how could they be—there was little stylish or expressive about their clothes, nothing sensuous or daring in their manner. They were solemn, dressed for a solemn occasion.

But what was intended as a solemn occasion became instead a carouse. In church it was the women who sang. The men mumbled or held back, embarrassed. Their toilet had not primed them for this frank, full-bodied expression of emotion. The women sang lustily, with florid vibrato. They leaned into hymns with nasal intensity. They held the tied whole notes bravely to the end. Then, during the sermon, some women wept. Whether they wept at the minister's message or for private griefs, no one could tell, but they were not ashamed. Nor were those brazen women who dozed, sunk in their gorgeousness. The rest, though more circumspect, were just as wicked. They quietly admired each other, letting the minister drone on unheeded, communing by glance and sideways smile.

Afterward, everyone had to shake the minister's hand. Ruthie and I dreaded this custom, but once past him, we were free. We ran wild with the others, played tag, gathered in a bright cluster behind our mothers, wanting to hear what they were saying about the minister's wife, wanting to know what dish each woman planned to bring to the pot luck supper. Their voices buzzed, rose to laughter, modulated down to gossip. They had waited a week for this meeting. They had prepared and saved remarks for this meeting. They were glad to see even their enemies. They were in no hurry to go home.

The men had to stand and smoke and wait. The men were boring. They didn't talk much. Also they seemed to have nothing to do. They stood with hands in their pockets, studied the sky. Ruthie and I hung at the edge of the circle of women. When they hugged us, we could smell their perfume, the powder they used to brush their teeth. Sometimes they would unpin the homemade corsages from their shoulders and give us the flowers.

The women made Sunday dinner, and the men had to sit and wait some more. They had to read the weekly paper and bide their time. Sometimes they tried to stroll in the yard, but they were stiff in their suits, and they still couldn't find anything to do with their hands. They talked about the weather and the price of corn, then lapsed into silence. As a last resort they walked to the barn, looked over the cattle, then came back to the driveway and kicked the tires of my father's car. They looked at the tractor. They looked at their watches. How implacably slow the earth's turning must have seemed to them.

How deliciously slow it seemed to me. Dinner was big, colorful, heavy. Afterward everyone took a nap. My mother and Hope lay on the bed, talking softly. Grandmother did embroidery. Aunt Mildred showed Ruthie and me how to crochet and to tat. Sometimes one of the women would read to us. Sometimes we lay on the bed with them, listening to them talk until we fell asleep.

I tried to stay awake, listening to the sound of my mother's voice. On these Sunday afternoons her voice had an easiness, a softness and grace I heard at no other time. Her words threaded the afternoon lightly, without tension or rancor. The sound of her voice left me with the impression of loosely woven cloth, a texture that would comfort the body.

I felt comforted there, lying next to her, or close by, within hearing. I believed this ease would continue, that we would not be tested. My grandmother's bedspread was printed with peacocks, those regal birds I had read about, but never seen. Their wide tails spread like full skirts seemed exotic beyond believing. I took it for granted all peacocks were female, and their images are imprinted on my memory still, an emblem of that uroboric feeling and that time.

I didn't worry about God and his ten inexorable commandments on those days. My grandfather did of course. He always did what he was supposed to do. The rest of us knew we were supposed to worry, but there in that inner chamber amidst down comforters, crewel pillows, blue glass perfume droppers and ivory combs, God and the fear he was to inspire seemed distant and unreal. What interested us was us. We were real, we were vibrantly alive, and we had let ourselves out of the bottles. We were genie women, and we wove our magic for a day among ourselves.

Linda Hogan

Linda Hogan is the author of CALLING MYSELF HOME, ECLIPSE, *and* THAT HORSE. *Her most recent book,* SEEING THROUGH THE SUN, *won an American Book Award from the Before Columbus Foundation. She is the recipient of a National Endowment for the Arts grant in fiction and the Minnesota State Arts Board grant in poetry. She teaches a course on Healing at the University of Minnesota.*

MEETING

It was a prayer meeting and it was Halloween and it was the women's gathering that had its roots in god-knows-where, but it was a tradition with the Indian women who lived in and near Seeker County.

All our cousins were going. I wanted to go, and so did my sisters. We wanted to see the town girls and what they were wearing. We wanted to see our cousin Evelyn who looked like Elizabeth Taylor.

Mom was there, sitting with her wide-hipped twin cousins. "I heard you two bet on those racing mules last week. Win anything?" she asked them. They wore mint green dresses and had identical rear ends. They told her they didn't; there was no use spoiling the odds.

And Ora Young was there carrying her fan of swan feathers that looked to be made of light just like Ora with her pale mottled skin and near-silver eyes. Ora stood beside Neva and the girls and told about people in town: This Indian woman had loved a black man who worked for the railroad, that one shot her husband, and didn't he just deserve it. That man stole his father's horses and sold them. This woman loved a Swede who was passing through town trying to document a story about rural something or other.

It was not gossip. It was the history of our living.

Ora was the keeper of records, the teller of lives, that woman who visited on and read to the elderly, that woman with bony knuckles, with hands that doctored sick cattle, shoveled the barn, gathered eggs.

Ora's husband, Darius Young, was a man who called himself preacher. He was both a Baptist and a Methodist; like everyone he was hedging his bets. Every year he fought with Ora not to attend the devil's meetings, as he called the women's prayers which took place irregardless of church, state, or husbands, but Ora's home life was worth a disaster so she went, as did the rest of us.

Occasionally I saw my sister Roberta and another girl elbow

one another and try not to laugh, but for the most part we walked with pomp and circumstance like the women, our skirts blowing against our legs.

In the clearing at Brook Hollow, women were already dancing in a circle and singing the rich low songs, the deer song, the trail song. They were warming up to the prayer songs, and so was the slow water lapping up the night beyond us.

These were the women who gossipped, laughed, baked bread, and complained. They were women who used to flirt with young men and still did. They gave birth to children, made beds, wrung laundry with stiff, arthritic fingers, and built chairs.

The night wind took away the noise that lived inside them, the worries about firewood in hard winters, and the internal, infernal chatter about this and that. For this one night there was no worry about love or money, no anger at the rich ones, no sorrow about what parcels of tribal land had been sold off by crooked chiefs.

We knew these women. Their hands drove horses, pumped water, killed and plucked chickens.

Mom was boiling coffee on the fire and serving it up. The women sipped it and warmed their palms over the fire. They were quiet but the lines of their faces spoke in the firelight, telling about stars that fell at night, the horses that died in the drought of 1930, and the pure and holy terror of gunshots fired into our houses. Roberta and I squatted by their legs and warmed our own hands just to look into those faces. We had misjudged them. Exhaustion had covered up all the mystery and beauty the women held inside. Cotton aprons full of lard and cornmeal hid the mighty life and glory of our neighbors.

When the wind died down that night even the trees were listening. The earth listened to the firesongs of women's voices that broke through the walls of skin. The heartbeat of the ground rose up. It was a sound, that drumming, that could have split the walls of Jericho.

Grandma Addie asked for another winter's strength and health. "And give us potatoes that don't rot," she prayed. "And birds that don't peck away the spring corn." There were long lists of thanks to earth and sky for easy births, for the new life carried inside, for all blessings we thank you mother. Gratitude like shopping lists.

280

Thank you father for the butter, for the laying hens, mother, for the fat old sow with piglets, grandmother, and for the boar whose days are numbered. For the shoes cousin Elmo sent that didn't fit his girls any more, for the can of grease and the little containers of snuff.

Ora shook the gourd full of small pebbles and they began singing, that song going up like we sang for our life, and we did. Evelyn's mom, looking like an elderly Liz Taylor, rattled turtle shells. Grandma rattled the deep purple bean pods, those pods so long that if they'd been edible, like green beans maybe, a single one would have filled an entire quart jar.

All the sounds of summer gone dry filled the air, along with the last of the insects and the wind.

Grandma had been speaking Chickasaw. We only knew a little of it but we listened hard. Then she turned to Roberta and said in English, "There's animals in you. I see them, little deers and snakes. Honey, they just move in, lock, stock and barrel, and there's nothing you can do about it." She pursed her lips. "It's a mixed blessing, but you will sure know whenever you take a wrong turn in your life because they'll fight you all the way. Well," she said, "I guess there's never an easy road to hoe." She squeezed Roberta around the shoulders. Roberta didn't smile. Then grandma gave me a hug, too.

I knew that Roberta was going to be a healer like Grandma. I knew she'd be one of those old women who traveled to the Glass Mountains where the sun and moonlight came from, those mountains like houseless windows rising from the red earth. She'd go there to collect mica, to take home sheets of that flaking light.

I knew Berta would become one of those grandmothers in that land of tarantulas, opossum, armadilloes, and mighty land turtles. She'd be like grandma when sick women gathered around her cooking stove. She'd hold her hands over sick people who were poor and who were losing children in labor, over women whose faces were white as powder, women who coughed and bled from the lungs, or who had too much sorrow. She'd carve mica into the shape of a hand and hold it over them until the sickness crept into the hand, and she'd look inside it and read it like a palm or a book. Afterwards she'd crumble the hand and bury it, but first she'd tell them what she saw, "It was the food you didn't have when you were a child. Be sure you eat plenty of greens and watercress now." She'd tell them not to give babies powdered milk with Karo syrup. She'd tell them to put their sadness away.

The women would cover their faces and cry.

I knew Roberta was always taking it in. She pretended not to listen, but she stood there swallowing pain, one of her run-over shoes making little circles on the floor and a downcast look on her face. Her dress ties undone, she watched.

When grandma blew smoke across the sick, Roberta kept track. There were times grandma knew she could do nothing but hold the women, times the only real help was love and compassion, so grandma held the women and Roberta gazed off out the window at chickens who had caught a frog and were pecking the life out of it, but Roberta had caught those two elements like they were the Asian flu. Like some people have signs in fire and air, Roberta was born in the sign of love with her moon in compassion.

I was jealous that night at the meeting when the women in their blowing dresses talked and sang and were silent. I was jealous that Grandma didn't say I had the animals in me. But healing is a calling, and I knew that much. It isn't something a person picks out for herself like an occupation, and I knew Roberta wouldn't have chosen it anyway, being the kind of girl who would like to do hair or work at the BIA, but there was that part of her that watched, sort of like an oversoul. She'd never have an easy go of it. I knew even then that Roberta was a kicker and fighter against fate. I also knew I'd be the one to search out some new ways to make up for not having the animals there to work with me, and that there's room for new ways too.

But the women were singing and there was that dancing and I learned that night what beauty lives under the high blood pressure and coronary blocks of our daily living, and that Evelyn didn't really look like a young Liz Taylor, and that grandma knew everything just as I'd always suspected. I met myself that night and I walked in myself. I heard my own blood. I learned all secrets lie beneath even the straggliest of hair, and that in the long run of things dry skin and stiff backs don't mean as much as we give them credit for. And I learned how the earth cranes its neck to hear our prayers.

Shay Youngblood

SHAY YOUNGBLOOD: *born 1959, Columbus, Georgia. Her fiction has appeared in* CONDITIONS *and* COMMON LIVES. *Shay is currently living in Atlanta where she is at work on a collection of memories about growing up with Big Mama.*

"Big Mama is a composite (fused with my imagination) of the Black women who raised me. They were some of the wisest women to see the light of day. I listened to them all through the years of my childhood, spellbound by their stories of physical, emotional and spiritual survival. One day I decided to give these women, my mama's, a voice. Luellen, Jennie Mae, Lillian, Bessie, Mary Lee, Myrtice and Nettie Mae need to be heard. Listen . . ."

BORN WID RELIGION

We didn't call her Big Mama cause she was big or even cause she was our mama, cause she wasn't either. She was just regular. A old black woman who had a gift for seeing with her heart. A brown skinned woman. Brother, who had a eye for color called her dark sienna. She kept her long, mixed gray hair plait up and wrapped across the top of her head. Her face was a place where deep lines drew high cheek bones that showed the Cherokee in her, and a place where dark knowing brown eyes showed their love for every living thing, 'cept maybe roaches. Her body was warm and full of soft places to lean into. In hard times folks be leaning on Big Mama. Like our blood mama, who left me and Brother with her, three years ago when I was six.

The story was told to me, that a slick talking beauty supply salesman driving a yellow convertible come to call on the shop where mama fixed hair. When he offered her a piece of the road, she dropped that greasy hot comb she was holding over some poor woman's head and they lit out of town in a cloud of fine red dust. Every now and then we'd get a post card from her saying how she was gonna send for us soon as "they" got settled, but times were still hard up north too.

Things be going bad for Big Mama she would up and go to the bible. She had faith in the power of the man above to work miracles, and me, I had faith in Big Mama.

Like the time Brother got put in jail for running numbers, Big Mama was up late every night reading out loud from the bible. She was doing some serious praying down there on her knees, eyes closed, work wore hands pressed together, pointed toward heaven, elbows digging deep into her side of the bed. About three days later Brother came stepping in the back door wid a plate of ribs smoking in one hand and a hat box in the other one. All he said was "thank you Big Mama." She said "Boy you better be thanking the lord." She was always giving credit to the lord.

When Aunt Viola got that growth in her stomach, everybody knew she was too old to have a baby. The doctor said it was a tumor and he was gonna have to cut her open, and that was gonna be risky since she was over 75 years old. Well Aunt Vi wouldn't hear about no surgery.

"I been wid a uncut belly this long I believe I'll just keep on till the lord takes me home." Aunt Vi had a way of keeping Jesus in every conversation. She sure was Big Mama's blood sister, them women loved the lord.

Now Aunt Vi believed that roots and herb medicines could cure anything. After the doctors' report she went to everybody in the neighborhood she knew could heal, then went to others she heard about. After a couple of weeks she looked about ready to deliver that tumor. Big Mama being her closest living kin, got worried and called a special meeting of the #2 Mission Prayer Circle to pray over Aunt Vi. Come dark, and just shadows apart, five elder sisters of the church eased in the back door. They would make their way through the kitchen to the front room, crowded with heavy, out dated furniture. Pictures of children Big Mama had raised covered the walls in frames of their own or stuck inside frames of the life-like portraits of Jesus or the gold framed double portraits of Dr. King and President Kennedy. Chairs were arranged in a raggedy circle. Aunt Vi was leaned back into the most comfortable chair, waving a funeral fan to knock flies from her swollen legs.

Miss Mary always showed up first. She looked like a skinny black gypsy. She had six gold teeth right in front, wore big gold earrings and bright colored scarves over her finger length plaits that stuck out from under. Then come Miss Alice, a light skinned sister wid the bluest eyes and hair I'd ever seen. Then Miss Tom come in. She was a mannish looking woman wid a moustache. She took the neighborhood kids fishing every summer. Then Miss Emma Lou come in, short dark and bow legged, still wearing her white maids uniform and carrying that spit cup. The woman didn't go nowhere without a tin of sweet georgia peach snuff in her apron picket and a old tin can that she kept under every chair and pew she took up space on. And late as always come Miss Lamama, her real name was Jessie Pearl Lumumba. In her youth she married a African and took to wearing African dresses and took on African like ways.

I got sent upstairs so the grown folks could meet, but I only went up halfway so I wouldn't miss nothing. There was a call to order to set old business straight and get on wid the new. Miss Alice reported on her visits to the sick members of the congregation. "Sister English is recuperating in satisfactory condition from her gall bladder operation and she 'preciates the chewing tobacco and peppermint candies that we took up collection to buy for her. Brother Solomon's cataract operation was a success, he says it scandalous though, how short them nurses are wearing their uniforms, he's seeing more now than he ever wanted to."

Then Miss Mary read a long passage from the bible. St. Matthew, 9th chapter, verses 1 through 27. It was about how Jesus cured the sick, raised the dead and healed the blind. Miss Mary got to reading loud in the end like she was about ready to start shouting. " . . . then the almighty Jesus said 'daughter be of good comfort; thy faith has made thee whole.' Halleluliah!" I couldn't hardly hear after that for the hand clapping, foot stomping and 'amens' that rocked the front room.

A low humming started around the edges of the room. The uneven sound of them old women calling on the spirit to move in them mysterious ways. It caught me by surprise and held me still. When I peeped around the corner of the stairwall, I saw Aunt Vi in the center of the circle moaning and singing and rocking back and forth. She started to testifying about how she had been afflicted for months with a tumor and a doctor, both who had given her nothing but misery. "Lord-Jesus-Mother Mary, bless this tired old body. I know you won't gimme more than I can bear Jesus, I just ask that this load of mine be lightened so I can continue to do god's work more better." The sisters shook they heads and threw they right hands in the air to testify to her speaking the truth. When Aunt Vi finished her prayer, everybody shook her right hand. Miss Lamama in African tradition kissed her on both cheeks.

Then Big Mama let out a song souls deep, "Precious Lord take my hand . . . " Made my knees shake. A chill went through me and I got hot, all at the same time. Right then something happened to me. Felt like I was falling back up inside myself. Felt funny, and tingly like I might've been hit by a streak of lightening.

My body started swaying and all I could think about or hear was the sound of Big Mama singing that song. When the song was over I came back to myself. Some of the sisters was crying and blowing they noses. Looking at Big Mama, nobody could tell just how much power she had over people. I promised myself from then on to do everything she said quick, before she spoke twice. She could move people. They didn't know it was Big Mama making folks feel the spirit and all that time folks giving credit to god.

Big Mama said a closing prayer for the health and strength of all god's children. Then the meeting was adjourned and the women started crowding around to touch or lay hands on Aunt Vi in the center of the circle.

I almost fell down the stairs when Big Mama called me. "Child come on in here and pour the ladies some tea." I thought she had seen me through the wall. There was iced tea, sugar cookies and my favorite, chicken salad on white bread. And there was some peach brandy Big Mama made out of peach peelings and plenty of sugar and water. She kept it in a covered jar in the pantry next to the water heater. The ladies started catching up on other folks business, home remedies and family problems. Just like Miss Mary always came first and Miss Lamama always came late, Miss Alice was always having troubles with her husband Mister Henry. One day, the week before, she came home to find her antique upright piano was missing. Come to find out Mister Henry had pawned it along with the breakfast dishes to pay off his gambling debts. Big Mama shook her head in disgust, told Miss Alice to have faith and pray over her troubles. "Either the lord will make a way or you gonna have to put a lock on the kitchen sink Alice."

"Or a knock upside his head," said Miss Emma Lou, taking aim at her old tin cup.

Even Miss Tom who didn't spare words, had to add, "A man is only good for a few things and if he can't do them right you don't need him. You can do poorly by yourself."

As usual Miss Alice started making up for all of Mister Henry's faults by saying he was a sick man and as usual nobody paid her no mind. If she hadn't been taking up for him all the time Big Mama might've fixed him.

It was almost midnight when everybody left, but Big Mama

didn't stop, she was up for hours praying over Aunt Vi's tumor. I watched her lips moving by the light of the big white candle my blood mama sent us Christmas last. She took a big breath and look right up in my eyes like she knowed I'd been studying her all the time.

"Chile, why you ain't sleep yet?"

"Cause I was thinking."

"What you thinking so hard 'bout?"

"Bout dying."

"You too young to be thinking 'bout dying sugar." She blew out the candle and got up in the bed next to me. My head found a warm soft spot on her chest that smelled a little bit like peach brandy.

"Not me Big mama. I'm scared you might die, then what I do." My eyes filled up and my throat got tight saying it out loud.

"Who said I'm going anywhere? You my sugerfoot. I wouldn't leave you for all the tea in China."

"What if you got sick like Aunt Vi and . . . "

"When the last time you knowed me to be sick? Listen baby, your Big Mama got a whole lot more living to do. I ain't going nowhere till the lord is ready for me. Stop worrying unnecessary and go on to sleep. You too young to be thinking thoughts like that."

She hugged me up close to her and hummed a little song. Finally I did go to sleep, with the smell of burning candles on the air and pictures of Big Mama laughing at death in my head.

The sisters of the #2 mission prayer circle kept coming to our living room every Tuesday night to testify, sing, preach and pray over Aunt Vi. In the middle of one meeting Aunt Vi fell out. She tipped over backwards on the floor holding on to her tumor. I started crying cause I knew she was dead. Miss Alice, who had some nurses training, said to be calm. Big Mama told me to hush. She took up Aunt Vi's hands and closed her eyes for a minute. Then she run a open bottle of green camphor oil wid cotton balls in it under Aunt Vi's nose. It brought her back to life. Big Mama be dealing serious. After that night I never worried much about losing Big Mama to death, she had too much power to go anywhere she didn't want to and I knew she never wanted to leave me.

Slowly, but surely Aunt Vi's stomach went down to its normal layered look. Eight weeks to the day after the first prayer meeting was called, she reported that her tumor had disappeared.

"That doctor said it was a miracle, but I told him it was the prayers of the faithful and the will of god that made me well," she said.

But me, I knew it was Big Mama again, shaking the mess out of misery.